An American Family Portrait

BOOK SIX

The Allies

Jack Cavanaugh

The Rasmussen Family
1712 Candler Lane
Modesto CA, 95355

RIVEROAK®
Good News in Fiction

An Imprint of Cook Communications Ministries • Colorado Springs, CO

River Oak™ is an imprint of
Cook Communications Ministries
4050 Lee Vance View
Colorado springs, CO 80918
Cook Communications, Paris, Ontario
Kingsway Communications, Eastbourne, England

Editors: Greg Clouse, Barbara Williams
Design: Bill Gray
Cover Illustration: Chris Cocozza
Maps: Guy Wolek
Production: Nancy Gettings

4 5 6 7 8 9 10 11 Printing/Year 08 07 06 05 04

THE
ALLIES

═══════════

Laurita Rasmussen

The Rasmussen Family
1712 Candler Lane
Modesto CA, 95355

This brother and sister story
is dedicated to my sister and brother—
Sandi and Dave

The Rasmussen Family
1712 Candler Lane
Modesto CA, 95355

ACKNOWLEDGMENTS

Special thanks go to Armando Martinez, Park Manager of Pancho Villa State Park, Columbus, New Mexico. And to Richard Dean, amateur historian, for taking the time to answer my questions regarding the town and that fateful night.

And although my family and friends always deserves thanks for standing behind me during times of deadline, this particular project took me away from them more than usual. God couldn't have blessed me with a more understanding support group.

And, as always, thanks go to Greg Clouse, my friend and editor; Barb Williams, who is a joy to work with; and the rest of the ChariotVictor staff. Thank you for believing in me and giving me the chance to do what I love to do.

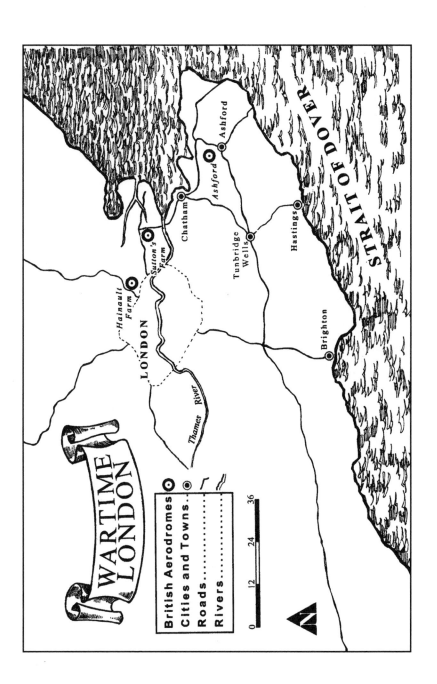

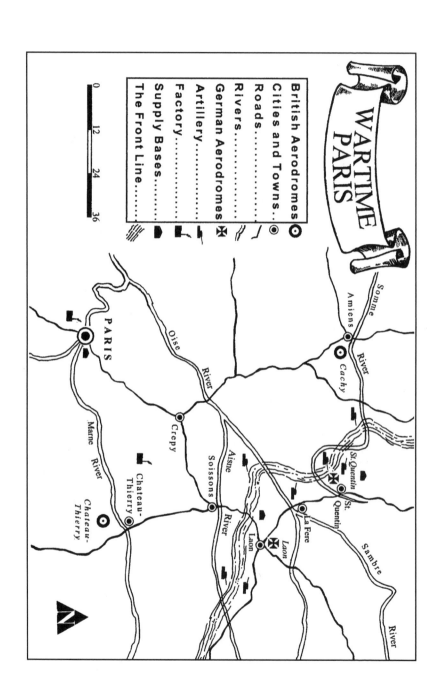

WARTIME PARIS

British Aerodromes......⊙
Cities and Towns....◉
Roads...........
Rivers..........
German Aerodromes....✠
Artillery.........
Factory..........
Supply Bases.......
The Front Line......

0   12   24   36

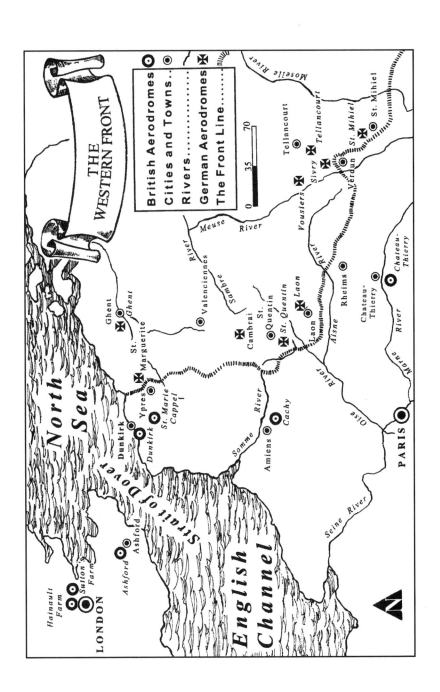

Chapter 1

NOTICE!

TRAVELERS intending to embark on the Atlantic voyage are reminded that a state of war exists between Germany and her allies; that the zone of war includes the waters adjacent to the British Isles; that, in accordance with formal notice given by the Imperial German Government, vessels flying the flag of Great Britain, or of any of her allies, are liable to destruction in those waters and that travelers sailing in the war zone on ships of Great Britain or her allies do so at their own risk.

IMPERIAL GERMAN EMBASSY

Washington, D.C., April 22, 1915

TORPEDO! The cry sent a shock wave across the deck. Couples strolling in the afternoon sun reacted with disbelief. Men's arms stiffened at the cry. Their mouths dropped open dumbly as though someone had slapped them, then froze their astonished expressions. Their eyes came alive with the horror realized.

Women likewise reacted to the cry of impending cataclysm. Gloved hands flew to gaping mouths. Instinctively
they nestled against their consorts.

For a split second all conversation on deck, all movement
ceased. There was no rustling of dresses. Patent leather
shoes no longer clicked against the hardwood surface.
Snippets of coy dialogue were swallowed. Merriment was
muzzled. For one silent instant, time itself was suspended
as every person who heard the cry groped for a fact—any
fact at all, no matter how farfetched—that would discredit
the cry. Something inside them demanded assurance, even
if it was fabricated assurance, that this sort of catastrophe
happened to other people, not to them.

Then the instant passed. The warning cry was real. So
was the torpedo. In the next few seconds every life aboard
the ship would be changed—their agendas, their values,
their priorities, their eternities.

Emily and Katy Morgan had just stepped from the
Grand Dining Salon on the upper deck when they heard
the cry. Word had reached them that the Irish coast was
visible from deck. Katy, anxious to get her first glimpse of
Europe, suggested they stroll the promenade. Mother and
daughter had been walking arm-in-arm, content following
the afternoon meal.

A few inches taller than her mother, Katy was every inch
a woman; intelligent, compassionate, beautiful, with dark
brown hair, dark eyes, full lips, and a striking figure in a
flowing white summer dress. She was indeed an answer to
her mother's prayers and more, a testimony in Emily's
opinion that God often blesses us more than we deserve.

Emily herself, now approaching her mid-forties, retained
the soft features and smooth pale skin that had characterized her as a youth, though a few wrinkles had begun making their debut in the corners of her eyes. Matching wide

brown eyes and dark brown hair linked mother and daughter in appearance. Heads turned as they passed, no doubt attracted by their outward gaiety and their matching summer dresses, Katy in white and Emily in peach.

The ocean crossing had been pleasant. The weather had been perfect, except for a few hours of fog the second morning out, and the sea smooth. Emily had been looking forward to this time alone with her daughter, whom she had rarely seen since Katy entered nursing school. The trip had not been disappointing. The two women, who had always been close, talked for hours and laughed even longer. One would have thought they were sisters, or best friends. Like most of the other passengers, they were relaxed and content as they neared the end of a six-day voyage across the Atlantic.

TORPEDO! TORPEDO! OFF THE STARBOARD SIDE!

It was a shrill cry. Frantic. The lookout on the bow leaned over the railing, pointing at the sea, shouting his warning, over and over. With each warning, his voice climbed the tonal scale until it reached a fevered pitch.

"Good Lord, no!" Emily cried softly, glancing at her daughter, her baby now grown. Katy broke free from her mother and leaned against the rail. She searched the sea for the torpedo.

All around her people on the promenade joined her at the railing. Taking a fix from the lookout's extended arm, they followed its line across the undulating surface of the ocean. Emily squeezed between a man with a bowler hat and her daughter to get to the railing so she could see for herself.

"There!" Katy pointed.

There was an amazing calmness in Katy's voice that surprised her mother, though it shouldn't have. Katy's tranquil response to emergency reflected her training. It also served to remind Emily that her daughter was no longer a little girl.

Off the bow, the torpedo looked like a slim dark porpoise with a white bubble train. It was headed straight for the ship. There was no way it could miss.

Emotions erupted the length of the railing. People cursed and cried and prayed aloud that God might save them from this mechanized instrument of terror and death.

The torpedo neared the ship, then disappeared in the starboard shadow. For a second there was nothing. Without exception those who stood against the railing hoped that they had been spared, that the torpedo wouldn't . . .

There was a deep thud, followed by a rumble, then a deafening explosion. The deck beneath their feet shuddered and trembled ominously, like the rattling cough of a dying man. Water and debris and black smoke flew skyward. A second explosion followed, worse than the first. The ship listed heavily to its right, tipping Emily and Katy and the other passengers on the starboard promenade precariously closer to the ocean's surface.

Passengers gripped the railing to keep from tumbling over the side. Those who couldn't grip the railing gripped those who could. Emily grabbed onto Katy as wails and screams and shouts from all parts of the ship mixed in a cacophonous symphony of human fear.

"Get inside!" Emily cried, pushing off from the railing.

The deck convulsed again and tipped starboard even more. Thick black smoke billowed from the side of the ship, funneling down the promenade, choking and blinding couples who just minutes before had been strolling arm-in-arm down the deck.

Bits of metal and wood rained down upon them. Emily grabbed Katy's arm, redoubling her efforts to get inside, seeking shelter from the deadly shower. The door to the dining salon, which opened outward, swung crazily back and forth with every shudder of the ship. Leaning into the angle of the ship, using the same posture they'd use if they were climbing an uphill grade, Emily and Katy stumbled and grabbed and pulled their way into the salon.

If the promenade had been chaos, the salon was bedlam. Well-dressed men and women were sprawled on the floor and across chairs and tables, slipping and sliding on mashed potatoes and vegetables and wine and bread and leafy lettuce. Had their faces not been twisted with the prospect of their own deaths, it would have been a comical sight.

"Mother, where are we going?" Katy cried.

Emily looked with growing panic at her daughter. *Surely, God, it is not Your will that my precious Katy perish at sea, is it? She has so much to offer. So much to give. There is so much life ahead of her. . . .*

"To the high side of the ship, dear," Emily said in response to Katy's question. "We'll look for a lifeboat there."

Katy nodded. Taking her mother by the hand, she led the way uphill toward the port side of the salon. Emily couldn't help but smile in admiration at her daughter's lack of fear. Katy's hand was warm, her grip firm, determined. There was absolutely no chill of trepidation in it. Not the slightest hint.

Emily grimaced as she stepped on something, then jerked her foot away. It had felt like someone's hand. Looking down, she grinned in relief. It was a steak. Filet mignon. Someone's dinner squished against a plush carpet in a gilded room that shouted elegance and luxury. . . a room that would soon be the dining area of fishes at the bottom of the Atlantic Ocean.

Why had she not heeded her instincts? They had tried to warn her. But earlier when she gave voice to her reservations, Jesse scoffed at her, and as usual, she gave in to him.

"This ship is unsinkable!" Jesse boasted.

"Father, no ship is unsinkable," Katy argued. Whereas her mother had the good sense to let Jesse's exaggerations pass, Katy loved challenging them.

"Don't take my word for it," Jesse defended himself. He leaned comfortably back in his chair in the ritzy first-class stateroom. "I'm merely repeating what the captain told me."

It was Saturday, May 1, 1915. Jesse Morgan had come to see his wife and daughter off as they sailed for England. While Emily unpacked, Jesse and Katy lounged on opposite sides of a walnut table laden with an oversized basket of fruit which was adorned with an equally oversized red ribbon. The words *Bon Voyage* sparkled in silver on the accompanying card. Sitting in front of the basket was an open copy of the *New York Times*. The current subject of discussion had been sparked by an advertisement and notice that the layout editor had positioned side-by-side.

The advertisement announced the departure of Great Britain's fastest and largest steamer, the pride of the Cunard Line; the adjacent notice had been paid for by the Imperial German Embassy. It reminded Americans that a state of war existed between Great Britain and Germany, stating that ships carrying the flag of Great Britain were liable to destruction.

"Do you want to hear what the captain said when he was informed of this notice?" Jesse asked, thumping the newspaper with his index finger.

He waited for a response. When there was none, he took his wife's and daughter's silence as assent.

"The captain said it was the best joke he'd heard in years, that he was confident his ship could outrun any submarine afloat!"

"What else would you expect the captain to say?" Katy cried. "He's just like every other male . . . overly boastful and proud about some machine, just like Johnny and his aeroplanes and you and your automobiles!"

Jesse feigned injury at the personal attack. "Me? Boastful of a machine?"

Emily grinned, folded a blouse and quietly placed it in the cedar drawer. This kind of lighthearted, antagonistic banter was not uncommon between father and daughter, especially during times that called for an expression of emotion. Both of them were deeply passionate individuals; both of them found it difficult to put their feelings into words. So instead of expressing their feelings, they jousted verbally. On this occasion it was their way of saying, "Good-bye. I love you, and I'll miss you."

"Don't pretend you don't love that automobile!" Katy asserted with a tell-the-truth-now grin.

"Of course I like automobiles!" Jesse cried. "What other method of transportation is as reliable? Or would you prefer we go back to the horse and buggy?"

"That black shiny contraption is more than just a convenience to you, Father. You love it! Admit it! Come on, admit that you have human emotions for that conglomeration of metal and wood and rubber!"

While Jesse pretended to have nothing more than admiration for the men who could build such a machine, Emily folded and stored more clothes. Her husband may have been easily distracted from the Imperial German Embassy's printed warning, but not her. She didn't take the German threat lightly, not after hearing of the atrocities they were committing in occupied Belgium. However, she alone seemed to be disturbed by the advertisement. Everyone else on board, including her two dueling magpies at the table, seemed unaffected by it. The mood everywhere onboard ship was gay and lighthearted and joyous.

The verbal jousting between father and daughter was turning physical. With arms outstretched and fingers wiggling, Jesse was threatening to come across the table and tickle Katy like he used to do when she was a child. She tittered and warned him back with a playfully stern look and challenging index finger.

"If the two of you don't settle down," Emily warned, "the captain will have you both thrown off this ship! And if he doesn't, I will!"

Scolded by Mother, Jesse and Katy dutifully folded their hands and pretended to behave. Their good behavior didn't last long. The moment Emily turned her back to place another blouse in the cedar drawer, they were at each other again.

Jesse was acting like an immature boy. New York seemed to have that kind of effect on him. Emily smiled to herself. It felt good to be back in the city that held so many memories for her and Jesse.

They had arrived in the city early to visit her parents who still lived on Fifth Avenue. Although their involvement was somewhat curtailed by failing health, her father was just as preoccupied as ever with his factories, likewise her mother with her art patronage. Too busy to find the time to wish their daughter and granddaughter a personal farewell on their voyage, but not so busy that they forgot to instruct a secretary to order them an ostentatious basket of fruit, so big it took two porters to deliver it.

That same afternoon, they drove past the Hester Street tenement where Jesse had been raised. The neighborhood was dirtier and its occupants more threatening than either of them remembered, so they didn't get out of the car.

However, Jesse grinned nostalgically when he saw the el train. He described to Katy how the train used to shower pedestrians with cinders and soot. Now, however, it ran much cleaner powered by electricity.

It was the first time Jesse and Emily had taken their daughter on a tour of New York. Emily only wished that Johnny had been with them. It would have done him good to see the boyish side of his father emerge. It seemed that the only side Johnny ever saw of his father was the stern disciplinarian side, or his professional side—his father's name in the newspaper, his father giving a speech, his father going off to Washington to consult with Secretary of State William Jennings Bryan or President Wilson. Whereas father and daughter had formed a mutual bond of love and respect, Jessie and Johnny were magnets with similar poles. Despite her best efforts, she could not bring them together. It was as though an invisible force prevented it, repelling them one from the other.

In the hallway outside their cabin a youthful male voice announced that the ship was about to depart. All persons who were not paid passengers were instructed to debark immediately.

Jesse pulled out a pocket watch.

"What time is it?" Emily asked.

"A few minutes past noon. Two hours late." He shrugged it off. "You'll make it up at sea. Did I tell you this ship can steam in excess of 25 knots?"

"Hundreds of times!" Katy cried in exasperation. In the tone normally reserved for a litany, she added, "And that it holds the record for being the fastest ship on the Atlantic run, and that it's 785 feet long and displaces 40,000 tons, and has a capacity of 2,000 passengers, and that . . . "

Jesse held up both hands in surrender. "Enough! Point taken!"

But Katy couldn't resist one last jab. Shaking her head in such a way to pronounce interest in such things as mundane and pathetic, she moaned, "Men and their machines!"

Turning to his wife, Jesse said, "I wish I were going with you." He stood and approached Emily with open arms.

"That makes it unanimous," Emily replied. She stepped into his embrace and closed her eyes. Years of love and warmth and comfort had been found here.

Even now her arms stretched all the way around her husband. Jesse was as thin as ever. At forty-five years of age, he still had a youthfulness about him, an infectious grin, and a lanky gait, though he wasn't in as much of a hurry to get places as he once was. Pulling away to kiss him, Emily saw affectionate blue eyes highlighted with middle-age wrinkles. Jesse was never one to peck. His kiss was warm and as passionate as a man can be in the presence of his offspring.

"Have a good trip, my love," he whispered. "And hurry home."

Jesse embraced his daughter. "I'm confident you'll do well during your interview with the London Missionary Society," he said. "Just be yourself. They'll love you."

"Thank you, Father."

"And take care of your mother," he said, resuming his playful tone. "She's your responsibility. I expect you to return her to me in this same condition."

"Yes, sir," Katy replied. She never called her father *sir* except in playfulness.

In the hallway, instead of taking the direct route to the exit, Jesse pulled Emily by the hand toward the middle of the ship. "I want you to see something," he said.

"Jesse! We don't have time!" Emily complained.

"We have time," Jesse insisted.

Katy shook her head. "Men and their machines," she muttered.

Jesse pulled his wife through a maze of passenger cabins and down a flight of steps. Katy trailed happily behind them. He didn't slow until they passed through the grand entrance into the First Class Dining Salon.

"So? What do you think?" Jesse cried. "Do you think you can learn to live in this kind of luxury for a week? It's a veritable floating palace!"

The salon was a vision in white and gold, in the style of Louis XVI. There must have been more than a hundred tables bedecked with white linen, gold-rimmed china, crystal goblets, sparkling silver, and fresh cut flower centerpieces. The predominant color of the room was rose, accentuated with magnificent mahogany sideboards with gilt metal ornaments. High above them, in cathedral fashion, towered a dome with picture panels painted in oils after the style of Boucher.

Overhead, the dining salon's Boucher dome tipped grotesquely starboard.

A siren wailed. All manners of screams and shouts could be heard. Babies cried. Children whimpered, frightened by the panic in their parents' voices. Ship's employees yelled instructions and waved arms, oftentimes in contradiction to one another.

"Mother, hurry! The ship's sinking!" Katy cried, clutching her mother's hand.

Suddenly, the passageway leading through the salon from port to starboard was flooded with people. For as many people who were battling to get to the port side, that many or more were traveling the downward slope toward the sinking starboard side. Those who were heading starboard puzzled Emily. It seemed common sense to avoid the water, to seek the highest ground to give oneself the greatest time possible to climb aboard a lifeboat and to keep from getting sucked into the inevitable whirlpool the ship would make when it sank. Still, as desperately as she and Katy worked to get to the port side, many others were working to get to the starboard.

A rush of starboard seekers crowded around them. Emily's link to Katy was broken.

"Katy!"

"Mother!"

Emily felt herself being pulled down the slope. She fought to get through the crowd, but was unsuccessful.

"Mother!"

Emily could see Katy's head bobbing above a sea of heads.

"Mother! Stay there. I'll come back for you!"

"No!" Emily cried. "Keep going! I'll catch up with you on deck!"

Either Katy didn't hear her mother, or she disobeyed. She elbowed and pushed and squeezed her way toward her mother.

Another explosion rocked the ship. Once again, the dying luxury liner shuddered beneath their feet and listed further still to the starboard side. Clearly the grand old lady of the seas was slipping quickly to her death.

Emily had no desire to accompany her. She redoubled her efforts to reach the port side and her daughter. Though a sea of bodies pressed around her, pulled her down, suffocated her, she kept pushing forward.

"Mother! Take my hand!" Katy was a little more than two arm length's away. She reached toward her mother, while Emily reached for her. Their fingers barely brushed each other.

"I've got you, Mother . . . I've got you!" Katy lunged toward her mother. Their hands touched, then grasped. The link between them was reestablished. They both pulled until, at last, they were side-by-side again.

"Let's join arms," Emily suggested. "It will be harder to separate us."

Katy agreed. Not only did they link their arms together, but they grasped their wrists to close the link and hold it shut. In this manner, they managed to inch their way across the ballroom-size salon until they reached the port side of the ship.

No sooner were they out the door when they realized why everyone was heading toward the starboard side. The radical starboard list of the ship caused all the port lifeboats to swing over the deck. They couldn't be lowered. Several of the boats were sprawled awkwardly on deck, testimony to failed attempts to launch them.

The two women looked at each other in horror. They had wasted all this time struggling to get to the wrong side of the ship! Emily looked up and down the deck, seeking an alternative route to the starboard side. All the passageways seemed equally crowded.

The two women stepped back into the salon, the one Jesse had been so impressed with, and worked their way down the slope toward the starboard side of the ship. Encountering several people working up slope, Emily tried to tell them that the lifeboats couldn't be launched from the port side. For her efforts, she got hostile glares and a few curses.

As it turned out, the starboard side did not hold much more hope. Although the lifeboats swung out over the water, the promenade was jammed with people waiting to board them. Inexperience and panicky decisions had scuttled some of the lifeboats. On one boat, the line was stuck. Passengers and crewmen hacked away at it, attempting to free it. Another boat in similar condition had successfully been freed, only to plunge into the ocean and float away empty.

In still another boat, a crewman let the line slip through his hands too quickly while his counterpart let the line slip too slowly. The boat dropped perpendicularly, spilling all its passengers into the sea.

"Mother!" Katy yelled. "Look! Over there!" She pointed toward the stern. A group of small children huddled together, no one attending them. They crowded in toward one another looking and sounding like a flock of frightened geese. Their faces were streaked. The fronts of their clothing were sopping wet. Most of the children had one or more parts of their hands in their mouths.

Emily pushed her daughter in the direction of the children. Katy needed no encouragement. When they reached the children, they counted eight in all. No amount of soothing talk from Emily or Katy had any effect on them.

"They probably wandered from the nursery," Emily said, scanning the immediate vicinity for someone who might be responsible for the children. She could find no one.

Katy busily dried faces and did her best to calm the children.

"Let's get them to a lifeboat," Emily said.

"What if someone comes back for them?"

"There's no time. At least this way, they'll be safe."

Katy nodded in agreement. Together the two Morgan women shepherded the gaggle of children down the promenade, carrying the smallest of them in their arms.

Almost miraculously, when people heard them coming, they stepped aside and cleared a path for them all the way to the closest lifeboat.

"What have we here?" said a clean-shaven crewman who looked like he had yet to emerge from his teen years. He was assisting people into the lifeboat. Despite the urgency of his task, he took time to wink at Katy. Lifting the first child out of her arms, he said, "Surely, they're not all yours!"

Katy gave the man a you're-not-funny smirk, one that she had practiced to perfection on her younger brother, and handed over the child. The ship shuddered beneath them, shaking the lifeboats. All levity dissipated.

"Here, let me help you!" A kindly middle-aged man with heavy jowls and an English accent stepped to Katy's side. A costly woolen suit was partially hidden by a bright-colored life jacket. He picked up child after child, talking kindly to them and lifting them into the boat.

Just as Katy was bending down to get the next child, she looked up. Something behind her mother caught her eye. "Good Lord, no!" she cried.

Emily swung around. An infant, not old enough yet to walk, was crawling toward the railing near the stern of the boat, reaching for the horizontal white bar. Emily's heart leaped within her. She was the closest to the baby. She ran toward it, calling out behind her, "Get in the boat, Katy! I'll be right there!"

"Mother!" Katy cried.

"Get in the boat!" Emily yelled again.

All the children were now seated inside the lifeboat. "Get in, miss," the middle-aged Englishman said, taking her by the arm to assist her.

"My mother..." Katy objected.

"Please step into the boat, miss," the boyish crewman insisted. His eyes, no longer distracted by Katy, were riveted on the bow of the boat from which issued a black column of smoke. "Hurry! Hurry!" he cried.

Katy had no choice but to climb aboard. She sat among the children.

The Englishman was right behind her. "Here, take this." He pulled the life jacket over his head and handed it to her.

Katy refused it politely, trying to catch a glimpse of her mother. Too many people blocked her view.

"I insist," said the Englishman, extending the life jacket toward her persistently. "You're caring for the little ones," he reasoned. "Should anything happen to this boat, you will need it to save some of them."

Relenting, Katy strapped on the life jacket, all the while craning her neck toward the stern of the boat in a desperate attempt to see her mother.

Just then, the young crewman signaled to his partner at the bow of the lifeboat. They began to lower it to the water.

"Wait!" Katy cried, standing up. "My mother hasn't returned!"

"Sit down, miss!" the crewman cried. Katy's action was causing the lifeboat to swing side-to-side.

"Pull us back up!" Katy demanded. "I'm getting out!"

Just then, the ship lurched violently. The lifeboat, still tethered to the ship, shook like a toy dangling at the end of a string. Katy fell down. She would have fallen overboard, had the Englishman not caught her. At the sudden movement, the children took up their wailing chorus again.

"Please, miss," the Englishman pleaded. "Sit down. For the children's sake. Your mother will see that you've done as you were told and will get on board another lifeboat."

Her heart racing, her stomach churning, Katy scanned the railing of the ship looking for her mother. The lifeboat hit the water and immediately the crewmen took the oars and moved away from the sinking ship. Still no sight of her mother.

"Take care of your mother," her father had said. *"She's your responsibility. I expect you to return her to me in this same condition."*

Katy did her best to comfort the frightened children, but not without continuing to scan the ship and nearby lifeboats for some sign of her mother. *Dear God, wrap my mother in Your loving arms and keep her safe,* Katy prayed silently.

Another explosion pulled everyone's attention to the ship. They watched in silence as the bow of the ship dipped beneath the surface. The ship rolled to its starboard side and in a half-spiral the hulking behemoth slowly sunk beneath the surface. The last thing Katy saw of it was its name printed on the stern: *Lusitania.*

A short twenty minutes ago, she and her mother had been strolling casually on deck, nearing the completion of an incident-free voyage across the Atlantic, Katy's first. Now, she was bobbing atop the waves in a sea of debris and oil and dead bodies floating face downward.

She sat in the midst of wailing children with no idea who they were or the whereabouts of their parents. Looking at their frightened faces, a horrifying thought struck her with such force she found it difficult to maintain her composure. *What if all their parents perished onboard the ship? Was she sitting in a boatload of the recently orphaned? Who would tell these poor children? Who would care for them now that their parents were dead?*

Suddenly her macabre thought turned into a nightmare. *Were there only eight orphans in the boat? Or were there nine?* Katy's eyes roamed the surface of the sea, staring at one life-less body after another, searching for a peach dress, hoping she didn't find one.

When Emily left Katy at the lifeboat, her one thought was to reach the infant before the infant reached the edge of the ship. It was a horrifying suspension of time. Emily straining to cover yard after yard of open deck while the infant inched toward the railing. It was as though she were looking down a tube—she saw nothing but the baby, crawling, reaching for the white railing, missing it, faltering, teetering . . . teetering, then disappearing over the edge.

"No . . . no . . . no . . . no, dear God, no . . . no . . . " The words tumbled from her lips, half prayer, half anguish.

Reaching the railing too late, Emily leaned over it, searching for the infant in the water. A white woolen jersey with matching leggings bobbed on the surface. The baby's head was facedown in the water.

There was no rational thought in Emily's actions. There was no thought at all. Emily didn't even feel the railing as she climbed over it. There was no fear of jumping. No fear of consequences. No fear of death. All she could think of was getting to the baby and lifting its head out of the water.

She fell to the water feet first. With a rush of wind, her peach dress rose up all around her, engulfing her in a linen cocoon. The next thing she knew she was several feet underwater. Looking up, she could see the pale blue sky on the breathing side of the ocean's surface. She could also see the baby, its face pointed her direction, its plump cheeks, its closed eyes. Bobbing. Lifeless.

A couple of determined strokes sent her toward the surface. She reached for the baby, turning its face heavenward.

Close by, the ship let loose with another explosion followed by several mournful groans. Emily did her best to put distance between herself and the dying hulk, all the while keeping the baby's head above water.

As the ship died and slipped down to its ocean-bottom grave, the baby choked, spit up some water, and bellowed angrily.

Emily's tears of joy added to the ocean's content. "Thank You, God," she cried. "Thank You for sparing this little one."

But after a time it seemed Emily's thanksgiving prayer might be premature. She found herself far from the nearest lifeboat. Her cries for help got lost among a hundred other similar cries.

Emily's saturated clothing soon grew burdensome. She found it increasingly difficult to keep her head above water. Still, all she could think about was saving the baby. Giving it a chance to live.

Her arms were growing heavier. Her legs felt like they were treading sand. Her head frequently slipped below the surface. She would give a little kick, take a gulp of air, then sink below the surface again. Each time she spent longer and longer beneath the surface of the water until she knew she could avoid the inevitable no longer.

Emily had always reasoned that death would be an intensely personal experience. From watching others die, she had observed that the closer people came to the moment of death, the more withdrawn they became. It was as if the soul was collapsing in, like a flower blossoming, only in reverse. Or better still, a collecting of oneself, packing one's bags for the journey into eternity.

Now, with her lungs screaming for air but finding only the thick liquid of seawater, she realized she had been wrong about death. Her thoughts were not on herself. Rather, her thoughts were on this poor child who would never have a chance to know life beyond infancy; and of Jesse, her beloved Jesse and how it pained her to think how he would grieve over her death; and Katy... dear Katy.

Beneath the ocean's surface, Emily wept, her tears absorbed instantly by the sea.

It would be easier for her to die if she knew that Katy was safe. And then there was Johnny—wherever he might be, whatever he was doing... Emily mourned the fact that she would never have the chance to say good-bye to him, to tell him that she understood his frustration, to let him know that in spite of all the pain and disappointment he'd caused his father over the years, that his father still loved him.

Her life was draining from her. Her thoughts focused on keeping her wrist and hand above water, for it was the baby's ark. She didn't know how much longer she could last. The grip of the murky waters was pulling her down. She looked for light, but saw only darkness until finally it consumed her.

Chapter 2

AS accustomed as Johnny Morgan was to Landis Wachorn's erratic flying, it wasn't difficult for him to know when something was wrong. The biplane was sliding in a crosswind and losing altitude. Johnny craned his neck to get a look at the pilot in the seat behind him.

Wachorn's head lolled to one side, bouncing with the vibration of the plane. Behind goggled eyes, the man's eyes were closed. His tongue protruded partway out of the corner of his mouth. A half-empty bottle of Scotch resting between his legs sloshed with the motion of the plane. Although the pilot's left hand was still on the neck of the bottle, his right hand was no longer gripping the stick that controlled the airplane.

"Not again," Johnny muttered. He turned forward and instinctively grabbed the secondary control stick between his knees. It flopped freely from side to side. Broken. Wachorn had promised to fix it at the next town if the receipts were good.

"Great!" Johnny shouted at the wind. It was his favorite expression. Sarcasm simplified. When things couldn't get any worse, pronounce them *great.*

He ran the fingers of both hands through sandy brown hair from his hairline all the way to the back of his neck. It was his way of showing exasperation. Lately, because of

Wachorn's increasing ineptness, he'd done it so often his hair was beginning to lay back naturally.

Having flown with the gray-haired aviator for more than six months, Johnny was accustomed to Wachorn's drinking bouts. But after his last crash which resulted in a split skull and a few broken ribs, the fear of God had entered the old daredevil and he swore he would never drink again while flying.

At the time Wachorn made his pledge, Johnny had no doubt the Gray Eagle, as he preferred to be called, was sincere. But the problem with the fear of God was that its power faded with time, while Wachorn's desire for drink increased. Johnny started finding empty bottles hidden among the tools.

Wachorn was an amiable and predictable drunkard. Unlike some men, drink didn't make him mean; instead, it inspired him first to song, then to sleep. Johnny depended on the order of Wachorn's drunkenness to keep them alive. Song then sleep. If the Gray Eagle started singing while on the ground, Johnny saw to it they stayed there, usually by manufacturing a mechanical difficulty. If the songs began in the air, Johnny had been able to coax the old flyer out of the sky before sleep overtook him.

Not this time. If Wachorn had been singing, Johnny hadn't heard it.

Loosening his harness, Johnny turned as far around in his seat as he could. The old man was just out of his reach.

"Wachorn! Wake up! Wake up!" he shouted.

The pilot didn't flinch.

Johnny pounded the flat of his hand on the canvas side. "Wachorn! Wachorn! Wake up!"

The man showed no sign of hearing him.

Wachorn had predicted this kind of thing might happen occasionally while they were in the air. "Don't you worry none if'n I should doze off for a spell whiles we're in the clouds," he'd told Johnny not long after they teamed up. "Nothin' like a little catnap in the clouds, I always say. Do it all the time! Think about it, boy. Who are we gonna run into at 2,000 feet? As for the aeroplane, this ol' Curtiss Jenny practically flies herself! Tell you what you do. If ever you catch me dozin' up there, just reach around and nudge the ol' Gray Eagle. Will you do that for me, boy?"

At several thousand feet above the ground, Johnny was hoping Wachorn's statement about the Curtiss Jenny was no idle boast. Right now they needed an aeroplane that could fly itself, because the pilot wasn't flying it, and Johnny's control stick was useless.

"Wachorn! Wake up!"

There was no stirring the man.

Unbuckling himself, Johnny turned completely around in his seat so that his knees were on the seat. He stretched himself over the portion of the fuselage that separated the two cockpits.

The air rushed madly past him, pushing up the bottom of his jacket and chilling his back. With his chest pressed against the fuselage, he could feel the pulse of the engine. At the moment, his pulse was racing faster. With no straps holding him in and little to hold onto, he prayed the aeroplane wouldn't do anything erratic.

With one hand, Johnny grabbed the pilot by the jacket. With the other, he slapped the Gray Eagle on the side of the face. "Wachorn! Wake up!"

The pilot's head took the blow. It waggled, then slouched to one side. A second slap yielded similar results.

Johnny began to fear the worst.

"Great!" he shouted. This time there were no hands through the hair; they were too busy holding him in the aeroplane.

"Think, Johnny, think!" he urged himself. "If you want to see your twenty-second birthday, think of something quick!"

He glanced over his shoulder toward the front of the plane. They were continuing to lose altitude, but more rapidly now. In the distance, he could see a row of trees lining a road. The plane was headed straight for them.

"Great!" Johnny muttered. "What are my options?"

He considered climbing all the way into the cockpit with Wachorn and sitting on the dead man's lap. No good. Even if he could manage to climb from one cockpit to the other without falling out of the plane, he doubted there was enough room inside the second cockpit to accommodate both of them. Wachorn was a large man with a protruding belly. There would be no room left for Johnny to maneuver the control stick.

What about unbuckling the dead man and throwing him out of the plane? No good. Wachorn was too large and Johnny was in no position to lift heavy objects.

He glanced over his shoulder again. The trees loomed larger than before.

There was only one other alternative. He would simply have to fly the plane from his current position. Backward.

Holding onto Wachorn's jacket with one hand, he braced himself as best he could with his legs against the inside of the forward cockpit. With his right hand, he reached down into the cockpit and slapped Wachorn's bottle of whiskey to the floorboard to get it out of the way. It landed on its side and gurgled until it was nearly empty, the odor of whiskey rising from the bottom of the cockpit.

He gripped the control stick, then looked over his shoulder to see where he was going. The trees were coming up fast. Johnny eased back on the stick. The plane plunged downward!

"Backward!" Johnny shouted. "Everything is backward!"

Quickly, he released the control stick, grabbed the throttle and pulled it out. The engine sputtered, then roared louder. The plane picked up speed. Grabbing the stick again, he shoved it away from him. The aeroplane responded, swooping upward.

There was a jolt as the landing gear brushed the tops of the trees. It knocked his feet loose. The aeroplane continued to rise. His only anchor was the grip he had on the dead man's jacket. Johnny's legs flailed helplessly, searching for something to latch onto, but finding nothing.

Level off! Level off! his mind shouted.

Pulling the stick toward him, the aeroplane assumed a gentler angle. His feet hit the sides of the cockpit, then found their position again.

His heart hammering in his chest, Johnny looked expectantly to Wachorn. There were no congratulations forthcoming from the experienced aviator. The Gray Eagle's lifeless expression served only to remind Johnny that unless he could land this bird, people would find two dead bodies in the crumpled fuselage.

Looking over one shoulder, then the other, he searched for a suitable field. Considering his flying position, it had to be something straight in front of him. Without access to the pedals which controlled the ailerons and stabilizers, he was limited to going up and down. There would be no circling, no side-to-side adjustments.

In the distance, he spotted a small town. He had no idea what town it was. In fact, he wasn't even sure what state he was in, or for that matter, if he was still in the United States.

"South!" Wachorn had bellowed two days ago. "South with the birds!"

There was a large dirt field just beyond the town. Unplowed. It had to be unplowed, otherwise the wheels would catch in the ruts and the aeroplane would nose over.

Pulling the stick back slightly, the Curtiss Jenny began to descend. After a few minutes, he passed over the eastern edge of the small town. The roar of the aeroplane engine brought people of all ages out of the buildings.

"No matter where you go, people are mesmerized by flying machines," Wachorn had told him. He mused philosophically, "The question is, why? You see, boy, I believe at one time we was like the angels, long, long ago. And for some reason, God done clipped our wings. But way back in our memory somewheres, we still remember what it was like to fly. That's why people are taken so by aeroplanes. It gives them a chance to fly again. Now some have forgotten so much, that they's scared to fly, but they loves to watch! Others aren't scared, there's lots of them! And boy, we can accommodate them! For a price, of course."

Johnny never did buy into the old man's story about the angels, but he could attest to the fact that people everywhere were fascinated by flying and aeroplanes. Himself included.

For as long as he could remember, he dreamed of flying. There was nothing else in the world he wanted to do. So when the Gray Eagle came to Denver one summer, Johnny went to the field every day to watch. Apparently, Wachorn could see the desire in his eyes, because he made Johnny a deal. If Johnny would cook and run the business—take the money, purchase parts and supplies, run errands, that sort of thing—and agree to wake Gray Eagle should he take a catnap in the clouds, Wachorn in exchange would teach Johnny to fly.

That was three years ago. Johnny dropped out of college, incurring his father's wrath, and went off to fly with Wachorn. He put up with the man's eccentric personality, his drinking binges, his frequent run-ins with angry creditors, and the life of a nomad for one reason. Wachorn had an aeroplane and Johnny wanted to fly.

Below him, people from the unknown town stared at the aeroplane and pointed and laughed. Johnny couldn't blame them. The sight of an aeroplane was exciting enough, but to have a man fly over the town straddling the fuselage of an aeroplane, backward . . . well, that was something you didn't see every day. A group of boys, looking like a school of fish, ran in circles and jumped and danced beneath the plane.

Having passed over the buildings, Johnny eased off on the throttle and descended even more. He fell from the sky ever so slowly. Beneath him the ground raced by at blurring speeds. Closer, closer.

The wheels hit. He bounced. Hard. Nearly knocking him from the fuselage. Gripping Wachorn's jacket and the control stick until his knuckles turned white, he tried again.

Another bounce. Not as hard. This time he was prepared.

The aeroplane jolted and bucked and bounced as it dashed across the field's rocky surface. Holding on with all his might, Johnny fought to keep from being thrown off. Now that he was on the ground, he had to cut the engine. Normally, he would throttle back, but in this case cutting the engine would be the fastest way to stop the aeroplane. However, with the engine still racing, each bump made the plane want to take off again.

Somehow, he had to free a hand to hit the cutoff switch. But which hand? His left hand gripped Wachorn's jacket, this was his anchor. But if he let go of the stick, how could he keep the aeroplane on the ground? He'd have to hit the switch fast.

He waited. One bump. Then another. Each time the aeroplane tried to rise off the ground. Another bump. Now! He released the stick and reached for the switch.

The aeroplane bucked. The switch jumped out of his reach. He reached again, another bump, another miss. The aeroplane rose up and back down, hitting the ground with a jarring crash. He felt like he was riding a bucking bronco. Another bump.

Then, he hit it!

The engine slowed and sputtered. The back skid hit the ground, causing another jolt. As the engine died out, the Curtiss Jenny aeroplane settled down and coasted to a stop.

For a long moment, Johnny just lay there, draped over the fuselage between the two cockpits, his hand still gripping the dead man's jacket. For the first time he could remember since he started flying, he looked forward to putting his feet on solid ground.

"That was some stunt flying!" a young male voice cried out.

Johnny lifted his head to see a young man in corduroys and a white shirt with rolled up sleeves running toward him. Johnny guessed him to be just a few years younger than himself.

"This your aeroplane?" he cried. "It's only the second aeroplane I've ever seen in my whole life. But the fellow who flew that first aeroplane was nowhere near as good as you! Why, the way he talked, flyin' was a hard thing to do. But you just made it look easy, riding on top of it and flyin' backwards like that! Never seen anything like it!"

With a groan, Johnny climbed down from the fuselage. His ribs ached from the pounding they took during the landing.

"I don't fly like that every day," he said. "It was something of an emergency." He motioned to the back cockpit. "I think my partner died on me."

The young man was right behind Johnny as they checked on Wachorn. The old pilot wasn't breathing. One eyelid had crept halfway open. The eye behind it stared coldly at nothing in particular.

"Don't get much deader than that," the young man said flatly. "He your father?"

"Good heavens, no!" Johnny cried.

"Friend?"

"More like a business partner. He's the one who taught me to fly."

"Were you close to him?"

Johnny looked at the dead pilot. "Not very," he said. Indeed, Johnny was being generous. He didn't dislike Wachorn, but neither did he like him. Emotionally, he was untouched by Wachorn's passing. In truth, he would have felt more anguish had the plane crashed or suffered damage.

"Just the same, my condolences," said the young man. "We should get him out of the aeroplane and into the ground. As hot as it gets around here, dead bodies tend to attract flies and other less pleasant insects quickly."

"You seem pretty knowledgeable about these things."

The young man shrugged. "We get them every now and again. Dead bodies, I mean. My parents own a hotel in town. When someone dies, I have to take care of them. My mother won't touch them, and my father, well, my father just tells me to take care of them. I don't mind. They're dead. What's a dead person going to do to you?" He offered to help Johnny lift Wachorn out of the cockpit.

Johnny took an instant liking to the young man. He had straight blond hair that parted on one side and covered a large head which sat atop a rather thin, if not frail body. He was taller than Johnny with large hands. A friendly enough fellow.

But it was the way the young man's eyes lit up every time he looked at the Curtiss Jenny that caught Johnny's attention. Johnny recognized the look; he knew what that look felt like on the other side of those blue eyes. It was more than just a simple attraction to a flying machine, it was a compelling fascination, almost bordering on reverence.

"By the way," the young man said, "my name's Percy. Percy Hill."

"Johnny Morgan."

Johnny removed his goggles, leaving behind a film of dirt on his forehead and cheeks. Unlike his new acquaintance, Johnny had a more serious look about him, characterized by a firm jaw, a sculpted nose, and a small mouth that was unaccustomed to smiling.

After shaking hands, the two extracted Wachorn from the cockpit and carried him toward town, Johnny holding his instructor under the arms and Percy carrying the dead man's feet.

"By the way, where am I?" Johnny asked.

"Columbus."

"What state?"

"You don't even know what state you're in?" Percy cried.

"From the air there are no border lines."

Percy nodded thoughtfully. "Never thought of that before," he said. "You're in New Mexico."

"Never been here before," Johnny said.

"Not many people have," Percy replied.

Landis Wachorn didn't have much of a funeral. No tears were shed. No eulogies given. Johnny and Percy dug the grave and placed him in it.

"Sure you don't want to say something?" Percy asked once the grave was covered.

"Can't think of anything," Johnny said.

"You could say something about how he taught you to fly."

Johnny shrugged. "For what purpose? He knows it. You

know it. I know it. Seems like a waste of breath." Tossing
his shovel aside, he added, "Do you know where I could
get a length of wire? The control stick in the front cockpit
needs fixing."

Percy watched as Johnny repaired the Curtiss Jenny,
assisting him when called upon.

"So I guess this is your aeroplane now," Percy said, handing Johnny a pair of pliers.

"Wachorn didn't have any kin, least that I knew of anyway," Johnny replied.

While Johnny grunted and pulled and twisted the wire,
Percy circled the aeroplane. He ran a tender hand across
the canvas. "I thought maybe Dr. Buckland owned the
aeroplane."

He was referring to an advertisement that was printed on
both sides of the fuselage. In fancy letters it read: "Dr.
Buckland's Scotch Oats Essence: Nature's Nerve and Brain
Food."

"That was on there when I met Wachorn," Johnny said.
"The way I heard it, Dr. Buckland paid for the repairs following a pretty severe crash in Oklahoma. Wachorn didn't
have the money to repay him, so they agreed on the advertisement."

"Have you ever tried it?"

"Tried what?"

"Dr. Buckland's Scotch Oats Essence."

"Can't say that I have. You?"

Percy's eyes half-closed, his mouth twisted grotesquely to
one side. He shook his head side-to-side convulsively. "Yes!
And I barely lived to tell about it."

Laughing, Johnny climbed out from beneath the aeroplane. "First chance I get, I'm removing that advertisement," he said. He climbed into the forward cockpit,

gripped the stick and pulled and pushed it in every conceivable direction. The ailerons and stabilizers responded accordingly.

"I'm going to take her up," he said. "Want to come with me?"

From the look on Percy's face, you would have thought that Johnny had just offered him a hundred million dollars. "You mean for free?" he cried.

"Of course for free. You helped me bury Wachorn, didn't you?"

Percy was nearly beside himself with excitement. He listened with rapt attention as Johnny demonstrated how each of the controls worked. He explained the gauges—tachometer, oil, and gasoline. Next, Johnny stepped his new friend through the ignition process.

Within minutes the two of them were racing across the field. With an excited shout from the first-time flier, the wheels of the Curtiss Jenny left the ground and the two young men sailed skyward.

They circled the town of Columbus several times. From the air, Percy pointed out Camp Furlong, the military outpost. Johnny made a low pass just before landing so that everyone could see that it was Percy in the front cockpit. A small army of children and none too few adults gathered near the railroad depot, racing across the tracks to the field where they landed. As far as anyone could remember, Percy Hill was the first resident of Columbus, New Mexico to fly in an aeroplane.

One of the Columbus residents rimming the field was Percy's father. He was not as excited as the other residents were about his son flying in an aeroplane.

"I'm surprised your father let me stay with you," Johnny said.

Lying on his back in the dark, he stared at the ceiling. Percy was on the other side of the room. A sliver of moonlight slipped through the window curtains and streaked across the floor between them. It was the only light in the room.

"My father takes pride in being a Christian man," Percy said. "You needed shelter; he provides shelter for a living. It's not a matter of liking you or not liking you."

"But he doesn't like me, does he?"

"No."

"Your mother?"

"Well, my mother's different. She's been around a lot of people, and she can usually . . . no, my mother doesn't like you either."

The darkness concealed Johnny's grin. He knew neither of Percy's parents approved of him; he just wanted to hear Percy admit it.

The aeroplane ride was just the start. At dinner Oscar and Pearl Hill were shocked at his lack of grief over Wachorn's death. After dinner, they were visibly displeased to learn that he had refused his father's offer to send him to college, that he failed to keep in contact with his parents, and that his only concern in life seemed to be a piece of machinery.

"I guess the topper was the chess game with your father," Johnny said.

"Do you always take games so seriously?" Percy asked.

"I don't like to lose."

"My father says you're out of control. That it's going to catch up with you."

Johnny grinned again. "Doesn't surprise me. Actually, I understand your parents. They're a lot like my parents. I guess that's why I left home. How's your backside?"

"It hurts. I'll get over it."

"Does he always beat you like that?"

"Only when I disobey."

"How did you disobey him by flying with me?"

"It was different this time."

"How so?"

Percy cleared his throat and thought a minute before answering. "You scare them."

"Your father beat you because I scare them?"

"They're afraid that, given the chance, I'll become like you."

"Would you?"

Percy didn't answer immediately. His words came out carefully measured. "If I had a chance to get away from Columbus and learn to fly an aeroplane? Yeah, I would."

Johnny didn't believe him. There was little doubt in his mind that Percy believed what he was saying. But he struck Johnny as the kind of guy who talked of getting away, but never would. Johnny could see him managing Oscar Hill's hotel someday. A leading citizen. Possibly even mayor. There was a solidness about Percy that he lacked.

Percy Hill and Johnny Morgan were opposites. Whereas Percy was a domesticated male who occasionally yearned to be wild, Johnny was a wild stallion who occasionally wanted to rest, to relax, to let his guard down. But Percy no more had it in him to be wild and free than Johnny had it in him to be respectable and domesticated.

Still, they had a common love. The aeroplane.

"Come morning I'll be heading out of here," Johnny said.

"Figured you would. Any idea where you're going?"

"Haven't given it much thought yet."

With his hands behind his head, lying in the dark, Johnny knew that Percy was wanting to go with him. He half expected Percy to ask to go with him tonight. But he didn't.

Come morning, he would though. Count on it. But Johnny had already decided that he'd fly away from Columbus alone. Percy belonged here. Besides, Johnny didn't want another set of parents angry with him.

But he couldn't blame Percy for dreaming. The mere presence of an aeroplane in a small town like this one was an exciting event. The freedom it represented got under men's skins, got them to thinking and wishing for things that could never be. That was the problem with small towns. Nothing exciting ever happened in them. So when it did, they didn't know how to handle it.

Chapter 3

GUNFIRE awoke them. Not the sporadic popping of a single gun, but a storm of bullets, accompanied by the thunder of horses' hooves and cries, *"Viva Villa! Viva Villa!"*

Johnny was up first, grabbing his clothes when Percy's feet hit the ground. It was still dark. The sliver of moonlight that had creased the floor earlier in the night was gone.

"What is it?" Johnny cried.

"Can't you hear what they're shouting?"

Johnny cocked an ear as he shoved a leg into his pants. The din of gunfire was predominant, coming from the direction of the front of the hotel. Percy's room was well to the back. He heard indistinguishable outbursts. Shouts. Panicky screams.

"They're yelling, *Villa!*" Percy said, his voice shaky. "Pancho Villa."

"The Mexican bandit? What's he doing on this side of the border?"

Percy burst out the doorway. "Sounds to me like he's sacking the town."

Being less familiar with the hotel layout, Johnny followed close behind his host. They had to push their way past hotel guests who were crowding the hallway in various states of undress. Recognizing Percy as the owner's son, they clawed and grabbed at him, dozens of hands all at once, demanding an explanation.

"Please," he insisted, trying to break free, "let me get to the front of the hotel. My father will . . . "

They wouldn't let him go. Nearly a dozen people shouting at once. Grabbing him. Demanding answers. Politely he pleaded with them They weren't listening.

Johnny grabbed one wrist at a time and pulled the hands off Percy. To each person whose arm he held, he stared them in the eye and said firmly, "It's not safe for you out here. Go back to your room. Stay low. We'll take care of it." If they asked him a question, he reaffirmed his grip on their wrist and repeated, "It's not safe for you out here. Go back to your room. Now!"

They did. One, sometimes a couple at a time.

Free to continue on their way, Percy nodded gratefully and led Johnny to the hotel lobby. It was dark, but not dark enough that they couldn't see that several bullet holes had already shattered some of the glass panes in the windows which faced the street. On the other side of the glass, horses sped by in both directions. Another pane exploded from a bullet, sending shattered glass skidding across the wooden floor.

"Keep down!" Oscar Hill motioned to them from behind the counter. Percy and Johnny made their way behind the counter where the hotel owner was waiting for them, his nightshirt hastily tucked into his trousers. He handed his son a rifle. "What took you so long?" He didn't wait for an answer. "Make your way toward the back," he ordered. "If they try to come in from the back, call me; if they try to come in the front, I'll yell for you." Looking to Johnny, he asked, "Do you know how to fire a pistol?"

"Yessir," Johnny said, though he'd never fired a pistol

before in his life.

Oscar Hill pulled a pistol from his waistband and handed it to Johnny. "You go with Percy. Protect the back."

Johnny took the gun. He was amazed at how heavy it was; he did his best not to show his surprise.

Percy and Johnny backtracked through the hallway. They weren't more than halfway down the hallway when a door cracked open. A round head poked out. An elderly woman, clutching the top of her nightgown closed with one hand.

"I told you to stay in your room and stay down!" Johnny shouted.

The woman saw the gun in his hand. Her eyes grew wide as a rabbit in the field when it spots a hunter. The door slammed shut and the locking mechanism clicked into place. Johnny rather enjoyed her reaction.

There was a single door leading out back with no windows. Percy hunched against the wall and pointed his rifle at it.

"Aren't you going to check outside first?" Johnny asked.

Percy shook his head. "Father said to guard the door. That's what I'm doing."

Johnny hunched against the other side of the hallway, also staring at the door. He waited. All the sounds were coming from the front of the hotel. Not a sound could be heard beyond the back door. Like all unused doors, it sat there doing nothing. But that didn't keep Percy from staring at it.

"Do you mind if I check outside?" Johnny asked.

Percy was unsure. His eyes narrowed and his head shook slowly back and forth as he considered the question.

Johnny stood. "I'll just poke my head outside. If it gets blown off, you'll know someone's out there."

Percy stared at Johnny incredulously, until he realized Johnny was toying with him. Then, he grinned.

Moving toward the door, Johnny put his hand on the latch. Percy hitched his shoulders and positioned his rifle. Slowly, Johnny turned the latch. The door swung outward. Standing to one side of the growing opening, Johnny poked his head slowly beyond the jamb.

The doorway opened up to nothing but dirt and cactus, open space and the night sky. Nothing moved. There were no signs of bandits.

"I'm going to check on my aeroplane," Johnny said.

"Father told us to guard the back of the hotel!"

"*Your* father told *you* to guard the back of the hotel. I'm going to check on my aeroplane." Not waiting for a response, Johnny took a step outside.

"Leave the revolver here."

"What?"

Percy had his hand out. "It belongs to the hotel. It will be used to guard the hotel." He was serious.

Placing the gun on the floor, Johnny slid it to Percy who placed it in his waistband. "I'll be back shortly," Johnny said.

The disappointed look on Percy's face told Johnny that Percy didn't believe him. "I know what you're thinking," Johnny said. "But I'll be back. I just want to check on my aeroplane. It's the only thing I have."

Percy's expression didn't change. Johnny closed the door on it.

Working his way down the street behind the buildings, Johnny made his way toward the train depot. His aeroplane was in a field situated on the other side of the main street, beyond the tracks and the depot, which meant that Johnny was going to have to cross the street occupied by hundreds of shooting and shouting Villa bandits.

He remembered seeing a military outpost from the air.

"Where is the army when you need them?" he asked aloud.

Johnny edged toward the main street up an alley, hugging the side of the building all the way. Should one of the raiders happen to take a side trip down the alley, he would be helpless.

Reaching the corner, he saw chaos through a cloud of gun smoke. Mustachioed bandits with sombreros rode horses every which way, firing into the air or at anyone who was foolish enough to appear in a window. From concealed places town residents fired back, but the presence of the bandits was so overwhelming the best the residents could do was to get off a quick shot without aiming.

Supply wagons were backed up to stores as the bandits loaded goods and ammunition. Pillars of smoke ascended in one or two places where businesses had been set on fire.

From the alley, Johnny surveyed the scene. Getting across the street without being shot would almost be a miracle. Backtracking down the alley, he made his way behind the businesses to the end of town, hoping that the traffic was a little less heavy there.

He came to the third to the last building on the street. He was in luck; there were fewer of Villa's men at this end. Still, it would be foolhardy for him just to make a dash for it. He needed some kind of cover.

A huge supply wagon with a high canvas profile lumbered down the middle of the street. He had an idea. It wasn't a good one, but it was the only one he had. If it worked, it would cut his dash across the street into two smaller halves.

He waited for the wagon to reach him, then pass. The wagon was tall enough that it hid him from the eyes of three or four of the bandits as it passed between them. There were two other bandits on this side of the wagon. He watched and waited for them to turn away from him.

They both had to be looking away at the same time before the wagon got too far down the road.

One bandit was looking away from him toward the outpost. The other bandit was scanning the buildings on Johnny's side of the street. Johnny couldn't move until both were looking away.

The wagon continued its ponderous course down the middle of the road.

"Look the other direction!" Johnny whispered.

The first bandit shouted something, pointing toward the outpost. The second bandit reined his horse around to take a look.

Now! Johnny leaped from the alley. He ran for the wagon, his eyes on the two bandits. Their backs were to him. Two other bandits sat on the wagon seat; he was behind their field of vision too. On the far side of the street, the other bandits were still cut off from view, unless he didn't catch the wagon. If he couldn't, his cover would roll away and he'd find himself standing defenseless in the middle of the street.

He reached the side of the wagon. He slowed down, matching its speed. The two bandits on his side of the wagon were preoccupied with the outpost. Now Johnny could see why. There were at least as many of Villa's men attacking the outpost as had attacked the town, occupying the army while the town was being looted.

Running beside the wagon, Johnny glanced behind him. The other three bandits should be coming into view any minute now. Previously, they had been staring at the center of town. He hoped they were still so occupied.

The last business on the far side of the street came into view. His plan was to get to the side of it, to let it shield him from the street traffic just as the alley had done.

Like before, he had to wait for the right moment when

the wagon, the bandits, and the building were all in position. He was in luck. Just as the wagon reached the end of the town, he slipped behind it, across the second half of the street, down the side of the building, and behind it before anyone noticed him.

I never knew crossing the street could be so hard, he mused.

However, the smirk on his lips barely had a chance to appear before it mutated into an open-mouth gasp of horror. From where he stood, he had a clear view of the field in which he'd landed the aeroplane. A ghastly column of black smoke rose from the flames that engulfed the fuselage. Ten mounted bandits surrounded it, watching it burn. Apparently, the gasoline tank had already blown, because all that was left was a skeletal shape of a flying machine that would never get off the ground again.

Johnny slumped to the ground, his eyes fixed in disbelief on the burning wreckage. *Why would they do that? What threat was the aeroplane to them?* He could imagine them being curious, possibly even wanting to steal it. *But burn it? Why? What sense did it make to burn it?*

Johnny's insides churned. His heart ached.

Slumped against the side of the building, Johnny mourned the loss of his aeroplane with an emotion he never felt at the death of Landis Wachorn, its former owner.

As the sun rose over Columbus, New Mexico, the center of the town lay in smoking ruin. The bandits had departed, shooting their rifles, whooping, shouting, *"Viva Villa! Viva Villa!"*

Johnny Morgan ambled down the back way toward the hotel, not wanting to accidentally encounter any Villa stragglers. He thought about going to pay respects to his aeroplane, but it was too painful for him to even think about it now.

As he reached the hotel, he saw another drama unfolding, a continuation of the Villa raid. Oscar and Pearl Hill's hotel was engulfed in flames. Percy was standing alone in the middle of the street watching it and weeping.

"Did everyone get out?" Johnny asked him.

Percy seemed startled to see Johnny at first. From the look on Percy's face, the tragedy was greater than just the loss of a building.

"They stormed the front," he cried. "Shot my father... I couldn't stop them ... I was too late ... too late."

"Did everyone get out? How about that woman, the one with the rabbit eyes, the one I told to stay..."

"I don't know," Percy cried. "I don't know... where my mother is...."

"Your mother's in there?"

"I don't know!"

"Have you seen her out here?"

Percy shook his head.

"You ask over there," Johnny said, pushing Percy in the direction he wanted him to go. "I'll ask over here."

Together, they queried the bystanders. No one had seen Pearl Hill.

"I'm going in," Johnny said.

Percy shook his head. "I already tried. It's too hot."

Johnny looked at the building. Tongues of flame licked the top of windows. Smoke poured out of every opening. Pulling his shirt over his mouth, Johnny said, "I'm going in to look for your mother."

Ducking his head, he charged through the front door into the lobby. Draperies, furniture, pillars, wooden window casings, all were in flames. Oscar Hill lay dead behind the counter, blood stained his shirt in two places on his chest.

Johnny felt something bump into him. It was Percy.

"Where would she be?" Johnny cried.

"I don't know!" Percy shouted. His eyes were desperate. He wanted to know where to start looking for his mother. He honestly didn't know where to start, given the morning's circumstances.

Acrid smoke burned Johnny's lungs. He began to cough. So did Percy. With each breath it felt like a portion of his lungs were cut away, leaving him less and less with which to breathe. They would have to move quickly, or they too would become casualties.

Johnny led the way down the hall. Most of the doorways were open. When he came to the old woman's door, the one that looked like a frightened rabbit, it was closed. He tried to open it. Locked. Either she took the time to lock the door on her way out, or...

"Help me break this down," Johnny shouted and coughed.

It took both of them several strong hits with their shoulders before the door gave way. The woman was laying in the middle of the room on the floor, curled up like a little child.

With Percy's help, Johnny managed to get the woman over his shoulder.

"You check the other rooms in this hallway. I'll take her out and be right back."

Percy nodded.

Laboring under his load, his breath cut short by the smoke, the heat as hot as an oven's insides, Johnny made his way down the hall and out into the street. He entrusted the woman into the care of two women bystanders and turned to go back into the blazing hotel. He ignored their shouts.

"What do you think you're doing?"

"Don't go back in there!"

"You're a fool!"

"He's crazy! He'll never come out!"

Coughing convulsively now, Johnny stumbled into the lobby. *Was it his imagination or was it hotter now than it was just a few minutes ago?* The heat was oppressive, nearly knocking him to his knees. Forcing himself to go on, he bent down low and made his way to the hallway.

Percy was slouched to the floor, propped up against a wall.

Johnny knelt beside him.

"I'm all right," Percy said, struggling to his feet.

"Let me help you anyway."

"My mother..."

Johnny led Percy to the lobby, fully intending on leading him out to the street. Percy had other ideas. "This way!" He pushed Johnny toward a door at the far end of the counter. Johnny noticed that Percy intentionally looked away when they were in view of his father.

Passing through the door, they came to an area that served as a dining hall. Through the smoke Johnny caught an occasional flash of light as the chandelier threw off reflections from the flames.

Both Percy and Johnny were coughing so hard, they could barely stand up straight. Johnny's lungs were so full of smoke it felt like he had less than a tenth of his breathing capacity. They were slowly dying and he knew it.

Leaning against one dining chair after another, they made their way, arms around each other's shoulders, toward the door at the far end.

"It leads to the kitchen!" Percy cried.

The kitchen door was blocked. As before, the two of them put their shoulders into it. But this time, the door moved on the first hit. It didn't swing all the way open; it moved as though something behind it was blocking it.

Percy stuck his head through the doorway.

"Mother!" he cried.

Pushing her out of the way enough to get both of them inside the kitchen, they picked up Percy's mother and, between them, carried her toward the front of the hotel. Like the rabbit-eyed woman in the room, Pearl Hill showed no sign of life.

Reaching the lobby, Johnny stopped. "Can you take her from here by yourself?" he shouted.

A puzzled look crossed Percy's face. "I think so."

Johnny transferred his portion of Pearl Hill's weight onto her son. "I'll be right behind you," Johnny shouted.

After assuring himself that Percy could carry his mother alone, Johnny went behind the counter and lifted Oscar Hill up from the floor and swung him over his shoulder. Blinded by smoke, nearly bursting from the heat, hacking so hard he couldn't walk straight, Johnny staggered to the front door carrying Percy's dead father.

Johnny found Percy sitting on the boardwalk, his shoulders slumped, coughing intermittently, staring at what was left of his father's hotel.

"Did your mother make it?" Johnny asked.

Tears filled Percy's eyes. He pursed his lips and shook his head.

After a coughing fit of his own, Johnny sat beside his friend. "I'm sorry," he said.

For a long time neither spoke a word. Johnny figured Percy needed to be alone, yet to know someone was near.

"The other woman. Did she make it?" Percy asked.

"No."

"I'm sorry."

"She did exactly what I told her to do," Johnny said.

"You did what was best for her at the time," Percy replied.

Johnny felt little comfort from his words.

"Johnny?"

"Yeah?"

"You knew my father was dead. Why did you go back for him?"

Johnny stared at the smoke-covered tips of his shoes. "Nobody deserves to be burned in a fire," he said.

"You're a good friend, Johnny Morgan."

Johnny didn't respond. He didn't feel like a very good friend at the moment.

Chapter 4

WE'LL take care of them from here, Miss."
"Oh, but I don't mind, you see I'm a nurse too and I . . ."

A kind but stern woman in a nurse's uniform bent down until her eyes were on the same level as Katy's. "We'll take care of them from here, Miss. Someone will be by to check on you in a little while."

Katy sat on the floor in the center of eight sleeping children, the children from the lifeboat. After they had reached shore, with no one to take care of them, Katy had taken it upon herself to shepherd them into an out-of-the-way corner.

An armada of ships, most of them from Queenstown, Ireland, had responded to the distress calls of the *Lusitania*. Katy had stayed with the children as they were transferred from the lifeboat to a fishing boat and then to the docks at Queenstown. The town was overwhelmed by the immediate care needed by the victims. So Katy took it upon herself to see after the eight children.

She checked them for physical injuries and, when she found none, did her best to keep them from being trampled by the onrush of emergency workers. They were frightened and tired—*who among them wasn't?*—and needed someone to care for them until their parents could be found. So she cleared a small corner in a docking office, gathered the children around her, held them, rocked them, sang to them, until finally they all fell asleep in a variety of positions around her.

Naturally, she wanted the best for them. But now that they were being taken from her, she realized how much comfort she herself had derived from them. A line of caretakers scooped them up one by one and carried them away. All of a sudden, her cozy little corner seemed barren and lonely.

Pulling a blanket—which had been given to her when she stepped off the fishing boat—tightly around her shoulders, she rose from the corner and stretched her legs. Her concern for her mother gnawed at her, but it seemed useless to rush around in a panic like so many of the others were doing. Their panic wouldn't change anything. It may hasten their knowledge of the truth, but at times like this maybe it was better not to know the truth for just a little bit longer. Katy knew that truth often came with jagged edges, bursting bubbles of hope.

She wandered past bruised and shuddering women; crippled, half-clothed men. Mothers clutching their children while anxious eyes searched for their husbands. As the hours wore on, signs began to appear in shop windows all over Queenstown:

> *Lusitania – missing baby, 15 mos. old*
> *Very curly hair. Rosy complexion.*
> *White woolen jersey & white woolen leggings.*
> *Tries to talk and walk.*

As more and more rescue ships docked at Queenstown, piles of corpses like cordwood appeared on the shadowy wharf. Katy stood solemnly and watched as they were stacked. She avoided looking at their faces. Instead, she looked for a peach dress, similar to the white one she was wearing.

By the end of the day, she knew no more of her mother's fate than she did drifting at sea aboard the lifeboat.

Three days later, on May 10, Katy Morgan stood alone with hundreds of other people beside a mass grave as the first group of victims were buried. Wooden caskets crowded each other at the bottom of the wide pit. The inscriptions on most of them were, at best, vague: Unidentified Male, or Unidentified Female.

Katy had stared at each one of the bloated, grayish faces. None of them was her mother. At least, she didn't think any of them was her mother. It was hard to tell.

She told herself she was attending the mass funeral out of respect for those who were not as fortunate as she to survive the sinking. But as her eyes scanned the inscriptions— Unidentified Female, Unidentified Female, Unidentified Female, Unidentified Female—a part of her conceded that one of those coffins, symbolically, if not in actuality, housed the body of her mother.

After all, it had been three days.

Jesse Morgan sat in a plush leather chair opposite the Secretary of State, William Jennings Bryan. The portly cabinet member, who had been sitting behind a massive desk, rose, skirted the edge of the desk, and took a chair next to Jesse. He placed a hand on Jesse's forearm.

"I'm sorry I'm not the bearer of gladder tidings," Bryan said.

Jesse held in his hand a telegram. "At least we know that Katy is safe," he said.

Bryan brushed a hand across his bald head, in a helpless

gesture. "There are times," he said, "when there is nothing we can do except trust God to work things out according to His will."

Looking at the state official, and his friend, Jesse could not help but grin. This was the kind of advice he might expect to hear from his minister, not from the Secretary of State. But considering who it was who was saying it, Jesse knew the words had been spoken sincerely.

"Have you made arrangements to go to Queenstown?" Bryan asked.

Jesse shook his head. "There's nothing I could do there that hasn't already been done," he said. "Katy thinks I ought to stay here. If anything needs to be done there, she can do it. And if, by some miracle, Emily is still alive, she may not know how to contact Katy. She may try here. So it looks like I'll stay for the time being."

Bryan patted his arm. "You do what's best for your family," he said.

"Thank you, Mr. Secretary. Especially considering recent developments here."

"There is little doubt I need you now, more than ever," Bryan said. "But your family comes first."

Jesse smiled warmly. "I know you mean that, sir, and I want to thank you. Meanwhile, get me up-to-date. I understand you have more information on German espionage in New York."

Returning to the business side of his desk, Secretary of State William Jennings Bryan opened a folder that lay atop his desk. He began briefing Jesse Morgan on recent developments in Germany and New York.

A daily list of names was posted at the Cunard offices in Queenstown. Katy checked it faithfully. Of the 1,924 people who sailed aboard the *Lusitania,* 1,198 of them did not survive. Sixty-three of the dead were children. One hundred and twenty-eight were Americans. None of the names matched that of Katy's mother.

Would she be number one hundred and twenty-nine?
And if not, where was she?

Chapter 5

F OUR newly filled graves appeared in the cemetery on the northern outskirts of Columbus, New Mexico. The earthen mounds represented a portion of the toll exacted by Pancho Villa on a town defending itself against his predawn raid. A total of seventeen people were killed defending the town, eight military and nine civilian.

Among the raid's casualties was Bessie Bain James and her unborn child. Bessie, her husband, and sister were running to the Hoover Hotel for its protective walls when she and her husband were shot as they neared the hotel's west entrance. Her husband managed to crawl in on his own; Bessie was helped by residents. Once inside, she looked up at those helping her and said, "We are now safe!" Then she died.

James T. Dean, a store owner, occupied one of the freshly dug graves. He was on his way down Main Street to help fight fires when he was shot. His body was found at daybreak at the intersection of Main and Broadway.

The two remaining graves were the final resting places of Oscar and Pearl Hill, hotel owners, parents, and casualties of the international crisis with Mexico that occupied more of President Wilson's time than did the war between the belligerents in Europe. As word of the raid spread by telegraph, these seventeen American lives served as kindling tossed upon the nation's flaming animosity for her southern neighbor.

The national passion for retribution burned in Percy Hill's eyes. Johnny could see it. Percy's oversized hands gripped and regripped a wooden shovel handle as he surveyed the somber handiwork of his parents' graves. His ears were closed to the words of comfort scattered by a clean-shaven, young minister among the mourners like so many rose petals, as though the fragrance of his words could somehow mask the stench of death, or sweeten the acrid tang of vengeance that permeated the gathering.

Johnny's palms were tender against his own shovel handle. His back still ached from digging Landis Wachorn's grave the day before. The Gray Eagle's earthen mound was lighter than the others. It served to remind him of his own loss— the gutted Curtiss Jenny in the field. Once a thing of beauty, it now resembled the skeleton of some prehistoric firefly.

Before the final Amen sounded, Percy fled the funeral service. Johnny followed behind him.

"Mrs. Ritchie offered us food and a place to sleep tonight," Johnny said in an attempt at conversation.

Percy gave no indication he heard. He strode purposefully down the middle of the street toward the remains of the hotel.

"She came up to me while you were digging. Said she made the offer to me because when she spoke to you, you didn't seem to hear her."

Percy continued walking.

"Sort of like the way you're not hearing anything I say right now," Johnny said.

Shovel in hand, Percy continued down the street and through the entrance of the building that had once been his parents' livelihood and his home. The adobe walls were still standing. Everything else was charred rubble littering the floor. There being no roof, not even any remaining structure of a roof, the rooms were well lighted and ventilated. However, there was not enough fresh air in all of Columbus to remove the gritty pungency of blackened wood. Its biting odor spurred frequent coughing spasms in both young men.

First with his shovel, then with his hands, Percy picked his way through the charred remains.

"What are you searching for?" Johnny asked.

The only sound Percy made in response was that of boards and books and pieces of furniture clattering atop other debris when he flung them aside.

"How can I help you, if I don't know what I'm looking for?" Johnny asked.

Without looking up, without slowing his search, Percy said, "Rifle. Pistol. Anything that shoots."

Johnny raised his eyebrows in interest. "Plan on shooting anybody I know?"

"Ah!" The sound Percy made was more of a grunt than an exclamation, not unlike a bull would make just before he charged. Reaching into the rubble he grasped something deeply buried and pulled and yanked it to the surface.

It was his father's rifle.

Percy examined it with a fiery look in his eyes which was quickly quenched by the rifle's condition. The wooden stock was charcoal black and just as brittle. The barrel was grossly discolored as was the breech. The firing mechanism was frozen.

With an anguished curse, Percy flung the rifle across the room. It smashed against the adobe wall and clattered to the floor. He resumed his search.

Wordlessly, Johnny helped him. The transformation that grief and anger had made in Percy intrigued him. He wondered if he would react the same way had it been his parents. Probably not. From what he had seen, Percy felt more deeply for his parents. Naturally then, his sense of loss was greater, more keenly felt.

The thought gave Johnny pause. He doubted that he would ever know the anguish Percy was feeling. For him to experience that level of anguish, he would first have to feel deeply for someone. That would never happen. Johnny neither sought nor desired close friendships. He didn't yearn to love or be loved. In this, he considered himself a unique breed of man. Stronger. Less vulnerable. Not subject to the irrational impulses that were driving Percy.

By nightfall, the last of the guns and rifles were found. Worthless. Every one of them.

Percy slumped against a wall, his hands and arms, face and neck blackened with charcoal smudges. He looked like he was deflating as his back slowly slid down the adobe enclosure. The fire that had been in his eyes had burned itself out. Now, his gaze was as empty and hollow as the gutted building in which he sat.

Clearing a space nearby, Johnny joined him. The remainder of the night passed in such solitude; at times Johnny thought for sure he could hear the stars in their courses overhead.

His own coughing woke him.

A slight breeze wafted through the skeletal remains of the hotel, bringing with it moments of freshness interspersed with the all-too-familiar odor of smoke that Johnny was sure had penetrated all the way to his bone marrow. It was this alternating condition of fresh and stale air that set off the burning in his lungs.

Expecting a coughing duet, but hearing only a solo, between spasms Johnny looked to the space where he had seen Percy last. It had been vacated. Doubled over by one extended cough after another, Johnny managed to get to his feet. He stumbled out of the room and down what used to be the hotel hallway. As he passed each doorway, he glanced in, only to find one room as empty as the other. Reaching the lobby, he found that room similarly unoccupied. He headed for the street and fresh air, gasping like a fish.

Once outside and away from the odor of burned timber, he managed to catch his breath and to catch sight of Percy. His smudged and darkened friend stood facing south, staring at the horizon.

The light of intelligence had returned to Percy's eyes. No longer burning with fire, no longer cavernous, they brimmed with pain and vulnerability.

"Did you really think you were going to ride into Mexico and hunt him down all by yourself?" Johnny asked. "He has hundreds of men. The army is massing at Camp Furlong. They'll go after him."

"I could join the army," Percy said, still staring at the horizon.

"You're not the Army type."

"Maybe I wasn't before, but I am now."

"Why? Because you feel like killing someone?"

"What else am I going to do?" Percy's voice trembled. Standing there, his hands in his pockets, with the morning sun casting a long sideways shadow, he looked lonely and pitiful. "I don't have a place to live," he continued. "I don't have a job, or a prospect for a job. All I've ever done is work at the hotel."

Johnny moved beside him. Staring with him at the distant south, he said, "We're quite a pair, aren't we? Yesterday I didn't even know the name of this town. Now I'm a resident—at least until I figure out what I'm going to do. Do you know where I might find an aeroplane?"

The ridiculous question brought a smile to Percy's face.

"Other than what's left of yours in the field, there isn't another aeroplane within . . ."

"Percy Hill!" a male voice boomed.

Both boys turned in the direction of the voice. A compact man with his trouser waistband pulled high over a protruding paunch approached them. He wore a white long-sleeved shirt with a bow tie and a hat.

"Mr. Mayor," Percy greeted him.

"Saw you standing over here and, well, just wanted to offer my condolences on the death of your parents. They were fine people, Percy. None finer than your father, or kinder-hearted than your mother. Known them many years. They don't come any finer than your folks."

"Thank you, sir," Percy said.

No doubt the expression of sympathy was welcomed, but it served as just another reminder that his parents were dead. Johnny saw a cloud of grief once again pass over Percy's face.

"And who are you?" the mayor said, turning to Johnny, forcing an introduction.

Johnny obliged the mayor with his name.

"You the flier? The one who flew that aeroplane into town the other day?"

"Yes, sir."

"Well, I guess when it rains it pours," the mayor said.

Percy and Johnny exchanged glances, each hoping the other knew what the mayor was talking about. They didn't have to wait long for an explanation.

"A few days ago Columbus had never seen an aeroplane except in pictures. Then, you fly over and . . . bam! Next thing we know we got ourselves a whole squadron!"

Johnny's eyes lit up. "A squadron of aeroplanes?"

"Eight of 'em. General Blackjack Pershing will use 'em to track down Villa. Oughta be here in a few days."

"What a sight that will be, won't it, Percy?" Johnny shouted. "Eight . . . " he turned to the mayor, "What kind of aeroplanes will they be?"

The mayor shrugged. "Aeroplanes are aeroplanes," he said.

Turning back to Percy, Johnny continued, "Does it matter? Eight aeroplanes in the sky all at once!"

"Well, they won't exactly be in the sky," the mayor said. "They're arriving by train from Fort Sam Houston, Texas."

"I don't care if they're coming in by pack mule!" Johnny cried. "Think about it, Percy! This way I can be back in the air and you can get your revenge!"

"But I don't know anything about flying," Percy said.

"You flew with me, didn't you? Besides, we're in this together. I'll teach you everything you need to know!" Turning back to the mayor, Johnny asked, "Who should we see about the aeroplanes? Who's in charge? Should we talk to General Pershing?"

"Doubt if Pershing would have time to talk to two boys," the mayor said. "The man in charge of the aeroplanes is Captain Benjamin Foulois."

"And where might we find him?" Johnny asked.

"Camp Furlong, I suppose," replied the mayor.

Grabbing Percy by the arm, Johnny pulled him up the street. "The military base is this way, isn't it? Come on, Percy, don't dawdle. We're going to get ourselves a couple of aeroplanes!"

After inquiring at the military base, Johnny and Percy managed to track down Captain Foulois at the train depot. He was emerging from the depot house when they eagerly accosted him.

"You want to what?" he bellowed.

Tightly focused eyes stared from beneath the rim of his

hat. He was dressed in a typical cavalry uniform with neat-ly tailored brown breeches and a shirt which was buttoned to the top button. His riding boots sounded heavy with authority as they pounded the planks of the depot floor.

"Fly," Johnny said simply. "We heard that you have eight aeroplanes scheduled to arrive from Fort Sam Houston. We want to volunteer to fly one of them for you."

"You do, do you?" Foulois said with just a hint of amuse-ment.

"Yes, sir," Percy said. "Johnny here is a real good pilot, sir. And, well, I want to learn how to fly real bad, and Johnny said he'd teach me everything he knows."

"So you have flying experience?" Foulois asked Johnny.

"Yes, sir!"

"How many hours have you logged?"

"Can't say as I rightly know the exact number of hours. But I've been flying for nearly a year now."

"You have, have you? In what aeroplane?"

"The one in the field over there, sir." Johnny pointed in the general direction of his aeroplane. "A Curtiss Jenny, sir. It was burned during the raid."

"I saw it," Foulois said. "So, that's your aeroplane?"

"Yes, sir. I sort of inherited it from a partner when he died kind of sudden. If you don't mind me asking, sir, what kind of aeroplanes is the army getting?"

"Curtiss Jennys," Foulois replied.

Johnny grimaced. "I was hoping for better, but I guess it's best to start out with what you know. So, when do we get started?"

The amused glint in Foulois' eyes was gone. "Son, I don't know where you got your information about our aeroplanes . . . "

"Mayor Hoover told us!" Percy said.

"He did, did he?"

The scowl on Foulois' face indicated he wasn't pleased with the mayor's ready distribution of army information.

"Be that as it may, gentlemen," Foulois continued, "the army doesn't let just anyone fly their aeroplanes. Eleven trained officers have completed a special flying school to qualify for this assignment. Needless to say, we won't be needing your services."

With a curt nod, he walked between Percy and Johnny in the direction of camp.

"Excuse me, sir," Percy called after him.

Foulois stopped, but he didn't turn around. Percy had to catch up with him in order to continue the conversation.

"If you don't mind me asking, sir," Percy said, "why are the aeroplanes coming in by train? Why don't they just fly here?"

"The answer is simple, son," Foulois said with forced courtesy. "They're not flying in because they're not yet assembled."

Foulois started on his way again. Percy jumped in front of him.

"Do you need people to help you assemble them?"

Foulois studied him a moment. "Do you know any qualified engineers?"

Percy grinned. "I don't know of anyone who's more qualified than Johnny over there. He was fixin' his own aeroplane all the time."

Foulois turned and looked at Johnny. "Is this true? You can repair a Curtiss Jenny?"

"I know every square inch of the Curtiss Jenny," Johnny replied, "but . . . "

Foulois nodded. "If that's true, you've got yourself a job as a civilian engineer." He told the boys the date and time of the aeroplanes' arrival.

Johnny shook his head. "I want to fly the aeroplanes, I

don't want to . . . "

Percy cut him off. To Foulois, he said, "He'll be there!"

Foulois took one last appraising look at Johnny, turned on his heel, and proceeded back to Camp Furlong.

"I'm a pilot, not an engineer!" Johnny cried to Percy. "I don't want to build aeroplanes, I want to fly them!"

"But don't you see? This way you will be around the aeroplanes! Captain Foulois can get to know you better . . . maybe give you a chance to fly the aeroplane, test it out, or something . . . then you can show him what you can do!"

"I don't know," Johnny said.

"Maybe the whole squadron will come down sick with something! Then they'll have to use you!"

"I just don't know if I can be around those aeroplanes all day watching other fellows fly them and not be able to take the stick myself."

"What else are you going to do? Stay with Mrs. Ritchie for the rest of your life?"

"If I do this, what are you going to do?" Johnny asked.

Percy shrugged. "There are two other hotels in Columbus. The Hoover and the Commercial. I suppose I could pick up a job at one of them."

"No," Johnny said.

"No? What else am I qualified to do?"

"You're qualified to be my assistant," Johnny said. "You helped me repair my aeroplane, didn't you?"

"What are you talking about? You repaired the aeroplane by yourself."

"You handed me the pliers when I needed them, didn't you? In my mind, that qualifies you as an assistant. And if Captain Foulois wants me to help them assemble eight aeroplanes, he'll have to hire the both of us."

"Really?" Percy said.

"Really!" Johnny replied.

Chapter 6

T HE U.S. First Aero Squadron flew its initial reconnaissance flight into New Mexico from Columbus on
March 16th. It was with mixed feelings that Johnny
Morgan watched the Curtiss Jenny he'd assembled take to
the skies with Captain T.F. Dodd at the controls and
Captain Benjamin D. Foulois as the observer. The next day,
General Pershing coordinated two columns heading due
south with orders to pursue Pancho Villa and disperse his
band or bands. According to their most recent report, Villa
has passed Casas Grandes and was moving south.

Two days later, Captain Foulois received orders from
General Pershing to proceed at once from Columbus to
Casas Grandes with his entire squadron. Upon receiving
his orders, Captain Foulois, ignoring Johnny's warnings,
interpreted them literally. He ordered all eight of the
Curtiss Jennys into the air despite the fact that it was after
5 P.M. and dusk.

The aeroplanes lifted off the desert floor and flew into
the darkening sky, each with a double-digit number painted prominently on its side, in the same place Landis
Wachorn's aeroplane had advertised Dr. Buckland's Scotch
Oats Essence. Johnny wiped his hands on a rag. To Percy
he predicted, "It'll be a miracle if we don't lose some aeroplanes and pilots tonight. Never fly in the dark."

Before long, they could hear the sputtering of an engine. A lone aeroplane approached the Columbus landing field. With a few good bounces it landed, having returned with motor trouble. As word came back about the fate of the other aeroplanes in the squadron, Johnny's prediction proved accurate.

Four of the aeroplanes managed to make it to La Ascencion where they landed in a pasture as darkness engulfed them. The three remaining aeroplanes got lost. One managed to land at Ojo Caliente, another at Janos, while the third one, aeroplane No. 41, crash-landed at Pearson, where it was fired upon by Mexican nationals. The pilot survived, managing to complete the trip to Casas Grandes on foot.

Three days later, Johnny and Percy were dispatched to Pearson to see what they could do to salvage No. 41. The damage was too great. After removing all the serviceable parts, they set fire to it.

The next day Captains Foulois and Dodd took off in aeroplane No. 44 at noon. Their orders were to seek out enemy columns in the foothills of the Sierra Madres. They managed to fly only twenty-five miles south of Casas Grandes before they encountered strong whirlwinds and vertical currents in the mountains. With only a 60-horsepower engine, they simply didn't have enough power to rise above the 10,000-foot peaks of the Sierra Madres. They had to return without accomplishing their mission.

Later that same day, Lieutenant Bowen wrecked aeroplane No. 54 when he tried to land it in a whirlwind. He managed to walk away with a broken nose and other minor injuries. So far in the expedition, the First Aero Squadron had been less than impressive.

Lieutenant Vernon Eastman sat in the mess shack with

his chair tipped back rakishly against the adobe wall. His right hand he held high, his palm suspended in midair. A sudden swooping motion brought it down level with the table.

He shared the table with four other fliers, but not the spotlight. With his foot planted on the seat of the chair, he sat where the top of the chair wedged against the wall. This placed him on a higher level than the four other fliers. While Eastman spun his yarn, they visualized his encounter with a desert whirlwind, his hand aiding the portrayal as it represented his aeroplane. To hear him tell the story, none of the other fliers would have survived the encounter.

Johnny and Percy entered the mess shack, trays in hand, and looked for a place to sit. The only table available was next to Lieutenant Eastman's one-man performance.

Every time Johnny saw the lieutenant, other than when he was strapped into the cockpit of his plane, there were at least three and sometimes five or more soldiers riding in his wake. Tall, muscular, and well-proportioned with short-cropped brown hair, Eastman was the epitome of the American male, that is if one were to believe the image portrayed in *Saturday Evening Post* advertisements. Eastman was attractive, intelligent, ambitious, and confident, if not cocky.

He had two facial characteristics that were unusually striking—steely, blue eyes and dazzling white, perfect teeth. He worked these two features in conjunction with one another with ease and confidence. While a sparkle in his eyes accompanied by a wide, easy grin charmed women and disarmed men, a hardened stare and clenched teeth signaled to opponents that a worthy adversary had arrived.

Johnny and Percy knew better than to attempt to join the fliers at their table. On base and off, the air squadron pilots were a group unto themselves. So the two young men had to satisfy themselves with sitting nearby and listening to the stories of those who were doing what Johnny and Percy only wished they could do.

"Hey, Eastman," one of the fliers said, "have you heard about that group of American fliers who are flying with the French in the war?"

Eastman nodded knowingly. "The Lafayette Escadrille," he said. "That's the Lafayette squadron for those of you with a lesser education."

The fliers laughed, each one accusing the others of ignorance.

"They're not actually doing combat," Eastman said, "just reconnaissance. Last I heard, their aeroplanes don't even have guns."

"But at least they're flying in combat conditions!" one of the soldiers cried.

"While over here pilots do battle with whirlwinds . . ." Johnny said, munching on a piece of bread, ". . . and lose."

"Did you say something, Morgan?" Eastman said.

Johnny sniffed, sopped his bread in his beans, and took a bite. He spoke and chewed at the same time. "Only that it seems strange to me that a group of so-called trained pilots don't know better than to fly in the dark, and that when they come head-to-head with a gust of wind, they crash; or, if they manage to survive, they think they deserve a medal."

Chairs scraped the floor. The attention of every flier at Eastman's table was now centered on Johnny.

"You know, Morgan," Eastman said, standing beside Johnny, towering over him, "for a mechanic, you have a big mouth."

"He's not a mechanic. He's a pilot," Percy said in Johnny's defense.

"A pilot?" Eastman cried in mock surprise. "Is that so? Well, let's compare qualifications, shall we? I received my training in Dayton at the hands of the Wright brothers themselves. Who taught you to fly?"

"Landis Wachorn," Johnny said nonchalantly, hiding his envy over Eastman's good fortune to have flown with Orville and Wilbur Wright.

Eastman gasped. "Not the legendary. . . " he screwed up his face comically, ". . . Landis Wachorn!"

While the other fliers howled with laughter, Percy cried, "I'd be willing to bet that Johnny Morgan's spent more time in the air than any of you, and that he could outfly any of you any day of the week!"

"You've actually seen Mr. Mechanic fly?" Eastman asked Percy.

Percy described the first time he saw Johnny Morgan, straddling his disabled Curtiss Jenny and flying it backward over Columbus.

"If that's true," Eastman said, "then what are you doing here as a mechanic?"

"Villa's men burned my aeroplane during the raid," Johnny said. "I tried to get Captain Foulois to let me fly for the army, but he seemed to think I was too intelligent and experienced for the job."

Johnny didn't expect anyone to believe his lie; he just couldn't pass up the opportunity to rattle a bevy of smug army pilots.

Eastman lowered himself until he and Johnny were on the same level. His eyes hardened. White teeth clenched visibly. "Anytime you think you're man enough to go up against me, you just say the word and we'll see who the real pilot is."

"Just tell me the word to say and I'll say it," Johnny replied.

Eastman was taken aback somewhat by Johnny's eagerness to accept his challenge. But he wasn't about to back down. "First chance we get, Morgan," he said.

"Better make it soon," Johnny replied. "At the rate this squadron is crashing aeroplanes, we'll run out before we get a chance."

Eastman's glare hardened. Balled fists indicated he was tempted to get violent. Instead, he spoke to the other fliers. "Let's get out of here." He started to leave, then turned and said, "Before I forget, No. 44 has been sputtering. Fix it." He turned and left the mess shack, his entourage following him.

"No. 44's not the only thing around here that's sputtering," Johnny muttered.

Percy nearly choked on his beans laughing.

In April, nearly a month after the First Aero Squadron's initial flight out of Columbus, mechanic Johnny Morgan reported to Captain Foulois the status of the squadron's aeroplanes. Five of the eight aeroplanes taken into Mexico had been wrecked. Another had been wrecked and abandoned, which left only two aeroplanes of questionable condition for field service.

The next day a report reached the camp that Lieutenant Eastman's aeroplane had gone down in the desert with engine trouble. Johnny and Percy were dispatched to evaluate the aeroplane's condition and, if at all possible, get it back into the air.

Johnny and Percy bounced in the back of the truck at the mercy of every rock and rut and hole along the Mexican desert trail. The heat was oppressive, the roar of the engine maddening. Between the incessant clanging of his tools in the box by his feet, the throat-burning odor of gasoline, and the dirty, gritty desert air, Johnny was getting a headache. Everything and everyone in the back of the truck was hot and sticky and coated with coarse sand.

To make matters worse, Captain Cavenaugh had stopped

to give some foot soldiers a ride. The commander of the unit would allow only those who were footsore or ill to accept the truck captain's offer, since they would normally ride an ambulance if one were available. He lined up his men and told the disabled to go to the truck and climb on. A footrace ensued, after which the commander ordered all those who forgot to limp to rejoin the company and continue on foot. However, there were enough soldiers who honestly qualified for the ride to pack the back of the truck. With quarters cramped, Johnny found himself suffocating between two other hot, sweaty bodies.

"Here's where we leave the trail!" Cavenaugh shouted over the engine to Johnny. "According to the report, it should only be a mile or two farther."

The truck lurched violently as it left the rutted trail. A soldier's head smashed against the bridge of Johnny's nose, jarring his already aching head. He gritted his teeth and forced a grin at the soldier's apology. He wished he'd taken a horse.

Captain Cavenaugh spied the aeroplane and the truck driver altered his course to intercept it. As they approached, the Lieutenant Eastman and his observer crawled out from aeroplane's shadow.

"What took you so long?" Eastman shouted as Johnny gladly hopped out of the back of the truck. Percy was right behind him, carrying the box of tools. The foot soldiers, at the end of their ride, climbed out too, expressing their thanks individually to Cavenaugh.

"I said, what took you so long?" Eastman asked again.

"What's the problem with the aeroplane?" Johnny asked.

His hands on his hips, his eyes and teeth in a coordinated sneer, Eastman stared at Johnny, apparently waiting for an explanation. Johnny wasn't about to give him one.

"Will it start?" he asked.

"Yes, it'll start."

"Let's hear it."

Eastman didn't move, nor did his withering gaze lessen.

"Percy!" Johnny shouted. "You grab the prop. I'll get the throttle." He stepped past the lieutenant blocking his path.

Eastman grabbed his arm. "It's my aeroplane. I'll start the engine."

Johnny motioned with his arms, suggesting that he get on with it.

The Curtiss Jenny's engine roared to life.

Johnny listened to it for a minute. Stepping beside the aeroplane's cockpit, he shouted to Eastman, "It sounds fine to me!"

"It cuts out at high altitudes!" Eastman shouted back.

Johnny listened again. He shook his head. "There's nothing wrong with that engine," he shouted.

Eastman cut the engine. Without a word, he marched past Johnny and spoke directly to Captain Cavenaugh. "Take my observer and this man," he motioned toward Percy, "back with you. The mechanic is my responsibility."

Cavenaugh nodded.

Percy looked at Johnny, his forehead creased with concern.

"I'll see you back in Columbus," Johnny said reassuringly.

Reluctantly, Percy climbed into the back of the truck. The observer joined him. Swinging around in a wide arc, the truck headed back in the direction from which it came.

"Rotate the prop," Eastman ordered. He climbed into the rear cockpit.

Once the engine was started again, Eastman motioned for Johnny. He tossed him a headgear and goggles. "Get in!" he shouted, pointing to the front cockpit.

Johnny stared at the goggles and headgear.

"Get in!" Eastman shouted again. "Let's see how good of

a flier you really are!"

Donning the headgear, Johnny climbed into the front cockpit. He had one leg inside when the aeroplane started moving, throwing him off balance. Johnny managed to catch himself. In the cockpit behind him, white teeth flashed in a devilish grin.

The aeroplane picked up speed and lifted off just as he was getting settled into his seat. Eastman pulled the aeroplane into a steep climb. Johnny felt himself being forced down into his seat. The air blasted against his face. The mesquite brush on the desert surface shrunk into little dots. Johnny loved it.

The control stick between his legs jerked to the right as though influenced by invisible hands. The aeroplane banked sharply to the right. Looking that direction, Johnny was staring straight down at the ground. The stick jumped left. The aeroplane banked sharply the opposite way. Johnny glanced over his shoulder.

Eastman flashed a superior grin.

The aeroplane leveled off. Its nose dipped. The ground came into view in front of the propeller, rushing fiercely toward them. With an increasingly high-pitched whine that caused the fuselage to shudder, the aeroplane pulled up several hundred feet shy of the desert floor. For about fifteen minutes Eastman circled left and right, climbed and dove.

"Had enough?" he shouted.

Johnny turned in his seat. "I could do this all day!" he shouted back.

The grin faded on Eastman's face. The aeroplane nosed upward and climbed to 6,000 feet. Leveling off, Eastman took his hands off the control stick.

"She's all yours!" Eastman cried. "That is, if you think you're man enough."

The lieutenant settled back into his seat, his arms folded across his chest. The pilotless aeroplane began to slip sideways in a crosswind.

Johnny turned back around in his seat. It was clear Eastman didn't believe he'd ever flown before. Eastman had done all of that up and down and left and right banking to intimidate him.

"You'd better take the stick!" Eastman shouted. "She can't fly herself for long!"

The aeroplane's control stick shuddered nervously between Johnny's legs. He let it shudder for a bit longer.

"What's the matter, Morgan?" Eastman shouted. "In the mess shack you were bragging about what a great pilot you . . ."

With a firm hand, Johnny gripped the stick and shoved it forward; at that same instant, he stomped on the left rudder pedal. The aeroplane nosed over and spiraled toward earth. Mesquite bushes and sand and dry riverbeds and rock outcroppings blended together in a clockwise blur.

Johnny couldn't help but glance over his shoulder at Eastman. Gone were the intimidating eyes and cocky grin. In their place were eyes stretched wide in alarm and a gaping mouth with cheeks that rippled with the onrush of air.

With masterful control Johnny stopped the spin and pulled up. The landing gear brushed a cluster of bushes. Easing back on the stick, the aeroplane ascended gradually to several hundred feet.

Suddenly, Johnny felt a resistance in the stick. *Had the cable jammed?* He glanced down at the floorboard for obstructions. There were none. Then, he realized what was happening. There was nothing wrong with the control stick. Eastman was trying to wrestle control of the aeroplane away from him.

"Let go of the stick!" the lieutenant shouted. "You're

crazy!"

Johnny grinned. Eastman's voice was high-pitched. There might have even been a quiver in it. He was scared.

Johnny eased the stick right. Eastman countered. The wings of the aeroplane wobbled but kept its straight course. Johnny tried to the left. Again, Eastman countered.

The compass indicated they were heading west. Given their current status—not able to turn to the left or the right—they would fly until they ran out of gas and then crash.

"You said you wanted to see what I could do!" Johnny shouted.

"This is my aeroplane! Let go of the stick!" Eastman shouted back at him.

Johnny thought for a moment. It was a stalemate. They could go neither left nor right, neither up nor down unless one of them released the stick. With a sigh, Johnny let go. He raised both hands so that Eastman could see them.

"That's better!" Eastman shouted.

The aeroplane rolled gently right as the lieutenant brought it to a heading that would take them back to Columbus. This was exactly what Johnny hoped he would do.

Placing his hand on the stick, he shoved it all the way to the right.

The aeroplane flipped over.

Eastman was caught by surprise. He tried to counter, but now Johnny countered his every move. It was just like before, only now they were flying upside down.

"Let go! Let go! Let go!" Eastman shrieked. He glanced upward and saw the ground racing over his head.

Calmly, Johnny fought all of Eastman's attempts to regain control of the craft. It was a stalemate. They could go neither left nor right, neither up nor down unless one of them released the stick. All they could do was fly upside down.

"I order you to release the stick!" Eastman bellowed.

"You can't order me, I'm a civilian!"

Eastman's voice turned conciliatory. "Please, Johnny, please release the stick!"

"Let me fly it!"

"It's my aeroplane!"

"It's your upside-down aeroplane!"

The stick in Johnny's hands jerked left, then right. Johnny held it firmly in place.

Suddenly, it was free. Eastman had released it. Johnny glanced over his shoulder. Both of the lieutenant's hands rested on the sides of the cockpit.

"If you crash my aeroplane and we survive," he shouted, "I'll kill you!"

Johnny grinned. He had no intention of crashing today.

With a quick move of his arm, he flipped the aeroplane over. Remembering his own tactic, he didn't want to give Eastman a chance to control the aeroplane. Pulling the throttle out as far as he could, he pulled back on the stick. The aeroplane responded with a sharp angle of ascent, shoving the two pilots back against their seats.

"Too steep! Too steep!" Eastman shouted. But he made no attempt to reach for the stick.

The altimeter indicated 5,000 and climbing fast.

"We'll stall!" Eastman screamed.

Seven thousand feet. The air was decidedly colder.

"Too much strain!" Eastman cried. "Too much strain!"

Nine thousand feet. The aeroplane slowed and shuddered. It was icy.

Nine thousand five hundred feet. Nothing but pale blue sky loomed ahead of them.

No matter how loud and hard the engine raced, the aeroplane slowed even more.

"We're stalling! We're stalling!" Eastman cried.

Johnny nodded his head. That was exactly what he wanted to do.

At 9,807 feet the aeroplane had reached its peak. Lieutenant Eastman screamed in terror. Had it not been for the roar of the engine and the fact that he was concentrating on the timing, Eastman's scream would probably have hurt Johnny's ears.

At the precise moment when the aeroplane had no more forward momentum, Johnny used full rudder, rolled it over, and zoomed downward maintaining perfect control.

For thirty minutes he flew one stunt after another. Slip turns. Barrel rolls. He used the rising winds off the mountains to perform a loop. He hadn't had such a great day since coming to Columbus. Behind him, Lieutenant Eastman had not said a word since the controlled stall. Through one maneuver after another he gripped the sides of his cockpit emitting an occasional whimper or yelp.

Just as Johnny was about to turn the controls back over to the lieutenant, he spotted something on the ground and swung east to investigate. He motioned to Eastman to look down.

Below them, they spotted Colonel G.A. Dodd's command. Johnny landed the aeroplane. After reporting to Colonel Dodd, they took off again and, without further incident, Lieutenant Eastman flew the aeroplane back to Columbus.

Without so much as a word to Johnny, Eastman climbed out of the aeroplane and went directly to Captain Foulois to report Dodd's location and his request for supplies. For locating the command, Lieutenant Eastman was awarded a citation.

On April 20, Johnny Morgan made his final report to

Captain Foulois at Columbus. Only two aeroplanes remained and they were in such condition as to be unsafe for further service.

Foulois nodded grimly. He ordered the aeroplanes condemned and destroyed. Newer aeroplanes had been ordered to replace them. The captain then informed Johnny that his and Percy's services would no longer be needed. Along with the new aeroplanes would arrive new mechanics specially trained in repair.

"One more thing, Morgan," Foulois said.

"Yes, sir?"

"Did anything unusual happen when you were up with Lieutenant Eastman?"

"Unusual, sir?"

Foulois' eyes narrowed. The pupils hardened into pellets. "Lieutenant Eastman reported that while the two of you were in the air monitoring the engine's performance, you attempted to commandeer the aeroplane and defied direct orders to release the controls to him. Is that an accurate report of the situation?"

"No, sir," Johnny said.

"Which part is inaccurate in your opinion?"

"I took the controls at his invitation. When Lieutenant Eastman did not approve of some of my maneuvers, he attempted to regain control of the aircraft."

"Did you surrender control?"

"Not until I was finished performing my maintenance check, sir."

Foulois stared at him. His gaze was so sharp and penetrating, Johnny felt like holes were being drilled through his skull.

"Do you have anything else to report, Mr. Morgan?"

"No, sir."

"What are your plans? Where will you go from here?"

"I don't rightly know, sir."

The captain shuffled some papers on his desk, read from one of them, cleared his throat and said, "I've flown with Lieutenant Eastman. He's a fine pilot. Handles his aeroplane well. I believe I have a grasp on his abilities."

Why was Foulois telling him this?

"And I have a report on my desk from some scouts in Colonel Dodd's command. According to their report, they were witness to some aerial stunts involving one of our aeroplanes that, quite frankly, I find impossible to believe. Yet I have no reason to doubt the accuracy of their report."

He picked up the report, read silently, then looked up at Johnny. His eyes were less hard. There was almost a glimmer of wonder in them.

"If this report is only half true, the pilot flying that aeroplane is an exceptional flier. As I said before, Lieutenant Eastman is good. He's not exceptional."

Johnny did his best to keep a grin from busting out on his face.

Foulois stood. An outstretched hand held an envelope. "Morgan, this is a letter of recommendation. Should you come across that pilot, I hope you will encourage him to take this letter to College Park, Maryland where he can enroll in army flying school. We need fliers of his caliber."

With a reverent hand, Johnny accepted the envelope.

"As for you, Morgan," Foulois said, "you're a competent mechanic. But if I ever hear of you ignoring or disobeying a direct order from one of my officers again, I'll have you thrown off base so quick your head will spin. Do you understand?"

"Yes, sir."

"Dismissed."

Johnny turned to leave. Before he reached the door, Captain Foulois stopped him.

"One more thing, Morgan," the captain said.

"What's that, sir?"

"There's a train leaving for the East Coast at 8 A.M. tomorrow morning. I suggest you take it."

"Yes, sir!"

Knowing the condition of the squadron's aeroplanes, Percy had concluded that he and Johnny were out of jobs even before Johnny gave his report to Foulois. He had already packed his things and was ready to relocate. It had been good for him while it lasted. He'd learned a lot over the last month. He knew more about aeroplanes than he ever dreamed he'd know. And the study had been good for him. It diverted his attention from his grief over his parents' death. He wondered if moving back into the town would reopen those wounds.

His increasingly somber mood burst like a soap bubble the moment Johnny barged into their quarters. Nothing could have prepared him for the excitement he saw on Johnny's face.

"We're going to flying school!" Johnny cried.

Johnny read the captain's letter of recommendation aloud.

"*You're* going to flying school," Percy corrected him.

"We go together," Johnny insisted. "I promised I'd teach you to fly, and that's what I'm going to do."

"But I don't even know if I'll be accepted into the school!"

"If Eastman and those other..." He stopped short of muttering a few colorful phrases, choosing instead to be magnanimous on his day of victory. "If the pilots that we've seen on this base can qualify to fly, so can you. You're going."

There was no dissuading him. Though, with nowhere

else to go, Percy didn't try very hard. At 8 A.M. sharp the next morning, the eastbound train pulled away from the Columbus station. Johnny Morgan and Percy Hill were on it.

Chapter 7

A BABY'S wail cut through the white fog that engulfed her senses. Her head throbbed with pain. Each shriek from the infant pricked it like a knife point on a boil. She was certain the next wail would lance her skull and the insides of her head would pour out all over the place, leaving an awful mess. But it didn't matter. If it did, at least there would be some relief.

Another wail. Another jab of pain. Her head didn't pop. She concluded that was a good sign. But she felt no relief. That wasn't good. Her pulse pounded in her head. Hands against her temples did little to stop the throbbing agony.

Emily moaned. She was laying on something matted and hard. Good. For her last memory was the undulating, floating feeling that comes from being engulfed by water.

She was beginning to remember. Water. A briny, salt taste coated her tongue and the inside of her mouth. Floating. No, not floating, sinking. Head under water. Deeper, deeper. Trying to breathe, sucking in water instead. Her arms, aching, raised.

The baby!

She had been trying to save a baby that had fallen overboard. As though it mattered that the baby fell overboard; the whole ship went down in the water moments later.

Another wail. Angry. Frightened. Hungry.

How did she know all this from a single, extended cry? Experience. Motherly instinct. The child needed her. Just like it needed her in the ocean, so it needed her now in the . . .

In the what? Where was she?

Emily forced open her eyes. They stung from the crusty sea salt that had crystallized on her eyelids. Feeling like huge rocks, grit and sand were lodged between her eyes and her lids. She tried to keep from rubbing them. It would only make them worse.

Batting her eyes several times, she managed to get them half-open. Everything was blurry at first. A few more blinks and she could see better. More blinks, better still. She saw the underside of a thatched roof.

The baby screamed.

Why doesn't someone take care of the child?

She turned her head in the direction of the scream. The pain inside her head complained, the throbbing increased, pounding harder, strangling her vision. She forced her eyes to focus. Wood grain. Dark. A box; more like a chest. Tall. With drawers. One drawer was pulled out. Above her. Tiny fists waved angrily from inside the drawer.

With a moan, Emily turned over on her side. She propped herself up on one arm. She was on the floor, lying atop a woven carpet. Her peach dress, still damp, clung to her, chilling her skin.

As best as she could tell, she was in a one-room house. At the far end was a pantry, a long wooden counter, a small table, two chairs. In front of her was the chest of drawers that was serving as a crib. A heavy-looking wooden door was to the right.

"Is . . . is any . . ." A catch in her throat that felt like a prickly brier provoked a violent coughing spasm, bringing up seawater which burned her throat and lungs. She tried again.

"Is anyone here?" Her voice was throaty, raspy.

The cry of the infant was her only answer.

Leaning heavily against the chest of drawers, and using the open drawer to pull herself up, Emily worked her way to her feet. Her head swam unsteadily and for a moment she felt faint. Gradually, though, her head cleared. The painful pounding was worse from the effort.

Nestled in a bed of woolen socks, the infant squirmed and screamed, its face beet red, its lower lip quivering with each fresh intake of air. It was still dressed in its white woolen jersey and matching leggings.

Emily reached into the drawer and picked up the infant. Still wobbly, she had to hold the child against her with one hand while steadying herself against the chest of drawers with the other. The infant was comforted only a little.

"I imagine you're hungry," she said.

Now that she was standing, she could see the rest of the house. A large curtained window was across from her, and facing it stood a wooden rocking chair and a telescope. To one side of the rocking chair was a round wooden table with a Victrola player on it. A stack of phonograph records was next to it. Also on the table was an open Bible, a pipe, and a tobacco pouch. Now that she saw it, she noticed the distinct odor of tobacco in the room.

To her left, at the far end of the house was a single bed pushed lengthwise against the wall. It was neatly made. A night table held a kerosene lamp. The door beside the chest of drawers was the only door. The window in front of the telescope was the only window.

"Let's see if we can find anything for you in the pantry," Emily said soothingly to the unhappy baby in her arms.

Canned foodstuffs were arranged neatly on shelves. Atop the bench was an overturned pail that was used for washing the dishes. A clean plate was propped against it. Nearby was an overturned cup and utensils. Apparently, the occupant of the house had washed them, then set them out to dry.

There was a wood-burning stove that had been partially hidden by a floor-to-ceiling drape. Its mate hung on the far wall which Emily hadn't noticed before. When the drapes were pulled, the kitchen area could be shut off from the rest of the house.

She found a stone enclosure in the right-hand corner. Its opening was covered by an oilcloth. Lifting the cloth, she spied a container of milk, butter, and a variety of cheeses.

"There it is!" Emily cooed to the crying baby. "Now, let's hope it's still fresh."

Bending down to retrieve the milk, she suddenly got dizzy again. She had to rest a moment before attempting to get up. The baby was unsympathetic.

"You're going to have to be patient with me, little one," Emily said woozily.

When the dizziness passed, she reached for the milk and stood. Dipping the tip of her finger in the container, she touched her tongue with it, testing the milk's freshness. The sweet taste of fresh cow's milk caused her own taste buds to tingle. It was such a refreshing taste compared to the briny taste of saltwater that lingered there.

Emily took the child and the milk and, after grabbing a small tin cup, moved to the rocking chair. Setting the milk and cup on the table next to the Victrola, she lowered herself gingerly into the chair. Her head pounded unmercifully from the exertion. The child's cry stabbed her ears, only making it worse. Still, Emily was encouraged. She had milk and a rocker, familiar tools with which to deal with her infant crisis.

Pouring some milk into the tin cup, Emily lifted it to the infant's lips. The crying ceased as the baby sucked eagerly at the rim. Taking too much in with a slurp, the baby choked and showered Emily with milk. Once the choking stopped, the screeching resumed.

"You're probably still on the bottle, aren't you?" Emily said, looking toward the pantry. She didn't think her chances were good of finding a baby bottle there. From the furnishings and general look of the house, there hadn't been a baby in it for some time.

Emily dipped a finger into the container of milk and touched the baby's lips. The infant sucked on her finger eagerly. Another dip of her finger yielded similar results with loud verbal protests every time she pulled her finger away from the infant's mouth.

Alternating between the finger method and the sipping method, Emily managed to feed the child. After a time, between the milk and the rocking, the baby settled down and fell asleep in Emily's arms. Now it was Emily's turn to take a few sips of milk. As it went down, it coated her scratchy throat. She could feel the coolness of the white liquid go all the way down to her stomach, which eagerly welcomed it with a satisfied growl.

Fatigue came over her like a blanket. She shrugged it off, not wanting to close her eyes until she knew who it was who lived in the house, and why she was brought here, and where all the other passengers had been taken, and where Katy was, and . . .

A hundred questions with no one to answer them.

At least I can see where I am, she said to herself, spying the closed curtains in front of her. Careful not to wake the baby, she got up and went to the curtains. She pulled one side back and stifled a small gasp. Pulling back the other side, she held the infant child close to her chest and stared at the scene that lay before her.

It was early evening. To her right an oversized orangish orb nearly touched the water. Its light spewed thousands of tiny orange reflections across the deep-blue expanse of the sea. The house in which she was standing was situated on its own private peninsula jutting out into the sea. Like fat earthen fingers, a series of similar peninsulas stretched to the horizon. Hazy, liquid blue filled the gaps between them. However, unlike the earthen finger upon which the house was situated, the other peninsulas were covered only with grass and rocks.

Emily slumped into the rocking chair. She knew now why the builder of this house had placed this oversized window here. But she still did not know where she was or in whose house she was staying.

After a time, as the sun disappeared and the sea turned dark, the fatigue which she had shrugged off earlier returned. It was heavier this time. Too heavy. Emily fell asleep with the baby lying on her chest.

In the morning, the baby lay hot against her, lethargic and soaked.

"You poor thing," Emily cried. She cast a glance first at the bed, then around the room. The bed was undisturbed. She and the infant were still alone. Emily stripped the woolen clothing from the baby.

"A little girl!" Emily exclaimed, amused that for all this time she hadn't even known the child's gender. To bring down the child's fever, Emily sponged her off, having found a well just outside the house. While she was outside, she also spotted a barn. Complaining cows could be heard inside; she'd relieve them of their milk later. Chickens pecked the ground hungrily outside the barn. The surrounding landscape was divided into sections by stone walls. A dirt road stretched to the horizon. Other than the house and the barn, she could see no other manmade structures.

While the mystery of the house's residents haunted

Emily, her first concern was the child. Throughout the day, she sponged and rocked and prayed and cared for the infant girl. Nothing she did seemed to relieve the fever.

As for her own condition, she was grateful that the pounding in her head had stopped. However, a residual aching remained, as though the pounding had bruised her brain. Emily found that she had to move slowly and deliberately. No sudden movements or jerking of the head.

She soon learned she had no stamina. Sponging off the baby exhausted her. After laying the infant in the drawer among the woolen socks, she had to rest. This became the pattern for her day. She fed the baby, and rested; milked a cow, and rested; dressed the child, and rested.

The day passed in this manner. No one came home or stopped by. Night fell and she was no closer to understanding how she managed to get where she was.

While the baby slept in the sock drawer, Emily rocked herself in the rocking chair and stared out the window at the starry expanse over the black sea. She had just awakened from a short nap and was feeling a little stronger. Strong enough to do some detective work. If the owners of this house weren't going to show themselves, maybe the house itself could tell her something about them. When she was younger, Emily had wanted to be an investigative reporter. This was her chance to test her skills.

Her first impression was that the house was occupied by only one person. There was only one bed. A single plate and cup and utensil setting had been found next to the wash basin. One chest of drawers. One rocking chair.

The occupant of the house was a man, a rather large one at that. The woolen socks in the baby's drawer were men's socks, much larger than Jesse's. Earlier in the day, she stripped herself of the damp peach dress she'd been wearing at the time of the sinking. Looking for clothes to wear, she found only men's clothes. The trousers she was wearing and the flannel shirt were huge on her. The only thing that kept her from losing her pants every time she stood up was a pair of braces she found in one of the drawers.

What did she know about this mystery man? He had a telescope positioned in front of a large window. Getting out of the chair, she stood behind the telescope. What was the last thing he'd seen before he left? Closing one eye, she peered into the eyepiece. Everything was black. Backing away, she peered in the same direction as the telescope. It was pointed at the sea. Not the stars. It was the ocean that fascinated him, not the heavens. That was, unless something had happened that distracted him from the stars . . . like a sinking ship? Was the telescope positioned on the very spot in which the *Lusitania* had sunk? Emily peered through the eyepiece again. She didn't really expect to see anything new this time. Her curiosity pulled her to the eyepiece like a magnet.

Had he watched the ship sink from here? Watched the lifeboats deploy? The bodies floating on the water? Then, after witnessing the event, did he leave this place to help rescue the victims? How else could she explain her presence here? But why did he leave again? And why hadn't he returned?

Unless he couldn't return.

Emily sat back down in the rocking chair. Her heart was pounding. Had the day of her rescue become the day of his death? Had saving her and the baby been the last thing he'd done in life? Was she waiting for someone to return who would never return?

She had seen no horse or carriage in or around the barn. And there was no telling how far she would have to go to find another house. She'd have to wait until the baby's fever was down and she was feeling stronger. If no one had returned by then, she would venture out on her own.

Her eyes fell upon the table next to the chair. The pipe. The Victrola. She reached for the stack of phonograph records. What sort of music did he like? She flipped through the thick heavy disks, reading their labels:

"I May Be Gone for a Long, Long Time"
Shannon Four

"Keep the Home Fires Burning"
John McCormack

"Roses of Picardy"
John McCormack

Another stack of phonograph records on the floor leaned against the leg of the table. They were spiritual in nature:

"In the Garden"
"Tell Mother I'll Be There"
"Old Rugged Cross"
"Make Somebody Happy Today"
"God Be with You Till We Meet Again"

Taking one of the phonograph records out of its sleeve, she placed it on the turntable and turned the crank on the side of the box. Positioning the machine's needle on the edge of the rotating disk, the scratchy sounds of music and John McCormack's tenor voice blossomed from the machine's speaker horn that looked very much like a lily.

Keep the home fires burning,
While your hearts are yearning.
Though your lads are far away

They dream of home . . .

The lilting music and the singer's words tugged at the strings of Emily's heart. Tears came readily as she thought of Katy. *O God, please let her be alive. How heartsick she must be to think that her mother drowned, for how can she think any differently?* And Jesse. Poor Jesse. For him to be on the other side of the ocean. Waiting for word. Hoping for the best. Fearing the worst. There was no doubt in Emily's mind that she would see her husband again, but he didn't have that same hope. Part of him had to recognize the possibility that she had died. She imagined the loneliness he must feel every night when he went to bed not knowing . . . not knowing! What agony that must be for him!

Please, Lord, somehow convey to him that I'm all right. Don't let him suffer. Please, Lord, don't let my Jesse suffer.

A tireless cycle of amplified scratching announced the end of the record. Emily replaced it with another, "Roses of Picardy." A sweet melancholy love song transported Emily back to special times with Jesse. A night alone on the Brooklyn Bridge when they were first attracted to one another. The Brown Palace Hotel in Denver when she surprised him on the day he was presented his family's Bible. The first time they held baby Katy between them, their foreheads touching as they gazed down at her chubby face; then again when Johnny was born.

As she listened and remembered and cried, it seemed as though all the water she'd swallowed in the ocean came pouring out of her eyes. For it seemed like a ceaseless stream.

Scratch . . . scratch . . . scratch . . . scratch . . . scratch . . . scratch . . . scratch.

Emily lifted the needle of the Victrola. This time she placed one of the religious phonograph records on the turntable. A female's voice wafted through the room. She sang of a quiet time in a garden in the early morning hours. It was there she felt so close to her Lord that it was as if He were walking beside her among the flowers.

There was a Bible on the table. Emily reached for it. Carefully opening the cover, she learned the name of the man whom she presumed had been her rescuer. There was an inscription written in a feminine hand.

My dearest Bryn,
May the words of this book bring as much light to your life as you have brought to mine. After my Lord, there is none whom I love more.
Forever and always,
Clare

"Bryn," Emily said aloud. She was sitting in his chair. Wearing his clothes. Listening to his phonograph records. Holding his Bible. Sharing in a personal moment between him and his wife. She just assumed that to be the case.

Her assumption was proved correct when she turned the page. There, she found a family record. There was a single entry.

June 17, 1902. My beloved Clare stepped into eternity on this day. After 57 years together, I could not find adequate words to tell her good-bye. I pray she understands and will for-give this slow-witted old man.

Emily reverently closed the Bible. She felt like she was trespassing in Bryn and Clare's personal affairs. Her heart ached as she imagined the scene that took place in this room every night for the past fourteen years.

A man grieving for his wife. Sitting here. Staring at the

sea night after night. Listening to phonograph records that reminded him of her. His heart aching with each melancholy measure.

Brushing the palm of her hand across the Bible's leather cover, Emily said softly, "Bryn, a part of me hopes you walk through that door. I'd like to thank you personally for saving my life." She gazed down at the Bible and thought of the inscriptions. "Another part of me hopes you're with Clare, because I have a hunch that when you see her again, you'll know once-for-all that there's nothing to forgive. She knows. She's always known."

Emily fell asleep in the chair with Bryn's Bible on her lap, oblivious to the sounds of the Victrola.

Scratch . . . scratch . . . scratch . . . scratch . . . scratch . . . scratch . . . scratch.

Chapter 8

ON the third day the baby's fever had broken and Emily was feeling stronger. Her instincts told her not to rush things. Her desire to ease the minds of all those who missed both her and the child prompted her to risk the journey. For all she knew, there was a neighboring farmhouse just over the next rise. Wrapping the child up in one of Bryn's shirts and covering the child's head with a dish towel, the two of them set off down the road.

The plan was to gauge her strength and not wander any farther than she could go comfortably and still make it back to the house. The moment they stepped from the house it was a grand excursion. The day was clear; the sun was bright. The fields stretched endlessly, carpeted with that deep-colored green grass that had come to be associated with Ireland. The breeze was fresh with just a tang of salt to it.

Even the baby seemed to appreciate the outdoors. Wide blue eyes stared wondrously at everything. She cooed and tried to talk, at least when she didn't have her fist in her mouth.

"We must look an odd sight," Emily said to the baby. "You dressed in a flannel gown with collar and buttons and me in sloppy men's clothing."

The baby gurgled a happy response.

Humming the tune of the hymn "In the Garden," the

two of them set off down the rutted road that was lined on both sides by a low stone wall. They walked nearly a mile when Emily's knees and legs first began to grow weak.

"Just a little farther, dumpling," Emily said. "To the top of that rise. Who knows what we might see from there?"

At the top of the rise they saw nothing that they hadn't seen already. Green fields. Gray stone walls. Blue sky. And a dirt road that seemed to stretch on forever leading nowhere.

"If we wander much farther, I don't know if we'd have the strength to make it back," Emily said to the baby. "Never seen so much of nothing since my days on the western prairie. Of course, it wasn't as green as this. But for a girl who was raised on the streets of New York, it's still hard to imagine so much land with so few inhabitants. Surely, there's a town or another farm around here someplace. And we'll find it. Rest assured. And we'll find your mother and your father. Don't you worry. We'll just have to wait a little while longer, that's all."

Emily turned around and headed back to the stone cottage by the seaside. She used conversation with the baby to fight the encroaching sense of disappointment she was feeling. Her limited abilities frustrated her. After all, she had crossed the great American plains, mostly on foot. Yet here she was barely able to walk a mile and back.

But there was no ignoring the symptoms. Her legs were shaky and growing weaker. Her lungs were beginning to burn with each breath. Even the baby's disposition had spoiled some. She wasn't as fascinated with things anymore. Curled up against Emily's chest she fidgeted, unable to get comfortable. She no longer made happy, gurgling sounds.

The walk back seemed twice as far as the walk out had been. Upon reaching the house, Emily fed the baby; then both of them took long naps.

It was dark when Emily awoke. The baby was still asleep.

Lighting a kerosene lamp, Emily went outside to get some wood from the woodpile so that she could warm the house and prepare supper. She set the lamp to one side, loaded one arm with wood, then bent over to pick up the lamp.

She saw something!

A face!

The wood in her arm tumbled to the ground. She held the lamp high to illuminate a greater area. Her heart was pounding so hard it caused the lantern to swing. She peered past the barn and the stone wall where she'd seen the face. Or, at least, where she thought she'd seen it. Nothing was there now. Just dancing shadows and she was creating them with the lantern.

"Hello?" she said, her voice uncertain. "Hello? Is anybody out there?"

No response. That was good, wasn't it?

She scanned the area again. Nothing but dirt and stone and shadow. Keeping a ready eye in that general direction, Emily bent down and retrieved the wood she'd dropped. She made one more cautious survey of the area, then went inside and bolted the door.

For the rest of the evening she was on edge. The baby was restless too. Emily kept the curtains to the window closed that night. She didn't play the Victrola in fear that it would cover up the sound of someone moving around outside. She decided to sleep in the bed, the chair growing more uncomfortable with each night. She kept the lamp nearby at all times. She kept trying to tell herself that it was just her imagination. But if it was her imagination, why was it she could still see the face so vividly in her mind? A balding head and squinty eyes.

It wasn't until the early morning hours that she finally fell asleep. She awoke with a start every time the baby turned over. It proved to be one of the longest nights of her life.

By morning Emily had convinced herself the previous night's fright was all her imagination. When she went outside the sun was bright, the air crisp—it was another perfect day. Her muscles were sore from the walk and she didn't have much energy, though she attributed most of that to her lack of sleep.

The baby crawled happily on the rug and made several attempts to stand up, using the chest of drawers to steady herself. Emily brought fresh milk and eggs in from the barn. Getting down on her hands and knees, she lifted the oilcloth of the stone cool box. Curious as to what items were inside, she pulled them out, one at a time. Mostly cheeses, and most of them sported a layer of gray, green, and blue fuzzy mold.

Reaching to the back of the stone box, her fingers caught the edge of one of the stones. It was loose. She shoved it back into place. It rocked and fell out a little farther. It was looser than she originally thought. Another shove failed to get it flush with the rest of the stones. It was almost as though something were pushing it out.

With the tips of her fingers, Emily fished out the rock. A small booklet tumbled out from behind it.

"What's this?" she muttered to herself.

Her curiosity piqued, Emily retrieved the booklet. She carried it to the window where she could get a better look. Sitting in the rocking chair, Emily opened the book. Several loose tissue papers tumbled into her lap—obviously not original pages—with India ink markings on them. Unfolding one of the pieces of tissue, she read the following notation:

10:15p I V. officers, 33 w. soldiers, 3 w. horses, 6 w. plats carts
Bruno

There were other similar pieces of tissue paper folded and stuffed between the pages of the small book, each with similar markings and most of them signed by Bruno. The book itself seemed to be a record of papers such as these. There were dates with similar notations written in the same hand that recorded Clare's death in Bryn's Bible. There were no entries that corresponded to the loose papers. Apparently Bryn had not yet recorded them.

Not knowing for sure what she found, Emily placed the tissue papers back between the pages of the little book. She stuck the book back into its hiding place and replaced the stone.

Another mystery. As if Emily needed another mystery.

It was midafternoon. The baby had been fed and was resting comfortably on Emily's chest as the two rocked gently in the rocking chair. The Victrola was softly playing, "Make Somebody Happy Today." Emily had just finished telling the sleeping baby that she had made this whole ordeal bearable.

"I don't know how I would have survived without you," Emily said softly to the sleeping child. She hummed along with the recording. "You're certainly doing what the song says," she said, kissing the top of the infant's head. "You're making me happy today."

Behind her, the door burst open.

Emily jumped. She held the child more tightly against her.

A man with a rifle burst into the room. He was elderly with a large, bulbous nose and was dressed in overalls and a plaid shirt. What few gray hairs that remained atop his head dangled down into his squinty eyes . . . squinty eyes! The face she'd seen in the dark! It wasn't her imagination after all! It was him!

Behind him were two women. They too were elderly and

both wore print dresses. Neither of them carried a weapon of any sort. They followed close in the man's wake, peering around him at Emily.

"Who are you?" the man demanded. The barrel of his rifle shook in his unsteady hands. The shaking seemed to be a physical malady, for there was no fear in the man's eyes or voice.

Before Emily had a chance to answer his first question, he fired a second question at her.

"What are you doing in Bryn Thomas' house?"

Instinctively, Emily turned to one side, placing herself between the gaping black hole at the end of the rifle barrel and the baby. The baby had jumped when she jumped, but didn't awaken. Emily stroked the baby's back reassuringly. The stroking calmed Emily as much as it did the baby.

"My name is Emily Morgan," Emily said. "I was on the *Lusitania,* the one that sank off the coast a few days . . . "

"We know all about the sinking of the ship," the man said brusquely. "That doesn't explain what you're doing here."

Emily took a deep breath and sighed as she returned the stare of three pair of hostile eyes. The breath was to calm herself. "I can't explain my presence here," she said. "The last thing I remember was being in the water. I was trying to keep this baby's head above the water and . . . "

"This baby . . . " the taller of the two women said. "The baby's not yours?"

"How do you know that?" The other woman stared at her partner through thick eyeglasses.

"A mother would have called the baby by name, or said 'my baby.' She said, 'This baby.'"

"You're correct," Emily said. She was as impressed with the taller woman's observation as was the woman with the thick glasses. "This isn't my baby. In all of the confusion, somehow she got separated from her parents."

"Do you know her parents?" the tall woman asked.

Emily shook her head. "Neither do I know if they survived the sinking."

"Then how did you end up with her?"

"She fell overboard. I jumped in after her."

The taller woman was taken aback. "You jumped overboard?"

Emily nodded. "To save the baby."

Impatient, the man interrupted. He waved the rifle barrel as she talked. "That still doesn't explain what you're doing in Bryn Thomas' house."

"I don't know what I'm doing here," Emily said. "The last thing I remember was being underwater, trying to keep the baby's head above water. Then, I woke up here, lying on the floor. I found the baby cradled inside one of the drawers in a bed of socks. There was no one here when I awoke. And you're the first people I've seen since then."

"It makes sense," the taller woman commented. She glanced at the telescope. "Bryn would have gone out to help."

Emily was drawn to the taller woman. She had a quick mind. And now that Emily had time to notice, she was more neatly attired and groomed than the other two. She was also taller. Her hair was white, short, and brushed back. Her eyes sparkled with intelligence. At the moment they were focused on Emily, evaluating, judging, trying to solve the puzzle of Emily's presence in Bryn Thomas' house.

"But the woman's taken up house here!" the man cried. "Why haven't you let your presence be known to the Queenstown authorities?" Suddenly, his eyes lit up. "Are you a kidnapper?" he cried. He turned to the women behind him. "She could be a kidnapper!"

"That's ridiculous," the tall woman said. "This young

lady is not a kidnapper."

"I assure you I am not a kidnapper," Emily cried. "I wanted to notify someone of our survival, but have been unable to do so. The baby has had a fever. And I myself have not fully recovered from swallowing so much seawater. Yesterday was the first day I felt strong enough to walk any distance. We didn't get far before we had to turn back."

"Poor child," said the tall woman.

"What do you mean, 'poor child'?" To Emily he said, "Why didn't you use the horse and carriage in the barn?"

Emily's eyes grew wide. How could she have missed . . .

The woman with the thick glasses slapped the man's shoulder. "How could she?" she cried. "The carriage is in town for repairs, and you have Bryn's horse yourself!"

From the sheepish expression on the man's face, Emily knew the woman was right.

The tall woman stepped beside the man. She placed her hand on the barrel of the gun. Without objection, the man lowered it.

In a kindly voice, the woman spoke to Emily. "Didn't you think it odd that the man who rescued you didn't return to his house?" she asked.

Emily spoke softly. "Yes, I thought it odd. After a time, I became concerned for him. I feared . . . "

The tall woman nodded. Her voice was solemn when she said, "Pieces of his boat washed ashore yesterday. We fear the worst."

"I'm so sorry," Emily said. "Now I'll never get a chance to thank him for rescuing the baby and me."

"Because of his failing physical condition, he wasn't supposed to sail alone anymore. But he did anyway. If you knew my brother, you'd understand. He was stubborn."

"That he was," echoed the man.

"At least he died for a worthy cause," the tall woman

said. To Emily, she said, "From the reports I've received, Bryn was on his way out to help rescue survivors. It was assumed he was heading out for the first time. Your appearance here indicates it was at least his second trip."

"Why do you think he would have brought me here?" Emily asked.

"It's closer than Queenstown. His boat was a small one. I assume he brought you here so he could go back and rescue more people." The tall woman's eyes fell on the flannel shirts both Emily and the baby were wearing, then on the oversized trousers.

All of a sudden, Emily felt self-conscious, even a bit guilty. She had been living in someone else's house and was wearing his clothes. Though she had nothing to feel guilty about, still the feeling was there.

"Our things were soaked," Emily stammered. "They should be dry by now. I can find them and we can put these clothes back where . . . "

The tall woman sensed her discomfort. "Bryn would have offered them to you," she said warmly. "By the way, I'm not his wife . . . "

"I know," Emily said.

Her response intrigued the tall woman.

"Clare . . . Bryn's wife . . . died nearly fourteen years ago."

"How did you . . . "

Emily looked over at the Bible on the Victrola stand.

The tall woman nodded in understanding. "I'm his sister, Maggie," she said.

"Pleased to meet you, Maggie."

"And these are Bryn's closest neighbors, Ian and Ethel Morehouse."

Emily nodded at each of them. They returned the nod, tentatively.

"I was coming to visit my brother when they intercepted

me," Maggie said.

Feeling more self-conscious than ever about standing in someone else's house, Emily shuffled from foot to foot and said, "I'll get out of your way as soon as I can... I'll just get our clothes and..."

A look of shock mixed with shame came over Maggie's face. "Dear child," she said to Emily, "your family must be worried sick about you."

Tears came to Emily's eyes. All of a sudden she realized that she would soon learn of Katy's fate and she could soon get a message to Jesse.

"I had a grown daughter traveling with me," Emily said. "We were separated."

"How awful for you!" Maggie cried.

"And a husband in America. I'll want to send a telegraph..."

"Of course you will! And this poor little one... we must find her parents! Are you able to travel by carriage?"

Emily nodded. "I think so."

Maggie turned to the Morehouses. "Would it be asking too much for you to take us into Queenstown? Would you mind getting your carriage and bringing it up here?" To Emily she said, "We left it a ways down the road. Didn't want to announce our approach, you see, not knowing what sort of monster we might find lurking in my brother's house!" She gave a comical wink to Emily.

"Ian, go get the carriage," Ethel said. "I'll..."

"Why don't you go with him, dear," Maggie said. "I'm sure Emily will feel much more comfortable while she changes into her own clothes. I'll just busy myself over here..."

"Of course," Ethel said, clearly preferring to stay. Nevertheless, she followed her husband out the door and closed it.

"I'll just go over here and pull these curtains," Maggie said. "That will give you the privacy you need to change."

"Thank you," Emily replied.

Maggie hurried across the room and disappeared behind the pantry curtains.

As Emily lay the baby down on the bed, she thought she heard rock scraping against rock behind the curtains. A minute later she heard more familiar pantry sounds. Canned goods shuffled around. Dishes and utensils clanking. Water swishing in the basin.

Removing Bryn's clothing, she dressed herself in the peach summer dress she'd worn aboard the *Lusitania*. She dressed the sleeping baby in her white woolen jersey with matching leggings. As she pulled back the curtains, Maggie asked, "Do you mind if I ride with you to Queenstown? I'd like to see how all of this turns out."

Emily hadn't known the woman but for a few minutes, but the thought of having someone nearby should she learn the worst about Katy was inviting. "I'd be pleased if you would accompany us," Emily said.

Maggie smiled warmly just as there was a tapping on the door. "Sounds like our carriage has arrived," she said.

As Emily left the house, she couldn't help but turn and take one last look.

The rocking chair. The telescope. The Victrola with its melancholy collection of songs. The Bible with Clare's inscription and the record of her death.

How happy Bryn and Clare must be, she thought. *Together again after fourteen years.*

Katy was standing facing the list of dead and survivors as a grim Cunard official updated it. Stoic yet composed, she watched as name after name was added to the growing number of dead.

Emily and Maggie had just stepped out of the carriage and were approaching the Cunard building when Emily spotted Katy. Beside her, Maggie followed Emily's gaze through the office doorway. "Is that your daughter?"

Emily was so overcome with emotion, she couldn't speak. All she could do was weep and nod.

"She's beautiful," Maggie said. "Quite the figure of a woman."

"Thank you," Emily managed to say.

How does one announce she is alive in a situation like this? Emily wanted to cry out, but she didn't want to shock Katy. *Would it be better to go up to her and tap her on the shoulder?* That might be even more of a shock.

Emily's dilemma solved itself when Katy turned toward the door.

For an instant there was disbelief. Then, she dared believe what she saw to be true.

"Mother? Mother!"

Katy flew out the doorway and into her mother's waiting arm, the other still carrying the baby. Graciously, Maggie took the infant to allow mother and daughter an adequate reunion.

"Mother, where have you been? Oh, it doesn't matter. You're here. That's all that matters. You're here. And alive!"

"I'm so sorry, baby," Emily cried. "I never should have left you."

No one rushed them. They didn't rush themselves. In the face of so much heartache and tragedy, a reunion like this needed to be savored.

After a time, Emily introduced Maggie and the Morehouses and, of course, her infant companion.

"The baby on the ship!" Katy cried.

Emily nodded.

Suddenly, a look of dawning awareness crossed Katy's

face. "White jersey!" she cried. "Mother, there are posters in nearly every window of Queenstown about this baby! Curly hair. White jersey. White leggings!"

"Her parents are alive?" Emily cried.

"It would seem so," Katy replied.

"Did you hear that, little one?" Emily cried, retrieving the baby from Maggie. "Your mother and father have been looking for you! Won't they be surprised!"

With Maggie and the Morehouses in tow—for no one wanted to miss the happy reunion this promised to be—Emily and Katy walked into the Cunard offices. First, they saw to it that Emily's name was listed among the survivors. Then, they told officials about the baby.

Within a short period of time, the parents were located. The entire Cunard staff joined Emily and Katy and the baby and Maggie and the Morehouses and several others who wandered in off the street when they heard the excitement as they rejoiced at the reunion between the infant survivor of the *Lusitania* and her parents.

Chapter 9

JESSE Morgan sat in the office of the Secretary of State and his long-time friend, William Jennings Bryan. He sat alone. Bryan had been detained by other business.

As Jesse glanced around the room at Bryan's collection of artifacts he shivered a patriotic shiver. The room and the man never failed to impress him. He was sitting in the midst of relics from Hawaii, Japan, Korea, China, the Philippines, Java, Russia, Austria-Hungary, and England. In a polished wooden frame hanging on the wall there was a photograph of Bryan standing in the snow next to Count Leo Tolstoy, author of *War and Peace* and *Anna Karenina*. Jesse could only imagine what it was like to travel so widely and to interact with so many famous people. The only famous person he knew was the one in whose office he sat.

He had first met William Jennings Bryan at a Chautauqua in Boulder, Colorado. He hadn't wanted to go. Emily dragged him there.

The Chautauqua movement was an adult education program that originated at Chautauqua Lake in New York State. It began after the Civil War as an assembly for the training of Sunday School teachers and church workers. Over the years it gradually grew beyond its original religious purpose to include general education and popular entertainment. It was a well-respected movement, not unlike the Lyceum movement of the previous century. One proponent of the educational movement dubbed Chautauquas, "the most American thing in America."

William Jennings Bryan was, without doubt, the most popular of the Chautauqua speakers. The first time Jesse saw the future Secretary of State, Bryan was standing on the Chautauqua platform at night under the electric lights and starlight. Jesse remembered grousing at Emily for insisting he accompany her. His attitude soon changed and before the evening was over, the speaker on the platform had gained another admirer.

People came from miles around to hear William Jennings Bryan speak. And hear him, they did. When Bryan began speaking, they forgot their hardships and the weariness of their travel. He began slowly, casually, like one neighbor talking to another. At some imperceptible point in the speech, the strength of his personality began to emerge. The longer he spoke, the more impassioned he became. His voice grew deep and solemn, at times urgent. He was speaking to the heart of America and the heart of America was listening. They recognized him for what he was—a rugged, honest champion of the masses.

Jesse was amazed at how Bryan always appeared perfectly at home on a platform, fortified by an ever-present pitcher of ice water. With a combination of humanity and humor, he had the ability to hold an audience's attention for two hours. His message was always simple, yet often keyed to some lofty issue. He never failed to find an eager response. And none more eager than Jesse Morgan.

Never before had Jesse written down a speaker's phrases or ideas. It was Bryan's speeches that got him started. In his trousers pocket Jesse carried a well-worn piece of paper of selected quotes, mostly from Bryan, which he reviewed frequently. The first bit of wisdom Jesse had recorded on his paper was a Bryan quote which literally changed his approach to life:

> *Destiny is a matter of choice; it is not a thing to be waited for, it is a thing to be achieved.*

Another of Jesse's favorites reinforced his belief in the eternal spirit of man:

> *If that vital spark that we find in a grain of wheat can pass unchanged through countless deaths and resurrections, will the spirit of man be unable to pass from this body to another?*

One of the humorous inclusions on Jesse's paper was this parody of a well-known cliché:

> *Do not compute the totality of your poultry population until all the manifestations of incubation have been entirely completed.*

Jesse was so captivated by the Chautauqua speaker and the movement's effectiveness in educating the common man that he volunteered to be a member of the local Chautauqua committee. He figured that this way he could help ensure the movement's success in Colorado.

Through Jesse's initiative, Bryan was also invited to speak at the Morgans' church on Sundays whenever he was in town. Following each of these occasions, Bryan was invited by the Morgans for dinner. It was over roasted chicken and mashed potatoes and green beans that a lasting friendship was formed.

When Bryan ran unsuccessfully for President in 1900, his second attempt at the office, Jesse spearheaded his campaign effort in Colorado. And again, in 1908 when Bryan ran for President, Jesse supported his cause. Again, Bryan's presidential aspirations were thwarted.

Following his third defeat, Bryan liked to tell the story of the drunk who tried three times to get into a private club, only to be thrown downstairs each time. On landing in the street following his third attempt, the drunk picked himself up, dusted off his clothes, and said thoughtfully, "They can't fool me! Those fellows don't want me in there!"

In 1912, another presidential election year, it was Bryan's influence that secured the Democratic nomination of Woodrow Wilson. When Wilson was elected, he rewarded Bryan by appointing him Secretary of State. In turn, Bryan enlisted Jesse's services by making him his personal assistant. In a career move Jesse Morgan never would have predicted, he left the Denver security agency at which he had worked all his adult life and joined William Jennings Bryan's staff in Washington, D.C.

The door to the office swung open. In strode the Secretary of State. Jesse remained seated. There was a time when he rose every time Bryan entered a room; even now his leg muscles tensed out of habit. It was the Secretary of State himself who had requested that their working relationship be an informal one. "There is enough pomp and circumstance outside of this office," he'd said. "Let's keep it there."

Jesse dutifully complied.

"Good. You're here," Bryan said, taking his place behind his desk. He dropped a couple of sheets of paper on top of an already paper-laden desk. Leaning back in his chair, the Secretary of State rubbed his eyes and moaned.

Bryan looked tired. More so than usual. He had every reason. Between the mess of warring leaders in Mexico, the conflict in Europe, the sinking of the *Lusitania,* increased U-boat activity in the Atlantic, charges by the German government that the United States was violating its own policy of neutrality, pressure by the Allied forces for more munitions and war matériel, plus the daily pounding he and the President took from the New York papers, there was little wonder he was showing symptoms of fatigue.

The man seated behind the desk was a big man. His cheeks and chin and neck were well filled. Bald on the top of his head, he let the sides grow enough that it curled. His eyes were sharp with intelligence, his nose prominent. He had a thin line for a mouth that stretched wide across his face and could open to enormous size, a family characteristic which they affectionately referred to as "the Bryan mouth." He wore his usual attire—white shirt with a black bow tie, black vest and coat, plain black or pinstriped pants. Outside, he always covered his bald pate with a black silk hat.

"Have you heard recently from Emily?" Bryan asked, his voice muffled by the hands in front of his face. They were still rubbing tired eyes.

"Yes, sir. She and Katy are fine. They're continuing on to England."

"Good . . . good. An answer to prayer."

"Yes, sir, it is. And I want to thank you for your efforts on their behalf. According to Emily, the Cunard people were beside themselves with joy when she turned up. She said your telegram put the fear of God in them, that they couldn't have been more intimidated had they been told they would have to give an account before the judgment seat itself."

Booming laughter came from behind the Secretary's desk. It was good to hear Bryan laugh. "I'll have to remember to tell Mary that one," he said.

Jesse's voice took on a concerned tone. "Were you and your wife able to get away over the weekend?"

Bryan dropped his hands to his side and gazed at Jesse warmly, obviously enjoying the temporary respite from the pressures of office this friendly exchange provided.

"We went away to Silver Spring, the home of Senator Blair Lee. We sat under that huge magnolia tree, ate a picnic supper, did a little reading, took a nap. At twilight we listened to the good-night song of birds. The entire day worked like an elixir. But do you want to know the best part of the weekend?"

"What's that?"

"No newspapermen!"

It was Jesse's turn to laugh.

Bryan sat up straight in his chair, pulled himself toward the desk, and picked up the papers he'd placed there. It was time to get down to business.

Beginning with a sigh, he said, "We have one report and two items of business to tend to, Jesse."

Jesse prepared himself for work. He pulled out a pad of paper and a pen to take notes if needed.

"First the report—and this pertains to you personally. I didn't tell you this before because of Emily." He paused, giving Jesse the impression that he still had reservations about sharing the information with him. "Mary and I were dining out on the evening we received word of the sinking of the *Lusitania*," Bryan continued. "On the way home a thought struck me. I remember wondering if that ship had carried munitions of war. I decided to have Lansing investigate it."

Bryan dug into a substantial stack of papers and pulled out what Jesse assumed was Lansing's report. Placing his pince-nez spectacles on the end of his nose, Bryan scanned the report as he talked.

"Lansing examined the clearance papers of the ship." He removed his spectacles and looked directly at Jesse. "You're not going to like what he found. The *Lusitania* was carrying ammunition on board. England was using our citizens to protect her ammunition. A note to this effect has been sent to the President. In it, I reminded him that it is imperative that we maintain, and enforce when necessary, our neutrality."

Jesse nodded grimly. He understood fully what the Secretary of State was telling him. The British had violated the rules of the game by transporting war matériel aboard a passenger ship. If the Germans knew this to be the case, they were justified in their actions. Innocent civilians were put at risk needlessly, among them Emily and Katy. Only by the grace of God did they survive. Most of the innocent civilians were not as fortunate.

Bryan allowed Jesse time alone with his thoughts. Not until Jesse nodded and thanked him for sharing Lansing's findings did he continue.

"The second item of business is this," Bryan said, picking up the papers he'd placed on the desk when he entered the room. "I don't think this will come as a surprise to you." Once again donning his spectacles, the Secretary of State read aloud:

My Dear Mr. President:

It is with sincere regret that I have reached the conclusion that I should return to you the commission of Secretary of State with which you honored me at the beginning of your administration.

Obedient to your sense of duty and actuated by the highest motives, you have prepared for transmission to the German government a note in which I cannot join without violating what I deem to be an obligation to my country, and the issue involved is of such moment that to remain a member of the Cabinet would be as unfair to you as it would be to the cause which is nearest my heart, namely the prevention of war.

I, therefore, respectfully tender my resignation, to take effect when the note is sent, unless you prefer an earlier hour. Alike desirous of reaching a peaceful solution of the problems arising out of the use of the submarines against merchantmen, we find ourselves differing irreconcilably as to the methods which should be employed

Dropping the letter and removing his spectacles, Bryan said, "That's the heart of the matter. It goes on from there. What do you think?"

Bryan was wrong in that Jesse was indeed surprised. *Why hadn't he seen this coming? Surely this was not a hasty decision on the part of the Secretary of State. Had he been so wrapped up in his personal problems that he missed the indicators that brought Bryan to this conclusion?*

Sensing some of Jesse's concerns, Bryan said, "I did not consult any of the Cabinet or you or others, because I did not want to implicate anyone else. Frankly, I do not see that I have any other choice. The President believes he is voicing the sentiment of the country with this second note to Germany. I feel that it is a certain step toward war. I'm also confident there are comparatively few Americans who want our country to be involved in this cataclysm. If I resign now, I believe it will be possible to bring the real sentiments of the people to the surface. The President may then feel at liberty to take steps which he now feels are unwise to take."

"Mr. Secretary. . . Will. . . "

Bryan smiled and nodded at Jesse's use of his first name.

". . . you know that I support you in whatever capacity you choose to serve, whether it be Secretary of State or private citizen. I am at your service and am willing to join you in the public sector."

"That brings us to the second matter of business," Bryan

said, his brow furrowing. "I don't want you coming with me."

"Sir?"

"I want you to stay here in Washington. Before the subject of my resignation came up, I was preparing an assignment for you. You are the perfect man for the job. I want you to stay behind and take it."

"But won't the next Secretary of State want to appoint his own man to the task?"

"You won't be reporting to the Secretary of State," Bryan said.

A clammy feeling came over Jesse. Why did he think he wasn't going to like what was coming next?

"For this assignment, you will be reporting directly to the President of the United States."

The clammy feeling was justified. "The President?"

"I've already discussed it with him. He agrees you are the man for the job. He's waiting for you right now to brief you on the assignment."

Jesse sat forward in his seat. "The President is waiting for me? You *are* going to tell me what this assignment is all about, aren't you?"

"The President will inform you of the assignment's nature and your role."

Everything inside Jesse signaled caution, if not outright danger. His mind didn't want to commit to a task without hearing about it first. His heart wanted to stay with Bryan. His knees . . . well, his knees were threatening to veto any movement that would lead toward the White House.

The President was waiting for him!

He shook his head slowly from side to side. This was too much, things were happening too fast.

Bryan leaned his forearms on his desk and clasped his hands in counselor fashion. "Jesse," he said in a calm, quiet voice, "I appreciate your loyalty to me, more than I can express. But your country needs you. This assignment is sensitive and dangerous. I did not recommend you lightly for the task."

"I appreciate your confidence, Mr. Sec . . . Will . . . "

"Jesse, listen to me. This may be our last chance for peace. I believe this second note to Germany regarding the *Lusitania* draws a line that as a nation we may stumble over at a later date. I believe it will force us into a war we don't want. I'm going to do all I can to prevent that from happening. Your task is just as vital. Your success can help keep us out of the war. Should you fail, our chances of going to war increase a thousandfold. Jesse . . . friend, it's the eleventh hour. As Christians we are faced with the horrible prospect of war. It is our duty to God to do everything within our power to prevent it, and then to trust God Almighty to do for us what we cannot do for ourselves."

It was clear to Jesse that his life was just about to take an unexpected sharp turn. *Sensitive* and *dangerous*. Those were the words Bryan used to describe the as-yet-unknown task.

"The President is waiting for you, Jesse," Bryan said. "Shall I tell him you're on your way?"

Jesse inhaled deeply. "My grandfather advised a President," he said. "It was an informal arrangement brought about by a chance meeting. My grandfather was giving an impromptu funeral oration for the soldiers who were killed during the battle of Antietam." Jesse chuckled at the remembrance. "The way I heard it, the organizers for the memorial service forgot to invite a minister."

Bryan chuckled.

"Anyway, President Lincoln was taking one of his carriage rides in the countryside. He saw the memorial service and stopped. No one knew he was there. Following the service, Lincoln invited my grandfather over to his carriage and then to share the ride back to Washington with him."

"Your grandfather was a fortunate man," Bryan said. "And if he was anything like his grandson, I'm sure Mr. Lincoln benefited from the encounter."

Jesse stood and offered his hand to the Secretary of State. "Sir, it has been an honor serving with you and for you. And, if you don't mind, I'd appreciate it if you'd inform the President that I'm on my way to the White House."

Bryan gripped Jesse's hand warmly. "And may God be with you," he said.

"May God be with us all," Jesse replied.

An automobile was waiting for Jesse at the bottom of the State Department steps. The driver was holding the door open for him. As the automobile merged with carriages and other automobiles, Jesse was mindful of the change in scenery. The State Department had been his home for two years. Now he was about to change addresses. He couldn't tell if he was more nervous or excited. Of one thing he was certain. He would miss the daily contact with William Jennings Bryan. He wondered if the United States would ever have another Secretary of State so outspoken in his Christian beliefs.

As the automobile rumbled and bounced down capital streets, Jesse smiled at Washington's initial exposure to Secretary of State Bryan. Specifically, he was thinking about the first state dinner. It was served without wine. The Secretary of State, an abstainer of alcoholic beverages, defended his alcohol-free dinners on numerous occasions. Jesse could still hear Bryan's booming voice: "Water, the daily need of every living thing. It ascends from the seas, obedient to the summons of the sun, and, descending, show-ers blessing upon the earth; it gives of its sparkling beauty to the fragrant flower; its alchemy transmutes base clay into golden grain; it is the canvas upon which the finger of the Infinite traces the radiant bow of promise. It is the drink that refreshes and adds no sorrow with it—Jehovah looked upon it at creation's dawn and said—'It is good.'"

A more amusing incident was the time Bryan was in Japan and toasted Admiral Togo with water. He was berated for not using champagne which all the other guests were drinking. To which Bryan replied, "Admiral Togo won his great victory on water, so I drink to him in water. When he wins a great victory on champagne, then I will drink to him in champagne!"

"Sir, the President is waiting."

The driver held open the automobile door. And when Jesse didn't jump out the moment the door opened, the driver felt it his duty to inform Jesse that the President's time was more important that his.

Jesse was hustled into the White House. He expected to be ushered immediately into the Oval Office. He wasn't. He was told to take a seat on a red velvet cushioned bench in a hallway. There he sat.

Ten minutes passed. Twenty. Forty-five. An hour. An hour and a half. An hour and forty-five minutes.

"Mr. Morgan? The President will see you now." A young man who couldn't have been any older than Johnny had been sent to retrieve him.

Jesse stood. His knee threatened to cramp from sitting on the bench for so long. "Just a minute," he said with a sheepish grin. He stretched his leg, working the cramp out of the muscle.

"Sir, the President's waiting," the young man said.

Jesse started to explain. Instead, he held back his words, nodded an acknowledgment, and let the boy lead the way. *What did a boy his age know of cramps?*

President Woodrow Wilson was seated behind his desk when Jesse entered. Immediately in front of the desk was a small grouping of chairs. One of them was occupied. Jesse recognized the man; white mustache, stern eyes, wide ears—Colonel Edward House.

The military rank was honorary, bestowed upon House by a grateful Texas governor for political services rendered. Without a doubt he was the most powerful unofficial government worker in Washington. An intimate friend of the President's, House served as Wilson's personal adviser. Jesse knew of him by reputation. And because of one particular service he performed for the President.

In late 1914, anxious to avoid America's involvement in the European war, President Wilson sent House as his unofficial emissary on a secret mission to the foreign offices of the major belligerent powers. House conferred with various foreign leaders in London, Paris, and Berlin. His goal: to secure a negotiated peace. He was not successful. Both the Allies and the Central Powers believed they could break the military deadlock by force of arms. The President's proposal, as presented by House, fell on deaf ears.

Within the administration itself, House's trip abroad created a whirlwind of controversy, not for its stated purpose, but because the President chose to bypass the office of the Secretary of State for this mission. At worst, it was an affront to William Jennings Bryan; at best, it was an admission that the President did not fully trust the Secretary of State's ability to perform such a sensitive assignment.

Wilson rose from behind his desk. The President was thin to the point of gaunt. He wore a neatly pressed gray suit. His hair was thin and gray, his cheek bones and chin sharply angular. Like his Secretary of State, the President wore pince-nez spectacles, only while Bryan wore his primarily to read, Wilson wore his all the time.

From Jesse's limited observations of the man, he knew Wilson to be stern and impassive, yet emotional; calm and patient, yet quick-tempered and impulsive. He could be unforgiving and fierce in his contempt toward those who dared disagree with him. Precise and businesslike, yet at times making decisions based solely on intuition. In short, he was a man known for his paradoxes.

"Do you know Colonel House?" the President asked, extending a hand toward his friend.

"By reputation," Jesse said. "I've never had the pleasure to meet him personally."

The three men exchanged handshakes. Jesse was led to the circle of stuffed chairs. The President motioned for him to sit in one. He and House sat side-by-side opposite Jesse.

"Let me begin by saying how surprised and saddened I am by the Secretary of State's decision to resign. I will accept it, of course, but only because he insists on its acceptance. Our two years of association have been very delightful to me. And our judgments have accorded in practically every matter of official duty and of public policy until now. William Jennings Bryan is a good and passionate man. And I know he thinks the world of you. Quite frankly, that is why you are here at this moment. Did he tell you what we are asking you to do?"

Jesse cleared his throat and fidgeted forward in his chair, clasping and unclasping his hands. "No, sir. He was insistent that I should hear of it from you."

"As it should be," the President said. "Colonel . . ." The President sat back in his chair, turning the briefing over to his adviser.

With a stern, no-nonsense demeanor, Colonel House opened a folder and began. He spoke rapidly with little inflection. "The President is concerned with the alarming increase in German espionage activity in the United States.

To date we have only suspicions, but here is what we believe is taking place:

"We believe that Germany has sent operatives to America with specific sabotage instructions and a bankroll with which to finance their efforts.

"We believe that there is an active sabotage ring operating somewhere in New York.

"We believe that specific orders have been given for the recruitment of anarchists in our country for the express purpose of sabotage and to foment worker strikes in factories.

"We believe that the Germans have covertly funded a munitions plant somewhere in Connecticut to divert war materials and drive up labor costs.

"We believe that there is a concerted effort to attach bombs to the rudders of ships in New York harbor.

"We believe that attempts are being made to breed anthrax among animals that are to be used by the military.

"And finally, we believe we will see more efforts to destroy factories and transportation routes."

"More efforts?" Jesse asked.

House flipped a page and read. "On February 2nd of this year, one Werner Horn was captured while attempting to blow up the Vanceboro Bridge which links the Canadian Pacific Railroad in New Brunswick to the state of Maine." He flipped another page. "And on January 1st of this year, the Roebling wire and cable plant in Trenton, New Jersey was blown up. We suspect German sabotage."

"I see," Jesse said, rubbing his chin in thought.

House handed him a thick folder. "In there you will find names and dates and a list of suspicious activities to the present. I want to emphasize that what you have in your hands is mere suspicion and speculation. It should never be given out to anyone, especially the press."

Jesse flipped through the pages. "And exactly what do

you want me to do with this?" he asked.

House looked to the President. "Mr. Morgan," the President said, "I want you to investigate these things. If there is a spy ring, I want to know who's involved and where they meet. If these suspicions are true, I want to know names and times and places. We must stop these things before any more of them occur. If we don't, I predict the American people will rise up in a fury of anti-German sentiment that will cause chaos in the streets and sweep us into the war."

Jesse sat there, dumbly flipping the pages of the report on his lap. The things he'd just heard, the task at hand, the President sitting opposite him, his immediate surroundings—the Oval Office of the White House!—all these things tumbled down on him like an avalanche. He didn't know where to begin. "I . . . that is . . . do . . . um, Mr. President, exactly what are you asking me to do?"

House gave Jesse a look that resembled the expression a schoolmarm would use on an obtuse student. "I think the President has been quite clear, Mr. Morgan. He wants you to investigate and report."

"Yes, I understand that part," Jesse said. "Who will I be working with?"

"You will be working alone," House said.

"Isn't there an agency . . ."

"We have operatives in the field, if that's what you're asking," House said testily.

The President interrupted. "On occasion, Mr. Morgan, I find it useful to assign certain tasks to individuals, tasks of a particularly sensitive nature. You will be acting as my personal adviser in this matter. This approach precludes a lot of bureaucratic nonsense."

"So I will be acting alone?"

The President nodded. "One man may be able to slip in and out of places unnoticed where a team of men would attract attention."

"And if I should bump into any of our operatives, will they know that I am working for you?" He chuckled self-consciously. "I wouldn't want to get arrested, or shot by one of the good guys."

"No one will be informed of your assignment," House said emphatically. "And should you 'bump into them,' you will not tell them."

"But what if . . . "

"As a last resort, and only as a last resort, you have permission to have them contact me," House said.

"I doubt it would ever come to that," the President said with a brush of his hand. "Mr. Morgan will be discreet, I'm sure."

Jesse didn't know whether the President was patronizing him or expressing confidence in him. "One more question?" Jesse asked.

"Go ahead," the President said, pulling a watch from his pocket. He looked at the time and frowned.

"Why did you pick me for this assignment?"

"Actually, it was the Secretary . . . " The President stopped himself and rephrased his answer, ". . . the *former* Secretary of State's recommendation. Naturally, we ran a check on you. Your security agency background, your upbringing in New York, we took these things into consideration. But in the end, I needed someone I could trust. And I trust Mr. Bryan to be a good judge of character. So, Mr. Morgan, do you accept the position?"

Jesse's impulse was to turn the position down and run out of the Oval Office and never come back. There was a time when he craved the very danger which loomed on the horizon. But he was older now. Wiser. Slower. At heart, a pacifist.

Still, he had his pride. And he hated to think of disappointing his friend, the former Secretary of State, on the day of his resignation.

"I'll do my best, sir," Jesse said.

The next thing he knew, he was hustled out of the White House and taken back to the State Department. As he stood in front of the State Department, the events of the last hour swirled in his head.

Bombings. Riots. Strikes. Anthrax. Spy rings. Sabotage.

All of a sudden, Jesse didn't feel safe standing on the street.

Chapter 10

DOES she handle rejection very well?" Maggie asked. Emily stared out the window of Maggie's London suburb house at her daughter. Katy wore a large-brimmed straw hat. She was trimming Maggie's rosebushes that had been neglected. Her movements were slow, pensive.

The two older women sipped tea around a small table positioned strategically near the window. It was Maggie's afternoon spot. There she would sit, sip her tea, and read or write letters or stare at her garden, as unkempt as it was. Today, she seemed especially pleased to be sharing this time with Emily, in spite of the bad news.

"Ever since she was eight years old, Katy has dreamed of being a missionary," Emily said, watching her daughter cut off a dead branch. "That's all she's ever wanted to do. So, you can imagine, how much of a setback this is for her."

Maggie nodded sympathetically. "From what I've observed, she seems an intelligent, capable young woman. Did the London Missionary Society tell her why they were turning her down?"

"They said that they couldn't receive all who offered their services for missionary work and were thus obligated to select only those who possessed the most promising acquirements."

"Pity," Maggie said. "It's their loss, to be sure."

Emily smiled in appreciation for her hostess' kind assessment of Katy. She was struck by how much she owed the Thomas family, first Bryn for saving her life and now Maggie for taking her and Katy under her wing. In Queenstown, Maggie insisted she escort Emily and Katy to London, and that they live with her during their stay in England. As it turned out, she was involved with the same humanitarian effort to Belgium as was Emily. So not only did they live together, they worked together.

"I'm curious," Maggie said. "What prompted Katy to want to be a missionary? Most young ladies her age dream of more romantic futures."

"Her Sunday School teacher used to tell stories of missionaries. And Katy has always been an adventurer. I'm sure the allure of foreign places has something to do with it." Emily's brow furrowed in thought. She took a sip of tea and cocked her head to one side with a new remembrance. "I do recall Katy predicting that someday Sunday School teachers would tell stories about her and the work she was doing on the mission field."

Maggie laughed. "We all have visions of grandeur at that age, don't we? I wanted to be Florence Nightingale."

Emily grinned. "I wanted to be an investigative reporter."

Drifting off into thoughts of the past, the women sat in silence for a few minutes. The clip, clip, clip of Katy's shears could be heard outside.

Setting her teacup onto the saucer with a clink, Maggie said with a sigh, "Well, we may not have become all we dreamed of, but we're doing a good work nonetheless."

"The Belgium relief effort," Emily said.

Maggie nodded. "You can't imagine what it's like over there, Emily. Farmers watching helplessly as German soldiers confiscate their livestock and their grain, leaving them with nothing to feed their families. Then, to see families lining the road as the farmers themselves were herded down the roads to do forced labor on German farms."

"It sounds horrible," Emily said.

"It was horrible."

"You were there?"

Maggie nodded. "My husband was one of those farmers. He wasn't well. A lung condition. I never saw him again. Two weeks later I received word he'd died in the field. I left my village. My home. Traveled in the dark of night with nothing but the clothes I was wearing. I drank out of streams and wells. I had nothing to eat for three days. But I managed to cross the frontier. An English night patrol found me curled up behind a barn. I knew some people here in London. They helped me start a new life. I considered living with Bryn in Ireland, but we never got along together when we were young. Besides, here in London I can do something to help my friends and neighbors back home."

Emily was aghast. She reached across the table and covered the older woman's hand with her own. "Maggie, I had no idea! You seemed so settled here. So connected. I just assumed you'd lived here all your life."

"Six months," Maggie said.

"I'm so sorry . . . for your loss, I mean. Your husband. Your home."

Maggie shrugged, resigned to her life. "After a time the tears no longer come. You just accept it. It's the images of what once was that drives me to do all I can in this relief effort. They come at unguarded moments—the image of German soldiers drinking and gorging themselves while Belgium children starve; the image of our little medieval town sacked, buildings that have stood forever, charred and engulfed with flames; our treasured library, filled with shelves of books that it took centuries to collect, now ashes. Classics and manuscripts that the world will never see again. Lost forever! It is these images that have scarred my mind. And I'll never be rid of them."

Emily squeezed Maggie's hand in comfort.

The door swung open and Katy stepped into the house.

"Katy, my dear!" Maggie said, jumping up. She took the shears from Katy's hands and lay them aside. "You are such a dear for tending my roses for me. But I wonder if I can impose upon you to perform a special errand for me."

There was a dullness in Katy's eyes that comes with disappointment. Still, she smiled and said, "What is it you'd like me to do?"

Taking a plate from the cabinet, Maggie loaded it with tea cakes. She covered the cakes with a napkin. Handing the plate to Katy she said, "You would be such a dear if you would take these cakes and deliver them to a Lieutenant Fred Radcliff. He's at Magdalene Hospital. You know where that is, don't you? It's just two blocks down the road."

Katy nodded. "On the left-hand side."

"Yes, dear, that's the one. I promised Edith . . . " To Emily, "Edith is my dearest friend. She's the one who set me up in this house when I came over; she and her husband, Charles." To Katy again, "I promised Edith that I would look in on him every day. It's really the least I can do for her considering all she's done for me. Fred is a fine young man. Wounded in the leg while he was . . . well, he can tell you all about that, can't he? Can you do this one thing for me, dear? I'd do it myself, but my schedule at the moment is simply impossible."

"I'll do it for you," Katy said. "The walk will probably do me good."

"And it will give you a chance to see inside a British hospital," Emily said. To Maggie, she explained, "Katy has had some training as a nurse."

"Then it's all settled!" Maggie cried. "Thank you, you

dear, dear girl!"

Emily and Maggie watched as Katy walked through the garden, through the gate of the white picket fence, and strolled dutifully up the road.

Maggie sat down at the tea table and took a leisurely sip.

"Is there something I can do to help?" Emily asked.

"Help?" Maggie asked.

"You said you had an impossible schedule."

"Oh, that!" Maggie scoffed. "The only thing on my schedule this afternoon was to take a plate of tea cakes to Fred at the hospital." She leaned forward and looked out the window. "I really do need to trim my roses, but it looks like Katy did a pretty good job of that too."

A sly grin crossed Emily's face. "This Fred Radcliff. He doesn't happen to be young and available, does he?"

Maggie scrunched up her face in an expression of extreme pleasure. "Ooooo, why didn't they make men that good-looking when I was young?"

"It won't work," Emily said with a grin. "Katy may be interested in changing his bandage, but that's where her interest stops."

Maggie gave a shrug. "It doesn't hurt to try. Besides, Katy needs a diversion right now. And Fred Radcliff qualifies as a top-notch diversion."

Emily laughed. For a woman who had seen so much pain and destruction, Maggie Thomas was certainly full of the joy of living.

Katy walked the brick road encompassed by a cocoon of self-pity. She knew it. She didn't like it. But she couldn't help it. That's how she felt.

It didn't matter that the sky was sparkling blue, that the air was crisp with a tang of salt, that she was walking a street in mystical London far from the everyday dusty plains that butted up against the Rocky Mountain peaks. It didn't matter that she walked among a people who dwelt in a war zone, that every day at any given house a mother could receive notice that her son had performed admirably in the service of his country even to the point of making the ultimate sacrifice; that people were hard-pressed for life's daily necessities due to the German U-boat blockade of the island; that on occasion death rained from the sky at night as German soldiers dropped bombs on the city from silver, cigar-shaped airships high overhead.

None of this mattered.

What mattered was that the London Missionary Society had rejected her.

"Obligated to select only those who possessed the most promising acquirements," they'd said. *What were they saying other than she possessed less than promising acquirements?*

All of her life she'd imagined the interview. She saw herself standing in a large room with sunlight streaming through cathedral-like windows. Behind a long wooden table, its edges adorned with exquisitely detailed carved scrolls, sat seven godly men, dressed impressively in three-piece suits. She even imagined being able to feel the spiritual presence emanating from these men of God whose responsibility it was to send dedicated workers around the world for the cause of Christ.

In her imagined interview, she would stand straight, tall, confident as they reviewed her written application, her references. They would be impressed. A good student. A hard worker. Faithful volunteer. Able to succeed in difficult circumstances. Dedicated. "Never before have I met a woman so totally dedicated to God's work," her pastor's letter of recommendation had said. "While other young women talk only of young men and marriage, Katherine Morgan talks of Africa and service to God in the tradition of Mary

Smith Moffat." (Katy had especially liked her pastor's reference to Mary Moffat, her role model and a London Missionary Society appointee.)

How dare they say she possessed less than promising acquirements!

In reality, her interview before the London Missionary Society resembled not her dream in the slightest detail. The interview took place in a small, cramped room with plaster walls that desperately needed patching. Hardly erect with perfect postures and a godly presence, the men who interviewed her sat slumped or hunched over a scarred table. They reviewed her written materials. There was not an impressed expression among them.

They asked her to describe her call to the mission field. With spiritual passion she described her lifelong dream. One of the men pulled out a pocket watch to check the time. Another nodded rhythmically without once looking at her. The worst, however, was the man who sat back, slumped in his chair, his coat unbuttoned and falling open, his hands interlaced over his belly, his eyelids drifting closed!

These were the men who said, "We are obligated to select only those who possess the most promising acquirements!"

Katy wanted to scream. She held it back. If she let one emotion out, the dam would surely burst and all her other emotions would follow.

It was better to encase herself in an emotionless cocoon. To give the appearance that she was maturely in control in spite of this disappointing setback. When, in reality, she wanted to run away to a place where no one knew her, to scream until she no longer had breath to scream, to weep until there were no more tears.

How was she going to face her father? How could she go back to the States now? She was a failure. And then there was Johnny. She'd have to face him someday. Of course, she didn't care what he thought of her. It was just that while he'd always been a disappointment to their parents, she'd been the one they were always proud of. And now she was a disappointment. . . .

Tears came unbidden. Biting her lower lip, Katy fought them back as she opened the door of the Magdalene Hospital.

"Fred Radcliff, please," Katy said to the ward nurse.

"Another one?" the nurse said, looking Katy over. She motioned with her finger halfway down the ward on the right side. "The one with the guitar."

Katy thanked the nurse. Magdalene Hospital was a two-story graystone structure. Open windows at each end of the floor allowed a sweet breeze to pass between the beds, clearing away the ever-present hospital odors of medicine, infection, and refuse.

Katy's heels clicked on the wooden floors as she passed between two rows of metal frame beds that lined the walls at right angles. Some of the beds had a box-like frame over them with ropes and pulleys stringing up an arm or a leg, keeping the soldier's injured limb immobilized. A pair of eyes from each bed followed her down the ward; the only exception were those beds whose occupants were sleeping.

"'ere comes another one for you, Radcliff!" one of the patients who'd overheard Katy's conversation with the nurse shouted. "'ow many sisters do you got anyhow?"

Laughter floated down the ward with the breeze.

The man with the guitar stared at Katy curiously as she approached. He was sitting atop his blanket propped against the metal bars of the headboard, wearing a navy-blue robe. His legs were crossed at the ankles. He cradled an acoustical guitar with six strings in his lap. Two robed patients sat on one side of the bed, while a third sat on the other. Patient Fred Radcliff seemed to be the center of attention of the entire ward.

Katy stopped at the end of his bed. A circle of silly male grins greeted her. "Mr. Radcliff?"

"Yes?"

Katy held out the plate of tea cakes. "These are for you. From Maggie Thomas. She asked me to deliver them."

"Ooooo!" one of the patients cried. "Now 'e's got one woman deliverin' things for another woman!"

The other male patients laughed at the observation.

Talking over their laughter, Radcliff said, "Maggie Thomas is me mum's friend!"

His explanation only served to increase the howls.

Radcliff ignored them. Katy wished she could. She extended the plate a little farther indicating she wanted Radcliff to take them. He did.

"It was nice meeting you, Mr. Radcliff," Katy lied. "I must be on my way now." She turned to leave.

"Wait!" Radcliff called after her. "Please forgive my boorish friends here. Maggie would never forgive me if I didn't give a proper thank-you to one of her friends who so graciously took the time to bring me these . . . " he peeked under the napkin, "tea cakes."

"There is no need to thank me," Katy said. She turned again to go.

"But I don't even know your name!" Radcliff called after her.

"I know," Katy called back.

"You're not going to make me get up on my bum leg and chase you down the ward, are you?"

Katy glanced over her shoulder. Sure enough, Radcliff had handed the guitar to one of his friends. With a wince he swung his leg over the side of the bed and was about to climb out.

"Stay in bed, Mr. Radcliff!" Katy said, turning to face

him.

"Only if you come sit awhile and let me thank you for the cakes."

The eyes of the other men in the ward swung back and forth from Radcliff to Katy. It looked like they were watching a tennis match.

Katy held her ground, her hands on her hips.

With another wince, Radcliff pushed off the edge of the bed and stood.

With an exasperated sigh, Katy retraced her steps. "Get in bed, Mr. Radcliff," she said.

A smile creased Radcliff's face, as they did on all the other faces in the ward that were awake. His victory was a victory for the entire ward.

Katy stood once again at the end of his bed.

Radcliff made shooing motions to the men who were seated around him. "Go along, mates," he said. "Can't you see I have a guest? Joey, give the lady your chair."

A boyish young man with a shaved head and big ears, without a doubt still in his teens, jumped up from his chair and offered it to Katy.

As the other patients cleared out, Radcliff motioned for Katy to sit.

She stood defiantly at the end of the bed, her arms folded across her chest.

With a silent, pleading look, he offered again.

Katy relented and sat in the chair.

"Are you always this stubborn?" Radcliff asked her.

"I could ask you the same question!" Katy cried.

"If you did, the answer would be yes. I *am* stubborn."

The man propped against the headboard of the hospital bed was a pleasant looking Englishman. Katy had seen handsomer men, though she took as much notice of them as she was taking of him. Radcliff's hair was dark brown, short, and combed neatly back. His eyes were dark, yet merry. A nondescript nose led down to a brown trimmed mustache that separated in the middle, making it look almost like two eyebrows on his upper lip. A thin line for a mouth could unexpectedly break open into a boyish grin showing even, white teeth. He was of average build, average height, with an above average air of self-confidence.

"Now, are you going to tell me your name, or do I have to ring up Maggie and ask her who it is that brought me these luscious tea cakes?" He made a motion toward an empty chair. The tea cakes were gone, but their disappearance was no mystery. The plate had already made its way up and down the ward where more than a dozen patients chewed with satisfied smiles and crumbs on their faces and beds. "Looks like the reviews are in," he quipped. "They were luscious."

Katy grinned without meaning to. Her grin pleased Radcliff.

"Much better," he said. "Now, would you grace that smile with a name?"

"Katy."

"Ah! Katy! And a Yank?"

"Yes, I'm from America."

"Thought as much. How is it that you know Maggie?"

Katy glanced around. Their conversation was being monitored by all the other men in the ward. She really didn't have to look around to know that, she could feel their eyes on her.

"By accident, actually," she said in a quieter voice. "Her brother rescued my mother when the *Lusitania* went down."

"The *Lusitania?*" Radcliff cried, loud enough for two wards to hear. "Your mother was aboard the *Lusitania?*"

The entire ward buzzed with excitement.

Katy nodded in response to his question, embarrassed at

the increased level of attention she was now getting. "We were coming over to . . . "

"We? Did you say 'we'? You were aboard the *Lusitania* too?"

Katy barely nodded.

"Did you hear that, lads?" Radcliff shouted. "Katy here was aboard the *Lusitania!*" To Katy, "What were you doing when the torpedo struck? When did you know for sure that the ship was sinking? Did you get into a lifeboat or did you have to jump?"

A thousand questions followed. From all over the ward, men got out of their beds and circled around Radcliff and Katy, listening intently as Katy described the events before and after the sinking of the ship.

Chapter 11

THE next day Katy returned to Magdalene Hospital with another plate of tea cakes for Fred Radcliff, compliments of his mother's friend Maggie. Katy left the house to an exchange of raised eyebrows and knowing smirks between the two older women. She didn't care what they thought. Katy found that she enjoyed the hospital surroundings. It diverted her from her personal misery. She was even thinking of doing some volunteer work there. This second visit would allow her to get a better look at the hospital and observe the staff with whom she'd be working.

The moment she stepped foot on the ward, she remembered what she didn't like about the hospital. The stares of all the men.

"Hey, Radcliff! Look who's back! Your *Lusitania* sweetheart!"

Katy was used to the crude, unthinking remarks of Neanderthals. She grew up with a brother. Still, it didn't make the walk down the middle of the ward any easier for her.

"You came back!" Radcliff said with a smile.

Katy extended the plate of cakes. "You missed out yesterday," she said.

Radcliff accepted the plate, tossed back the napkin and took a cake before passing the rest along to the other patients in the ward. Katy sat down in the chair beside his bed before it was offered to her.

"How are you feeling today?" she asked.

"I'm being released," he said.

"That's wonderful news!"

Radcliff nodded with cake crumbs in his mustache. "Two days," he said with his mouth full, "and I'll rejoin my squadron."

"Mechanic?" Katy asked.

Radcliff frowned. "Pilot."

"Oh." Now it was Katy's turn to look disappointed.

"Why would you think I was a mechanic?"

Katy shrugged. "Just hoping."

"Hoping I was a mechanic? Why?"

"My brother flies aeroplanes," she said. "He's an uncouth bore who thinks only of himself."

Radcliff laughed heartily. "Then he's probably an excellent pilot! Is he?"

"He thinks he is."

"He wouldn't happen to be one of the Lafayette Escadrille pilots, would he?"

Katy shook her head. "I don't recognize the name, but I don't think so. Last I heard, he was flying away with some drunken aerial daredevil named Blackhorn, or something like that."

"The Lafayette Squadron is a bunch of American chaps flying with the French," Radcliff explained.

"That's certainly not Johnny," Katy said. "He'd never survive in the military. He's as undisciplined as they come."

An awkward pause hung between them.

"You never told me how you hurt your leg," Katy said.

"An aeroplane fell on it."

"What?" Katy started to laugh at the image of an aeroplane spiraling out of the sky and crashing on Fred Radcliff's leg.

"It may sound funny to you," Radcliff said with a grin, "but it hurt!"

Katy sobered immediately. "I didn't mean to laugh at your pain," she said.

Radcliff waved off her apology. "Actually, the wheels hit a rut and the plane tipped over. I was pinned beneath the engine. Ripped up the muscle a bit. Nothing that will keep me out of the sky."

Nothing that will keep me out of the sky. Radcliff was beginning to sound like Johnny. Katy sobered even more.

"Hey, Freddie boy!" the man in the bed next to him cried. "Tell her about how you almost got captured by the Huns."

Radcliff wrinkled his face in disgust. "She doesn't want to hear about that."

"On the contrary," Katy said, "tell me."

He shook his head. "I'd rather talk about you," he said. "So you came over here to London with your mother to help with the Belgium relief effort."

"No, actually, she came over for the relief effort. I came to be interviewed by the London Missionary Society."

Radcliff's expression soured. "Whatever for?"

His reaction raised Katy's defenses. "To be placed as a missionary!"

"You? A missionary?"

"And why not?" Katy cried.

"You're too beautiful for one thing," he said. "It would be a waste!"

"A waste of what?" She was genuinely angry now.

"A waste of a beautiful woman, that's what!"

Katy's face felt fiery red. Her breathing increased. She considered stomping out of the ward, but chose not to. She had locked horns with an ignorant brute and she intended to hang him up to dry.

"Let's ignore your cheap attempt at a compliment and get to the heart of the matter, shall we?" she seethed. "In your opinion, exactly what are beautiful women good for?"

Catcalls and whistles echoed up and down the ward. As before, she had managed to provide afternoon entertainment for the ward.

"What do you mean, cheap compliment? I meant it!"

"Meant what?"

"When I called you a beautiful woman, that's what!"

His sincerity unnerved her. Anger she could handle and give back in full measure. But she had never considered herself attractive. She glanced self-consciously around the hospital ward. Unanimously, the men in the beds were agreeing with Radcliff, some with grins and nods, others with a thumbs-up sign.

Lowering her voice, she cried, "That still doesn't excuse the fact that you think my going to the mission field would be a waste of my life."

It was Radcliff's turn to look sheepish. "You're right," he said. "It was insensitive of me. It's just that . . ." He considered explaining, then thought better of it. "When do you leave?" he asked.

"Leave?"

"For the mission field."

Katy lowered her head and stared at her hands. "I don't. They rejected me."

"Then what's all the fuss?" Radcliff cried.

"The fuss is your attitude! I've worked hard to become a nurse so that I could serve on the mission field. It's been my lifelong dream. And now I'm not going!"

Katy was close to tears, prompted by the fresh reminder of her rejection by the London Missionary Society.

"You're a nurse?" Radcliff asked.

Katy nodded.

"Well, you don't have to go to India or China or..."

"South Africa," Katy said.

"... or South Africa to be a nurse. There's a war going on here! There's plenty of need for nurses!"

Katy pulled out a handkerchief and dabbed her nose.

Radcliff leaned back and sighed. "What is it with nurses and all this spiritual nonsense?" he said. "Do you know you're the second nurse I've met who gets all emotional over all this..."

"Spiritual nonsense?" Katy asked.

"Religious stuff. You know what I mean," he said.

"Who's the other nurse?" Katy asked.

"A woman in Belgium," Radcliff answered. "She was always reading the Bible to us, those parables mostly, and also from another book... *The Imitation of Christ.* I think that was the name of it. Ever hear of it?"

"I've heard of it. Never read it."

"She used to read to us from that book to keep us occupied, I guess."

"Who was she? Your nursemaid?" Katy said, attempting to be humorous.

Her humor failed. Radcliff's face turned more serious than Katy had ever seen it before. "She saved my life," he said. "Me, and about a hundred other men."

"I'm sorry," Katy whispered. "That's not to mean I'm sorry she saved you, but that I'm sorry I made light of someone who..."

Radcliff shook his head. He'd taken no offense in her comment.

"What's her name?" Katy asked.

"I can't tell you."

"Oh?" She was a little hurt. "Why not?"

"Because she's still over there, still helping French and British soldiers who are caught behind the German lines escape."

"I see," Katy said. She didn't stay much longer than that. Radcliff had lost his desire for company, encompassed by a memory that stirred very deep emotions for him.

Three days later Fred Radcliff appeared on Maggie Thomas' doorstep to thank her for the tea cakes and to ask Katy out to the theater. Katy had to admit to herself that Fred Radcliff looked quite dashing in his military uniform with the wings featured prominently over his left breast pocket. Quite an improvement over his navy-blue robe.

He took her to see a production of *Twelfth Night*. It was a marginal performance. Most of London's finest actors and stage personnel were in some way occupied by the war effort. The most memorable part of the performance for Katy was the irony she found in one of the Bard's more famous lines: "Be not afraid of greatness; some are born great, some achieve greatness, and some have greatness thrust upon them." Still stinging from her recent rejection, she thought it appropriate to rewrite the line to: "Be not afraid of obscurity; some are born obscure, others achieve obscurity, and some have obscurity thrust upon them."

"Have a good time?" Radcliff asked as they stepped from the theater.

"Yes, thank you," Katy replied politely.

He offered her his arm. She took it out of politeness. It was nearly midnight. The street lamps burned brightly. An occasional motorcar disturbed the night, but for the most part couples walked. With the rationing of gas, motorcar transportation for leisure endeavors was curtailed.

"So you're rejoining your squadron tomorrow," Katy said.

"That's right."

"Where?"

"Ashford, for now. But I expect to be transferred to France within the month. Dunkirk. Possibly St. Marie

Cappel."

"I see," Katy said.

They strolled through the night. The air was chilled and thick with fog. The only sound was the scrape of their feet on the bricks and a distant humming sound.

"And you?" Radcliff asked. "What are your plans?"

"At the moment I don't know," Katy said. "Probably back to America, though I don't know what I'll do once I get there. I may do some volunteer work at the hospital to pass time before I leave."

"Magdalene Hospital?" Radcliff asked.

Katy smiled and nodded.

The humming sound grew louder. It came from above.

"Will you be back in London any time soon?" Katy asked.

Radcliff didn't answer her. He stopped and cocked his head to one side.

"What is it?" Katy asked.

He held up a hand to shush her.

The hum turned to a droning sound.

"Zeppelins!" he cried.

The moment he announced their presence, the airships loosed their bombs. There was a series of thuds, each one getting closer. Louder.

Katy looked up. Against the black, star-spangled sky, there were two silvery Zeppelins holding stationary as though they were hanging by ropes from the stars. It was an eerie, unearthly sight.

A block down the street the fire bombs hit a factory. Glass and wood flew everywhere. Brick crumbled. Flames and smoke belched from the now jagged edges of the walls.

Radcliff grabbed Katy's arm and pulled her into the door-way of a darkened merchant's office, sheltering her from the debris with his own body.

The falling bombs weren't frequent, but when they fell, they fell three and four at a time. With a pause in the bombing, Radcliff looked around, then pulled Katy out of the doorway. They began running up the street.

A middle-aged woman, curious to see what all the noise was about, ran from her house wiping her hands on her apron. She stared at the inferno that had moments before been a factory. "Did the factory explode?" she yelled to Radcliff.

He shook his head. "Zeppelins! Get inside!"

The woman looked up. When she saw the silver airships, her mouth hung open in a mixture of fear and wonder.

Bombs fell behind her.

The woman screamed.

Her house exploded in flame.

"Joseph!" she cried. "Joseph! Nellie! Thomas!"

It took both Radcliff and Katy to restrain the woman, to keep her from running into her house which was completely engulfed in flames. It was obvious from the first blast that there were no survivors in the house. After the second blast, there was barely any house left.

Like fiery footprints, the destruction from on high marched down the street.

Katy saw a couple huddled under an overhang at the entrance to a bank. From the distance and line between the factory and the burning house, it looked to Katy that the bank was in the exact spot where the next bombs would fall.

"Get out!" she shouted to the couple.

They didn't hear her.

Radcliff saw what Katy was thinking. "You hold on to her," he said regarding the woman. He ran toward the bank yelling to the couple.

Katy watched as he got their attention. The horror showed on their faces as they understood what he was saying. They bolted from the doorway.

The bank erupted. Flames spit out the shattered windows. Wood and rock debris blasted across the street like cannon fire, taking out doors and windows of neighboring buildings.

The couple went down. So did Radcliff.

"Come with me!" Katy shouted to the woman.

"My children!" she screamed, trying to pull away, to get back into her house.

"There's nothing you can do to help them!" Katy cried.

She wasn't getting through. The woman was hysterical. Katy couldn't let her go; the woman would run into the burning house for sure. But Radcliff and the couple needed attention.

Katy peered through the smoke. Three forms lay on the ground. Motionless.

"My children!" the woman cried, trying to pull away.

With all her strength, Katy pulled the woman with her. She had to help Radcliff and the couple. She had to.

Chapter 12

KATY slumped against the hospital wall between two litters. Radcliff lay on one; the girl he was trying to save from the Zeppelin's fire bombs lay on the other. The stone-walled room was filled with litters laden with victims from the bombing. Some, who had straggled to the hospital on their own accord, lay on the bare floor, squeezed in narrow spaces between the litters, making it difficult for hospital workers to get from one victim to another. Some of the injured were propped up in sitting positions, dazed and disoriented; those with lesser injuries stood or leaned against walls.

Moaning was the night's anthem. Mournful sounds of agony. Expressions of grief for loved ones lost. Commingling with this lamentation were the sharp acrid odor of smoke that permeated the clothes of so many of them and the sickening sweet stench of burned flesh.

An elderly man who had been tossed into a corner close to Katy sat with his knees pulled up against his chest. His face was buried in glistening red and black hands. One leg of his darkly stained woolen trousers was shredded at the knee; his foot was bare. From the edge of his shredded pants down his calf to the tips of his toes, his white hairy flesh was charred black and blistered. The man's shoulders shook uncontrollably as he sobbed into his cupped hands.

Hospital nurses and doctors rushed from patient to patient in an attempt to assess their needs. *The night shift,* Katy thought. There were far too few of them. Katy could only assume that word had been dispatched calling more doctors to duty. But would they arrive in time? Some of these people needed medical attention immediately.

The cries of the victims called to her. She hesitated. A combination of thoughts and remembrances held her back. She was trained, but lacked experience. She was in a foreign country; this was England, not America. Until a few days ago, she'd never heard of Magdalene Hospital. She didn't know their procedures, didn't have access to supplies, didn't know the staff. And of the four people she'd already tried to help, two of them were dead and the other two unconscious.

On the street, seconds after the Zeppelin's bombs turned the bank into an inferno, she had tried to reach Radcliff and the couple who had moments before been cuddled in the archway of the bank's entrance. In her haste to help them, she lost her grip on the hysterical woman who had witnessed the fiery death of her family.

Having wrenched herself free from Katy, the woman ran into the flames with no more care than if she were running into a sunlit meadow. The house swallowed her up and she was gone. Minutes later, the entire structure collapsed.

Katy had stared helplessly at her hands. Clawlike. Her grip broken. She was supposed to save the woman, but her attention had been diverted. And now the woman was dead. For all she knew, so was Radcliff and the couple. In her desire to save them all, she wondered if she had killed the only one she could have saved?

She turned to Radcliff and the couple lying in the street. They were as still as the debris piled all around them. What had moments earlier been a quiet London street was now a war zone.

Katy had seen war pictures of similar destruction in the newspaper. Black and white, blurry representations of French towns in ruins. Reality was sharply focused and all too graphic. The newspaper pictures didn't convey the ear-shattering boom of the explosion, or the crumbling sound of brick falling upon brick, or the crackle of fire, or the suffocating feeling of smoke, or the grittiness of dust and soot in the air. They didn't show the town moments before the bombs fell as ingenuous men and women and children walked the streets, greeted their neighbors, and conducted their day-to-day affairs. Now that she was standing within a picture of destruction, the emotional blast that hit her affected her more directly than the Zeppelin's bombs.

Her vision now blurred with tears, she had picked her way over stone and brick and bits of burning lumber, stumbling toward Radcliff. He was unconscious; breathing, but unresponsive to vocal or physical stimuli. She found no major external wounds, only minor cuts and abrasions. The young woman was in similar condition. Unconscious. She, however, had suffered a severe gash on her leg. There was also an abrasion on her forehead that was raising into a sizable welt. Katy used the woman's woolen scarf to wrap the leg. The young man who had shared the arched doorway of the bank building did not fare as well. His right arm had been severed and a large wooden splinter had pierced his neck. He was dead.

When an ambulance came, Katy continued to minister aid, checking the woman's scarf-bandage and trying to get both her and Radcliff to awaken. The ambulance corpsman helped Katy into the back of the truck and told her to lie down. Katy identified herself as a nurse. Not at the moment, he told her. As of now, she was a patient. When she begged to differ, he called her attention to a gash on her own forehead and a bloodied right sleeve.

Katy remembered wiping her forehead with her sleeve. She'd thought it was sweat from exertion and the heat of the fire. Now that the corpsman had corrected her misconception, she also realized she was feeling a bit dizzy. Accepting a bandage from the corpsman, she lay down in the back and accepted her new role as patient.

Now, having had time to think about it, she realized the corpsman had been right. She was a victim. The bombs hadn't been meant for her. She was American, not English. This wasn't her war. It was better to stay out of it.

The scene before her was chaos. Doctors shouting long strings of orders to nurses. Nurses stepping over people while the broken and bruised and burned cried out for help, begging for relief from their pain.

"Welcome to the war."

Radcliff's groggy voice, weak though it was, rose up to her ears.

Katy shifted to her knees and bent over him. "How do you feel?" she asked.

"Like a boxer who has just been KO'd," he replied, wincing. Apparently, talking hurt his head.

"Just lie there quietly," Katy instructed. "You may have a concussion."

A moan came from the litter on her other side. The young lady's eyes fluttered open, then stared wildly from side-to-side, confused.

"Where am I?"

"Lie still," Katy said softly. She placed a comforting hand on the girl's shoulder. It seemed to help the girl as she navigated her way from unconsciousness to conscious thought.

She was young, probably no more than eighteen or nineteen years old, still wearing her straw hat of a simple inverted bowl design that flared at the brim. A wide peach ribbon encircled the hat and drew up into a bow. Poking out from beneath the hat's brim was curly brown hair with flashes of red. Her eyes were wide and innocent. Thin lips pressed together with concern; it was an adult expression on a cherubic face. She pulled her heavy tan woolen coat around her defensively.

"Where am I?" she asked again.

"Magdalene Hospital."

The girl stared up at her. She blinked repeatedly, attempting to focus on Katy. "You're not a nurse," she said.

To Katy, the girl's words sounded like an accusation, and a confirmation of what she was feeling. Her words pricked Katy's pride. It was one thing to admit to herself that she was shaky about her abilities, quite another to admit it to a stranger.

"Please lie still," Katy said. "I am a nurse. I'm just not wearing a uniform."

"No, you're not," the girl insisted. She attempted to get up. It wasn't difficult for Katy to hold her down by the shoulders.

"I'm not going to argue with you," Katy said.

But the girl refused to give up. "I work at Magdalene Hospital," she said. "I know everyone on the nursing staff. You're not a nurse." The girl looked past Katy. She saw someone she recognized. "Miss Cantrell!" she cried.

"Please," Katy insisted. "You need to be quiet. You may have a . . . "

"Laura?"

The nurse the young girl had called bent over both of them.

"Laura! Is that you? Are you hurt badly?" The nurse's eyes ran up and down the length of the young woman on the litter, searching for signs of injury. The eyes stopped twice: once when they came to the bandaged leg, and again when they came to Katy's hand that was pinning the girl against the litter.

"She's been unconscious for some time," Katy said in a professional manner. "She may have a concussion. She also has a gash on her right calf. I bandaged it as best I could on the street. It will need stitches and a fresh dressing."

The nurse stared at Katy through mere slits between her eyelids. "You a nurse?" she asked.

"I've been trained as a nurse," Katy explained, "but I haven't had much actual . . . "

"Why didn't you identify yourself to us?" the nurse barked. "We need every hand that's available!"

"But I'm not sure I can . . . " Katy stammered.

The nurse cut her off. She lifted the bandage on Katy's forehead and evaluated it. "Do you have any other injuries besides this?" she asked.

"Not that I . . . "

"Do you feel dizzy?"

"Not any more, but I . . . "

"Good. See what you can do with that man in the corner."

The nurse wheeled around and returned to the woman whose arm she had been dressing when Laura called to her.

Katy released Laura's shoulders. The girl made no attempt to get up. "You *are* a nurse," the girl said.

With half a grin, Katy nodded agreement.

The room was nearly cleared of litters and injured patients. The worst of them had been taken to surgery or transferred to wards after being treated.

Following orders, Katy had attended to the man in the corner. His burned hands were now thick with bandages; his leg, also burned, was now bandaged. Katy learned amidst a steady flow of tears that the man was burned while pulling two of his three sleeping grandchildren from their beds. The structure collapsed before he could rescue the third. His oldest grandchild. A boy. Ten years of age. Earlier that evening the boy had played his first clarinet solo at a family reunion.

"How did you lose your shoe?" Katy asked.

"I took it off," said the man.

"Took it off?" Katy cried, wrapping the badly burned foot. "Why would you do that?"

Fresh tears streaked his already stained cheeks. "I was so angry," he said, gritting his teeth. "So angry at those Huns that they would do this to my house, to my family. I had to do something. So I threw my shoe at them!"

Katy nodded her approval. She understood the need to strike back, however futilely or irrationally. In fact, not only did she empathize with the barefooted man, she thought that his throwing his shoe was one of the saner, more heroic things she'd heard all night.

After he'd been carried off to a ward, Katy turned her attention back to Radcliff and the girl whose name she now knew.

"Can I help you with something, Laura?"

The girl had raised up on one arm and was looking about for someone. She had been doing this off and on for some time. Suddenly, it dawned on Katy for whom the girl was looking. Katy had been so busy, first being a victim, and then attending the barefooted man, that she'd forgotten that in the street before the bombs fell, Laura had been one half of a couple.

"The young man who was with you in the archway?" Katy guessed.

Laura's eyes grew wide. "Yes! You know about him?"

"Only that the two of you sought shelter in the doorway of the bank."

A studied look came over Laura's face. She looked at Katy's face, then her clothes. It was her clothes that helped the girl remember. "You were in the street!" she cried.

Katy nodded. "So was Radcliff . . . um, Fred."

She motioned toward the next litter. Laura's head turned and inspected him as well. Radcliff was still heavily dazed. He lay staring at the ceiling, his eyelids blinking purposefully, each blink attempting to bring the world into focus.

"It was you who warned us!" Laura said. "Then you know what happened to Taffy!"

"Taffy? The young man you were with? Is he your . . ."

"Friend. Just a friend," Laura said quickly, her cheeks blushing. "We grew up together. Taffy . . . Ira, really, his name is Ira Shields, but he's been called Taffy all his life . . . he was just given his first orders. Infantry. We were celebrating. Has he already been taken to a ward?"

Katy lowered her eyes. "No . . . I doubt that he . . . you see, Laura, I treated you and Radcliff on the street . . ."

"My leg . . . you did that on the street? Then you must have also . . ."

"Laura, he was already dead by the time I got to him."

The news hit her hard. An invisible blow, but just as painful and debilitating as any physical punch. She collapsed back onto the litter, too stunned to cry at first. She looked like Radcliff, blinking her eyes. But unlike Radcliff, she wasn't trying to regain her physical sight, she was trying to regain her emotional balance.

Unsuccessfully.

Hidden springs behind her eyes burst forth. "He was the first man in his family for seven generations to qualify for the infantry," she said of Taffy. "The whole family has a history of weak eyes. Taffy was so proud. He would be the first of the Shields to fight for England in seven generations. And he was so close . . . so close."

"I'm so sorry," Katy said. She took Laura's hand in her own and held it.

"Katy?" Radcliff's head was turned toward her. "Katy?"

"I'm here."

His eyes were focusing better now. "You're hurt," he said, looking at the bandage over her eye.

"I'm fine," Katy said.

Radcliff reached out his hand. Katy took it. With both hands occupied, she sat between the litters and attended her two patients until the hospital staff came for them.

They took Radcliff first to the men's ward. The doctor expressed concern about Radcliff's inability to keep his eyes focused for any length of time.

When two corpsmen came to move Laura to the women's ward, the young woman clung tightly to Katy's hand. "Come see me tomorrow?" she asked.

Katy agreed to visit.

The corpsmen proceeded to take her away.

"Wait! Wait!" she cried. "Katy! Are you working at another hospital?"

Katy shook her head. "I'm just visit . . ."

"Could you fill in for me while I'm laid up? It would mean so much to me. I'm just a volunteer, but they're so shorthanded and I'll feel guilty lying in bed knowing that I should be helping out . . ."

"You have no reason to feel guilty," Katy said.

"I'd feel so much better if I knew someone was filling in for me. I know it's asking a lot. You hardly know me. Just until I'm able to be on my feet?"

The corpsmen looked at each other. A silent agreement passed between them. They started down the hallway to the ward.

"Please consider it," Laura called from halfway down the hall.

"We'll talk about it tomorrow," Katy called back.

The nurse, Miss Cantrell, approached her. Katy was the

sole patient left in what had earlier been a crowded room.

"Let's take a look at that," the nurse said, pulling up the bandage on her forehead. "Two, maybe three stitches. Not bad. Head ache?"

"A little."

The nurse led her to a treatment room. "I want to thank you for helping us out tonight," she said. "You're a Yank, aren't you?"

"Yes."

"Could tell by your accent."

Katy was seated on a stool while the nurse prepared a tray for the doctor.

"So Laura is a volunteer nurse?" Katy asked.

"A good little worker," the nurse said, selecting a needle, lifting the bandage once more, then selecting another, larger needle.

Katy considered asking Miss Cantrell if a Yank could volunteer in an English hospital. Several times, while her forehead was being stitched, the question was on her lips. The words never formed. When the stitching was done and her head was bandaged, she quietly walked home to Maggie's house.

Chapter 13

I n her dream Katy sat on the cold brick street in front of the bombed-out bank building. She sat between two piles, both of which towered over her head. One pile was hundreds of scarves; the other, an equal number of human legs.

She picked up one leg and examined it, then another, and another. They all had an identical gash on them. Numbly, she reached for a scarf and bound the wound on one leg and set it aside, starting a third pile.

While she bound the wounds, she lifted her head and shouted, "I'm not experienced enough to be doing this!" Her voice bounced off the smoking ruins of the buildings and down the dark street.

Her work soon took on a rhythm. Grab a leg. Wrap. Toss. Grab a leg. Wrap. Toss. Before long the piles of wounded legs and wrapped legs were almost equal in size.

A rumbling sound interrupted her. A motor. Its chugging echoed down the street, growing louder and louder. Soon a truck appeared, belching black smoke from its exhaust. It came toward her backward bearing a massive pink load, laboring under the weight. Legs. More legs. A pile twice the size of the original pile. The truck dumped the fresh load of legs next to Katy.

Katy jumped up, trying unsuccessfully to stop the flow of legs from the back of the truck. "No!" she cried. "I'm not supposed to be doing this!"

She shouted in the direction of the truck's cab, though she couldn't see the driver. She shouted as the legs continued to tumble from the back of the truck.

"I can't do this! These are British legs!" she screamed. "Look! Look for yourself!"

Snatching a leg from the pile, she turned it so that the arch of the foot pointed toward the cab of the truck.

"See there?" She pointed to the bottom of the foot. "Do you see that? This is a British leg!"

Indeed, Katy had a point. On the bottom of the wounded leg was a blue, white, and red Union Jack.

The interior of the truck cab was dark with barely an outline of the driver visible. The driver gave no indication of having heard her. As the last of the legs tumbled out of the back, the truck roared to life and rumbled down the street.

"Come back!" Katy yelled. "This is wrong! Didn't you hear me? I'm a Yank! These are British legs! British legs!"

The truck shifted into another gear, belched smoke, and picked up speed. The shadowy visage of the driver filled the side mirror. Dark eyes stared at Katy.

Thinking further proof might convince him to stop, Katy dropped to the ground and hastily pulled off her shoe. "Look here! See? I'm a Yank! A Yank!"

However, when she looked at the bottom of her own foot, to her dismay, it was bare. There was no American flag as she'd expected, no symbol, no mark, only the wrinkled lines that had been there since birth. At first, the absence of a flag on the bottom of her foot perplexed her. Then, intuitively, the answer came to her. The London Missionary Society! She must have left it there! Come morning, she could return there and ask the interviewers to give it back to her. That would prove conclusively that she was not supposed to be binding British legs!

Another truck rumbled toward her. It carried another load of legs. The pile was just as tall, if not taller, than that which the first truck delivered. No amount of pleading on Katy's part could stop the truck from delivering its load.

Legs were piling up all around her. All of them with wounds. All of them needing to be bound. But who would bind them? There were too many. Katy was not experienced. She was a Yank! These were British legs! Why was this happening to her?

In desperation, Katy picked up the shoe that she had removed from her foot and threw it at the cab of the truck.

It sailed through the air slowly. End over end. It seemed in no hurry to reach its target, yet its course was determined. End over end it sailed.

Then, the driver of the truck stuck her head out the cab window. Katy recognized her. The woman who had run into her flaming house! The woman she couldn't hold. The shoe tumbled slowly straight toward the woman's head.

Katy reached out as though she could call the shoe back. There was no stopping it. It tumbled, end over end, on its course toward the woman. Katy shouted a warning. The woman did not pull back. Katy saw that the woman saw the shoe, she looked at it tumbling end over end toward her, but made no effort to duck or move out of the way.

The shoe found its mark. It hit the woman squarely in the forehead.

Thump.

The woman's head registered the shoe's impact with a backward jerk. The shoe, its forward momentum blocked, fell to the brick street. The woman looked at it, then looked at Katy. She smiled. A gap-toothed, black teeth, taunting, wicked smile.

The truck exploded. An enormous ball of flame billowed skyward between the broken buildings on the London street. Windows shattered again. Flaming debris rained down on the street. Walls toppled. Once again, the woman died a fiery death.

And it was all Katy's fault.

She screamed. Her mouth opened but no sound came out. She screamed again and again. The best she could produce was a dry, raspy croak that was barely audible.

Katy awoke. She bolted upright. Perspiring. Disturbed. Frightened. Her throat was scratchy. She remembered screaming. Had she really screamed, or was it just in her dream? Glancing about the room she saw nothing but dark shapes in a dark room. She could hear her mother's gentle slumber coming from the bed next to hers.

Katy fell back onto her pillow and stared at the textured ceiling with wide-open eyes. She was shaking. Her heart pounded against her chest as though trying to escape. Tears formed in the corners of her eyes.

Several ragged breaths held back tears and eased the pounding in her chest. But try as she might, she couldn't stop from shaking. She lay awake until dawn slowly filled the room with a diffused light, listening to the ticking of the mantel clock in Maggie's drawing room at the end of the hallway.

All through the morning, though the London sky was sparkling clear, Katy felt like she was walking around in a fog. At the slightest moment of inattention, her eyes would lose their focus and her mind would wallow in a miry bog of . . . of what? Of nothing. It was as though she was neither awake nor asleep, but caught between those two realms.

Her mother and Maggie noticed her lack of attentiveness. They attributed it to the wound on her forehead and doted over her all morning. Katy was content to let them think the bump on her head was to blame for her foggy state of mind. She knew the gash was only partly to blame. The images and emotions of her nightmare still haunted her.

When Katy announced she was walking to the hospital, her mother and Maggie exchanged motherly glances. Her mother offered to accompany her, saying that she had yet to see the inside of the Magdalene Hospital. After assuring her for the hundredth time she could walk the short distance unassisted, Katy was finally allowed to leave the house alone.

The walk to the hospital did her good. Though her head was pounding in rhythm with her pulse by the time she ascended the hospital steps, the brisk fall afternoon, the turning leaves, and the physical exertion strengthened her enough to shrug off most of the tiresome effects from the previous night's dream. She went to Laura's ward first.

The curly headed girl was sitting up cheerfully in her bed when Katy arrived. Spotting Katy in the doorway, she stretched both hands toward her.

"There you are!" Laura said happily, bouncing slightly in the bed. "I'm so glad you came to see me! I want to apologize for last night."

"Apologize?" Katy said, offering her hands to Laura in kind. "Whatever for?"

Laura squeezed Katy's hands warmly and held on to them. "Why, for imposing upon you last night! It was selfish and utterly ghastly of me to attempt to press you into service like I did. Can you ever forgive me?"

Katy shook aside the apology and wondered when she was going to get her hands back. "There's nothing to forgive," she said.

"Nothing to forgive!" Laura cried. She gripped Katy's hands even tighter and shook them as she spoke. "You bandage my leg in the middle of the street; you do what you can to save Taffy and that other fellow..."

"Radcliff," Katy said, beginning to feel uncomfortable about having lost possession of her own hands.

"And how do I thank you for your kindness?" Laura cried. "I try to talk you into doing my job! Believe me, I was raised to be more polite than that!"

Katy stared at her hands. She stared until Laura looked to see what she was staring at. Suddenly, Laura understood. Blushing, she released Katy's hands.

"I interpreted your actions last night as a sign of responsibility," Katy said. "You're concerned that your inability to do your job will put an extra burden on the other nurses."

"That's exactly how I feel!" Laura said, surprised and pleased that Katy understood.

Katy couldn't help but smile at the young lady in the bed. Her back was board-straight, delicate fingers were folded and placed ladylike in her lap, hints of dimples punctuated each cheek. Even the girl's hair appeared happy with its curls bouncing every time she spoke. It was clear to Katy that the young lady before her was one of God's special creations whose personality was blessed with a double dose of goodness.

It was beyond Katy's understanding how the girl, or anyone for that matter, could be so buoyant this soon after a night of terror. And though she risked dousing a happy flame, Katy had to ask: "Laura, are you all right? You had a frightful scare last night with the bombing and…"

"Taffy's death?"

"You must miss him."

The flame flickered, but didn't go out. "His parents were here earlier," Laura said solemnly. "I cried with them. Taffy and I were friends, but never very close. Our fathers have been best of friends since their university days."

She reflected silently on the boy and their fathers.

With a sharp breath and a smile, Laura seemed to set

aside her somber emotions as easily as a person would shelve a book. "And how about your Mr. Radcliff," Laura said, "is he your..."

"Oh, no!" Katy cried. "He's not my anything. We have a mutual friend."

"Pity," Laura said with a feminine grin. "He's rather striking, don't you think?"

"I wouldn't know," Katy said.

Shapely eyebrows pulled together in a puzzled response to Katy's answer, but Laura didn't pursue the matter. "How long will you be in London? Are you looking for a nursing position?"

"Not exactly," Katy said. "I came to be interviewed by the London Missionary Society."

Laura clapped her hands happily. "You're going to be a missionary!" she cried.

She brought it on herself. Still, Katy wondered how many more times she would have to admit her failure. "I was," she said. "They turned me down."

"Turned you down?" Laura cried incredulously. "Turned you down? What were they thinking?"

Katy liked this girl the more she talked to her.

"Just look at you!" Laura carried on, rising up to her knees. With an outstretched hand she motioned from Katy's head to her toes as though she were displaying a prized horse. "One look at you and anyone with sense can see that you would make a perfect missionary!"

Her neck warmed by the way Laura was carrying on. Other women in the ward were staring at her. Apparently they wanted to see what a missionary was supposed to look like. The thought struck Katy that Laura might be having fun at her expense. The sincerity of Laura's eyes dispelled that notion.

Plopping down on her bed, Laura said, "I always dreamed

of becoming a missionary for the London Missionary Society. I just never thought I was holy enough."

Katy said, "I'm sure that's not the . . . "

"Who is your favorite missionary?" Laura cried.

"There are several," Katy replied. "But I think the most inspirational to me is Mary Moffat."

Laura squealed and clapped her hands. "Mine too! Mine too! The way she sailed from London to Cape Town to marry Robert! Then, as a newlywed, to travel 600 miles inland by ox-drawn cart . . . "

". . . to Kuruman," Katy said.

"Kuruman!" Laura cried, pointing happily at Katy. "What's your favorite Mary Moffat story?"

"Well . . . " Katy searched for a chair, found one, and pulled it beside Laura's bed. "I think my favorite Mary Moffat story would have to be the time she heard a strange noise coming from beyond the edge of the garden compound in the jungle. She paused in her work to listen. It sounded like a baby's cry, but there was something odd about the sound. Thinking it might be an animal, she picked up a garden tool for protection as she investigated. She followed the sound. It led her to a pile of stones stacked neatly at the foot of a small hill. Carefully, Mary began lifting the stones, one by one. The sound grew louder. The more stones she lifted, the clearer the sound. It was a baby! Working as quickly as she could, she removed stone after stone to find a naked baby lying on top of its dead mother, because that was the tribal custom of the natives in that part of the world. If a woman died, they buried her children with her. Naturally, Mary snatched up the infant and cared for the child from that day forward as if it were her very own."

Laura's shoulders and back slumped in satisfaction as the warmth of the story covered her. Suddenly, she sat up straight. "That's it!" she cried.

"What's it?"

"You! That's why I said anyone should be able to look at you and see that you are supposed to be a missionary. You are exactly how I've always pictured Mary Moffat would look."

The fog in Katy's mind had lifted by the time she made her way across the polished wooden floors from the women's ward to the men's ward. In a reversal of roles the patient had bolstered the visitor's spirits, and Katy was feeling good for the first time that day. She entered the men's ward smiling.

Radcliff was on the opposite side of the aisle from where he had been the first time she came to see him. Unlike that first encounter, there was no gathering of patients around his bed. There was no guitar. No gaiety. The ward was strangely devoid of banter or conversation of any kind. Had it not been for the patients' open eyes and an occasional movement or cough, the ward could have easily been mistaken for a morgue.

The sound of Katy's footsteps clicked clearly as she made her way down the aisle between the beds. There was an empty chair beside Radcliff's bed. She sat down.

Radcliff was lying on his back, covers pulled up to his chest, his arms and hands resting on top. Beneath his right hand was a small brown book. With clear, focused eyes he stared at the ceiling. He didn't acknowledge his visitor.

Katy leaned toward him with a smile. "How are you feeling?"

A blank stare was her answer.

Leaning forward even more, Katy studied Radcliff's eyes. They looked clear, responsive; not like the night before when he kept blinking, forcing them to focus.

A young bushy-haired boy with freckles propped himself up on one elbow in the bed next to Radcliff. "He's had a bit of bad news," the boy said.

Katy looked at Radcliff—there was no reaction—then back at the boy. "From the doctor?" she asked.

The boy shook his head. "No, that's not it. The doctor said he'd have a nasty knot for a time, ringing in his ears, that sort of thing, but that's all."

The corpse-like figure on the bed belied the boy's report. Since Radcliff didn't seem to be speaking, Katy conversed with the one who was. She asked the boy, "What sort of bad news?"

This time, Radcliff answered. With a voice that sounded like he'd dragged it up from a well, he said, "They executed her." Tears formed pools atop his eyes.

"Executed whom?" Katy asked.

Radcliff raised his hand, lifting the small book.

Katy cocked her head to read the title. *"Of the Imitation of Christ."*

Once the book was identified, Radcliff's hand went limp.

"It was Edith Cavell's favorite book," the boy offered. "She was a British nurse in Belgium, the one who helped Radcliff get back to England when his aeroplane was shot down. The news came in just a little while ago. The Germans shot her as a spy."

Raising a hand to her chest, Katy sat back in the chair, absorbing the news. A nurse like herself. Executed. "She was the person you couldn't tell me about before," Katy said to Radcliff.

"I never knew a finer woman, or a braver person," Radcliff said, his voice hollow and wooden.

Katy placed her hand on his. It was deathly cold and clammy. She fought the impulse to pull her hand away. Radcliff's lips and jaw moved, but no sound was forthcoming. It was as though they were working up to something. Katy waited. The words would come when Radcliff was ready.

"It was a gray, dismal night," he said. "There were two of us. Me and Tommy Budds. After our aeroplane went down, we managed to crawl out of the wreckage and hide in a nearby forest before the Huns arrived. We hid under bushes and covered ourselves with leaves, shivering all night long.

"In the morning, we stole some clothes from an outlying house so we looked like Belgian factory workers. Tommy stuffed an extra shirt between his shoulders. He thought that being a hunchback would throw off any inquisitive Germans who thought we looked fit enough to be in the army. For three months we hid out in the forest and countryside, eating only what we could catch with our hands. We knew better than to appear in any of the nearby villages. The Huns would be looking for us.

"We made our way to Brussels. There were German patrols everywhere. It took us three nights and three different routes before we managed to slip into Berkendael Medical Institute, a training school for nurses on the outskirts of the city. We'd heard from others who had made it back that if we got shot down, we could find help there."

Radcliff chuckled at his remembrance. A tear rolled down his cheek. "She looked like one of those nurses who would rip your arm off and beat you with it if you didn't do exactly what she said. A no-nonsense kind of person, if you know what I mean."

"Edith Cavell?" Katy asked.

Radcliff nodded. "But she was a godly woman if ever there was one. She used to read to us at night from this book." He lifted *Of the Imitation of Christ* again.

"How did you manage to escape?" Katy asked.

"Miss Cavell arranged for two locals to guide us out of the city. We sneaked aboard a coal barge going to Holland, jumped off just before the Germans inspected it. From there, a Belgian man met us who smuggles newspapers across the frontier. He helped us cross over into neutral territory."

Radcliff stared vacantly at the ceiling, reliving the memory. Katy sat quietly, leaving him alone to his thoughts.

"We must have hidden in the surgical house a month or more before we escaped," Radcliff said. "We kept watch by peering through slits in the boards. Without question, Miss Cavell treated everyone who came to her. Belgian peasants. English. French. We watched her patch up German soldiers! German soldiers! What kind of animals would shoot a woman who treated their own kind?"

Katy was struck by another thought. *This isn't my war! These are British legs! There must be some kind of mistake! I'm a Yank! I'm a Yank!* The memory of this selfless nurse . . . no, more than that . . . this selfless martyr made her ashamed of her feelings. While Radcliff ruminated silently over his memories of Edith Cavell, Katy was haunted by her dream. The feelings she'd felt the night before washed over her afresh, leaving her weak and trembling.

Radcliff was immersed in his own suffering. He didn't notice Katy's sudden change in mood. He thumbed through the small brown book. His words cut into Katy's thoughts. "I was going through this book, finding portions she had read to us."

He paused and brushed a memory tear away. As he did, the pages flipped. It took him a moment to find his place again.

"It's remarkable. She read these things to strengthen us inside." He tapped his chest with the book. "Looking back on it now, she was being strengthened for what was to come. Listen to this." He sniffed, sat up slightly in bed, and began to read. The men in nearby cots strained to hear the words.

"Occasions of adversity best discover how great virtue

and strength each one hath. For occasions do not make a man frail, but they shew what he is."

Here's another: "Thou must pass through fire and water before thou come to the place of refreshing."

He flipped a few pages and read again: "It is no small prudence to keep silent in an evil time, and inwardly to turn thyself to Me, and not to be troubled by the judgment of men."

A few more pages flipped: "Then with full resignation and with thy entire will, offer up thyself to the honor of My name, on the altar of thy heart a whole burnt offering, even thy body and soul, faithfully committing them unto Me."

Radcliff sniffed and wiped away another tear. "This is the one I was reading when you arrived. It seemed prophetic. 'Without a combat thou canst not attain unto the crown of patience. If thou are unwilling to suffer, thou refusest to be crowned. But if thou desire to be crowned, fight manfully, endure patiently.'"

Katy wanted to respond immediately, so that Radcliff would not know how powerfully the words had been to her. She felt humbled and ashamed. It took a moment to compose herself, and then all she could say was, "That's lovely."

"Here!" Radcliff handed the book to Katy. "I want you to have this."

Katy held up a refusing hand. "I couldn't. It means so much to you."

"I'll get another one," Radcliff insisted. "You wanting to be a missionary and all, I figure you'll get a lot of use out of it."

Gratefully, Katy accepted the book. Weighing it in her hands, she received the impression that the words contained therein had just begun to shape her life. "This is sweet of you, Fred. Thank you."

A half-grin spread across his tired, pained face. It was clear he needed time to rest; his eyelids were weighing heavily.

Katy stood. "I'll come back tomorrow," she said.

Radcliff was hovering between wake and sleep. "Promise?" he said thickly.

"Promise."

His eyes were closed and his breathing heavy before she reached the end of the bed. Katy's heels clicked down the ward. She held her new treasure tightly in her hands. How different she felt from the time she walked into the hospital. Two visits. Two emotional boosts. One in attitude, the other in devotion.

The pain she felt in her heart for the death of Edith Cavell, a woman she'd never met, sparked a determined fire. It was the same kind of passionate blaze she felt when she heard stories of Mary Moffat. How similar the two women were. And how desperately Katy wanted to be like them.

She stopped at the administration office before leaving.

"Is Miss Cantrell on duty?"

A male attendant with a wide mustache looked up from a hospital chart. He grinned. "Your accent. You're a Yank, aren't you?" he asked.

"Yes, I am. Is Miss Cantrell available? I'm a nurse, and I want to volunteer my services."

After two days of hasty orientation, Katy began her duties at Magdalene Hospital. Laura Kelton returned to work that same day. At Laura's request, she and Katy were given the same schedule. With the heavy traffic of casualties that came through the hospital from the front, Katy was glad to have a friend with Laura's sunny disposition working close by.

Both girls were probationers, housed and fed by the hospital. Their lives were regimented. A bell rang at 6 A.M. to awaken them. Breakfast was at 6:30 and they were on-duty at 7, with a half hour for dinner, tea on the ward, and two hours off duty. They went off shift at 9:20 P.M. with lights out at 10. All lectures were attended on off-duty time.

Each nurse had her own room which she was required to keep clean as well as sweeping and dusting the wards and cleaning all the brass plaques over the beds. Their meals were plain and unvaried—porridge and cold sausage, porridge and cold beef, porridge and mince. Occasionally, they were treated to bread pudding.

Leisure hours were usually spent in the hospital garden which the nurses had dubbed, The Garden of Eden. The garden consisted of beautifully arranged flowerbeds, small decorative ponds, little bridges, and a Japanese summer house where they could make tea. No men were ever allowed in the garden, other than the gardener, whom the nurses playfully nicknamed Adam.

On days off there was an occasional launch down the river to Tilbury with a lovely basket of cakes, sandwiches, and tea provided by one of the hospital's wealthy patrons. Other days-off activities involved a bus or a train. The bus drivers and conductors of London, recognizing the distinctive bonnets and cloaks of the nurses, frequently refused to accept the standard fare of one penny.

The most sobering of times for Katy was not the actual hospital work, but when details of the events of Edith Cavell's capture and execution became available. Written accounts circulated among the hospitals and were read aloud to groups of nurses in the Magdalene Hospital garden. Among the accounts was a composite of four eyewitnesses to her execution.

Two hundred and fifty troops had been paraded to witness the event. A German officer stood to address them. Before he could say anything, Philippe Baucq, who had also been arrested with Miss Cavell, shouted to the German troops: "Comrades! In the presence of death we are all comrades!" He was prevented from speaking further. The officer then read the sentences which were translated by an interpreter into French. It was announced that the soldiers need have no worries at the thought of shooting a woman, owing to the heinous nature of the crimes she had committed.

After that, Edith Cavell and Philippe Baucq were allowed a last word with a clergyman. Pastor le Seur ministered to Miss Cavell. He pressed her hand and repeated in English the Grace of the Anglican Church. To him, Edith replied, "Tell my loved ones that my soul I believe is safe, and that I am glad to die for my country."

Pastor le Seur then led Miss Cavell to the execution post, to which she was lightly bound. Her eyes were bandaged. A few seconds passed while a Catholic priest spoke longer with Baucq, then, the prisoner was placed in front of a post next to Miss Cavell. Philippe Baucq pitched forward and yelled, *Vive la Belgique!* One sharp command was given. Two salvos rang out from two parties of eight men barely six paces away. Both of the condemned sank silently to the ground.

The account of Edith Cavell's last moments alive had a sobering effect on Katy and Laura and the hospital staff that lasted for days.

Two days after the reading of the account was a day of good-byes for Katy. First, Fred Radcliff was released for a second time to return to his squadron in Ashford. Though it was not a tearful farewell, Katy knew she would feel his absence. The two of them made no promises to write to each other. He made no promise to return to London should he be granted leave; if he had, she was prepared not to promise she would be there when he returned.

The closest Katy came to spilling her emotions was when she thanked him for the book, *Of the Imitation of Christ.* It had become part of her daily reading and it never failed to give her strength to face the day.

Then, Fred Radcliff walked out the door into the bright sunlight. Katy figured that was the last time she would ever see him.

The second farewell that day came in the form of a letter written by Edith Cavell to her nurses a few days before her death. Like the execution account, Miss Cavell's letter had been copied and was circulated widely among the London hospitals.

It was an emotional reading for Katy. For some time now she had been inspired by reports about the woman. This letter was far more personal. These were Edith Cavell's own thoughts, her own words. As the letter was read, Katy listened as though it had been written just to her.

My dear Nurses,

This is a sad moment for me as I write to say good-bye. It reminds me that on the 17th September I have been running the School for eight years.

I was so happy to be called to help in the organization of the work which our Committee had just founded. On the 1st October 1907 there were only four young pupils, whereas now you are many—fifty or sixty in all I believe, including those who have gained their certificates and are about to leave the School.

To my sorrow I have not always been able to talk to you each privately. You know that I had my share of burdens. But I hope that you will not forget our evening chats.

I told you that devotion would bring you true happiness and the thought that, before God and in your own eyes, you have done your duty well and with a good heart, will sustain you in trouble and face to face with death. There are two or three of you who will recall the little talks we had together. Do not forget them. As I had already gone so far along life's road, I was perhaps able to see more clearly than you, and show you the straight path.

One word more. Never speak evil. May I tell you, who love your country with all your heart, that this has been the great fault here. During these last eight years I have seen so many sorrows which could have been avoided or lessened if a little word had not been breathed here and there, perhaps without evil intention, and thus destroyed the happiness or even the life of someone. Nurses all need to think of this, and to cultivate a loyalty and team spirit among themselves.

If any of you has a grievance against me, I beg you to forgive me; I have perhaps been unjust sometimes, but I have loved you much more than you think.

I send my good wishes for the happiness of all my girls, as much for those who have left the School as for those who are still there. Thank you for the kindness you have always shown me.

Your Matron,
Edith Cavell

After hearing Miss Cavell's letter, from that day forward Katy Morgan considered herself one of Edith Cavell's girls. And she made a pledge to God and to herself that she would live a life worthy of that calling.

Chapter 14

My dearest Jesse,

I hope this letter finds you well. For that matter, I hope this letter finds you, given the disruption of services here in England and your peripatetic responsibilities in Washington.

You can't imagine my amazement when I received your last letter. My husband, Jesse Morgan, a personal aide to the President of the United States! Even as I write the words I find it difficult to believe. Truly Noble would be jealous. In all his adventures, never once was he an aide to the President. Despite your assurances that this new position is nothing that should cause me worry—or should I say, because of your assurances—I have to admit an element of trepidation that you are unable to communicate specifically your current responsibilities.

Be that as it may, your news prompted me to reevaluate my stay here in London. Darling, though I miss you terribly, I have chosen to extend my stay here. The relief work is going well and my responsibilities will soon end. However, other considerations encourage this course of action.

First, Katy has taken a position at Magdalene Hospital as a volunteer nurse. It has been wonderfully therapeutic for her following her devastating disappointment with the London Missionary Society. Never have I seen her so

*impassioned about her work . . . and, as you know, pas-
sion has not been one of Katy's shortcomings.*

*Which reminds me . . . have you heard from our son? I
pray for him daily. Long ago I learned there was little
more I could do as his parent than to pray that God
would keep him from killing himself long enough to
learn the joy of relationships. But it would do this aching
mother's heart good to hear from him.*

*As for London and my decision . . . I have found such a
good friend here in Maggie Thomas. And since there is
no place for me in your current work in Washington, and
not wanting to go back to Denver all alone, if it's all the
same to you, I'll stay on here with Maggie a while longer.*

*Maggie is such an inspiring woman. She has suffered so
much in this life, yet she maintains a godly optimism
that is contagious. I told you in my previous letter how
she moved back to London following her husband's death
at the hand of the Germans. Her trip to Ireland, during
which she found me in her brother's house, was part of a
semiannual journey she took simply to check up on him.
Bryn had not been healthy and did not take care of himself all that well. And though their upbringing was horrendous to say the least (I'll fill you in on the details
when I see you next), she saw it as her family responsibility to care for her brother.*

*Here in London, she is a whirlwind . . . going every-
where, involved with everything related to the war. I
can't keep up with her and she must be at least twenty-
five or thirty years older than me.*

*Just between you and me, she has a mysterious side to
her. I don't know if it's her old-world ways (you know how
it is . . . there are some family matters that others must
never know) or whether she is dealing in black market
goods for some reason, but there is a part of her that she*

hides from me. I pretend not to notice.

I must say, though, she was as thrilled as I was when she heard of your new position with the President. She has taken an interest in our family as though we were her own. I'm hoping to talk her into returning with me to America for a visit so you can meet this dear woman yourself.

Don't worry about me in London. If the Zeppelins get too numerous or an invasion seems likely, I'll hightail it home immediately. I hasten to add that I pray America will stay out of this war. The daily news of death and constant shortages takes its toll on one's attitude, making life here rather bleak. I would hate to see our country suffer in the same way as England and France.

My darling, you are always on my mind and in my heart.

Be careful.

I will always love you,
Emily

Jesse sat alone at a café table and read the letter a second time. Two things Emily said brought a grin to his face—the reference to Truly Noble, his boyhood fictional hero, and her parting admonition to be careful. She worried about him more than she was letting on. And she had reason to worry, more than he would ever tell her.

Folding the letter and placing it in his vest pocket, Jesse turned his attention to the *New York Times.* He had been rereading William Jennings Bryan's explanation for his decision to resign as Secretary of State.

The resignation was secondary in Jesse's mind, though a large measure of criticism had been leveled at Bryan for resigning during a time of crisis. The primary issue as Jesse saw it was the maturing of a nation. It was Bryan's printed defense that helped him to see that. Bryan insisted that he

and President Wilson were in perfect agreement regarding
their intent: the peaceful solution of the dispute that had
arisen between the United States and Germany. Where
they differed was in which system would they use to
address these differences.

The old system was based upon power and confrontation.
Threats leading to counter-threats in an unending cycle,
until war became inevitable. According to Bryan, this system was the basis for the President's *Lusitania* notes to
Germany. There was a better way. Bryan called it the system
of persuasion.

Bryan preferred to champion this new system as "a humble follower of the Prince of Peace." According to Bryan,
the new system of persuasion employs argument, courts
investigation, and depends upon negotiation. In the old
system war was the chief cornerstone; the new system con-
templated a universal brotherhood that led through example. In the essay, Bryan had written:

"Some nation must lead the world out of the black night
of war into the light of that day when 'swords shall be beat-
en into plowshares.' Why not make that honor ours? Some
day—why not now?—the nations will learn that enduring
peace cannot be built upon fear—that goodwill does not
grow upon the stalk of violence. Some day the nations will
place their trust in love, the weapon for which there is no
shield; in love, that suffereth long and is kind; in love, that
is not easily provoked; that beareth all things, believeth all
things, hopeth all things, endureth all things; in love,
which though despised as weakness by the worshipers of
Mars abideth when all else fails."

Jesse looked up from the paper and peered through the
plate glass window onto the New York street. People of all
colors and sizes and shapes and education and social and
economic status walked by. Would Bryan's new system

work with these people? Could it work among nations?

"Why not?" he muttered softly.

"Why not what?"

Jesse looked up as Colonel House took a seat opposite him. He folded the newspaper and set it on the seat beside him. "Just thinking out loud," he said.

Colonel House had arranged for this meeting. He had documents and information to pass along to Jesse that would help him in his task; documents that were too sensitive to entrust to ordinary carriers.

House got right to the matter. He placed a satchel on top of the table and pushed it toward Jesse. "Here's what we have," he said. "Two of our operatives were tailing Dr. Heinrich Albert, based on your report. He boarded a streetcar carrying a case. Apparently, he dozed off for a while. When his stop was called, it roused him. He jumped up and got off the streetcar, leaving his case behind. Before he realized his error and got back on the streetcar, our operatives had recovered the case."

Jesse nodded, inwardly pleased. He had suspected Dr. Albert and alerted House. Had the case contained nothing of importance, House wouldn't be sitting opposite him right now.

"You'll find the details in there." The colonel motioned to the satchel.

Jesse moved the satchel from atop the table to his side. He kept one hand on it at all times.

House got up to leave. "Do you have anything else for me?" he asked.

"Maybe. I'm going to the opera tonight."

"The opera?"

Jesse nodded. "If I hear any good tunes, I'll recommend it to you."

Chapter 15

IT'S stuck!" Percy cried.

"Get out of the way!" Johnny shoved the taller boy aside.

Grabbing the wrench which was already fit on the propeller bolt, he pulled downward with a grunt. The bolt didn't budge. He pulled again, harder this time, with a scream. The bolt remained frozen.

Percy stood by helplessly, his hands, black with grease, dangling at his side. There was nothing he could do to help until the propeller was removed. Like an engine idling, his hands twitched, his feet shuffled. His entire body was in motion, anxious to be thrown back into gear.

With another grunt and another failed effort, Johnny glanced over at the progress of the teams on either side of them. Teams three, four, and five to his left were no threat. Too much head scratching and arguing to be taken seriously. Team one to his right was a different story. The lead he and Percy had established over the team-one mechanics was quickly vanishing.

"Calahan has the second wing off," Percy reported.

"I'm not blind!" Johnny shouted. Another pull and grunt on the wrench yielded the same time-consuming result.

Percy moved next to him. Shoulder to shoulder. Reaching up to add his hands to the wrench, he said, "Maybe if together..."

Johnny elbowed him hard in the ribs. "How can I get a grip if your enormous paws are draped all over it? Back away! I'll get it!"

Percy stepped back without comment.

Repositioning the wrench up higher, Johnny pulled. His eyes squeezed shut from the exertion. Veins bulged in his neck. His feet raised off the ground.

Suddenly, the bolt broke free. Johnny landed back on the ground with a soft thud.

"You got it!" Percy shouted.

Without so much as a smile of celebration, Johnny spun the wrench furiously until the bolt dropped onto the dirt. His hands already on the propeller, Percy yanked it off and set it aside. By the time he turned back around, Johnny had another wrench and was working on the bolts that would free the engine.

Five aeroplanes were lined up side-by-side in front of three large hangars. Each one of the aeroplanes was in a varying state of disrepair. Fifty feet to one side stood a raucous crowd of smoking, swearing, wagering soldier spectators, separated from the flight training school competition by a thin white rope.

Four-man teams buzzed around the aeroplanes. Their goal was to be the fastest team to disassemble, then reassemble an aeroplane. Once an aeroplane was disassembled, it had to be approved by an adjudicator before it could be reassembled again. The team that successfully started its reassembled aeroplane was declared the *unofficial* winner. *Official* declaration of the winner came when one of the team members flew the aeroplane the circumference of the field once and landed it safely. The prize for which they were competing was an extra weekend pass and class bragging rights. Additional winnings included side bets which were officially discouraged.

For this class of pilots there was an added attraction. Team two was comprised of only two men, Johnny Morgan and Percy Hill. It was Morgan himself who requested this exemption to the rules. And it was Capain David Knowles who approved it, hoping that a defeat would in some small way humble the immature and arrogant Morgan.

The captain was not alone in his desire to see team two fail. More than a score of soldiers were eager for the chance to get the best of Johnny Morgan, who had been a loud-mouthed thorn in their side since the first day of flight training.

"Can't you work any faster?" Johnny yelled at his partner.

Percy's arms had disappeared up to his shoulders as he reached under the engine cowling. Johnny steadied the engine to keep it from rotating while Percy worked feverishly to free it.

Beside them, Calahan—a burly red-headed Irishman who had bet heavily against Johnny—was removing the propeller of team one's aeroplane while another team-one member matched Percy's position under the cowling.

"Come on . . . come on . . . what's taking you so long?" Johnny shouted.

"There!" Percy pulled away from the cowling.

"Get over here! I can't lift the entire engine myself!"

Percy ran to Johnny's side, donning gloves. Together they slid the engine forward until the shaft cleared the front of the fuselage. Ordinarily, because of the weight of the engine, this was a three-man job. Both men moaned as the engine fell free and the full weight was upon them. Metal bit into their gloved hands. Their back muscles screamed at the strain. It was all Johnny could do to keep his knees from buckling. They inched their way to the wooden mount that would cradle the detached aeroplane engine.

The instant the engine hit the mount, Johnny shouted, "The aeroplane is disassembled, sir!"

This was the required signal that would bring an adjudicator to inspect the team's progress. He would determine if all the required pieces had been removed from the aeroplane.

Panting heavily, his knees still trembling from the weight of the engine, Johnny leaned against the mount as their paunchy adjudicator, Captain Knowles, ambled toward them.

Next to them Calahan shouted, "The aeroplane is disassembled, sir!" The adjudicator for team one stepped up smartly and began his inspection.

"You look tired, Morgan," Knowles said casually. A sly grin spread across his lips as he carefully perused the aeroplane's disassembled parts.

"Just resting for my victory lap, sir!"

Johnny's remark was met by a stony stare.

Beside them, team one's adjudicator shouted: "This aeroplane is disassembled!" The four-man team jumped into action, hoisting the engine back into place and fitting the wings in position.

Captain Knowles gazed unhurriedly at team two's wingless and engineless craft. He counted the various parts that were laid out precisely on the ground. He examined the engine on the block. He looked again at the array of parts.

"You're doing this on purpose, aren't you, sir?" Johnny said.

Knowles, half a head taller than Johnny, took offense at the remark. He moved slowly and deliberately toward him until his nose was inches from Johnny's face. Johnny could see bread crumbs in the captain's neatly trimmed mustache. The adjudicator's breath smelled of knockwurst. Behind him, Johnny could see team one attaching the propeller.

"This aeroplane is disassembled!" Knowles shouted in Johnny's face.

Percy was already in position to lift the engine when

Johnny turned around. Within moments the engine was back on the aeroplane and Percy had slipped under the cowling while Johnny replaced the propeller. They worked wordlessly, using every bit of their Camp Furlong mechanic experience to close the gap between them and team one.

While Johnny and Percy affixed the last of the wing struts, Calahan jumped into the cockpit of his aeroplane. Two team members grabbed the propeller and primed the engine.

"Get in the cockpit!" Johnny shouted to Percy.

"This strut isn't . . . "

Team one's engine sputtered, coughed, belched smoke, and died.

"GET IN THE COCKPIT!"

With a shake of his head, Percy dropped his wrench and climbed into the cockpit. Johnny ran to the front of the plane and grabbed the propeller.

Beside them, team one's engine sputtered. It roared to life.

A cheer erupted from team one. Behind the rope winning soldiers whooped while the losers groaned. Calahan, sitting in the pilot's seat, thrust his hands victoriously into the air.

Johnny and Percy exchanged glances. It was over. They'd lost.

Then, team one's engine failed. It cut out, sputtered, and died. Likewise, the celebration. Calahan looked to the adjudicator.

The judge shook his head. The contest wasn't over!

Flush with renewed hope, Johnny grabbed the propeller. With a kick of his leg to gain leverage and momentum, he pulled down with all his might. The aeroplane engine wheezed, but failed to ignite. He tried again.

Next to him team one attempted to restart their engine. It coughed and sputtered, nearly catching on again.

Johnny kicked his leg and pulled.

A cough. A wheeze. A chug. Another chug. The engine sputtered. Percy nursed the throttle. Black smoke belched from the exhaust. The engine caught hold. With a roar, it sprang to life. To Johnny, it was the most beautiful sound in the world.

Everyone waited, mindful of the premature celebration moments before. All eyes were fixed on the nearly invisible whir of team two's propeller. It purred contentedly.

When it was obvious the engine was not going to die, Captain Knowles reluctantly raised his arm, signaling team two as the provisional winners.

Calahan cursed and swore at his team members who were still attempting to revive their aeroplane's engine.

Captain Knowles made a circling motion with his arm. Johnny and Percy understood. To this point they had only earned the right to be the first team to take off. In order to seal their victory, the aeroplane had to circumnavigate the field successfully.

Grabbing his headgear and goggles, Johnny climbed onto the wing. With a grin and a thumbs-up signal to Percy, he stood to one side so that Percy could climb out of the cockpit. Percy made no effort to climb out.

With the howl of the engine making verbal communication difficult, Percy pointed emphatically at the strut he'd been working on just before they started the engine. "It's not secure!" he yelled.

Leaning over the fuselage, Johnny inspected the strut. Percy was right. The strut was attached, but not secured. With a nod, Johnny acknowledged its condition. He waved Percy out of the cockpit.

"Not . . . safe!" Percy yelled, emphasizing each word.

Johnny nodded again, this time more emphatically. Yes, he understood. With a determined motion, he waved Percy out of the cockpit.

Clearly displeased that Johnny was going to take the aeroplane up anyway, yet resigned to the fact that he was not going to change Johnny's mind, Percy climbed out of the cockpit. He walked along the wing and jumped clear, but not without first taking another look at the unfastened strut.

Easing himself into the metal seat, Johnny strapped himself in, checked his gauges, and prepared for takeoff. Beside him, team one's engine started up.

Johnny grinned at their success. They were too late.

As Percy pulled the blocks from in front of the wheels, Johnny looked triumphantly around. Captain Knowles scowled at the apparent winner. Calahan shouted something to Johnny which he couldn't hear. Clearly, though, the red-headed Irishman was not wishing him *bon voyage*. Behind the rope, the majority of the soldier spectators stared at him sullenly.

Johnny never felt happier.

Members of the ground crew grabbed the aeroplane's wings and swung it around toward the open field. Johnny pulled back on the throttle. The engine responded with power and the aeroplane wobbled across the grass.

Taking off from a grassy field was a bumpy affair at best. Johnny liked to think of takeoffs as the storm before the calm in which a bone-jarring, teeth-rattling jaunt across an open field was rewarded by the inexplicable thrill of taking wing. Who could put into words the feeling of those first few seconds in the air? The final ground jolt was a leap onto a cushion of cloud that carried him into the sky. The earth, its people, and all the problems that came with relationships grew smaller and less significant the higher the aeroplane climbed.

For Johnny Morgan life was at its best when he was flying. He was alone. There were no expectations. No disappointments. No forced or unwanted conversations.

Here, he was free. Racing with the wind, dodging clouds; soaring gently sunward, or plummeting madly downward, or simply hovering effortlessly between heaven and earth; at ease with himself, at ease with his surroundings.

While other pilots flew white-knuckled and in constant fear that at any moment something might go wrong, Johnny sailed invisible streams of air with the confidence of a bird, always in control.

Except now.

Something was wrong. The frame to which his seat was attached shuddered like a child with fever. Johnny checked the first thing that came to mind—Percy's unfastened strut. He didn't like what he saw. The strut had worked itself undone, probably during takeoff. It dangled from the upper wing like a loose tooth.

Suddenly, with a loud cracking and ripping sound, the wind tore it off. It spiraled downward, taking portions of the upper right wing with it.

A preview of events to come?

Johnny inspected the damage. Large sections of the wing's skeletal frame were visible where the fabric had been torn away. Wires dangled and flapped in the wind.

This isn't good . . .

There was only one way to assess the damage. He shoved the control stick to the right, adding a little rudder bar pedal. Ordinarily, the aeroplane would bank to the right and make a turn. It didn't. Instead, it skidded sideways like an automobile on an icy road.

Whoaaaa!

He corrected the skid and tried turning left. Another skid. He shoved the stick forward, the aeroplane's nose dipped. Back, the aeroplane leveled off.

So, I can climb and descend. I just can't turn. He chuckled, reminded of his intended purpose. *Makes flying in a circle a little more challenging, doesn't it?*

The edge of the field and his first turn was approaching. Glancing over his shoulder, he looked behind him at the assembly of pilots and soldiers on the ground. He knew all eyes were on him.

Options. What are my options? I can land in the first field that presents itself and walk back in humiliation. Or, I could fly straight until I run out of gas and am forced to land. Or . . . A thought occurred to him. He grinned. *Who said an aeroplane needs ailerons to make a turn?*

He eased off on the throttle and hit the left rudder bar pedal. The tail swung around behind him. When it traveled roughly ninety degrees, he corrected the rudder and increased the power to pull out of the turn.

Ha! It works! Sort of like taking a corner wide in your father's automobile! Not pretty, but it will get you around the block.

At the next turn, he repeated the procedure. He eased off the power, gave the rudder bar pedal a shove, let the tail swing around, corrected the rudder, and pulled out of the skid by giving the aeroplane a little gas.

He was ecstatic. *Is there anything I can't do in this aeroplane?*

Just then, more fabric ripped from the right wing. The wing flexed unnaturally, cracking two struts. The shuddering increased dramatically.

Instinctively, Johnny slowed the aeroplane's speed to reduce the force of the wind against the weakened and deteriorating wing.

Whoa, Johnny boy! Skidding around corners is one thing. Flying with only one wing is . . . well, let's hope you never have to try. Speaking to the tattered wing he said, "Stay on there baby . . . stay on there. Only two turns to go."

The shuddering continued. It shook him so badly, his instruments looked blurry. Coaxing the aeroplane around the third turn, he heard a snap and groan from the right wing.

The voice of reason told him to land the plane immediately. But Johnny rarely ever listened to his voice of reason. He entered this competition intending to win, and that's exactly what he was going to do.

The shuddering continued. Each time the right wing flexed, the jagged cracks opened and closed, looking like tiny animals baring their teeth at him.

He needed something to occupy his mind, to keep him from panicking between turns three and four. He started to whistle, then thought of a song the pilots sang in jest. It was ideal for the occasion.

> *Take the cylinder out of my kidney;*
> *the connecting rod out of my brain.*
> *From the small of my back take the camshaft,*
> *and assemble the engine again.*

He laughed more at the shaky sound of his voice caused by the aeroplane's vibrations than at the lyrics. The fourth turn approached. He skidded into it. The loose fabric of the right wing flapped furiously. The frame groaned. But nothing broke. Nothing fell off.

Immediately, Johnny began his descent, landing well short of the aeroplane hangars. The initial bounce of the wheels against the field—which always signaled his return to a world that didn't like him—was, for once, a welcome feeling. The aeroplane waddled, not unlike a penguin, for a good 500 yards back to its point of origin.

With a sigh of relief, Johnny cut the engine. He made it! More importantly, he won the competition!

"What were you doing up there?" Captain Knowles screamed, charging toward the cockpit. Then, noticing the damaged wing he bellowed, "Look at this! Look at this! This aeroplane was in no condition to fly!"

Calahan jumped into the uproar, his face as red as his hair. "Morgan should be disqualified!"

Knowles agreed with him, but it would take a majority vote of the five adjudicators to disqualify a team.

The five adjudicators huddled. After several anxious moments, by a vote of four to one—Knowles casting the lone dissenting vote—it was determined that team two was indeed the winner of the competition.

With the announcement came a reprimand to team two for knowingly flying an unsafe aeroplane; however, they observed there was nothing in the rules that said the aeroplane had to bank on the turns as it circled the field. Therefore, the weekend passes were awarded to Johnny Morgan and Percy Hill.

For Johnny, the real prize came afterward when soldier after disgruntled soldier filed past him and handed him cash or cigarettes, his winnings from the bets.

His pockets bulging with cigarette packages, Johnny strolled back to the barracks with his teammate.

"What are you going to do with all those cigarettes?" Percy asked. "You don't smoke!"

"Probably trade them for something," Johnny said. "You know they're as good as cash."

Percy's hands were thrust in his pockets. He was abnormally quiet.

"By the way," Johnny said, "you did good out there today. We really showed 'em, didn't we?"

Percy shrugged. "I guess we did all right."

"You guess we did all right? We did fantastic! Two against four and we beat 'em! Every one of them!"

"That part was fun."

"You bet it was fun!"

"So, why don't I feel good about it?"

"What are you talking about?"

Percy stopped walking. Two steps later, Johnny pulled to a halt and turned to face him.

"Johnny, you know you're my best friend. And there's no way I would have made it through flight school without your help."

"I just showed you the ropes. You did the rest."

Percy didn't look convinced.

"What are you worried about?" Johnny cried. "We'll both graduate tomorrow. We'll be assigned to a squadron . . . is that it? Are you afraid we might not be assigned to the same squadron? Leave that to me. I'll talk to Captain Knowles . . . "

"That's not it," Percy replied.

"It's not? Then what's sticking in your craw?"

Percy grimaced. It took him two aborted attempts before he could get the words out. "I'm not sure I want us to be assigned to the same squadron."

The verbal blow rendered Johnny speechless.

"I'm tired of people always hating us!" Percy cried. "Why do you always have to make people angry at us?"

"First, they're angry with me, not you. Second, they're just sore losers, that's all."

Percy shook his head. "It's more than that. Don't you realize that I'm the only person in this whole place who likes you?"

"So?"

"So? Doesn't that bother you?"

Johnny shook his head. "I don't care if people like me. Never have. All I care about is flying and getting over to Europe so that I can fly against the Germans. Show those Lafayette Escadrille fellows a stunt or two."

An aide from Captain Knowles came running up to them. "Captain wants to see you right away, Morgan."

The aide noticed all the packs of cigarettes Johnny was

carrying or had stuffed away. His eyes grew even wider as Johnny unpacked his pockets and handed the packs to Percy.

"Take these back to the barracks for me, will you?" Johnny asked. "The captain probably wants to wish me a personal farewell."

The joke failed to strike Percy as funny.

"You wanted to see me, sir?"

"I'll make this quick, Morgan."

Captain Knowles sat behind his desk, his attention buried in a sheet of paper. Never once did he look up. Not when Johnny entered the room. Not as Johnny stood in front of the desk. Not when he addressed Johnny. With the captain's hat setting off to one side of the desk and his head lowered, his receding hairline was unavoidably pronounced.

"You won't be graduating with the class tomorrow."

"What?"

"You heard me." Still, he didn't look up. His tone was calm. Even.

Johnny was ready to do violence. "I'm the best pilot in this school!" he shouted. "Present company included."

Knowles bolted from his chair. His eyes were daggers. Leaning over the desk on fisted hands, his mustache stretched out like two tiny arms holding him back, he yelled, "Yes, you are a better pilot! But there is more to being a pilot than flying an aeroplane." Referring to the sheet of paper in his hand, he read: "Candidates must be naturally athletic and have a reputation for reliability, punctuality, and honesty. They should have a cool head in emergencies, a good eye for distance, a keen ear for familiar sounds, a steady hand, and a sound body with plenty of reserve. They should be quick-witted, highly intelligent, and tractable."

"What's tractable?"

Knowles ignored him. He continued reading, emphasizing each word: "Immature, high-strung, overconfident, and impatient candidates are not desired!" He slammed the paper down on his desk. "A perfect description of you, Mr. Morgan."

"I'm not high-strung," Johnny shouted. "And I'm probably the most tractable person in this squadron, whatever that means."

"Believe me, you're not."

"I'm still the best pilot you've got! Isn't that what this is all about? Say you're a pilot in the skies over France facing a German squadron, who do you want up in the air with you? Me? Or someone who is always punctual?"

"You're dismissed, Morgan."

"I logged more hours in the air before I got here than most of those Lafayette fellows have flown their whole lives! You saw my abilities the first day you allowed us to climb into an aeroplane!"

"You were instructed to fly around the field three times and land."

"Which I did!"

"Upside down!"

"You didn't say we had to fly right-side up!"

"You're dismissed, Morgan."

"I can't believe you're doing this!"

"Then it's high time the shoe is on the other foot, because I can't believe you think you're pilot material with all the stunts you've pulled. Including that one today during the competition."

"I won . . . we won . . . Percy and me. Two against four! That ought to prove something!"

"It proves you were willing to take unnecessary shortcuts to win. What if Percy had flown the aeroplane instead of you? Would he have made it back alive? Or would your desire to win at all costs cost him his life?"

"I'm a better pilot than Percy. I wouldn't have let him go up in that aeroplane."

Knowles composed himself. "Percy Hill may not have your abilities. But in my estimation, given these guidelines . . . ," he rattled the sheet of paper listing a pilot's qualifications, "he is a superior candidate. He will graduate flight training school and go to France for further training and service. You will not. You're dismissed, Mr. Morgan."

Chapter 16

The sky was clear, the air crisp. A perfect day for graduation exercises in Captain Knowles' estimation. It seemed as though the resident population agreed with him. Nearly all of College Park and half of Washington, D.C. were pouring into the stands for the event. They came not only to honor the new pilots, but to see the newly arrived Nieuport 17s from France, and possibly to get a glimpse of the President of the United States.

President Wilson had arrived early in the day by motorcar. Throughout his tour of the flight training facility, he took keen interest in the program and the machinery. He tried his hand at tracking a model aeroplane through the sights of a machine gun as it simulated flight by sliding along a string. He ran his hand along the sleek lines of the Nieuport 17 and sat in its cockpit.

Had he not been attending the President of the United States, Knowles would have found the incident amusing. The President, looking like a bespectacled scarecrow, doffed his top hat and, with the assistance of nearly a half-dozen nervous aides, climbed into the Nieuport cockpit.

Standing on a ladder beside the fuselage, Knowles pointed over the President's shoulder, giving him a simplified version of a pilot candidate's first lesson. *This is the gas gauge. This is the altimeter. This is the throttle. This is the oil pressure gauge.* And so on.

After several minutes of playing with the control stick and working the rudder bar pedals back and forth and back and forth, the President was lifted out of the aeroplane whereupon he was immediately presented with his honorary wings.

The privilege of giving the President of the United States his first flying lesson was indeed an accolade for Captain Knowles. And he beamed appreciably when the President thanked him and shook his hand. But, for Knowles, the best of the day was yet to come—the graduation review and air show.

"Presidents don't follow printed programs," Knowles was told. It was his job as commandant of the flight training school to stand alongside President Wilson and personally tell him what was happening and what would happen next at each stage of the program.

Knowles' timing and luck couldn't have been better. He had personally orchestrated the program, giving special attention to the air show. Copiously, he had studied the most recent developments in military aviation on the European continent. He had chosen this review to introduce synchronized flying formations to the school. It was his intention during the air show to prove the advantages of this new tactic.

The press would be there. In a release statement he promised them a spectacle they would never forget. Then, when the President announced he would attend the graduation ceremony, Knowles knew that his career was on the verge of greatness. With any luck, one of the flying formations would be named after him.

The Knowles Flying Wedge. It had a good ring to it.

Shielding his eyes from the sun, Captain Knowles–the

creases in his pants never sharper, his shoes and medals never shinier—leaned toward the President's ear and pointed northward.

"Sir, the candidates will approach from that direction flying in a single-line formation. They will then proceed to land, one after the other, and taxi into position until they are all lined up wing tip to wing tip facing the reviewing stand."

The President nodded his acknowledgment, his eyes fixed on the northern sky.

First there was a speck. Then the slightest hint of a drone.

"There, sir!" Knowles pointed to the lead aeroplane.

The buzzing sound grew louder as the aeroplanes approached. Flying just beyond the eastern edge of the review field, the parade of aeroplanes passed the review stand.

A cheer went up from the enthusiastic crowd.

Following the lead, the line of aeroplanes circled around and approached the field. Descending, they landed one behind the other in an unbroken line, taxied down the middle of the field, then turned toward the crowd and moved into position side-by-side along a white chalk line, just as Knowles said they would.

Not until the last of the aeroplanes had landed and was on the line did they simultaneously cut their engines. The pilot candidates jumped out of their cockpits, removed their headgear and goggles, and stood at attention in front of their aeroplanes.

"Ladies and gentlemen," the public address system boomed. "The graduates of this year's flight training school, and America's future flying aces!"

The crowd erupted with raucous applause and cheers.

Clapping enthusiastically, the President glanced at Captain Knowles. "Impressive," he said.

Knowles suppressed a grin. After all, he was a military man. "Thank you, sir," he said crisply.

One by one the candidates were called forward to get their wings.

"Calahan!"

The red-headed Irishman moved smartly between the stands and the aeroplanes to enthusiastic applause from the crowd.

"Our top graduate," Knowles said to the President.

The President nodded.

"Putnam! Creech! Clay! Beane! Landis! Swaab! Hill!"

Knowles watched with special interest as Percy Hill received his wings. It seemed odd to see Hill by himself. From the moment he stepped on the flight school grounds the boy had been Johnny Morgan's shadow. And Knowles fully expected to lose Hill when Morgan was dismissed. Yet here he was, graduating with the class. *Good. The boy was a competent pilot.*

"Kindley! Springs! Biddle! Sewall! Robertson! Stovall! Baucom!"

Twenty-three men in all received their wings that day.

Three Nieuport 17s approached from the north flying in a V formation. A lone Nieuport 17 approached from the south. It was painted black.

Originally, Knowles had planned on having the lone attacking Nieuport painted red to represent Germany's celebrated ace Manfred von Richthofen, who used the bold color to taunt his Allied enemies. But when Knowles was presenting his plan to his superiors, they reminded him of the President's repeated admonitions that the United States always portray a neutral image in keeping with her neutral status. Accordingly, the attacking Nieuport was painted black instead of red.

"Mr. President, note the strength of the V-shaped formation," Knowles said.

Shielding his eyes against the brightness of the day, President Wilson peered skyward intently through mere slits for eyes.

Knowles continued: "A hostile lone scout, represented by the black Nieuport to your right," he waited for the President to locate the black scout, "is forced to deal with all three aeroplanes as a unit instead of challenging any one of them at random."

Side-by-side the President and Knowles watched as the opposing aircraft approached each other from opposite directions. Head-to-head, the distance between them decreased dramatically.

"Now watch what happens as the single attacker encounters this superior formation," Knowles said.

The aeroplanes continued their head-on collision course.

"Any moment now..." Knowles said in anticipation. "Any moment..."

The lone scout should have broken to one side by now.

"Any moment..." Knowles was keenly fixed on the black scout. *Why hadn't he broken off?*

High above the review stand, collision seemed imminent.

"Come on...come on..." Knowles said, his voice panicking.

The black scout held its course. Straight at the formation.

"Come on...."

The lead aeroplane pulled up, high and away. Not a second to spare. The aeroplanes on either side fell off to their respective sides. Like a bowling ball mowing down pins, the black scout plowed through the three opposing Nieuports. Breaking the formation. Sending them scattering every which way.

The crowd gasped. Then cheered.

"Impressive!" President Wilson shouted, clapping his

hands with the audience.

Captain Knowles didn't respond. Dumbfounded, he stared skyward at his broken formation.

"Whaaaaaahoooooo! That was close!" Johnny shouted, his face split with the biggest grin of his life. Gripping the control stick of the black Nieuport 17, he executed three barrel rolls to celebrate. "I could grow to like these new machines!" he shouted, as he swung around to engage the three opposing aeroplanes.

With no guns mounted on any of the aeroplanes, the resulting dogfight was staged. The rules were that if you could hold an opposing aeroplane in your sights . . .

" . . . to the count of five," Knowles explained to the President, "it is considered a kill and the downed aeroplane must land."

"How does the pilot normally get an aeroplane in his sights?" the President asked.

Knowles used his hands, both stretched in a flat position, to simulate the aircraft. He positioned the tips of his fingers on one hand behind the heel of the palm of the other. "A superior position is one that is directly behind the enemy aircraft, like this . . . " he demonstrated. "In this position it is possible to sustain an attack on the fleeing aeroplane for an extended time."

"Like that?" The President pointed upward.

The black scout was on the tail of one of the three aeroplanes. The pilot under attack banked left, then right . . .

"You can't lose me that easily," Johnny cried.

He followed his frantic prey as they plummeted from 6,000 to 5,000, to 4,500, twisting this way and that. Johnny stayed on his tail.

"One . . . two . . . three . . . "

" . . . four . . . five!" The President shouted. "That's a kill, isn't it?"

The spectators in the reviewing stand cheered lustily, indicating they were convinced it was a kill.

"Yes, Mr. President," Knowles said sullenly. "It looked like a kill to me."

To the pilot in the sky, as well. He broke away from the action and maneuvered to land.

"Wheeehaaawww!" Johnny shouted, pulling up. "Too easy! Too easy!"

He scanned the sky around him for the two remaining aeroplanes. One was off at a distance. The other one buzzed past right in front of Johnny, a direct challenge.

"Calahan!" Johnny shouted, recognizing the pilot. "Don't mind if I do. . . ."

He fell in behind Calahan, maneuvering to get on his tail.

Knowles signaled to an aide. "Get me the pilot of that first aeroplane," he whispered through clenched teeth. "I want to know what's going on!"

"Captain, what are they doing now?" the President asked.

Knowles scanned the sky, reviewing the situation. He smiled at what he saw. "Teamwork, sir," he said. "See that lead plane?"

"The one about to be shot down by the black scout?"

Knowles shook his head knowingly. "Bait, sir. He taunted the black scout into coming after him. Look over there."

The President followed Knowles' pointing finger off to one side. The distant aeroplane was coming on fast.

"While the black scout occupies himself with one aeroplane, another sneaks in behind him and blasts him out of the air! Watch what happens!"

"This is going to be a pleasure, Calahan," Johnny said, pulling up behind his next intended victim.

Just as he was about to get Calahan's aeroplane in his sights, the lead aeroplane would dart one way or the other. Erratic enough to keep Johnny guessing. But somewhat lazy too.

"Too easy," Johnny said. "I thought you were better than. . . ."

The President stared at the three planes lined up, one behind the other. "Is that last fellow close enough to start counting?" he asked.

"I believe he is, sir."

"One . . . two . . . three . . . "

"Calahan, you're a disappointment," Johnny said. "I expected more from . . . wait a minute!"

Johnny's head whipped around. Someone was on his tail!

He pulled up hard, giving the engine full throttle. There was nothing but sky in front of him. He climbed, losing speed steadily. Glancing over his shoulder, he looked behind him. No one was there. He checked the other side. Two aeroplanes on a parallel course.

His aeroplane stalled. He let it roll over on to its back, then banked into an upright diving position. He was closing fast on the tail of the third aeroplane. It was in his sights.

"One . . . two . . . "

". . . three . . . four . . . " the crowd shouted.

"Five!" said the President. "Wonderful! Masterful flying!"

Knowles wasn't as pleased.

An aide approached him and whispered in his ear. "It's

Morgan, sir."

"What?"

"Morgan," the aide repeated. "The pilot of the black scout aeroplane."

"Are you sure?"

"Beane got a good look at him in the air," the aide said, "and we found Sewall tied up in the hangar."

Knowles cursed as he turned his attention skyward again. The second of the downed aeroplanes was making an approach to land, leaving only two aeroplanes left in the sky. Calahan and Morgan.

"Nice try, Calahan, old boy," Johnny said. "But now it's just you and me."

He tried slipping in behind his lone opponent. For fifteen minutes Calahan managed to stay out of his reach. Like an albatross ballet, the two aeroplanes dove and rolled and feinted this way or that, neither one able to get the advantage over the other.

After a particularly close pass, Johnny pulled back on his stick to gain as much altitude as quickly as he could. He positioned himself so that he stayed in the line of sight directly between Calahan and the sun. He held that position for as long as he could.

Below him, Calahan banked this way and that.

"You've lost me, haven't you?" Johnny said.

Pushing the stick forward, he began his descent coming directly out of the sun.

"Look there!" the President cried excitedly. "The black scout is gaining the advantage! Why doesn't the other aeroplane use evasive tactics?"

"He doesn't see him," Knowles moaned. "Morgan's hidden by the sun."

"Morgan?"

"The black scout. Morgan is the name of the pilot."

The President nodded and looked up admiringly.

Johnny was on top of Calahan before he was spotted.

"Got you!" Johnny cried.

Instead of pulling behind Calahan, Johnny literally descended on top of him. Calahan didn't know he was there until the shadow of Johnny's aeroplane eclipsed him. The astonished look on the lead pilot's face was worth whatever trouble awaited Johnny once they landed.

Calahan tried to dive away.

Johnny stayed right with him, descending until his wheels nearly touched the top of Calahan's wings. The lead pilot shouted, though Johnny couldn't hear what he said, and shook an enraged fist. Johnny pointed to the ground. He wanted Calahan to land.

At first, Calahan refused. But Johnny had him covered. Calahan couldn't get away. He had no choice but to bank slowly until the field came into sight and come in for a landing.

"What's he doing?" the President asked. "He can't shoot from that angle."

"It looks like he's trying to force Calahan to land," Knowles said.

"Outstanding!" cried the President. "He not only captures the pilot, but the pilot's aircraft as well! Outstanding!"

Leaning over the edge of the cockpit, Johnny watched below him as Calahan's aeroplane landed on the field. To his left was the reviewing stand overflowing with cheering spectators. Unable to resist, Johnny flipped his aeroplane upside down and flew the length of the field, waving to the crowd. A few rolls and spins and stunts later, he landed and taxied toward the reviewing stand to be arrested. The cheer that greeted him as he climbed down from the aeroplane was deafening.

He was met by two silent armed guards who escorted him, not to the brig, but to the reviewing stand. They marched him up the steps to the platform where he was met by the President of the United States.

"Well done, son!" the President cried.

Beside the President stood Captain Knowles, glowering at him with such burning hatred that Johnny could nearly feel the heat.

"As I was telling your commandant," the President said to Johnny, "you couldn't have made your point any clearer than that!"

"Point, sir?" Johnny asked.

"That no amount of formations or strategy and such can compete against a single well-trained pilot. Congratulations, son, you are an honor to your graduating class."

Johnny shook the President's extended hand. "Thank you, sir," he said tentatively.

Turning to Knowles, the President said, "You're doing a quality work here, captain. Keep it up!"

"Thank you, sir. I will, sir."

To Johnny again. "By the way, son, would you happen to be any relation to one Jesse Morgan of Denver, Colorado?"

Johnny was taken aback. "Yes, sir. He's my father."

"And my personal aide!" said the President. "Good man! Now I can see where you get that steel nerve of yours. I suppose you'll be going to France now?"

"Well . . . I'm not . . . "

"Yes, sir, he is!" Knowles cut in.

"Fine!" said the President. To Knowles, he added, "I want to be kept informed of this boy's progress, Captain. Our aviation future is indeed bright with men like him flying our aeroplanes."

"It is indeed, sir," said Knowles.

"Strange that your father never mentioned you," the President said to Johnny. "Of course, I heard of your mother and sister because they were passengers aboard the *Lusitania.*"

"Yes, sir," Johnny said. But the *Lusitania* comment was news to him. The President said they were passengers. He didn't say survivors. Did that mean . . . ?

The President's motorcar was barely out of sight when Knowles turned on Johnny. For a good ten minutes he screamed and ranted and cursed until he was nearly exhausted. As he was winding down, he said, "You didn't tell me your father was a personal aide to President Wilson."

"I didn't want it to influence the way my performance was evaluated," Johnny lied. In truth, he hadn't known either. Just like he didn't know about his mother and sister. But now that he knew, it was about all he could think about. *How could he go about finding out if they were alive?*

"Get your bags, Morgan," Knowles said.

"My bags are already off-base, sir," Johnny said.

"Well, get them back on-base, then."

"Sir?"

"You sail for France in three days."

"With my wings, sir?"

Knowles made a face that looked like he'd just bit into a sour pickle. "What choice do I have?" he groused. "But believe me, Morgan, for the next three days I'm going to make you wish you had real wings, because life for you on the ground is going to be one very long nightmare."

Chapter 17

I T was a perfect night for sleeping. Cool. Clear. A slight breeze off the ocean was a welcome reprieve from the summer heat that had blistered the city for at least a week.

Jesse pulled out a pocket watch from his tuxedo pocket. Angling the watch face to catch the soft glow of the street lamp, he checked the time. 1:52 A.M. He slipped the timepiece back and sauntered from one diffused circle of light to another along the promenade of the Brooklyn Bridge, stopping mid-span.

His back against the railing, he gazed nostalgically down the deserted promenade toward the Manhattan side. He was beginning to wish he hadn't come. He had hoped the memories associated with the bridge would soothe his longing for Emily. Instead, they were having the opposite effect on him.

"Come here often?"

The voice, though soft and pleasant, startled him. The face that accompanied the voice was equally pleasant. A young woman. Innocent, wide brown eyes. He'd seen her before.

"Emily... Emily..."

"Barnes," Emily Austin said. She repeated it for him. "My name's Emily Barnes."

"The young lady with the police whistle!"

She pulled the whistle from her waistband. Holding it

between two fingers she smiled impishly. "A woman can't be too careful," *she said.*

"Barnes . . . " Jesse smiled and shook his head. It had been Emily's *professional* name. The name she used when she pretended she was an investigative reporter while in reality she was a neglected only child of wealthy parents, trailing Jesse because she'd fallen in love with him.

Emily laughed. Jesse was taken by the sound of her laughter and the way her eyes sparkled when she laughed. She caught him staring at her eyes. Neither she nor he looked away. Jesse felt like he was being drawn into two glistening brown pools. He knew he could drown in those eyes and die a happy man.

She glanced away. Jesse caught his mouth hanging open. He closed it and cleared his throat.

"Well, good-night," he said.

"Good-night."

"And don't worry. Your secret's safe with me."

"Secret?"

"Being undercover as a typist."

"Oh! Yes, yes . . . " Emily sputtered. "Sometimes I get so caught up in my own cover that I forget it's a cover. Thank you for keeping my secret."

"Well, good-night."

"Good-night, again," Emily said. Her fingers fluttered a little wave and she turned and left Jesse standing alone.

Again he was left standing alone on the bridge. Only on this night more than a few city blocks separated them.

He thought of Emily in England. Her decision to stay there longer than planned had stung him, more than he cared to admit. It was his own fault. She was right. Given the unpredictable nature of his current assignment it would do her no good to stay alone in some New York apartment, each night wondering if he would come home.

In England she had Maggie. And Katy.

Turning around and resting his forearms on the railing, Jesse stared downward at the black liquid that coursed beneath the bridge. He tried to brush aside feelings of envy for Maggie. Tried, and failed. He didn't even know the woman. It was ridiculous for him to feel this way. But the feeling persisted.

It was Maggie—not he—who was sharing Emily's forced attempts at civility first thing in the morning. Her witty, at times acerbic, but always entertaining commentary in the afternoon. Her more reflective thoughts over a cup of coffee at night.

Jesse's heart ached for Emily's company as the lights of the city reflected in the river, as the horn of a boat sounded, as Miss Liberty stood in silent silhouette a few miles farther down the harbor.

There was no one to blame but himself. It was he who wanted to come to Washington with William Jennings Bryan. Emily didn't object, but at the time she knew better than he the price they would pay being separated. Now, he knew too. It was a higher price than he'd anticipated.

All he wanted at this point was to go home to Denver with Emily. If he never traveled again, he would be happy. If adventure and notoriety passed him by the rest of his life, he would be content. A quiet life with the woman he loved. That's all he wanted.

A young couple shuffled down the promenade. Huddled closely together, their hushed but giddy conversation ceased as they passed quietly behind him, giving him a wide berth. The giggling began again, then faded as they grew distant. He watched them.

"Emily . . . Emily . . . "

"Barnes," Emily Austin said. She repeated it for him. "My name's Emily Barnes."

"The young lady with the police whistle!"

She pulled the whistle from her waistband. Holding it between two fingers she smiled impishly. "A woman can't be too careful," she said.

Jesse roused himself from the memory. Maybe he would feel better if he went back to his apartment and wrote Emily a letter.

The thought reminded him of the letter in his pocket. From Johnny, delivered to him by way of the White House. He pulled out the letter. It was folded in thirds.

Dear Father,

I assume congratulations are in order since you are now working for President Wilson. As for me, my life too has taken a turn for the better. Landis Wachorn died on me in Columbus, New Mexico. Through a chain of events that are too numerous to mention in a letter, I ended up here in College Park where I just completed flight training and earned my wings. Now it is on to France. I know you won't agree with this, but we pilots are hoping America gets into the war real soon. We would rather shoot Huns with bullets than shoot them with film in reconnaissance missions.

I don't know exactly how to put this, so I'll just ask it plainly. Are Mother and Katy alive? I just learned they were on the Lusitania, *but didn't hear if they were among the survivors or not. Please let me know as soon as possible.*

I know that if I were a better son, I wouldn't have to be asking this question. I'm not going to start making excuses for myself now. Be that as it may, I am sorry that I'm such a disappointment to you. I hope you see fit to reply to my letter.

Johnny

Folding the letter, Jesse returned it to his pocket. He had already replied to Johnny's letter, informing him of his mother's and sister's safety. He also congratulated Johnny on completing flight training. Secretly, Jesse hoped the discipline of the army would mold his son into a man. He feared, however, that Johnny's rebellious streak against authority would quickly prove to be his undoing. Frankly, he was surprised the boy had made it this far without getting tossed out.

Jesse's dilemma was whether to include Johnny's letter along with his own to Emily, or simply to comment in his letter that he'd heard from Johnny. He knew certain phrases would upset her: . . .we pilots are hoping America gets into the war real soon . . . I know that if I were a better son . . . I am sorry that I'm such a disappointment to you.

With a final tuck of the letter in his pocket, Jesse decided not to forward the letter. He'd simply tell Emily that they'd heard from Johnny, that he had completed flight training, and that he was shipping out to France.

Johnny's letter had prompted no small emotional stir within Jesse. There was relief the boy was still alive, considering he flew off in a rickety aeroplane with a drunkard for a pilot. The report that he'd completed flight school brought a tinge of pride and hope that the boy might yet straighten out.

I am sorry that I'm such a disappointment to you.

Being sorry was one thing; doing something about it was an entirely different story. It would take more than a letter to convince Jesse his son had changed.

Jesse blamed himself as much as he blamed the boy. As a father he had failed to instill the proper spiritual values into Johnny. This was not only his responsibility as a father, but as the keeper of the Morgan family Bible.

As such, he had been charged with the preservation of the

Morgan family spiritual heritage. Johnny, being his only son, was the next in line to receive the Bible and the charge. But how could Jesse entrust the Morgan family heritage to a son who cared for none of the values it represented?

Names of those who had gone before them came to mind. Heroes. Pioneers. Spiritual leaders. There was Drew Morgan, the founder of the spiritual heritage. It was he who courageously led the English town of Edenford across the sea to resettle in the new world. Following in his spiritual footsteps was Christopher Morgan, the missionary to the Indians; Philip and Jared Morgan, one a missionary, the other a pirate, both of them men of God; Jacob and Esau Morgan, twin brothers who fought in the Revolutionary War; and Benjamin Morgan, Jesse's father, who turned his back on a life of wealth to minister to the poor and downcast living in the New York tenements. This was their heritage.

Jesse did not feel worthy to be included with these men. Nevertheless, his name was printed in the front of the family Bible beneath theirs, though he had done nothing extraordinary to warrant the honor other than being Benjamin Morgan's son. But it was an honor he took seriously, as he did the Morgan family tradition.

He could not say the same for Johnny. And in all good conscience, Jesse could not bring himself to pass along the Morgan family Bible, the symbol of their Christian heritage, to his son.

Maybe my branch of the Morgan family tree was never intended to have the Bible in the first place, he concluded. Following this assignment, he would return the Bible to his uncle J.D. Morgan and thereby give the responsibility of the family heritage to another branch of Drew Morgan's descendants.

He sighed heavily and looked at his watch. 2:05 A.M.

Came here lonely, he muttered, *leaving lonely and depressed.* With another sigh he sauntered homeward. His thoughts wandered back to the events earlier this evening. A feeling of anxiety rose within him, the very feeling that had kept him awake. The feeling he'd come to the bridge to escape.

Yet, even now he couldn't shake it. Something was in the wind. He could feel it. But that was all he had. A feeling. Getting worked up over a feeling could drive a man crazy. *But what else was there?* Bits and pieces that didn't fit. Not enough to formulate a working hypothesis, more than enough to feel certain that something was about to happen. Soon. It was maddening.

Jesse came to a halt. Deep in thought, he stared at the city lights that flickered in the river. He didn't look to them for some sort of magical key that would unlock the mystery. The light simply provided a convenient focal point while his mind turned inward and examined—for the hundredth time tonight—the pieces of information at hand.

First, there was the *Deutschland.* For the last three weeks it had been moored up the Chesapeake Bay at the port of Baltimore. This German merchant submarine had just completed its maiden Atlantic crossing and was taking on commercial cargo. She was also undergoing emergency repairs to her engines—plates and batteries as permitted under the neutrality laws.

The U-boat's skipper, Captain Paul Koenig, was readying his vessel for a dramatic dash down the Chesapeake Bay and out beyond the Atlantic's three-mile limit toward home. Waiting for the *Deutschland,* like dogs guarding a rabbit hole, were British and French cruisers bent on capturing or sinking her.

It wasn't the submarine itself that made Jesse uneasy, but the movements of her skipper. During his stay Captain Koenig was a frequent patron of Hansa Haus, a favorite gathering place in Baltimore for German sailors and shipping officials. There, in conversations with American merchants of notable German sympathy, the captain displayed a special interest in the geography and facilities of the port of New York. *Professional curiosity? Or was the German captain's interest more than that?*

Then there was the sedate brownstone house on West Fifteenth Street in Manhattan, also frequented by the captain. During the day it was the home of former German opera singer Martha Held. During the night, it was well known as a house of ill repute where Miss Held wined and dined German dignitaries. It was not uncommon for those who lived on West Fifteenth Street to hear powerful operatic arias from the booming voice of the hostess, or the boisterous singing of patriotic German songs from her male guests lasting late into the night.

Jesse, however, had it on good authority that merrymaking was not the only business transacted behind the shuttered windows of Miss Held's brownstone address. According to one eyewitness—a drugstore delivery boy whose services were used frequently by Miss Held late at night—there were several occasions when large maps were spread across tables, blueprints and photographs were scattered across the floor, and the evening's patrons were locked in animated discussion the tone of which did not resemble the usual late night merriment.

Then there was the anonymous phone call that sent him to the Opera House.

Mr. Morgan. If you want to curtail Martha Held and her band of German saboteurs, attend the opening performance of Tannhauser. *Stand outside the west exit during intermission with a program scrolled in your left hand.*

The voice was male, deliberately disguised. Considering the risk to himself minimal, Jesse attended the opera. Martha Held was also in attendance, the opening night guest of honor. Seated in the front row, she stood and basked in the thunderous ovation that surrounded her when she was introduced immediately preceding the performance.

For Jesse, it was an uncomfortable first act. He didn't know opera, didn't like the music, didn't understand German, and hated being dressed in formal wear. As best as he could deduce from what he saw, there was this fellow Tannhauser who woke up in the cave of Venus, sang to the goddess who was reclining on a couch, and asked her to send him back to earth where he could experience pain again and sing in a contest and win the hand of a fair maiden named Elizabeth. What he couldn't figure out was why it took them so long to tell the story.

At intermission, he worked his way to the west exit as instructed with the night's program scrolled in his left hand. Surrounded by other people's swirls of cigarette smoke, he casually stared into the night. Pockets of people stood here and there. Laughing. Talking. Some waved their hands like a conductor when they spoke. Others broke into portions of song, in Jesse's estimation doing the music greater justice than the actors on the stage.

His contact approached him from behind, close enough to whisper in his ear. He was told not to turn around. A folded newspaper was placed under his arm from behind. Four words were spoken. *Bruno sends his greetings.*

Jesse waited for more. There was none. Furthermore, he realized he was now standing alone. He turned around. The Opera House lobby was crammed with well-dressed New Yorkers enjoying an evening out on the town. Any one of them could have been the messenger.

Taking the newspaper from under his arm, he unfolded
it. *The New York Times.* Today's edition. Cradled inside the
fold of the newspaper was a pocket dictionary. A slip of
paper with a vertical row of what appeared to be hand-
printed random numbers served as a bookmark.

A newspaper. A dictionary. And a bookmark. Jesse wondered how many big words in the newspaper Bruno
thought he didn't know. Whoever Bruno was.

Jesse didn't return to his seat for the second act. Instead,
he pocketed the dictionary and found a local cafe where he
could sit down and study the newspaper, hoping that
something inside would direct his attention to Bruno's
intended message.

Three cups of coffee later, he folded the newspaper and
gave up. Nothing was circled or marked in any way. As far
as he could determine, the numbers on the bookmark had
no direct connection with the newspaper. Nor were there
any particularly hard words that would require a dictionary.
And other than an advertisement announcing opening
night of *Tannhauser,* he could find nothing of relevant
importance.

On the front page American relations with Mexico commanded the spotlight. President Wilson had agreed to the
appointment of an international joint commission to work
out the evacuation of forces in Mexico. Locally, a strike was
underway by the employees of the Third Avenue Railway
Company which ran many of the city's streetcars. There were
shark sightings off Brooklyn and Long Island beaches. There
was an epidemic of infantile paralysis. And Casey Stengel,
pinch-hitter for the Brooklyn Robins, belted a triple that
broke an eighth-inning tie, giving the league-leading Robins
a narrow victory over the St. Louis Cardinals.

Discouraged and frustrated, he returned to his apartment. He wished Emily were with him. She was better at

this sort of thing than he was.

Opening his apartment door, suddenly he understood. Enlightenment did not come in a flash of inspiration, but in a folded scrap of paper that had been slipped under his door. A series of numbers was written on it.

Tossing the newspaper aside, Jesse reached in his pocket for the dictionary. He matched the numbers on the scrap of paper with the numbers on the bookmark. They matched, with the exception that the numbers on the scrap of paper had one or two additional digits appended to it.

Page numbers?

Jesse held up the rectangular piece of paper in triumph. Not a bookmark, a code breaker! Excitedly, he rushed to the dining table, switched on a light, grabbed a pen, and began decoding. The first word took the longest because it had to be spelled out letter-by- letter.

B - R - U - N - O

The last three words were easy, but with them came a flood of satisfaction. With the dictionary and the hand-printed list of numbers, he had been given a code breaker. The newspaper itself was irrelevant, merely a covering for the true delivery.

Jesse held up the decoded message and read it again: *Bruno sends his greetings.*

The message begged several more questions for which he had no answers. *Who was Bruno? What kind of information did he possess about Miss Held and Captain Koenig? When and how could he expect to hear from him again? And why Jesse? Why did Bruno choose him?*

Jesse went to bed, but not to sleep. His mind was a whirling engine, cranking out thought after endless thought. He tried focusing his thoughts on something other than Bruno and the coded message. He thought of Emily.

That's when the loneliness struck. And that's when he decided to take a midnight stroll across the Brooklyn Bridge.

Jesse pulled out his watch and looked at it again—a form of self-torture practiced by those who cannot sleep. 2:08 A.M. Gratefully, his eyelids were beginning to feel slumber's weight. Pocketing his watch, he turned toward . . .

A brilliant flash of light lit up the harbor.

Ear-splitting thunder in one explosive blast threw him across the promenade.

The bridge itself, that giant edifice, swayed and shimmied at the impact.

From behind his back, Jesse could see flaming rockets and screeching shells piercing the sky. Dazed, he lifted his arm over his face to protect himself from fallen wood and metal debris.

His ears ringing, he managed to get onto his hands and knees, then with one tentative foot placed on the promenade, he succeeded in standing. He stumbled to the railing as a fireball rose from a promontory that jutted into Upper New York Bay.

Black Tom Island! Jesse muttered. They got the munitions plant!

Chapter 18

MAGGIE Thomas, I do believe you're a spy!" With a knowing grin, Emily took a sip of tea, then nearly choked on it when she saw Maggie's reaction. Her host's face drained of color. The woman's blue eyes stared in the direction of the tabletop, at nothing in particular, as her mind and mouth fumbled for some kind of response.

Hastily setting her cup in its saucer, Emily reached across the table and took Maggie's hand. "My dear, dear friend," she cried apologetically, "I didn't mean a German spy!"

The elderly woman was slow to respond. She held a wrinkled hand against her chest. Her head fell backward. Her mouth gaped open as she struggled to inhale.

Instantly, Emily was kneeling by her side, clasping the old woman's hand. "My dear, are you all right? Please forgive me," Emily pleaded. "I had no intention of startling you this way!"

A trembling smile formed on Maggie's thin lips, signaling forgiveness. Tentatively, a shaky, brown-spotted hand returned Emily's reassuring pats. "You did give me quite a start, I must say!"

"Please believe me, Maggie, that was not my intention!"

The smile broadened. Color returned to Maggie's cheeks. "What do you say we finish our tea?" she suggested with another reassuring pat on Emily's head.

Feeling somewhat sheepish now, Emily returned to her side of the table. The clinking of teacups against saucers was the only sound for the next several minutes. Emily peered over the rim of her cup at the woman opposite her. Maggie's hands shook slightly as she stirred her tea.

"So tell me, dear," Maggie said, "what makes you think I'm a spy?"

Emily was slow to respond. There was something about the woman's shaking hands that gave her pause. "We don't have to talk about this now," she said.

"By all means, let's do!" Maggie set down a trembling spoon and lifted a trembling cup to her lips. "It will be great fun!"

Emily smiled at her host. From her observation of the woman, this approach was typical of Maggie Thomas. Always face things head-on.

"Let's hear it!" Maggie insisted. The control of her voice was forced, but its tone genuinely lighthearted.

"Well, let's see . . . " Emily said reluctantly. If she thought there was a way to change the subject, she would. But Maggie would never allow that. Not now at least. "You are coming and going quite a bit. Suddenly. Unexpectedly and without explanation. That sort of thing."

"Oh, yes, we spies do a lot of that," Maggie said. "What else?"

Emily laughed. The Maggie she knew was slowly returning. Confident. In control. Quick-witted. "Then, there's the number of hours you spend alone in your room at night embroidering . . . "

"Spies love their embroidering!" Maggie interrupted.

"I just find it odd that you never produce any work," Emily said. "There are no embroidered tablecloths or napkins or handkerchiefs or anything else that I've seen. A person who spends as much time embroidering as you do ought to have something to show for it."

"We spies hate to show other people our embroidering."

"And the sounds that come from your room when you're embroidering aren't embroidering sounds. More like tissue paper sounds. The kind of paper spies use to record their messages so that they can be folded into tiny pieces and hidden in unusual places too small for regular paper."

Emily expected Maggie to make a spies-love-tissue-paper remark. But there was not one forthcoming. So she continued.

"The kind of tissue paper that Bryn had in the little book hidden behind a loose stone in his kitchen cool box."

All levity left Maggie's eyes. "I see," was all she said.

"I found it when I was looking for milk for the baby," Emily explained. "And when we were preparing to leave Bryn's house and you pulled the kitchen curtain closed, I heard you pull out the stone. What other reason would you have to do that unless there was something behind it that was important to you?"

"And did you see the markings on the tissue paper?" Maggie asked.

"It had a time and some cryptic remarks about soldiers and horses and carts."

"Did you understand it?"

"Not really." Emily shrugged. "But it wouldn't be too hard to figure out. Probably some kind of report on troop movements, or something like that."

Maggie's eyebrows raised. "I'm impressed," she said, calmly. Her hands were no longer shaking. "You would have indeed made an excellent investigative reporter."

Emily smiled a half smile at the compliment. "Maggie, I know it seems like I've been snooping . . . but believe me, you have been so wonderful to Katy and me . . . "

"No need to apologize," Maggie said. "You are not a

snoop. You are a woman with a keen sense of observation."

"Then, you *are* a spy?"

"An undercover carrier."

"Through the relief effort," Emily said.

Maggie nodded. "I receive messages through Belgium and see that they get into the right hands here in England."

"And Bryn? Was he involved too?"

"He assisted me at times," Maggie said.

Emily leaned forward on the table. The longer they talked, the calmer Maggie became with the topic. With her friend at ease with the subject, Emily allowed her excitement to mount.

"Do you have a code name?" she asked.

"A code name?"

"I know what it is!" Emily squealed.

Arched eyebrows invited Emily's guess.

"Bruno. It was on the papers in Bryn's house. Your code name is Bruno, isn't it?"

For an instant, there was a spark of alarm in Maggie's eyes.

Understandable, Emily thought. *Hearing one's code name spoken aloud by someone who isn't supposed to know it must be unnerving.*

Maggie leaned toward Emily and whispered, "You must never speak that name to anyone. Never!"

"Then, you *are* Bruno?" Emily whispered.

Lifting her cup, Maggie took a long sip of tea. With a twinkle in her eye, she nodded affirmatively.

"Are you bored? I'm bored," Katy said.

Laura sat beside her, composing a letter to her parents. The hospital garden at this time of early evening was cool and refreshing with long shadows and deep colors. The scent of the roses and daisies, even the fresh-cut grass, was a welcome change to the medicinal and bodily odors of the ward.

"Do you want to say anything to my parents?" Laura asked, her head down, continuing to write.

"Where do they live again?"

"Exeter."

"Where in England is that?"

"Southwest."

"On the River Exe?"

Laura lifted her head. A look of pleasant surprise formed on her lips. "Do you know the River Exe?"

"I've heard my father speak of it. Our ancestors come from that part of England."

"They do? What town?" Laura said, her giddiness causing her to bounce on the stone bench.

"Edenford," Katy replied.

"Edenford! That's just up the river from us! Have you ever been there?"

Katy shook her head. "You?"

"Ridden past it. The road crosses over the river to the town, then crosses back on the way to Tiverton! And your ancestors are from there?"

Katy nodded.

Laura returned to her letter, busily scratching the news that Katy Morgan's ancestors originated from Edenford.

"This isn't exactly what I'd hoped it would be," Katy said while Laura wrote. "The hospital, I mean. I know we're doing a good work, healing soldiers and all that, but there's something missing."

"Too many nurses," Laura said.

"Huh?"

"There are too many nurses. Almost anybody can be a nurse on a ward. You're getting lost in the everyday duties of a nurse. That's fine for me. But you were destined for more than that."

Katy looked at her friend with a smile.

"What are you grinning at? You know it. I know it. You're destined for greater things. Didn't you tell me that someday Sunday School teachers are going to tell stories about you?"

Katy examined her friend to see if she was poking fun at her dreams. There was no hint of insincerity on Laura's face.

"So then, what am I supposed to do?" Katy asked. "Since it seems you have all the answers."

Laura folded her letter and stood. "No answers, just observation."

The two nurses walked side-by-side through the garden and into the dormitory hallway.

"All I know is that you'll know when it's time for you to leave, to move on to something greater than this."

"That's it!" Katy said, running to a bulletin board.

"So soon?" Laura followed her.

Katy pulled down a notice that was tacked to the board. "This is what we're supposed to do!" she cried. "I know it!"

"*We?*"

"Yes, we."

Katy shoved the flyer at Laura.

Laura shook her head. "Oh, no, I don't think I could do that!"

"Sure you can!"

Laura shoved the poster away. "It's in the war zone!"

"I know!" Katy cried.

"In France!"

"I know!"

"Where they're shooting guns and cannons! We could get killed!"

"We can help a lot of men who desperately need our help!"

"But I don't know how to drive an ambulance!" Laura cried.

"Come on, silly! They'll teach us!"

Chapter 19

WATER cascaded from the sky in sheets, pounding against the roof of the ambulance with a deafening din. Katy gripped the steering wheel with gloved fists, fighting every inch of the narrow, slippery, muddy road. The vehicle bounced and lurched and slid through ruts and potholes.

Beside her, a wide-eyed Laura clinched the side of the passenger seat with one hand and the metal windscreen with the other. It was the only way the petite girl could keep from being thrown from the open cab.

Wind and water whipped all around them. Everything was drenched. The seat. Their heavy nurses' cloaks. Their faces. On the instrument panel droplets of water trickled down the glass-covered gauges, shivering in their courses from the engine's vibration.

The land through which Katy and Laura traversed was anything but the idyllic flowered French countryside of poem and fable. A slick, gray-brown terrain stretched endlessly in all directions—denuded of vegetation, scarred with trenches, pockmarked with blast craters, and girded with barbed coils of wire. Settling upon the land like a shroud was a blanket of white mist. Or was it poisonous gas?

The wind moaned over lifeless forms that littered the field. Fallen soldiers. Mules. Horses. Carts. Equipment.

Black branches and roots protruded from the earth grotesquely like skeletal hands reaching up from their graves to claim the things that now rightfully belonged to them.

Overhead, German shells scratched the sky. Muddy geysers erupted where the shells hit, digging new craters that filled quickly with water. The ambulance shuddered with each blast. Gravel and clumps of mud splattered the large red cross painted on the ambulance's paneled sides.

Between the din of the rain and the thunder of the artillery shells, Katy could barely hear the ambulance's engine. She knew it was laboring. It smelled hot. Shifting to a lower gear, she slowed as they passed a platoon of soldiers marching toward the front and ducking instinctively at the scream of each overhead shell.

Steadying herself with a single hand on the windscreen, Laura waved and smiled at the men. Their joyless expressions, heavy from the ordeal of war, brightened instantly. Several of them called out to her, asking her name. Others whistled or howled like wolves.

Katy grinned at the exchange. It typified Laura Kelton's contribution to the war. She was an ever-present ray of sunshine in an otherwise dreary undertaking.

Having passed the platoon, Katy swerved around a team of twelve mules pulling a hulking cannon, its deadly end pointing at them as they approached. She then slipped and slid her way past a lorry that was mired in the mud up to its rims. The muddied and soaked driver scowled at her as she skirted the hazard that had claimed his vehicle. Katy ignored him. She'd come to expect it. His response was common to women ambulance drivers.

"Are you bored?" Laura shouted.

A shell screeched overhead.

"What?" Katy responded, without taking her eyes from the road.

"I said, 'Are you bored?'"

"What kind of question is that to ask?"

"If you'll recall," Laura shouted, "you dragged me over here because you were bored. I was just wondering where we'd go next if that were still the case."

Katy laughed, then winced as the front wheel slammed into a pothole, jarring both of them. She hadn't seen that one coming. Filled with muddy water, it blended smoothly with the slick, muddy road. "I'm no longer bored," she shouted.

"A relief!" Laura shouted with a smile.

Hitting a muddy patch, the back wheels slid to the right of the road. There was a distinctive thump as the right wheel fell off the edge of solid ground into a muddy pit. Katy acted instinctively. She turned into the direction of the skid, jammed in the clutch, dropped to a lower gear, released the clutch, and accelerated. The tires spun. She could feel the back end of the ambulance sinking.

"Come on!" she coaxed.

The wheel spun, gripped the edge of solid ground, and vaulted out of the muddy hole.

"Close!" Laura said.

Katy nodded.

"How much farther?"

Squinting, Katy stared hard through the filter of falling rain. Everything was blurry blue and gray. She thought she could see huge cauliflower shapes lining the road in the distance.

"Looks like the town ahead," she said. "Then, we look for a cathedral. That's all the directions Mrs. Jones gave me."

Mrs. Graham Jones was the organizer and driving force behind the Women's Voluntary Aid Detachment Motor Ambulance unit in France. Based at a large hospital in northern France, she directed the work of thrteen girl drivers. "The motor cars themselves were big and powerful, and the girls had entire charge of them, not only for the driving but for cleaning and all except heavy repairs.

A believer in strict and unquestioning obedience to army discipline, Mrs. Jones exemplified the strength of character, self-control, and nerve that characterized her female volunteers. The women had to load and unload their human cargo as well as transport the patients from dressing stations near the front to hospitals or hospital trains and ships.

The demand on ambulance drivers required that the women were obliged to work in shifts of eight hours on and four hours off, night and day. It was not unusual for them to drive as much as a hundred and thirty miles a day and then clean and service their car for the next shift.

"There it is!" Laura cried, pointing in the distance on her side of the ambulance.

The rain had let up. A temporary reprieve, if the swollen black clouds were any indication.

Katy turned right at the next road. Bombed-out houses and businesses lined their way. Rising smoke from the ruins made the town look like it was peopled with ghosts.

A half a mile down the street on the left-hand side, the remains of a once-proud cathedral dominated the view. Nearly one whole side was blasted away, exposing interior Corinthian columns and majestic arches that supported what was left of the roof. Under the covering, wounded-bearing stretchers were jammed side-by-side with barely any space between them to walk. A massive oil-painting of Christ ascending into heaven presided over them.

"What took·you so long. . ."

A bellowing sergeant, short and bristling with energy, bounded across the rubble toward the ambulance as Katy shut off the engine. A wisp of steam rose from the radiator.

It wasn't the only thing steaming, especially when the sergeant noticed that the ambulance drivers were women.

Interrupting his own rebuke, the sergeant launched into a string of curses. Speaking to no one in particular, he cried, "What are they doing sending me women?" He motioned in disbelief to several soldiers who were standing nearby. "Look at this! Women! I ask for an ambulance and they send me women!"

Actually, the sergeant didn't have to announce Katy and Laura's presence, or their gender. If open-mouthed gawking was any indication, most of the soldiers had already noticed that two women had arrived.

The sergeant was shorter than Katy and compact. Rolled-up sleeves revealed thick forearms covered generously with a carpet of black hair. Underneath his helmet that swung back and forth like a bell, the man's face was round and clean-shaven. It was also flushed red with anger.

Wanting to get past this man and on with the work at hand, Katy said, "If you would be so kind to point out Sergeant Gillette to me . . ."

"I'm Gillette!" the man shouted, stabbing his chest with his thumb.

"And we're the ambulance drivers," Laura said sweetly. "Now, if you'll show us which of these men you want transported . . ."

"Sarge! Sarge!"

A private with the face of a teenage boy ran toward them, out of breath. He didn't salute. He didn't wait to be acknowledged. Doubled over, he spoke between gasps.

"Captain Quigley! . . . we found him . . ."

"Where?" Gillette shouted.

"In the trees . . . edge of a field . . . about a mile from here . . ."

"Is he dead?"

The boy shook his head. "Alive . . . just barely."

"Then why didn't you bring him back with you?"

"Can't . . . trapped . . . beneath his engine . . . we tried to move it . . . too heavy."

"Mules . . . " Gillette looked around.

"None available," the boy wheezed. "I checked."

"We can use our motor car," Katy said.

Gillette looked at her, reluctant to admit it was a good idea.

"Let's go!" he said. "Maxwell, get a rifle and a rope and jump in the back."

The private saluted, still doubled over slightly. He disappeared into the cathedral. Laura climbed into the passenger seat. Gillette jumped behind the steering wheel.

"You'll not be driving my ambulance, Sergeant," Katy said.

"Just watch me!" He punched the starter. The engine revved impatiently.

"Sergeant, I'm warning you. This vehicle is my responsibility."

Gillette growled, "Either jump in the back or step away!"

Katy grabbed Gillette by the wrist. "Commandeering an official army vehicle without proper authorization is a serious offense, Sergeant. You leave me no other choice than to report it stolen."

Gillette glared at her. Katy met his gaze with equal intensity.

Maxwell reappeared from the cathedral. He jumped into the back of the ambulance. Seeing the stalemate in the front seat, he said, "Captain Quigley's hurtin' real bad, Sarge!"

With a loud curse that had something to do with the stubbornness of women, Sergeant Gillette pounded the steering wheel with the flat of his hand, cursed again, then slid over on the seat. Katy climbed behind the wheel and slipped the gearshift lever into first gear.

Captain Quigley's aeroplane stood at the far end of a muddy field, tail-up, wedged between two juniper trees in a long row of trees. One of the aeroplane's wings was broken at the fuselage. Upended like it was, it looked like a wounded bird.

Abandoning the road, Katy cut across the field, heading directly toward the downed aircraft. As they drew closer, a torso could be seen jutting out from beneath the engine at the base of a tree.

Rope and rifle in hand, Maxwell jumped from the ambulance before it stopped moving. Laura was right behind him.

"Told you I'd bring help, Captain!" Maxwell shouted.

While Laura evaluated the captain's condition, Katy and Sergeant Gillette worked to pull the aeroplane off of him. It took several attempts, but Gillette managed to lasso the tail section. Then, he tied the rope to the back of the ambulance. He started toward the driver's seat, then stopped. To Katy, he said, "Do you know what to do?"

"Take up the slack, keep it in low gear, go slowly, and hope there's enough traction to pull that thing off him."

Gillette grunted. "Don't stall it!"

Laura ran up to Katy. "His legs are crushed and he's lost a lot of blood. Keeps drifting off. His complexion is pasty."

"Wrap him in blankets. Let me know when you're ready and we'll try to get that machine off him."

Laura grabbed blankets from the back of the ambulance. A few moments later the captain was wrapped and she signaled she was ready.

With Maxwell guiding the fuselage and Gillette watching the rope, Katy sat behind the wheel. *I must have been absent the day they taught us this in ambulance school,* she thought. After uttering a quick prayer, she eased out the clutch. The ambulance inched forward. There was a slight jar when the rope pulled taut. Katy pressed the accelerator and eased out on the clutch a little more.

The tail of the aeroplane came down with ease. Progress slowed when the full weight of the aeroplane engine was felt. Katy gave the ambulance more gas. The motor strained. Back tires spun in the mud.

Even more gas, more clutch.

A little movement was felt.

The tires spun, then caught.

The ambulance crept forward. One foot. Two. Three.

"He's clear!" Gillette shouted.

With a sigh, Katy applied the brake and cut the engine. She ran to the back of the ambulance, untied the rope, then circled the vehicle around toward the trees and the injured man.

CRACK!

This close to the front the sound was unmistakable. Gunfire!

Gillette spun around. His helmet went flying. He collapsed in a heap. Lifeless.

At the foot of the juniper trees, Laura was bending over the captain. Maxwell was crouched in a firing position, his rifle at the ready, his eyes scanning the terrain for a target. With a free hand he was waving at Katy.

"Get down! Sniper! Sniper!" he cried.

Get down? How does one get down when they're driving a . . .

CRACK!

Ping!

A bullet ricocheted off the front fender of the ambulance. Katy ducked, her eyes barely peering over the steering wheel. She accelerated. *Can't he see that this is an emergency vehicle?*

Maxwell spotted something. He raised his rifle and fired. His target, the sniper, was 200 yards away in a shell hole beyond the last tree in the row. Using her vehicle for cover, Katy drove the ambulance between the sniper and Sergeant Gillette. She tumbled out of the cab, landing on the ground next to him. He was moaning. A red line creased the side of his head.

"Sergeant! Sergeant!"

All the sergeant could do was moan and roll his head.

"This is going to be a lot easier on both of us if you can help me," Katy muttered.

Gillette stirred. His eyes opened but refused to focus.

Katy pulled the sergeant's arm around her neck to lift him up.

CRACK!

Bam!

One side panel of the ambulance erupted with splinters which rained down upon Katy and the sergeant.

"Private Maxwell! I need help! The sergeant's been hit!"

When no response was forthcoming, she craned her neck in the direction she had last seen Maxwell. Laura sat with her back against a tree trunk, cradling the head and shoulders of the captain in her lap. Maxwell was no longer with them. He was working his way up the row of trees in the general direction of the sniper.

CRACK!

Bam!

Another hole in the side of the ambulance and another shower of splinters.

"Come on, Sergeant," Katy moaned. "Let's get you in the ambulance."

"My helmet . . ." the sergeant muttered.

"Good. You're coming around. I'm going to try to get you on your feet. Do you think you can help me?"

At the sound of her voice, the sergeant swung his face toward hers. With his arm draped over her shoulder, they were cheek-to-cheek. He looked at Katy and cursed women in general. Then said, "My helmet . . ."

"Sergeant. There's a sniper. We have to get you into the back of the ambulance. But I can't do it alone, you've got to help me."

Something she said got through to him. His eyes focused with intelligent thought. Without a word, he pushed himself off the ground in an effort to stand.

"Whoa!" Katy cried. "Wait for me!"

He was woozy, unstable, but mobile. She helped him climb into the back of the ambulance.

CRACK!

Bam.

Two holes. One in each side. The bullet had passed through the ambulance directly over them.

Gillette threw a beefy arm around Katy and pulled her down on top of him. This close to the sergeant, she could feel his heart pounding against his chest. He could undoubtedly feel hers too.

"Where's Maxwell? The others?"

Hasty hands shoved against the sergeant's chest to get away. Katy swallowed an instinctive protest to the sergeant's unwanted familiarity. His action had been protective, not romantic.

She described to him the situation. His eyes blinked several times. He wiped his forehead with a sleeve and winced. He was having a hard time thinking. "We've got to . . . got to . . ."

CRACK!

They ducked. Nothing hit.

"I got 'im, Sarge! I got 'im!" Maxwell's voice carried clearly across the field.

"Maxwell!" Pain cut short Gillette's order. He cringed and held his head in his hands. To Katy, he said: "Tell him to stay low. There may be more than one sniper."

Katy shouted the message. Gillette winced at the volume of her voice too.

"Is he staying down?"

Maneuvering herself so she could see around the back of the ambulance, she scanned the trees. "He's moving from tree to tree in a crouched position. He's staying low."

"Privates!" Gillette cursed. "Not a brain in them. If I don't mother them, they go and get themselves killed."

Maxwell's voice carried across the field again. "There's only one of 'em, Sarge. I got him in the head. He's still alive!"

Gillette tried to get up. "Get me over there," he said.

Katy held him down. "I'll drive you over. You lie down."

The sergeant didn't put up a fight. He laid down on one of the stretchers in the back of the ambulance.

First, Katy drove to where Laura was sitting. The younger nurse's face was a combination of fear and relief. Unrestrained curls that had escaped from beneath her head-covering dangled as she looked down with compassion at the man in her lap. Blood stains smudged her coat, white apron, and hands.

Until now the full impact of Katy's decision to come to France had not hit her. Her mother had tried to talk her out of coming to the front. It was a token objection. Already, she had given her daughter up to the African mission field and life-threatening danger. What did it matter whether the danger took the form of a German rifle or a bushman's poison arrow?

Unlike Katy, Laura was reluctant to come. Her parents were ardently opposed to it. Over a period of weeks Katy wore her friend down with arguments and pleas. Then, in an attempt to soothe her conscience and knowing how difficult it had been for Laura to go against her parents' wishes, Katy made a pact with herself that she would protect Laura at the cost of her own life. It was a pact she fully intended to keep. But now, seeing Laura bloodied and shaken at the base of a tree, Katy realized how foolish her pact had been.

The blood on Laura's arms and hands could have easily been her own. She survived a sniper attack today, but what would happen tomorrow? An artillery shell? A cathedral caving in on top of her? There were any number of ways Laura could die in a war. And there was nothing Katy could do to stop it. Nothing.

"How is your patient doing, dear?" Katy asked.

"He slips in and out of consciousness. If we don't get him to the hospital soon, he isn't going to make it."

Katy retrieved a stretcher from the ambulance and while Maxwell guarded the German sniper, the two women loaded Captain Quigley into the back of the lorry next to Gillette.

"Where's Maxwell?" Gillette asked.

"He's our next stop," Katy answered.

Private Maxwell was proudly waiting for them at the rim of the shell crater. He held two rifles, his own and the sniper's, one in each hand. Beneath him lay the German sniper, his face covered with blood.

"Got him in the head," Maxwell boasted.

Laura stepped over the rim of the crater and slid down beside the sniper.

Maxwell was taken aback. "What do you think you're doing?"

Speaking to Katy, Laura said, "He has a head wound. I think he's blind. Get me some bandages." To Maxwell, she said, "Help me get this man into the ambulance."

Maxwell scowled at her. "He's a Boche!"

"He's a man!" Laura shouted. "And if we don't get him to a hospital, he'll die!"

"Let 'im die!" Maxwell shouted back. "He shot Sarge! And would have killed all of us if it hadn't been for me."

"Are you going to help me or not?" Laura asked.

Katy returned with bandages and a stretcher. Handing the bandages to Laura, she saw a fire in the girl's eyes that she had never seen before. For the moment at least, friendly, cheerful, lighthearted Laura had become a lioness.

"Leave him alone!" Maxwell ordered.

Laura continued bandaging her patient. "Can't do that," she said.

Turning to Katy, Maxwell asked, "If he were dead instead of wounded, you wouldn't take him in the ambulance, would you?"

It was clear what Maxwell was thinking. "But he isn't dead," she answered.

"I can fix that." Maxwell shouldered his rifle and aimed at the top of the German's head.

"Put that rifle down, Private!" Katy ordered.

"No, ma'am. That there is the enemy."

"I said, 'Put that rifle down!'" She reached for the rifle.

Maxwell deflected her hand. He grabbed the barrel and, using the rifle as a staff, he shoved Katy away, knocking her to the ground. Once again, he took aim at the German sniper.

"You might hit Laura!" Katy shouted.

"I'm an excellent marksman, ma'am."

Laura stared defiantly at Maxwell. Calmly, she stretched herself over the German, shielding him with her body.

A befuddled, frustrated expression formed on Maxwell's face. "Get off of him!" he shouted. "I'm going to shoot! Get off of him!"

Laura stared directly at him. "The bullet will have to go

through me first!"

"Put the rifle down, Maxwell," Katy shouted.

The private trembled with indecision.

"Maxwell! Put the rifle down!"

The order came from the direction of the ambulance. Sergeant Gillette stood there, steadying himself against the panel siding.

"Maxwell, put the rifle down!" he said again.

"But, Sarge, he. . . "

"I'm giving you an order. Put down the rifle!"

Slowly, with great reluctance, the barrel of the rifle lowered. Katy jumped up and stepped between the private and the sniper. She grabbed hold of the rifle and tried to take it from him. Maxwell tensed.

"We need you to help us carry him out of there," she said.

Maxwell looked to Sergeant Gillette, who nodded his agreement. Frustration turned to anger as he surrendered his rifle and the sniper's rifle to Katy who gave them to Gillette. Then, with Katy and Laura on one end of the stretcher and Maxwell on the other, they lifted the German sniper out of the shell hole and into the ambulance.

Wordlessly, Maxwell climbed into the back with the captain, Gillette, and the sniper. Katy and Laura took their places in front. As Katy turned the vehicle in the direction of the bombed-out cathedral, the dark skies overhead opened up. Once again a deluge fell from the heavens.

As Sergeant Gillette climbed out of the back of the ambulance, his eyes were clear and sharp, though he still had to nurse his pounding head with each step. Katy checked his wound before she would let him get away. It was a clean crease. He waved aside as inconsequential any expressed concern from the men who gathered around the ambulance.

Maxwell gained an instant audience as he related the events in the field, displaying his two trophies—the German rifle and the sniper himself—as testimonies to his noteworthy actions. Nothing was said about the incident on the ridge of the crater.

The German sniper was not the greatest attraction, though. An even greater number of soldiers gathered around the back of the ambulance to get a glimpse of Captain Quigley.

"An ace if there ever was one!"

"Thirty-two kills!"

"Thirty-three! Downed another Fokker a couple of days ago."

"Back away, boys!" Gillette shouted.

Katy winced for him. "You really ought to lie down for a while, Sergeant."

"Tend to your other patients," Gillette groused. He supervised the loading of two more stretchers onto the ambulance. "What about the sniper?" he asked. "How bad is he?"

"If he doesn't get to a hospital, he'll die."

Gillette glowered at her. "He's taking up the space for one of my boys."

"Do you have anyone worse off? Or can they wait for the next ambulance?"

He thought for a while, then looked up at the clouds. Rain splattered his chin and cheeks. "Doesn't look like it's going to let up. Roads are going to be as bad as I've ever seen them. Are you sure you can . . . " He stopped himself. The faintest hint of a smile formed on his lips. "Be careful on the roads," he said.

Katy smiled. "Thank you, Sergeant. And thank you for stopping Private Maxwell."

Gillette glanced over at the lanky private who was eagerly retelling his story to a new group of listeners. "He's a good kid. He wouldn't have fired."

"On that, we don't agree," she replied. "But thank you,

anyway."

The back doors of the ambulance were closed.

"We're ready," Laura reported.

Drenched, cold, and shivering, Katy climbed into the ambulance and started the engine. The tires spun in the mud as she started out. She slipped and slid her way carefully onto the road. In her side mirror, she saw Sergeant Gillette standing with his hands on his hips watching them leave.

The skies opened up. Visibility was no more than a dozen feet. Katy glanced over at Laura. Her head was bowed, her eyes closed. She held herself and shivered. It was going to be a long trip back to the hospital.

Chapter 20

D UE to the inclement weather, the return trip to the hospital took more than twice as long as it did under drier conditions. Add to that the amount of time that had been spent retrieving Captain Quigley from his aeroplane and Katy wasn't surprised that a large contingent of workers rushed out to them when they arrived.

The trip had been the most difficult journey Katy had ever made. To begin with, her nerves were on edge and her attention was heightened to a wearying degree simply in her attempt to keep the ambulance out of the ditch. Lives were depending upon her. One slip might mean hours of delay and possible death for any one of their patients.

Laura, normally a refreshing breeze in any situation, was a burden. For the entire journey she sat hunched over with her hands folded and clenched between her knees. Shivering. Her eyes were downcast and locked. She spoke not a word, not even in answer to a direct question. A castle gargoyle would have been more lively company.

Despite her best efforts, the ambulance jolted and rocked mercilessly. Katy flinched with every unexpected lurch, knowing that each jar meant agony for her patients. Their cries and moans tormented her.

The doors to the ambulance flew open the instant it came to a stop. Attendants she expected. Armed soldiers surprised her. Two contrasting choruses hit her.

"Where is the German sniper?"

"Where is Captain Quigley?"

In any other situation, Katy might have reproved them for their lack of professionalism. In accordance with procedure, each of the patients had been tagged at the cathedral. Each tag bore the patient's name and listed the patient's wound. *Name Unknown, German* had been written on the sniper's tag. However, considering the frenzied nature of the reception, she merely pointed to each one.

Quigley was whisked away first. The German was second to be pulled out.

"Morgue," the attendant said. "This one's dead."

The other two patients were removed and processed according to their wounds. Then, everyone rushed off. Other than the heightened frenzy, this was a typical hospital reception. A few moments of breathless action followed by a calm as everyone disappeared into the hospital leaving Katy and Laura with the ambulance.

Katy closed the back doors and walked to the passenger side. There, she saw Laura in the arms of Mrs. Graham Jones. The supervisor was whispering something in Laura's ear. The young girl nodded and thanked her with a weak voice.

Mrs. Jones looked up at Katy. She glanced at the bullet holes in the side of the ambulance, then said, "I understand you've had quite an adventure today, Miss Morgan."

"Yes, ma'am, we have," Katy replied.

"Has the ambulance sustained any damage other than these holes?"

"The radiator has been smelling hot all day. It probably needs to be serviced."

Mrs. Jones nodded. "Clean the vehicle as usual, then take it to maintenance. Take a few minutes to clean up yourselves," she glanced at the blood stains on Laura, "then come to my office. I want to talk to you."

"Yes, ma'am," both women said.

Mrs. Jones gave Laura's shoulder one last squeeze, then turned and entered the hospital.

"Are you all right?" Katy asked Laura.

"Let's get the ambulance cleaned," Laura said, refusing to look at Katy.

"Laura . . . " Katy pleaded.

"I'll be fine!" Laura insisted, grabbing some rags out of the side equipment box.

Katy wasn't so sure. She got the impression Laura said that just so that she'd stop asking.

"Miss Morgan, give me your impression of Sergeant Gillette."

Katy and Laura sat side-by-side in straight-back chairs facing Mrs. Graham Jones. A desk separated them. Actually, it was two barrels and a horizontal door, with the latch still in it, that served as a desk. The room barely accommodated all of them. Katy's knees rubbed against one of the barrels. She had to stand up and move her chair to open the door to get out.

Stacks of papers towered on the desk and in arrays against one wall. Motor gears and hoses and a variety of parts lay here and there. The walls were stained from leaks in the roof and the only thing attempting to cover them was a heavily marked-up rotation schedule for the drivers.

Hardly ever had Katy seen a room or an office that was so out of character for its occupant. Mrs. Jones was an organized, meticulous, disciplined woman. When it came to the task at hand, she was making the proverbial silk purse from a sow's ear.

"Your impression of Sergeant Gillette," Mrs. Jones said.

The supervisor's hair was brown and short, curled under neatly to keep it out of the way. Her eyes were serene and brown. Her manner, soft and compassionate. Yet despite her genteel appearance, she had a way of getting things done.

The question was a little unnerving. In all of Katy's debriefings, she had never been asked to give an impression of a person with whom she had worked. Naturally, she wondered what prompted the question now.

"He . . . Sergeant Gillette . . . is a capable leader, in my opinion," she said. "He took control when we pulled the aeroplane off Captain Quigley. And when we had a little difficulty with Private Maxwell, he stepped in and brought order to the situation."

"Difficulty?" Mrs. Jones said.

Mrs. Graham Jones was not one to toy with people. By asking the question, it was clear to Katy that she was not aware of the situation.

"Private Maxwell objected to Laura treating the German sniper."

Mrs. Jones leaned forward. "Did he threaten Miss Kelton?"

"Not directly," Katy replied. "He was threatening the German. Laura was getting in the way."

"I see. And that's when Sergeant Gillette stepped in?"

"Yes, ma'am. Having been wounded, he was lying in the back of the ambulance. When he heard the trouble, he came out and addressed the situation."

"I see." Mrs. Jones wrote on a pad of paper. "So you found working for Sergeant Gillette to be a pleasant experience?"

Katy wasn't ready to go that far. "In all truthfulness, Mrs. Jones, it took a while for us to prove to him that women could do the job of ambulance drivers, but once he saw that we were trained to do our jobs, he was supportive."

Mrs. Jones nodded. "I think you'll find that to be true in

most of the situations you will face, Miss Morgan."

"If I may . . . " Katy asked.

Mrs. Jones nodded, giving her permission to proceed.

"Why are you asking me questions about Sergeant Gillette? Has there been some kind of complaint?"

A warm smile was the initial response. "On the contrary," she replied, "it seems our Sergeant Gillette was quite taken by you and your abilities. He radioed us of your situation, alerting us of both Captain Quigley's and the German sniper's presence."

"That was kind of him."

"Kind is hardly the word I'd use," Mrs. Jones said, chuckling. "How about *unusual, unheard of,* or *miraculous?* More than one of our ambulance drivers has returned in tears from the cathedral and our Sergeant Gillette."

Katy didn't know what to say.

"He has requested you and Miss Kelton whenever your schedule permits. Any objections?"

"Not from me," Katy said.

Laura shook her head slightly.

"Very well, then," said Mrs. Jones. "You are both to be congratulated. You have done exemplary work. Now you'd both better get some sleep. Your shift starts again in less than four hours."

Laura led the way down the hospital hallway to the nurses' quarters.

"Laura?"

The girl didn't slow down.

Katy ran to catch up. "Laura?" She grabbed the girl by the arm. Laura stopped in the middle of the hallway and sighed in resignation.

"Laura, dear, please tell me what's bothering you," Katy said.

Laura wouldn't look her in the eyes. She said, "I'm tired and want to be alone, that's all."

"Have I done something to hurt you?"

In response, Laura resumed walking.

Katy let her go.

"Miss Morgan! Wake up! Miss Morgan!"

A hand rocked her side-to-side.

"A train will be here in ten minutes, Miss Morgan!"

Katy glanced up at the woman shaking her. A short-haired, stocky orderly. Nodding, to indicate that she was awake, she swung her legs over the side of the bed and looked at the clock. Five-thirty A.M. She moaned and rubbed tired eyes. Though she had gone straight to bed, she had slept less than an hour.

By the number of drivers pouring out into the hallway, Katy surmised the evacuation train was a huge one. They were all headed toward the garage to sign out their vehicles. Katy saw Laura ahead, buttoning her coat. She quickened her step to catch up with her.

Exiting the building, Laura walked several strides before she realized someone was beside her. She greeted Katy with a weak smile.

"At least the sun's out today," Katy commented.

Laura looked up at the sky. It was patchy with clouds. The day could go either way. The clouds could disperse and give them a sunny day, or they could join forces and persecute the land once more with more rain than it could absorb.

"Feeling better?" Katy asked.

Laura nodded slightly.

"Listen, Laura, if I've done anything . . . "

"It's not you," Laura said. "It's me."

"Would you like to talk about it?"

"Maybe later. No promises."

"No promises," Katy replied.

Compared to the day before, their shift was an easy one. A taxi service basically. The wounded were lined up on stretchers in front of the hospital. A long string of ambulances lined up to carry them to the evacuation train. From there they would be ferried across the channel to London.

Katy and Laura would wait in line, load up, drive to the station, unload, and come back for more. The streets were paved, though still wet; the patients were stable and, for the most part, in a pleasant mood because they were going home.

"Reminds me of freight," a private with a leg wound said, taking a last look around as he was loaded into the ambulance.

"Freight?" Katy echoed.

"I worked at a train yard one summer," the private replied. "Spent all day checking tags and loading boxes. Same as here, only instead of boxes it's human freight."

"Hopefully, we take a little better care of you, Private."

"Roger. Call me Roger."

"Sorry, I can't do that, Private."

For the entire ride from the hospital to the train station, Roger saw fit to entertain everyone within hearing distance with his hospital experience. Two of the other patients were so heavily drugged, they didn't mind what he did. If the third patient, a chest wound, minded, he didn't say anything.

"The day I was brought in, it was pounding rain something awful! 'Course, the first thing they do after taking your name—which they will never use while you're with them—is to dehumanize you. You know, they reduce you to vital statistics. Regiment. Rank. Nature and date of the wound.

"Then, they stripped me and rubbed me with a warm sponge. Ahhhh, now that was a heavenly experience! None of us in the trenches had been able to wash for days! Not for lack of water, mind you. We're up to our waists in it.

"'Course, after such a glorious experience the nurses are quick to remind you you're in a hospital, not some resort. It was a very pointed and unwelcome reminder, if I do say so myself."

"The anti-tetanus injection," Katy offered with a grin.

"Torturers! All of you!" he cried. "Well, let's see, after that, we were put on a stretcher again and moved to a waiting room. In the army you stand in line for everything, but I never thought I'd have to stand in line to be operated on! While I was there, I heard someone call my name. It was this fellow from my old battalion! Imagine running into old friends waiting to be operated on.

"Well, they put me on the table and decided I didn't need an operation after all! Put my leg in a splint and sent me on my merry way, they did! And then! Then!" He cupped his hand to one side of his mouth like he was sharing secret information. "You have to know what it's like day after day living like a gopher in miles of trenches and caves to appreciate this . . . Sheets! They put me between sheets! I was so happy, I almost cried!

"Living on the hospital ward was a depressing bother, though. I don't know how you nurses stand it, day in and day out. Beside me was an officer who was shot through the stomach. He was dying and there was nothing anybody could do about it. Right across from me were two other officers. They were coming out of ether and were always asking the nurse to hold their hands or smooth their brows. From what I hear, I had a good ward. The one next to me was pure bedlam. Blokes were crying and moaning and screaming all the time.

"This morning we had pancakes for breakfast. They attached new cards to us. Our travel orders. Then we were set outside to wait for you ambulance drivers. At least it wasn't raining. I've heard that even if it's raining, they don't move you back inside. . . ."

Katy interrupted him. "All aboard evacuation train number ten!"

Private Roger strained to see his tag. "Ten! That's me. How many stretchers do they load in a single car?"

"Sixteen," Katy said, climbing out.

Private Roger continued to talk while he was unloaded and was still talking as he was carried away and loaded onto the hospital train. Katy and Laura looked at each other and laughed.

"Are you sure that fellow was British?" Laura asked. "The way his tongue was wagging, I could swear he was Irish!"

Katy laughed, harder than the humor warranted. It was just good to see Laura happy again.

They rode in silence on the way back to the hospital to get their next load. About halfway back, Laura said softly, "It's nice, isn't it?"

"What's that?"

"The silence."

The two of them laughed again.

"Katy?"

"Yes?"

"I want to apologize for yesterday."

"Apologize? My dear, whatever for? You did nothing wrong."

"I was angry with you."

Katy looked over at her friend. Laura's eyes were downcast. One hand picked self-consciously at the fingernails of the other.

"Actually, I was scared," she said. "Scared more than I've ever been in my life."

Nodding, Katy indicated she understood.

"When that German sniper started firing at us and Sergeant Gillette went down . . . then Private Maxwell left me at that tree by myself . . . and when you were inside the ambulance and it was hit . . . I thought we were all going to die."

She began to weep. Katy reached over and took her hand. Laura wiped tears away with her other hand.

"It was as though life was unraveling and I couldn't stop it! It was dark. I was sitting under a tree in a field I'd never seen before, in a land not my own, with a half-dead man in my lap, not able to see what was going on behind me because if I leaned one way or the other I knew I'd get a bullet in my head.

"I began to shake. And I couldn't stop shaking. I knew I was going to die. I knew I'd never see my parents again. In my mind I could see them reading a letter from Mrs. Jones telling them that I had died in a French field. I could see my father putting his arm around my mother to comfort her. I could hear my mother saying over and over, 'She never should have gone. We tried to tell her, but she wouldn't listen! She never should have gone! She never should have gone!'"

Katy released Laura's hand and covered her mouth in an attempt to hold back her own tears.

"And all I could think," Laura said, "was that God was punishing me for disobeying my parents. He was going to let me die in a muddy French field far away from my parents and I'd never be able to tell them that I loved them again, or that they were right and I never should have come to France. And then I thought of you and concluded that this was all your fault. I was happy in London. I didn't want to come to France. You made me. I didn't want to come. I should have listened to . . . "

Sniffles turned to sobs.

Katy joined her. She drove down a blurry road. "You're absolutely right," she said. "I sensed it in the field too. I was being selfish. I never should have talked you into coming with me."

"No," Laura said, wiping back tears. "It's not your fault."

"But you just said . . ."

"Yesterday I blamed you. Yesterday I was convinced it was your fault. But it's not. I know that now."

"Why the change of heart?"

"The German sniper."

Katy shot Laura a quizzical look.

"When we reached him and I slid down into that crater, I realized he was just a boy, not God's angel of judgment! He was whimpering when I first got to him. His eyes were fixed and filled with blood. I knew he couldn't see. But he could sense that I was there. He lifted his hand to me. And I took it. It was as cold as a dead man's hand. He knew it. I knew it. And he was scared. O Katy, he was so scared."

They reached the hospital. Katy pulled behind the last ambulance in a long line of ambulances as they waited their turn for their next load. She was relieved. The steady flow of her tears had been making it more and more difficult for her to see to drive.

"Do you understand what I'm saying, Katy? That German boy was afraid, just as I had been afraid. He was in a field far from his home, from his parents and brothers and sisters. I knew just how he felt! He was scared. And there was no one there for him, except me. When I held his hand, I could feel him relax. He knew he wasn't going to die alone. Someone was there who understood. Who cared."

As the line of ambulances pulled forward, Katy moved their vehicle forward.

"His name was Wilhelm," Laura said. "He told me when we were at the cathedral. Of course, most of what he said I couldn't understand, but there was no mistaking the tone of his voice. He was grateful that I was there. He was holding my hand when he died. I didn't tell anyone, because I was afraid of what Maxwell or some of the others might do to his body."

Laura sniffed and wiped her nose.

"It took me awhile to sort through all that," she said. "But I know beyond any doubt that this is where I'm supposed to be. I believe God allowed me to feel what I felt in that field to make me a better nurse. Katy, please forgive me for being so hard on you. I don't know what I'd do without you. You're so strong. You're my inspiration."

Katy shook her head, her eyes overflowing. "No, dear, it is you who are the inspiration."

They hugged as best they could in the cramped quarters. The last of the ambulances in front of them pulled away with a full load, so Katy and Laura jumped out—both with red, puffy eyes—to load up with patients waiting to be shipped home.

Katy glided down the hallway, her head buried in her daily driving log, giving it one last review before delivering it to Mrs. Jones. She rounded a corner and ran headlong into four RAF pilots.

"Well, I'll be!" one of them exclaimed.

"Do you know the lady, Freddie?" a short redhead asked.

Katy pulled back and gathered her papers and her wits.

"Gentlemen, allow me to introduce Miss Katy Morgan. An American."

"A Yank!" cried the redhead. "And a good-looking one too!" He launched into his rendition of a popular song, "K-K-K-Katy, beautiful Katy..."

His three comrades groaned. They all put hands on him, one pair around his throat, to shut him up.

"Stop drooling, Smythe," Radcliff said.

"Introduce us to this fair maiden!" the tallest of them said.

Radcliff conceded with obvious pleasure. With a sly wink he said, motioning to his friends, "Miss Morgan, allow me to introduce the most disreputable band of pilots you'd ever want to meet. This rather tall but decidedly ugly gentleman is Cedric McCubbin."

A rakish grin from the thin pilot pulled back leather cheeks in folds as McCubbin nodded his greeting.

"And this fellow," Radcliff put his hand on a black-haired man his own height who sported a box-like jaw, "is probably the worst dart player in the history of Great Britain." Hoots of good-natured derision came from the other two friends. "His name is Albert Staton."

"Pleased to meet you, ma'am," Staton said. "And if indeed you have the misfortune of knowing Freddie Radcliff here, you have my sympathies."

Radcliff laughed. "And this redheaded weasel," he motioned toward the shortest among them, "is Willy Jordan."

Jordan took Katy's hand and dropped to one knee. "I do believe I've met the woman I'm going to marry!"

Katy nodded to them all. "Gentlemen," she said. "It's been a pleasure. Now if you'll excuse me. . . ." She tried to retrieve her hand. Jordan wouldn't let it go.

"Unhand the fair maiden!" the lanky McCubbin said. When Jordan refused, he grabbed the smaller redhead from behind and pulled him away. "I believe our good friend Freddie here would like a moment with this young lady."

Radcliff nodded appreciatively as McCubbin and Staton pulled Jordan away.

"I'll expect this favor to be returned someday," McCubbin said.

"You'd better be a gentleman with my future wife,

Radcliff!" Jordan cried. "If I hear otherwise, I'll come back and . . ."

McCubbin clamped a hand over Jordan's mouth. They disappeared around a corner. The slam of a door signaled their exit.

Radcliff shrugged somewhat sheepishly. "They're good blokes," he said. "They just get a little bonkers around women."

"Odd," Katy said, "I would have guessed they acted that way around everyone. I'd love to stay and chat, but I have to get this report to my supervisor." She attempted to move forward. He intercepted her.

"So you're assigned here? To this hospital?"

Katy nodded. "I'm an ambulance driver."

"An ambulance driver? That's rather dangerous, isn't it?"

Katy smiled. "To quote a mutual friend: 'Occasions of adversity best discover how great virtue and strength each one hath. For occasions do not make a man frail, but they shew what he is.'"

"Thomas à Kempis!" Radcliff's eyebrows raised in delight. He was clearly impressed.

"Laura is here too."

"Laura?"

"Curly hair. Always smiling. The young lady in the archway with her male friend the night the Zeppelins attacked."

"Laura! Yes, now I remember! An ambulance driver too?"

"We're a team. And how about you? I thought you would have had your fill of hospitals in London."

"I'm stationed at the St. Marie Cappel," Radcliff replied. "The other blokes and I came to visit our commanding officer. His plane went down a few days ago."

"Captain Quigley?"

Radcliff's entire face brightened to a degree Katy had never seen before. "You know the captain?" he cried.

"Laura and I were the ones who brought him in."

"No!"

"It's a matter of record."

"But we heard there was a German sniper and . . . you! It was really you?"

Katy nodded.

"Well, well, we have come a long way from London and that old Yank 'this-is-not-my-war' attitude, haven't we?"

Katy was not amused at being the source of his humor. "It was nice seeing you again, Lieutenant Radcliff," she said coolly.

"Wait, please wait," Radcliff cried. "That came out all wrong. What I meant was that you seem a much stronger woman than you were then. You're taking quite a risk doing what you're doing."

"Thank you. Now if you'll excuse me, I really . . . "

"Are you free this afternoon?" Radcliff asked.

She had the entire day off. She just didn't know if she wanted to give that information to Fred Radcliff. Laura had gone shopping with some of the other nurses and Katy was catching up on her paperwork. "I might be free . . . " she ventured.

"There is a concert here at the hospital this afternoon," Radcliff said. "Miss Lena Ashwell arranges them. She's a friend of my mother and . . . "

"Who isn't a friend of your mother?" Katy cried with a grin.

"Who indeed?" Radcliff laughed with her, in no way offended. "Anyway, I promised my mother I would attend one of Miss Ashwell's concerts. It would be so much more palatable for me if you would attend too. Please say yes."

Katy hedged. "I don't know . . . I have a lot of paperwork to catch up with . . . I'm not sure I have time to go out with . . . "

"Don't think of it as going out with me," he interjected. "Think of it as part of your nursing duties. I know I'll be sick if I have to attend one of Miss Ashwell's concerts alone!"

"You exaggerate," Katy said.

"Unfortunately, I do not. For if you do not go with me, I will be forced to drag McCubbin or possibly even Jordan along with me."

Shaking her head, Katy laughed at the mental image of Jordan at a concert. She felt herself giving in to Radcliff. She resisted. She didn't want to go with him. But he looked so puppy-dog sad.

"What time?" she asked.

Radcliff interpreted her question as an acceptance. "Great!" he cried. "On the green. One o'clock. I'm forever in your debt!"

He was gone before she could say anything else.

Chapter 21

AS the hour of one in the afternoon approached, Katy wished she hadn't agreed to attend the concert. Actually, she hadn't agreed. But then, she didn't stop Radcliff from believing she'd agreed. But did that mean she was irrevocably stuck?

She considered not showing up. There was her paperwork that needed to be done. Hospital business. Certainly he would understand that. But then not showing up, or at least by not informing Lieutenant Radcliff that she would not be attending, would be rude. Such a cowardly approach might reflect on her character as a nurse.

As the hour loomed closer, the more irritable she became. *When am I going to learn to say no to people?* She looked at the unfinished report forms stacked on the small wooden nightstand next to her bed. Reaching for a pen and a piece of paper, she began to write –

Dear Lt. Radcliff,
   It is with sincere regret that I inform you I will be unable to accept your kind offer to accompany you to the concert this afternoon. Unfortunately, my work demands prohibit me from attending. Thank you for understanding.
               Sincerely,
               Miss Katy Morgan

The concert had not yet started when Katy arrived.

Several hundred patients and hospital staff had gathered on the grassy courtyard for the concert. Lieutenant Fred Radcliff waved to her from the far side of the green. Weaving her way between stretchers and around portable hospital beds and chairs occupied by hospital patients with every conceivable wound, she finally reached him while members of the small orchestra tuned their instruments and warmed up.

"I was afraid you wouldn't come," Radcliff said, taking her hand.

"What gave you that impression?" Katy asked.

He offered her a seat on a blanket spread out on the grass. A plate of cheese and grapes was laid out. Two glass goblets filled with clear liquid were carefully nestled in the grass.

"I'm afraid it's only water," Radcliff said. "It was the best I could do on short notice."

Pulling her legs under her, Katy reached for a goblet and sipped. "This is fine," she said. "Very thoughtful."

He was pleased that she was pleased.

The orchestra instruments grew silent as a petite woman with short brown hair appeared from one side and stood in front of them. She folded her hands and rested them against her midsection as she prepared to speak.

Radcliff leaned toward Katy and whispered, "Miss Lena Ashwell."

His breath tickled Katy's ear. She resisted the urge to rub it. More uncomfortable to her than the itching ear was how close Fred Radcliff was sitting to her. He leaned on one hand, his head and her head inches away. A little too familiar for Katy's comfort.

"Isn't this a gorgeous day?" Miss Ashwell said, doing her best to project her voice so that all could hear. "As you know we have had some horribly gray days earlier this week, and I feared we would have to cancel today's concert. But look at this!" She held her hands upward. "Not a cloud in the sky!"

The audience applauded enthusiastically.

As Katy applauded, she increased the distance between her and Radcliff. The lieutenant had to sit up to applaud. When the applause died down, he leaned back on his hand, closing any additional distance Katy had created between them.

Did he do that on purpose? Katy glanced at Radcliff, fully prepared to tell him to stay on his own side of the blanket. The lieutenant was focused completely on the speaker. He gave no indication that he was aware of what he'd done.

"Allow me to introduce myself," Miss Ashwell said. "My name is Miss Lena Ashwell and it is my . . . "

She was interrupted by applause.

"Thank you. Truly, thank you," she said. When the applause died down, she continued. "It is my pleasure on behalf of the Ladies' Auxiliary Committee of the Y.M.C.A. to welcome you to today's concert."

More applause.

Miss Ashwell then proceeded to introduce the concert members. There were four vocalists: a soprano, contralto, bass, and a tenor. Instrumentalists included two violinists, a cellist, a clarinetist, a trumpeter, and a pianist.

"Let me tell you about the sacrifice these fine people make on your behalf," Miss Ashwell said. "It is not uncommon for them to perform three times a day. After this concert, they will pack up and travel 30 kilometers to the front where they will give another concert tonight. It is not unusual for them to perform under shell fire."

The courtyard filled with appreciative applause.

"We have another troupe who performs plays. It's a small group of actors, but we have done *Macbeth* and *The School for Scandal.*" She laughed good-naturedly. "I remember one performance of *The School.* We performed in the woods. Half our audience was seated on the grass, like here; and the other half was dangerously perched on tree limbs! I thought for sure someone would fall out of a tree before the performance was over! Another time, we performed *Macbeth* in a great aeroplane hangar with army blankets for the walls of the great banquet hall scene and a sugar-box for the throne!"

She laughed at the memory. Her audience laughed and applauded.

"Why do we do it?" Miss Ashwell asked. "Why do we put ourselves at risk? Why do we endure such primitive artistic settings? We do it for the men who wait for hours just to get a seat at one of our concerts. In fact, one soldier told me that he would rather miss a meal than one of our concerts. Why do we do it? We do it for the soldiers who write letters of appreciation like this one—"

She extracted a piece of paper from the belt of her dress, unfolded it, and read:

> *Dear Miss Ashwell and members of the concert orchestra,*
> *How can we ever thank you? Your concerts hearten the men on the front and send us back to the firing-line happy and with the feeling that the people who are home really do care for us and are trying to do something to help.*

Gripping the letter between her thumb and forefinger, Miss Ashwell lifted it high and said, "Why do we do it? We do these concerts for men like this. For men and women like you here today who are risking your lives for the cause of freedom. We're here because you're here! This concert is for you. May God bless you!"

The orchestra struck up the first chord before Miss Ashwell got off the stage area. The applause that accompanied her nearly drowned out the music.

"She has always had a flair for the dramatic," Radcliff said, leaning into Katy's ear.

Katy didn't look at him. She merely nodded her head.

The program that followed was a varied one. It contained classical pieces, selections from operas, solos, duets, and trios; old ballads and folk songs, as well as ragtime tunes and modern choruses.

The concert itself was wonderful. Between the waves of music washing over her and the afternoon sun warming her, it was sheer heaven. Katy closed her eyes and relaxed for the first time in months.

Just when she would reach a point when she was about to be absorbed completely by the melody or lyrics of a particular piece, Radcliff's whispering voice would sound in her ear, rudely breaking the melodious spell.

She learned two significant things about Lieutenant Fred Radcliff's personality that day. He was not a lover of music and he had a short attention span.

"Are you enjoying yourself?"

It was intermission and Radcliff had leaned toward her to ask the question. Katy stood up.

"The music is wonderful! Very therapeutic," she said, stretching.

Radcliff stood and stretched with her.

"Then you're glad you came?" he asked.

"I haven't felt so relaxed in a long time."

Her answer pleased Radcliff.

"So, tell me about your family," Katy said. "And this mother of yours who knows everybody." Her question was purely an offensive maneuver. She wanted to control the subject of their conversation, preferring to talk about him, not her, and by all means to keep from talking about *them*. Since, in her opinion, there was no *them*.

"Not much to tell," Radcliff began in a matter-of-fact way. "My mother is a patron of the arts and something of a good-natured gadfly. She enjoys supporting causes and is quite good at it. Father is a banker. Quite successful."

"Are you? Will you be going into the banking business?"

"Heavens, no!" Radcliff cried. "I despise all that financial rubbish. Give me an open field, an aeroplane, and the sky and I'm happy."

"Hmmph," Katy grunted. He was just like her brother in that.

"But tell me about what happened the other day with Captain Quigley," Radcliff asked, folding his arms across his chest.

He'd changed the subject. Brought it back to her. But it was a safe enough topic. Her work. The war. She narrated the events of Captain Quigley's rescue.

"Tell me," she said, "what was he doing up in the air in the first place? The weather was horrendous!"

"Not when he took off!" Radcliff rose quickly and passionately to his captain's defense. "He'd been down a good day and a half when you found him."

"I didn't know that."

Radcliff nodded vigorously. "He'd gone on a scouting mission. Signaled the rest of us to return to base. We figured he'd spotted something of strategic importance on the ground that he wanted to investigate before returning."

"When he didn't return, didn't you go looking for him?"

"It was dark by then. Besides, we'd encountered heavy ack-ack on the way."

"Ack-ack?"

"Antiaircraft fire," he said. "Most of our squadron took at

least one hit. Besides, the storm had come in. There was nothing we could do but wait. To tell you the truth, most of us thought we'd lost him for good. Being around the barracks was something awful that day. You would have thought royalty had died."

"How is the captain now? I haven't had a chance to check in on him."

Radcliff sobered. "He lost both of his legs above the knee."

"At least he's alive."

Shaking his head, Radcliff replied, "He'll never fly again. Might as well be dead."

"Nonsense!"

He took a good hard look at her. "Apparently, you don't know pilots," he said.

"On the contrary, I'm afraid I know them all too well," Katy scoffed.

"That's right, your brother..."

"Believe me, I understand them completely. But understanding them and sharing their values are two different things!"

They stood in silence. For the first time that afternoon, Radcliff was subdued. Katy knew she had overreacted, but maybe it was just as well. Maybe by pointing out their incompatibilities, she had accomplished what she needed to accomplish. She had discouraged his advances.

Radcliff stood there, his hands in his pockets, and sulked. Katy felt bad. He was decent enough, for a man. Handsome enough with his brown mustache, standing there in his uniform. He was considerate. After all, he'd brought a blanket, cheese, and goblets for the afternoon. But he was a man. And a man of the worst sort, a pilot. And Katy was not interested in men. She had seen too many women abandon their noble efforts for the sake of a man, and she was determined that was not going to happen to her.

Miss Lena Ashwell walked to the front of the staging area. It was time for the second half of the program to begin. She started to say something, then spotted Radcliff. Interrupting herself, she dashed over and hugged him happily.

"Freddie! It's so good to see you!" she bubbled. "Your mother told me I might run into you here! How is she? Have you heard recently?"

"Mother's fine," Radcliff said. "Busy, as usual."

"I've never seen a woman with so many irons in the fire all at once!" Turning to Katy, she said, "And who might this be?"

Radcliff introduced her.

"Why, she's lovely, Freddie! And a nurse!"

"We're just friends," Radcliff said.

Katy was glad to hear it. She wanted to say it, but thought it might hurt him and she'd hurt him enough already for one afternoon.

Miss Ashwell shrugged her shoulders and smiled, as though she knew a secret they didn't know. "My advice? Give it time! It wouldn't be the first time friends turned into lovers! Maybe our music will help get you started in a romantic direction. It could happen, couldn't it?"

Katy blushed. So did Radcliff. It was evident his mind was racing for something to say in response. His lips moved, but there were no words.

"Got to go!" Miss Ashwell said. "They can't start without me!"

While the vivacious Miss Ashwell announced the second half of the program, Radcliff looked over at Katy and shrugged apologetically. "I'm sorry..."

Waving a hand, Katy said, "She meant well. She obviously likes you."

Radcliff started to say something when the tenor, a tall balding man, let loose with a voice that overpowered every other sound in the courtyard.

Katy turned her attention to the music. So did Radcliff.

They were only three selections into the second half when an arm-waving woman on the other side of the courtyard caught her eye.

Mrs. Graham Jones.

She was motioning to Katy. Turning to Radcliff, she pointed to her supervisor and excused herself. Radcliff acknowledged her departure.

"Thank you for inviting me," Katy said. But he didn't hear her. He was listening intently to the soprano soloist who's voice was so strong it made the tenor sound like a muffled child.

Mrs. Jones apologized for calling her away from the concert, then said, "I need an answer from you right away. I have been asked to select my best team for a special training project with the French. Do you speak French?"

Katy shook her head.

"You will soon."

Chapter 22

"I'M cursed! There's no other explanation for it. I'm cursed!"

The American base squadron commander halted two-thirds of the way down the row of his most recent batch of pilots, recent graduates of College Park, Maryland. A full head taller than the new arrival that stood at attention before him, the muscular commander stared at him with steely blue eyes.

"Morgan," he said as though the word was a piece of filth that he was trying to work off his tongue.

"Johnny Morgan, sir!"

"And Hill, isn't it?"

"Percy Hill, sir!"

"Gentlemen . . . is this a joke?" the commander asked. Turning around and looking for someone who wasn't there, he shouted, "Is this a joke? Someone, please tell me this is a joke!"

No one answered him. The new arrivals stood ramrod straight in a perfect line. Four enormous hangars arched side-by-side in front of them. Aeroplanes of French design were lined up impressively for inspection. Behind them a grassy green field stretched eastward, in the direction of the enemy.

The commander's shouting brought a French general scurrying from the nearest hangar.

"Is something wrong, Captain?" the general asked.

The commander snapped to attention. "No, sir!"

"Then why are you yelling like that?"

"Just disappointment, sir."

"Disappointment?"

"Yes, sir. Disappointment in the quality of the men they sent me."

The French general scanned the row of pilots. His shaking head indicated he saw nothing wrong with them.

"Only two of them, sir. Previous acquaintances."

"Which two?"

Captain Eastman introduced the French general to Lieutenants Percy Hill and Johnny Morgan. "Are you two troublemakers?" the general asked.

"No, sir!" Percy shouted.

"Not troublemakers, General," Johnny said. "Pilots. Excellent pilots, sir."

One eyebrow raised on the general's forehead. He was obviously not pleased with Johnny's arrogance.

"Sir, if I may . . . " Eastman tried to interrupt.

The general stepped in front of Johnny. Toe to toe. "You are a superior pilot?" he asked.

"Yes, sir."

"And for this, your commanding officer is displeased?"

Johnny grinned. "My commanding officer is displeased because I gave him a flying lesson in Mexico that he will never forget."

Johnny Morgan's first night in France at the American 59th Pursuit Squadron based just outside of Amiens was spent on KP for insubordination.

Johnny Morgan sat securely in the mount of his Spad 7 aeroplane. He flew the right wing side of a three-aeroplane formation. Percy Hill flew the left wing side. Captain

Eastman flew center position.

"I want to keep an eye on you," he said.

It felt good to be in the air again. The voyage over, holed up in the belly of a ship for days on end, was unbearable. This was where he was supposed to be, doing what he was supposed to be doing with the ground thousands of feet below him, the roar of the engine in his ears, and the rush of the wind against his face. There was nothing in life comparable to flying.

The Spad was a good plane. It couldn't out-turn a Nieuport or most of the German aircraft, but it could handle steep dives without losing a wing. Durable, reliable, fast.

Now if it only had a gun.

Being a neutral in the war had its disadvantages. American fliers flew French aeroplanes under French control and then only reconnaissance. Instead of a gun, the Spad was armed with a camera.

As good as it felt to be in the air, flying in formation with Eastman was boring. No sooner had they reached 7,000 feet when Johnny wanted to test the Spad. He waggled the wings. Eastman shook his head no, ordering Johnny to stop. He tightened the formation, seeing how close he could get to Eastman's wing. The commander motioned him to move away. If Eastman had his way, they would do nothing more than fly a few miles over the enemy lines, snap a few pictures of the troops below, then fly back and land.

Johnny wanted more. He hadn't trained to be a flying photographer. He wanted action. He longed to get into a dogfight with some German aeroplanes.

It would help, though, if he had a gun.

If they were to encounter hostile aeroplanes, their orders were to turn back immediately. Under no circumstances were they to engage the enemy. After all, they had no guns.

Eastman waved a hand to get Johnny's attention. He

pointed down at the ground.

Johnny sighed. Time to get to work. He readied his camera, and leaned over the side.

Click.

Pulling the camera back into the aeroplane, he advanced the film. Leaning over again, he took a second shot.

Click.

At this rate, I'll be an ace in no time.

Eastman was signaling again. Johnny ignored him. He probably wanted pictures from the other side of the aeroplane.

Click.

Eastman's hand was waving furiously.

Johnny glanced over. Even at a distance with goggles covering the commander's eyes, Johnny could see the fear. Eastman's hand was pointing upward at a one o'clock position.

German Fokkers! Three of them!

Three against three. Even odds. We can take them!

If they had guns.

Hill and Eastman banked, descended, and raced toward friendly airspace. Johnny stared at the Fokkers. His blood raced. More than anything he wanted to engage them. To test his skills against their skills. To blast them out of the sky.

Think of it! Three of them! I could return three-fifths of the way toward becoming an ace!

If his Spad had a gun.

He had an idea. He didn't have a gun, but he had a camera. If he could get close enough to take their picture . . . it might not count as a kill, but he would know he could have downed them. If he had a gun!

They hadn't spotted him yet. Accelerating, Johnny approached them from underneath. Three Fokkers. In formation. Johnny Morgan coming up fast.

He was on them before they knew it.

Click!

Johnny split their formation between the two aeroplanes forming the V. The expression on their faces was priceless!

He singled out one of them. Got on his tail and closed in for the kill.

Click!

"Got him!"

The sound of machine-gun fire came from behind him. Pieces of fabric from his right wing went flying as bullets ripped through it. He'd been hit!

Johnny dove left. He looked behind him. The Fokker was still on his tail!

Feinting right, he pulled the stick hard left and accelerated. The Fokker was fooled!

Again, he heard the repeating thud of machine-gun fire. The second Fokker strafed his tail. His controls were damaged. The third Fokker was closing in on him. A hard right turn barely avoided its deadly stream of bullets.

He was outnumbered and . . .

If I only had a gun!

But he didn't. They did.

Leveling his aeroplane, he slowed. He waggled his wings. Two Fokkers took up positions beside him, one behind. Johnny signaled to them by pointing down. He was going to land. He was offering them a captured pilot and a captured aeroplane in exchange for his life.

The pilot on his right nodded, giving him permission to land.

He found a large field and made his approach. One of the Fokkers split off. Apparently, he was going to report the good news to their superiors.

Johnny landed on the German field. The two remaining Fokkers landed behind him. He taxied a short distance and stopped. He waited.

The German pilots shut off their engines and climbed out of their planes.

Johnny smiled. He knew he had them now.

Drawing revolvers from their uniforms they approached him. He let them get about a hundred feet from their aeroplanes, then he pulled out the throttle as far as it would go. His Spad rumbled across the field. Behind him, the two German fliers chased him on foot. Shouting. Shooting at him with their pistols.

Johnny swooped into the air. He circled the field and strafed the two embarrassed German pilots who were furiously attempting to start their engines.

Click.

With a friendly wave, Johnny Morgan flew back to his aerodrome on the French side of the war. For his disobedience to an order from his commanding officer, Johnny Morgan was given eight days house arrest. But the pictures he took circulated around the squadron long after he was released.

Chapter 23

COLONEL Edward House strolled casually alongside Jesse on the Manhattan side of the East River. It was a sunny Sunday afternoon and the boardwalk near the tip of the island was crowded with recreational traffic.

Freshly relieved of their stiff church clothes, children skipped and hopped and whooped and hollered on their way to the beach, a park, Coney Island, or any number of weekend amusements. Men wearing straw hats pitched balls and swung bats in anticipation of the upcoming baseball season. Women strolled the boardwalk, the wind whipping the edges of their dresses and the ribbons in their bonnets. The streets were teaming with vehicles—streetcars, buggies, and automobiles. It was an unusually warm weekend for early spring and everyone had someplace to go.

Colonel House tipped his hat to a stylish young couple walking the opposite direction. Both man and woman were pushing a baby carriage. He paused and watched them pass before resuming his stroll with a sigh.

"Enjoy it while you can," he muttered loud enough only for Jesse to hear.

Jesse studied the man walking beside him. House had become his regular contact with the White House. The man had aged in the time Jesse had known him. Probably due to the pressures of his position. It would not be exaggerating to think that House knew everything President Wilson knew. The President consulted with him on every decision.

His relationship to Jesse was professional. House made it a point always to ask after Emily and Katy and Johnny, but Jesse wouldn't say that he and House were close friends. The man was business-minded, efficient, and thorough. But not warm.

This was the first time Jesse had seen him subdued to this great a degree. *Something important must be coming down.* And it wasn't hard for Jesse to guess what it was.

At all their previous meetings, House had determined the agenda. The meetings concluded with him giving Jesse an opportunity to bring up anything they might have missed. Jesse never did because House never missed anything. So Jesse concluded that if House wanted him to know the reason for his enjoy-it-while-you-can remark, he would tell him. When he was ready, and not before.

House paused once again. Shielding his eyes with his hand, he stared into the distance at the promontory that stuck out into the harbor. "I read your report to the President regarding the Black Tom incident." He dropped his hand and looked Jesse in the eye. "The explosion from there," he pointed to the promontory, "actually knocked you off your feet all the way over there?" He turned and pointed to the Brooklyn Bridge.

"Yes, sir," Jesse said. "It was quite a series of blasts. Shrapnel chipped Miss Liberty all the way out at Bedloe's Island."

"But her torch remained lit?"

"Yes, sir."

"Amazing! Tell me, Jesse, what were you doing on the bridge that late at night?"

"Couldn't sleep. A number of things were on my mind. Emily. My family. A coded message from Bruno. That was the night I was given the dictionary and code strip."

Colonel House nodded. "What was the first thing you did when you saw what had happened?"

Jesse laughed. "I thanked God I was still alive!"

House laughed with him. "Then what?"

"Well, the whole harbor seemed to shudder. The bridge swayed."

"It swayed?" House cried incredulously.

"Hard to believe, isn't it? Then, an eerie quiet settled over everything for a moment. Not long. A series of explosions went off at the factory with rockets and metal pieces flying everywhere. It was as though we were under attack by an invisible armada.

"I ran toward the street and tried to hail a cab. Drivers were racing to the scene. They weren't interested in fares. People were running into the streets, many of them having been thrown from their beds. All over the city, burglar alarms were blaring by the hundreds. Fire alarms too. It was chaos!

"By the time I reached Black Tom, it was an inferno. Apparently, the first large explosion was a boxcar of black powder."

"I read that in your report," House said.

"Several other freight cars were on fire. Tugs were trying to pull ammunition barges into the bay and away from the fire. One of the barges was ignited. Men were blown into the air and fell in the water.

"The men in those tug boats were the heroes of the night. They boldly braved explosions and shrapnel bombardment as though they were under fire to save people from what could have been even bigger explosions.

"It was a charred ruin. The whole place. Thirteen huge warehouses were leveled. Six piers destroyed. Fire swept through the remains of railroad cars and other barges tied to the docks. A huge cavern was hewed out of the earth by the explosions of some eighty-seven dynamite-laden railroad cars. The hole was so deep, it was below sea level. Water seeped into it to create a pond littered with all sorts of debris. There must have been 200 or more barges and houseboats in the bay filled with people fleeing from the destruction. Many of them were frightened, screaming immigrants from Ellis Island. The place looked like a floating village."

"We got a taste of war that night," House said with a philosophical tone.

Jesse agreed with him. In the lazy sunlight, surrounded by a carefree Sunday population, it was hard for him to imagine that the night of terror at Black Tom had taken place not far from here.

"The President has asked me to express his congratulations to you for your part in rounding up that gang at Frau Held's residence. As you might expect, the case against them is complicated and fraught with international significance. It will take time for justice to be done. But the President is confident we can bring the whole matter to a satisfying conclusion."

"That's good to hear, sir."

House resumed his stroll. Jesse fell in step with him. "Congratulations are also in order for your other successes. The President is quite impressed with you."

"Thank you, sir, but I find it difficult to take the credit. I happen to have a reliable source."

"Ah yes, Bruno."

Jesse nodded.

"And you have no idea who this Bruno is or why he has chosen you to be his contact here in the States?"

"No, sir. I was hoping you might be able to shed some light on Bruno's identity."

"I sent memos to the appropriate agencies. Without exception, they have never come across a contact by that name before. Do you have any idea from where Bruno operates?"

Again Jesse shook his head. "He could be anywhere. Germany. France. Belgium. England. All I know is that since he has contacted me, his information has been timely and accurate."

"From the kind of information he passes along to us, our intelligence operatives believe he is a disgruntled German army officer."

"Whoever he is," Jesse said, "he's good."

Using tips from Bruno, Jesse had orchestrated Federal Secret Service operatives in several successful efforts to thwart German espionage attempts. In one incident, two Germans, Robert Fay and Walter Scholz, were arrested as they attempted to buy ten pounds of picric acid, a chemical used in the composition of high explosives. In a coded message, Bruno had informed Jesse of their presence in Weehawken, New Jersey, and their intended purpose to disrupt the flow of goods to England.

When investigators searched the apartment where the two men lived, they learned that Fay was a lieutenant in the German army. He had fought in the Battle of the Marne and came to the United States six months previous to his arrest. Other documents found in the room connected him to the German Foreign Office.

The two gave not the slightest resistance when arrested. In fact, Fay gave himself up with a quiet smile and remained unruffled after hours of grilling by the Secret Service. They learned he was a man of culture and refinement. He spoke English fluently and possessed a striking personality. His accomplice was a mechanic who entered the country two years before him.

Altogether, five explosive mines were discovered in their possession. The mines were designed to be fastened to the rudders of steamers. When the steamer's engines started, a rush of water from the propeller would activate a clock mechanism which would then, after a certain time, detonate the mine as the ship steamed out to sea.

The arrest of Fay and Scholz was Jesse's most noteworthy success. Tips from Bruno also prevented bombings in two factories and a canal.

"Do you ever send Bruno messages? Or is your communication one-way only?" Colonel House asked.

"So far, I've only received messages. They appear under my doorstep. Inside a magazine or newspaper. I never see who is slipping me these messages, if indeed it is only one person."

"I see," said House.

"On a personal side, this whole thing of coded messages has a special interest to me."

"How so?"

"One of my ancestors, Drew Morgan, a Puritan who did some spying for Bishop William Laud then later broke with him, used a similar decoding device with the bishop, only instead of a dictionary, they used a Bible."

"So secret codes run in the family."

"You might say that."

"If you were to attempt to contact Bruno, how would you go about it?"

Jesse's forehead bunched up studiously. "I'd have to give that some thought. Bruno seems to be the kind of person who is particular about his anonymity. Any attempt to contact him might dry up the source."

"We may need to take that risk," House said. "We believe some German agents have infiltrated the intelligence network in England. It's low-level, but still of some concern. Three of the agents have recently been found murdered, all in the general vicinity of London. The fear is that this breach in security might grow wider. If it does, the entire

Allied effort might be compromised. Codes. Agents—
French and American, as well as British. War plans. It's
imperative that we stop this leak before it gets out of hand."

"And you want me to ask Bruno if he knows of any
German operatives in England who might be killing these
British agents."

"Do you think he'll tell us?"

Jesse shrugged. "I don't know. So far the communication
has been all one-sided."

"See what you can do."

"Yes, sir."

They walked in silence awhile. Colonel House stopped
and stared for a good long time at Lady Liberty. After a
time he glanced one way, then the other. Given their location, it was merely a check against casual eavesdroppers.

"We can't stay out of the war much longer," he said.

Jesse frowned in thought. *Was this an opinion expressed by
Colonel House the man, or was it official news that was merely awaiting its time?*

"Something is going to break . . . and soon. Possibly
tomorrow. You should know about it." He pulled a piece of
paper from his coat pocket and handed it to Jesse. "The
British intercepted and decoded it. It is a communication
between Berlin and Mexico."

The sheet of paper was a typewritten note, hard to read
because of the glare of the bright Sunday afternoon sun.
Jesse squinted. Eventually the black ink markings formed
words he could read.

*Strictly secret, yourself to decipher. We intend from the
first February unrestricted U-boat war to begin. It will
be attempted to keep United States neutral nevertheless.
In the event that it should not succeed, we offer Mexico
alliance on following terms. Together make war. Together*

make peace. Generous financial support and understanding our part that Mexico conquer back former lost territory in Texas, New Mexico, Arizona. Settlement in the details to be left Your Excellency.

You will inform your President of the foregoing in strictest secrecy as soon as war's outbreak with United States is certain and a suggestion that he immediately join in inviting Japan and at the same time mediate between us and Japan. Please inform the President on this point that ruthless employment of our U-boats now offers prospect England in few months to be compelled to peace. Acknowledge receipt. Zimmermann.

The resumption of unrestricted submarine warfare was old news. It was the German response to a note from President Wilson to the belligerent nations in which he called upon them to state their terms by which the war might be ended. Since that time German U-boats had sunk without warning the Cunard ship *Laconia* with a loss of American lives, the liner *California,* and three American steamships, the *City of Memphis, Illinois,* and *Vigilancia.* In response, diplomatic relations with Germany were broken off and Count Johann von Bernstorff, the German ambassador in Washington, was handed his passport.

Jesse stared at the note in disbelief. "This is . . . this is . . . "

"The proverbial straw that broke the camel's back," House said.

"Inviting Mexico to attack us, and Japan to join them! Promising them three states in return!"

"It makes sense for them," House said. "A two-front war would keep that much more attention, matériel, and personnel from going to Europe. Actually, the note was intercepted some time ago. The British held onto it for a while."

"Why?"

"Their dilemma was how to release it. By releasing it outright, the Germans would know that the British have obtained their code books and cipher keys."

Again Jesse looked surprised.

"Oh, yes! They have been cracking the enemy's communications for some time now. So they were looking for a way to get the information out without compromising their advantage. As it turns out, the Germans are so arrogant about their codes—they think their codes and ciphers are so cleverly conceived that no mere non-German could ever break them—that they have concluded the telegram was stolen after its arrival in Washington or Mexico City, or leaked by a faithless embassy employee. The President plans to release it to the press any day now."

"Think of the popular reaction," Jesse said, shaking his head.

"Outrage. It will make it that much easier when the President calls for a war declaration."

"He's really going to do it?"

"The decision has been made."

Jesse stood at the foot of Manhattan on an indescribably beautiful day. Now he understood Colonel House's somber mood. He shared it. Now he saw the carefree people on the boardwalk like Colonel House saw them. He understood the colonel's sigh, when the young father passed by with his infant children.

The faces . . . the faces of all the young men that passed by him. Like sheep to the slaughter? They were going to war. They just didn't know it yet. How many would die? Which of the laughing faces he saw today would breathe their last, cheek-down in the dirt on some French battlefield? Would the young father return home to his children? Would the baseball players?

The shadow of war and death was looming over the land,

but the day was too nice and the mood so untroubled that nobody noticed.

Jesse Morgan stood with his back against the wall in the gallery of the House chamber. Like all the other spectators, he was allowed half the space his body required. For this historic occasion people had been stuffed into the gallery like olives in a jar. The heat was awful, the air stifling.

Below them assembled the members of Congress. President Wilson, gray and gaunt, had just taken his position at the podium to deliver his address.

"Gentlemen of the Congress:

"I have called the Congress into extraordinary session because there are serious, very serious, choices of policy to be made immediately, which it was neither right nor constitutionally permissible that I should assume the responsibility of making.

"On the 3rd of February last I officially laid before you the extraordinary announcement of the Imperial German Government that on and after the first day of February it was its purpose to put aside all restraints of law or of humanity and use its submarines to sink every vessel that sought to approach either the ports of Great Britain or Ireland or the western coasts of Europe or any of the ports controlled by the enemies of Germany within the Mediterranean. . . .

"The present German submarine warfare against commerce is a warfare against mankind. It is a war against all nations. American ships have been sunk. American lives taken, in ways which it has stirred us very deeply to learn of . . . .

"The challenge is to all mankind. Each nation must decide for itself how it will meet it. The choice we make for ourselves must be made with a moderation of counsel and temperateness of judgment befitting our character and motives as a nation. We must put excited feeling away. Our motive will not be revenge or the victorious assertion of the physical might of the nation, but only the vindication of right, of human right, of which we are only a single champion. . . .

"With a profound sense of the solemn and even tragical character of the step I am taking and of the grave responsibilities which it involves, but in unhesitating obedience to what I deem my constitutional duty, I advise that the Congress declare the recent course of the Imperial German Government to be in fact nothing less than war against the Government and people of the United States; that it formally accept the status of belligerent which has thus been thrust upon it. . . .

"The world must be made safe for democracy. Its peace must be planted upon the tested foundations of political liberty. We have no selfish ends to serve. We desire no conquest, no dominion. We seek no indemnities for ourselves, no material compensation for the sacrifices we shall freely make. We are but one of the champions of the rights of mankind. We shall be satisfied when those rights have been made as secure as the faith and the freedom of nations can make them. . . .

"It is a distressing and oppressive duty, gentlemen of the Congress, which I have performed in this addressing you. There are, it may be, many months of fiery trial and sacrifice ahead of us. It is a fearful thing to lead this great, peaceful people into war, into the most terrible and disastrous of all wars, civilization itself seeming to be in the balance.

"But the right is more precious than peace, and we shall fight for the things which we have always carried nearest our hearts—for democracy, for the right of those who submit to authority to have a voice in their own Governments, for the right and liberties of small nations, for a universal dominion of right by such a concert of free peoples as shall bring peace and safety to all nations and make the world itself at last free.

"To such a task we can dedicate our lives and our fortunes, everything that we are and everything that we have, with the pride of those who know that day has come when America is privileged to spend her blood and her might for the principles that gave birth and happiness and the peace which she has treasured.

"God helping her, she can do no other."

Support for the President's speech erupted all through the chamber. Small American flags appeared from nowhere: senators, congressmen, pages, and spectators waved them and cheered lustily.

Jesse couldn't help but think of his friend, William Jennings Bryan. Events had unfolded just as he had warned. The President had delivered an ultimatum to Germany regarding the U-boats. Now that the Germans had crossed the line, he had no other choice than to ask for a declaration of war.

Whether war could have been avoided through other peaceful methods was now a moot point. The nation— pending congressional approval that would surely be given—was at war.

As Jesse left the historic building, his thoughts turned to Johnny in France.

I know you won't agree with this, but us pilots are hoping America gets into the war real soon.

Johnny and the other pilots had just gotten their wish. Now they would have to live—or die—with it.

Chapter 24

"KATY! You promised you'd come!"

"I changed my mind."

"It's too late for that," Laura insisted. "They're waiting for us."

"Go ahead without me. I have to study."

"Now how would that look? A single young woman strolling around Paris with two men? If my mother found out, she'd have apoplexy! She would say, *'C'est déshonorant!'*"

Stretched out on a bed in the Hotel American, Katy had an open French language textbook and memory cards strewn in front of her. She and Laura had been chosen to be part of an exchange program with the French equivalent of the British ambulance program. The training included learning each other's language. Katy clamped her eyes shut in concentration as she searched through the French vocabulary words she had just stuffed into her head. "Your mother would say... 'It is ... it is ...'"

"She would say, 'It is dishonorable.'"

Clapping her book shut, Katy whined, "French comes so easily for you!"

Laura smiled gleefully. She was perched on the edge of her bed, arranging her hair for the twelfth time. "It does, doesn't it? I don't know why. It just sticks in my head."

"I don't think that's fair."

Laura's smile disappeared as a look of realization dawned on her face. "It bothers you that I can do something better than you, doesn't it?"

"No, it doesn't bother me."

"You're a very competitive person, Katy Morgan. I don't understand why it would bother you that I can pick up languages faster than you. You're a better nurse. A better driver."

"It doesn't bother me. And I'm not competitive!"

"Can't you be happy that finally I can contribute something to the team?"

"It doesn't bother me!"

Laura fell silent.

"Laura . . ."

Pursed lips were Laura's only response.

"Don't be like that. I didn't mean to hurt you. It's just that, well, look at this." She opened her textbook, found a sentence, and read aloud haltingly, *Tous les dimanches matin, il partait avec une casquette neuve; tous les dimanches soir, il revenait avec une loque.*

Without the slightest hesitation, Laura translated: "Every Sunday morning, he went out with a new cap; every Sunday evening, he returned with a rag."

"See?" Katy cried, extending an open palm in Laura's direction. "Now why should I care that some nameless fellow ruins his hat every Sunday? I'm a nurse, not a hatter!"

A tiny grin crossed Laura's lips. "Then you'll go sightseeing with us?"

Katy tossed the textbook on the bed. "Yes, I'll go. But I can't promise I'll have a good time."

Laura beamed as she put the finishing touches on her hair. "And don't worry about Fred Radcliff. I won't tell him you went out with another man."

"Wait a minute! First, I'm not going out with another

man. I'm going sightseeing with my friend and her friend. Second, you can tell Fred Radcliff whatever you want! I have no designs on him."

"He does on you."

"Nonsense."

"He does!" Laura insisted. "If you'd open your eyes and look at the way he stares at you."

"Fred Radcliff doesn't stare at me."

"It's almost indecent!"

"Laura!"

The younger woman giggled as she crossed the room and swished her dress back and forth before a full-length mirror. Katy had never seen Laura this giddy before. Happy. Effervescent. Bubbly. Always smiling. These words described Laura's daily emotional fare. But this was different. Greater than before. The girl was intoxicated with glee.

Katy first noticed something was different two nights ago when Laura returned from a Y.M.C.A.-sponsored dance. Katy hadn't gone. She'd stayed home to study. When Laura returned, she was floating on air and didn't come down for the rest of the night. She said she'd met a young man. An American in the army.

"You'll like him," Laura said, brushing the front of her pale yellow chiffon dress with a flat hand. "He's so kind. Considerate. And tall!"

Standing in front of the mirror, Laura looked heavenly, like an ancient Greek goddess who had deigned to grace the earth with her presence. Puffed sleeves, a double strand of simulated pearls, and broad-brimmed straw hat adorned with colorful silk flowers completed the ensemble. Rarely had Katy seen her when she was not wearing her nurses' uniform. In the yellow chiffon, Laura looked the picture of wide-eyed youth.

"And he says his friend is very nice," Laura continued,

unaware that Katy was gazing at her.

"I don't know how I let you talk me into this," Katy said, straightening the wrinkles from her simple light-blue cotton dress. She adjusted the white lace trim and checked her hair in the mirror. Passable. Especially since she was not trying to impress anyone.

A stray thought struck her. *What if... just for argument's sake... what if she was about to meet the man she would one day marry? Not that she was looking to get married. She wasn't even sure she wanted to get married. Ever. Marriage would put an end to her goals. Her dreams. Certainly, no man was worth that. It was best for her not even to consider marriage an option.*

Still... what if the man she was about to meet was someone special?

"*Allez!*" Laura said.

"Let's go," Katy translated.

"Very good!"

"Do I have time to change my dress?"

Laura grinned.

"This one is all wrinkled!" Katy protested. "You don't want me walking all over Paris in a wrinkled dress, do you?"

The grin grew wider.

"Oh, for heaven's sake!" Katy cried. "It's not what you think!"

Laura said nothing. She only grinned.

"It's not!" Katy insisted. "Stop grinning like the Cheshire cat and unbutton me!"

Two men in American uniforms were waiting for them a block from the hotel in front of a sidewalk café. One was tall and blond, the other was shorter with brown hair and a strong jaw.

"There they are!" Laura squeezed Katy's arm excitedly.

She pointed to the tall one. "Isn't he handsome? And his friend . . . " She looked up at Katy with wide expectant eyes. "What do you think? He's even more handsome than Fred Radcliff, don't you think?"

Katy stumbled over nothing in particular. She stared at the men, who had now spotted them too.

Sensing Katy's hesitancy, Laura said, "The wings. You see the wings. O Katy, I know I should have told you they were pilots, but I was afraid you wouldn't come if you knew."

Laura walked ahead. The tall pilot greeted her with a kiss on the cheek.

"Well," Laura said, bouncing excitedly on the balls of her feet. "This is my friend. The one I've been telling you about. This is Katy."

"Pleased to meet you, Katy." Laura's friend held out his hand.

Katy took it. Her hand was swallowed up in his grasp.

Turning to the young man beside him, he said, "And I'd like you to meet . . . "

"My brother," Katy said.

A dumbfounded expression fell over the tall pilot's face. It must have been contagious, because Laura wore the same expression.

"Hello, Johnny. What are you doing in France?"

"I was about to ask you the same question, Katy."

"This can't be!" Laura said in laughing disbelief. "This isn't really your brother! Is it?"

With a lackluster wave of her hand, Katy said, "Laura . . . Johnny Morgan. Johnny . . . Laura Kelton."

"And I'm Percy. Percy Hill." He extended his hand to Katy a second time, his face split wide with a grin. "It's so good to make your acquaintance. Johnny has told me . . . "

" . . . virtually nothing about his sister, or his parents I daresay. After all, he lives as if we don't exist."

Johnny didn't respond. Folding his hands in front of him, he stared placidly at his sister.

"Who would have thought this would be a family reunion?" Laura squealed, still taken aback by the turn of events. "Well, why don't we . . . um, why don't we . . . " She looked to Percy.

"Why don't we sit down over here," Percy said, motioning to a table in front of the café, "and get better acquainted. At least, for some of us, that is . . . and then . . . then, well, we can decide where we're going to go today."

"That's right!" Laura chimed in. "Why not? We can still go sightseeing. Now, it's a family event. I mean, after all, how many people get a chance to see Paris with their brother?" She looked at Katy.

"Or sister?" Percy said, nudging Johnny good-naturedly.

"*Oui! Asseyons-nous!*" Laura looked to Katy for a translation. When one was not forthcoming, she translated the phrase herself, "Let's sit down!"

Percy and Laura shepherded the dispassionate Morgans to a table. Greeted by a waiter, Percy ordered coffee for everyone and pulled out a chair for Laura. He was about to sit in the chair next to her when he realized that by doing so it would put brother and sister side-by-side. He hastily offered his chair to Katy. This way, he sat across the table from Laura which put Katy and Johnny on opposite sides of the table as well.

"Thought you'd be in Africa by now," Johnny said to Katy.

Lowering her eyes, Katy said, "The London Missionary Society didn't want me."

"I know," Johnny replied. "Father told me."

A tide of red rose in Katy's face faster than the antediluvian flood. "Then why did you . . . "

"It was their loss!" Laura interjected. "I, for one, am glad things worked out as they did. Otherwise, Katy and I never would have met!"

"Last I heard," Katy said to Johnny, "you were flying around Colorado in a crate with an old man begging for food."

"We never begged for food!" Johnny objected. "We *earned* our living. And that Curtis Jenny may have been slow, but it wasn't a crate!"

"Did you know that's how Johnny and I met?" Percy said in a lighthearted tone. "He and Mr. Wachorn were flying into Columbus—New Mexico, not Ohio," he said to Laura, who nodded with great interest. "And . . . " Percy started laughing, ". . . you should have seen this . . . " He laughed harder. "While they were approaching the town, old Mr. Wachorn died in the mount, leaving Johnny with no way to fly the plane from his seat in front!"

"No!" Laura shouted incredulously. To Johnny, "What did you do?"

Percy answered for him. "He turned around, straddled the fuselage, and landed the aeroplane flying backward!"

"Really? No! You didn't, really?"

Johnny shrugged.

"First time I ever saw him," Percy said, "he was sitting backward on an aeroplane flying over the town!"

Percy and Laura laughed.

When the laughter died out, there was silence. Bristling, caustic silence. In comparison, a toothache would have been a pleasant change of pace.

Laura was the first to break it. "So, Johnny, tell me, what is it like to fly?"

"Don't encourage him, Laura," Katy said.

"I really want to know!" Laura said innocently. "I've often imagined what it must feel like to soar above the clouds. Is it as pleasurable as it seems?"

"You don't have to do this on my account," Johnny said,

scooting his chair back.

A large paw fell on his shoulder, keeping him from getting up. "If Laura said she was interested in knowing what it is like to fly," Percy said in a low, serious voice, "she's genuinely interested."

The two men locked eyes.

"Percy, if he'd really rather not talk about it . . ." Laura said.

"Do you really want to know?" Johnny said in all seriousness, scooting his chair back to the table. "Because most people when they ask, are just passing the time of day. But if you really want to know . . ."

Laura nodded reluctantly. If she'd wanted to know before, she wasn't so sure she wanted to know now.

"All right," Johnny said. "Here are the answers to the questions most frequently asked about flying." He began a count using his fingers as a visual aid.

"One. Yes, sometimes it is dangerous. Sometimes it is not.

"Two. Yes, the higher we fly, the colder it gets. We notice this by the fact that we start freezing when it gets colder.

"Three. Yes, we can fly several thousand feet in the air. And yes, we can see things on the ground at that height, although not as well as we can see them from a hundred feet.

"Four. We cannot use telescopes to help us see because they shake.

"Five. The observer sits in the front of the aeroplane and can see a hit. We cannot talk to one another well because the engine makes too much noise.

"Six. We don't have telephones in the machines, but we are provided with electric lights.

"And seven. No, we do not live in caves."

With a look of pure disgust, Katy folded her arms. "You haven't changed, have you?"

"Haven't seen the need."

"Well," Percy exclaimed. "Who's ready to see the Eiffel Tower?"

The waiter arrived with their coffee.

"Our coffee! Mmmm, smells wonderful!" Laura said. "First we drink, then we see the sites." Taking a sip, she turned to Katy. "The other night, Percy was telling me how wonderful their hotel is. Anything they want, day or night, all they have to do is push a button and someone comes running."

"The room service at our squadron barracks isn't quite as good," Percy said jokingly. He and Laura laughed.

Then the killer silence returned.

"I'm sorry," Katy said to no one in particular. She shook her head as though coming out of a trance. "You must forgive me," she said to Percy. "I've been horrible company."

A relieved smile spread across Laura's face.

Reaching across the table, Katy touched Percy's arm. "Naturally, Laura has told me a lot about you, but she hasn't said where you are from."

"Born and raised in Columbus, New Mexico. The place where Johnny . . . "

"Yes, I remember the story," Katy interrupted. "What was your father's profession?"

"Owner and manager of a hotel, as was his father before him."

"Do your parents still live there?"

Percy shook his head sadly. "They died the night Pancho Villa raided the town. You probably heard about it."

"Yes, I did. And I'm sorry for your loss," Katy said.

Laura's face clouded with sympathy. "I didn't know that," she said.

"Johnny was there that night too," Percy added, "having arrived the day before."

The two women glanced at Johnny. He sat back in his

chair, his arms folded with a bored look on his face. His coffee was untouched.

"And so now you're a pilot," Katy turned her attention back to Percy. "Where did you learn to fly?"

"Actually, most of what I know about aeroplanes and flying I learned from Johnny. We did mechanic work together during Pershing's Mexico expedition. Then, we went to flight school together in Maryland, although it seemed a waste of time for Johnny to attend. He could fly better than our instructors when he arrived."

Again heads turned toward Johnny.

He smiled smugly.

"But now you're the same rank," Katy said, comparing the insignia on the two men's jackets.

"But that doesn't mean we're equal in the air," Percy replied. "Johnny is the best there is when it comes to flying. I never would have made it through flight training if it hadn't been for him."

If smug could get any more smug, Johnny did.

Katy gave up. Every comment she made, every question she asked, every compliment seemed somehow to work its way around to her brother.

"Percy and Johnny are in Paris for two weeks!" Laura said.

"Two weeks? How did you wrangle a two-week furlough?" Katy asked.

"We're the captain's favorites," Johnny said. It was meant to be humorous. Nobody laughed.

On long summer evenings, back at her family's home in Colorado, Katy used to sit on the back porch under newly emerging stars and stare at the mountains. She would dream of faraway places and what it would be like to go there. She imagined the unforgiving deserts and dark jungles of Africa. The mysteries of forbidden China. The exotic wonders of South Sea Islands. The barren frozen tundra of Alaska. And the romance of Paris.

And now, here she was strolling down the Champs Élysées.

"You know that song with your name in it, 'K-K-K'-Katy?" Johnny asked.

"Yes, I've heard it."

"It's sung a lot at our squadron barracks."

"Oh?"

"With a few variations, of course."

Katy knew it would be expecting too much to think she might escape hearing the variations.

Johnny sang:

"K-K-K-K. P!
Dirty old K.P.,
That's the only Army job that I abhor;
When the m-moon shines over the guardhouse,
I'll be mopping up the k-k-k-kitchen floor!"

"That's lovely, Johnny."

"Wait, I have another one. This is my favorite."

Katy held up a hand. "You don't have to sing it on my account."

"C-C-C-Cootie,
Horrible cootie,
You're the only b-b-b-bug that I abhor;
When the m-moon shines over the bunkhouse,
I will scratch my b-b-b-back until it's sore!"

As the late afternoon sun reflected gold and orange on the historic River Seine, Katy became painfully aware that it is not *where you are* that counts nearly as much as it is *who you are with* that counts.

Percy and Laura walked ahead of them—more like float-ed ahead of them—holding hands, basking in the charm of Paris. Katy walked a dozen or so steps behind them. Johnny trailed behind her.

They had been to the Eiffel Tower, the Louvre, and the Arc de Triomphe. Now Percy and Laura were talking about getting tickets to the theater. That was where Katy was draw-ing the line. She'd had enough of her brother to last her sev-eral years. The last thing she wanted to do was sit next to him in a theater and listen to his inane comments through-out the entire production. Even if she had to fabricate a headache, she was going back to the hotel.

She glanced again at Laura and Percy. They looked so natural together. The two of them needed to be alone.

Laura turned around. "Katy! Percy and I have been talk-ing. First, we'll find some out-of-the-way little French restaurant. While we're eating, we can ask the maitre d' to recommend a theater. What do you think?"

Katy met the proposal with a furrowed brow and a hand to the forehead she hoped portrayed headache pain. She never got the chance to voice her excuse.

An American army corporal was running down the street shouting happily. "America has declared war! America has declared war!"

Spotting the two familiar American uniforms, he ran up to Percy and Johnny. He was short and young. His face full of freckles. Gaps showed between his teeth as he shouted, "Have you heard? America declared war! It's official. The Senate voted 82 to 6. We're in it! We're in the war!"

Not waiting for their reaction, he ran up the street in the direction of more American uniforms.

"It was just a matter of time," Percy said. He squeezed Laura's hand between two enormous paws.

"Does this mean you have to go back right away?" Laura asked.

"Not unless they cancel all leaves," Percy said.

"I'm going back," Johnny said.

The three others looked at him. His jaw was set. There was a hunger in his eyes that went beyond the competitive hunger Katy had seen so many times while they were growing up. This look had an animal quality to it. They were the eyes of a predator on the prowl. Without so much as a good-bye, he turned and marched—almost ran—in the direction of the hotel.

"Are you sure you can stay?" Laura asked.

"It's going to be months before our aeroplanes can be out-fitted for combat. There'll be nothing for him to do when he gets back to the squadron but wait. And he gets testy when there's nothing to do. That's why Captain Eastman gave us two weeks furlough, to get Johnny out of his hair. Johnny didn't want to come. The captain made him. I doubt that Captain Eastman will be pleased to see him return after just a few days."

"I'm glad you're staying," Laura said, looking up into Percy's eyes. Her head barely reached his chest, so it was a long way to look. She didn't seem to mind the eye strain though.

"I'm glad I'm staying too," Percy said, his chin touching his chest as he looked down at her. Their eyes locked in silent communication.

Katy cleared her throat. "Well, I'm going back to the hotel," she said.

"No, Katy," Laura pleaded. "Stay with us. You'll have fun."

"Please," Percy added. "It will give me a chance to get to know you better."

"Thank you, but no," Katy said. "I'm sure you've had your fill of Morgans today. I really do want to apologize.

We're just not at our best when we're around each other."

"There's no need to apologize," Percy said. "I've been living with Johnny long enough to know what it's like. There's something inside of him. Almost like a fire. It drives him and consumes him all at the same time. One minute I think he's the greatest. The next minute I wish nobody knew we were friends."

Katy chuckled. "That's my brother, all right. Still, you and Laura should be alone for a while. And I have studying to do. I'll leave a light on for you, Laura."

"At least let us walk you back to the hotel," Percy said.

Katy checked the amount of daylight left in the sky. "That's not necessary. I'll be fine, really. Go on, have fun. When this furlough is over, Lord knows when you'll be able to see each other again."

She'd meant the statement to be nothing more than one additional argument why the two of them should not worry about her. But as the words were spoken, they had a gravity that was far more weighty than she'd intended. It was an affirmation that they were at war and that people die in war.

Even though Katy had been involved in the war with the British, there was something different about America being involved. All of a sudden the war was much more dangerous. It was personal now. American lives were at stake.

Percy felt it too. Katy could see it in his eyes. Amidst the sparkle for Laura, there was a sadness. A funereal kind of sadness. A foreshadowing of death. Men in Percy's squadron would die. There was no way of knowing who, or how many. But some of them would die. It was inevitable. This was war.

Laura felt it too. She moved closer to Percy, entwining her arm with his.

"Enough of these somber thoughts," Katy cried. "There will be time enough for war. The two of you need to make the most of tonight. Have fun!"

Waving good-bye, she turned and left Percy and Laura standing beneath an ancient shade tree. When she reached the corner, she couldn't help but look back. Percy and Laura were still standing beneath the tree, facing one another, holding hands. He whispered something. She laughed. They looked so happy. So right for each other.

When they resumed speaking in normal tones, Katy could faintly hear their conversation. She knew better than to eavesdrop, but the two unchaperoned young lovers held a fascination for her.

"I'm afraid for you," Laura said. "We just found each other."

"I'll be careful," Percy said. "Now, more than ever. You've given me something to live for."

Laura's head lowered shyly. "If it were just up to you, I wouldn't worry," she said. "But I've heard enough stories about those machines you fly. I just don't trust them. And I certainly don't like the idea of other men shooting at you!"

Cradling her head in his huge hands, Percy lifted her face to his. "I can't promise you that nothing will happen to me," he said, "just as you can't promise me that nothing will happen to you. This is war."

She lifted a hand and brushed away a tear.

"I just think it's cruel that America is getting into the war now. Why couldn't your Congress wait a few months longer? You'd think they could at least do that for us."

Percy laughed softly.

"I have every confidence that both of us will come through this war in fine shape," he said.

"Oh? Do you know something I don't know?"

"Look at it from this perspective. We survived the Morgan war today, didn't we? How bad can the Germans be?"

Laura laughed softly.

Katy strode toward the Hotel American with quick determined steps. With each step, she walked faster, her heels
clicking angrily on the street. Her anger was not directed at
Percy and Laura, but at herself and her brother. She was
ashamed. They'd both acted shamefully, like children.

*What was it about her brother that brought out the worst in
her?* The instant she was around him, she acted like a completely different person. Everything he said or did grated
on her nerves. Nobody else affected her like this. Only
Johnny.

She thought she had grown since the last time she'd seen
him. She thought she'd matured beyond this level of petti-
ness. But if today was any indication of her maturity, she
hadn't made much progress at all.

Upon reaching her hotel room, Katy threw herself onto
the bed. She flung open her textbook and channeled her
anger and self-disgust toward something productive, learning the French language. She studied until she fell asleep
on her bed, still clothed and with the textbook draped
across her abdomen.

It was late when Laura returned. She did her best to be
quiet and not wake Katy.

"Did you have a good time?" Katy asked, setting the
book aside.

"I'm sorry! I didn't mean to wake you!"

"That's all right. I haven't dressed for bed yet."

"I had a wonderful time!" Laura squealed. "Better than
wonderful. Fabulous! Better than fabulous! It was . . . " She
searched for the right word, but failed to come up with
one. "What's a word that means better than fabulous?"

Katy smiled and yawned at the same time. "How about
really, really good?"

Laura laughed. Grabbing her pillow she hugged it. "I had a
really, really, really good time!" She climbed up on top of her

THE ALLIES § 308

bed. "I mean a really, really good time!" With each *really*, she bounced. "A really, really, really, really . . . "

"I think I get the idea!" Katy said, laughing as she watched Laura jumping up and down on the hotel bed.

Chapter 25

HIS Spad slipped fluidly through the sky. Johnny closed his eyes and commanded the aeroplane by feel alone. The throb of the engine and the beat of his heart matched each other in perfect rhythm. The wings were an extension of himself. It was as though all he had to do was think of a maneuver and the aeroplane responded.

Sailing high above a carpet of cauliflower clouds, he rolled left, then right, then left, then right, back and forth, back and forth in a rocking motion. Each rock was higher than the previous one until he slipped over into a barrel roll. Then another. And another. Effortlessly.

Opening his eyes, he squinted at the bright light until they adjusted. This was his world. Clouds below. Above him only sky. Floating through a layer of atmospheric ether. Here, he had no troubles. No bothersome sister. No arrogant squadron commander. No friends who acted hurt whenever you spoke your mind. Here, he was king.

His engine sputtered. Choked.

Johnny adjusted the throttle. Gave it more fuel.

The sputtering became worse.

He backed off on the fuel.

The engine seized and died. The propeller froze. The nose pitched downward.

The king had a problem. He was falling out of his sky.

It was a well-known fact among aviators that more deaths were caused by mechanical malfunctions than enemy bullets. As Johnny's crippled aircraft nosed toward the ground, he acted calmly. He was not going to let an engine failure deprive him of his life before he had a chance to do battle with the Germans.

He entered the clouds. Blinded, plummeting downward at a steep dive, he fought to keep his craft from going into a spin. He waited to clear the clouds, knowing that once he did, he would have to find a suitable place to land. Quickly.

Moisture accumulated on his goggles. He wiped it away with a gloved hand. A frigid wind roared madly past him, chilling his arms and hands and face. He'd always imagined death would be a cold experience as life drained from one's limbs.

Just another enemy, he told himself. He would fight the Germans tomorrow. Today it was a dogfight with death.

The lack of engine sound was unnerving. No power. But that didn't mean no control. The ground rules were different, that was all. The earth was pulling the front of his aeroplane to the ground like a magnet pulling a metal bolt. Unlike the bolt, he had wings with which to fight the pull of the earth. This he did, fighting to keep his descent as shallow as possible. Waiting for a break in the clouds. Praying it would come sooner rather than later. A low cloud ceiling would be to the enemy's advantage.

The earth appeared below him as through a fog. Then it disappeared. A moment later, he saw it again. A flicker. Then another, and another, until he broke through the clouds.

He had several hundred feet to play with. Not much.

The ground beneath him was barren, undulating hills with trenches. Barbed wire. He was over the front!

A bullet whizzed past him. Then another.

Johnny threw the stick to the side, banking hard. Away

from the source of the bullets. Beneath him, French soldiers stared up at him. Their mouths open at the sight of a
silent aeroplane. Beyond them were German trenches. The
source of the gunfire.

"Help me out, *mes amies!*" Johnny shouted, knowing they
could hear him.

Ping! A bullet ricocheted off the engine cowling.

Beneath him, the French troops opened fire at the German
lines. Up and down the line he could hear the pop, pop, pop
of gunfire as he turned his tail toward the enemy urging his
powerless craft to put as much distance between him and
them as quickly as possible.

He raised a hand of thanks to the French infantry.
"Merci!" he shouted. *"Merci!"*

The length of the trenches, hands raised as they followed
his descent.

With the ground coming up fast, he was running out of
options. There were houses and trees to his right. A tree-
lined road on his left.

Why do the French have to line all their roads with trees?

He banked left, looking beyond the trees. A field!

*Not good. Recently cultivated. Furrows. Soft ground. Not good
at all.*

But he was running out of time and choices. He looked
around and saw a creek, more houses, more trees. He'd run
out of options. It would have to be the furrowed field.

His current approach met the furrows at a right angle.
Like trying to land on a washboard. He banked left, held it,
then banked back. He'd lost altitude, but gained a better
approach to the furrows in the field. But at what price?

A high hedge bordered the field on the side of his
approach. Had he gained a better angle only to slam into a
hedge? Johnny pulled back on the stick, hoping to gain a
little altitude. There was no significant response. The earth's

pull was too great.

Beneath him, the ground began to race until it was a blur. The hedge and the field loomed in front of him. Thoughts of the wheels catching the hedge came to mind. He'd topple over and cartwheel. Not an attractive thought. Better to plunge into the hedge and take his chances.

No. Over. He had to make it over. He pulled back on the stick knowing it would not help, but he had to try. He had to do something.

The ground raced faster.

The hedge flew toward him.

SLAP! The wheels hit the hedge. There was a jolt, but the aeroplane stayed its course. He'd cleared it! Now to land. To land.

Keep the wings level . . . level . . .

The wheels hit the dirt. Hard. Jarring Johnny nearly senseless. The aeroplane bounced back up.

Level . . . keep the wings level . . .

He hit again. Not as hard. Bounced. Not as high. Dirt and dust flew everywhere. Johnny was thrown forward against his windscreen. He felt the ground trying to grab the wheels, to upend the aeroplane as they plowed two new parallel rows.

The craft bounced and lurched violently. Johnny held on with all his might.

Suddenly, he felt his seat rising from the back; like it was spring-loaded, the tail rising up behind him; he was going over! Visions of pilots crushed beneath their engines flashed in his head. His hands flew out in front of him, instinctively reaching, grabbing at anything that might anchor him in his seat.

Then, as suddenly as the tipping began, it stopped. There was a final thud and a short skid. Then, everything was still except for the billowing cloud of dust that surrounded him.

His cheek was pressed against the windscreen. Out of the corner of his eye he could see the tail of his aeroplane pointing at the clouds.

Slowly, he tested his arms. His shoulder was jammed against the instrument panel. Bruised, but nothing broken. He wiggled his left foot, then his right. Bracing himself with his arms, he pulled himself up to give his legs room to work. When needed, they performed as usual, if not a bit shaky.

Johnny climbed out of the Spad and surveyed the damage. All in all, it wasn't bad. The right wing had a couple of cracked struts. The propeller had broken. Fuel poured out of the engine and ran down one of the farmer's newly made rows.

His hands on his hips, Johnny stared upward at the clouds. *Strange,* he thought. *Had I lost the battle, death would have been credited with one more kill. But death lost the battle. So why am I not credited with a kill?*

As he walked toward the nearby farmhouse, he pondered his question. When the answer came to him, he didn't like it.

Someday death will get the kill and there's no escaping him. Today wasn't a victory over the enemy. It was merely a temporary escape.

The fuel truck saved him five miles of walking.

Flying is better than walking, he'd decided. Accustomed to sailing across terrain at more than a hundred miles an hour, walking was the pace of snails.

"You headed toward the aerodrome?" the driver asked, speaking English.

Johnny thought it was rather obvious where he was headed. Not many people walk down French roads on a warm day with a leather jacket slung over their shoulder and carrying a leather helmet and goggles. But he said nothing. He didn't want to insult someone who could save him from five miles of dusty country road.

"I'm with the 59th squadron," Johnny replied.

The driver threw open the passenger door. "Hop in!" he shouted. "That's where I'm headed."

Johnny climbed into the cab of the truck. With a grin and a nod, the driver rammed the gearshift lever into place and released the clutch. The truck shimmied in complaint at the heavy load, then resigned itself to the task at hand and picked up speed.

The thing Johnny noticed most about the driver was that he had a large cigar protruding from his lips. He thought it dangerously odd that a driver of a fuel tanker would smoke a cigar, until he noticed the blunt protruding end. It had never met a match.

Thin, with hollow cheeks, the driver nevertheless had large forearms. He was clean shaven with a nose that arched over his lips and nearly touched his chin. When he spoke again, Johnny noticed the reason for such an unusual facial arrangement. The man had no teeth.

This being a five-mile relationship, the man didn't ask Johnny his name and Johnny didn't offer.

"Aeroplane go down?" the driver asked.

"About ten miles back in a farmer's field. He wasn't too happy about it."

The driver chuckled. "Survived this one, did you?"

Johnny turned his head and stared at the passing scenery while he suppressed a chuckle. This man had an uncanny knack for asking obvious questions. He wanted to say, *Nah, I didn't survive this one. It only looks like I did. And that's the third time this week I didn't survive. But I'm going to keep trying until I get it right.*

Instead, he said, "Yes, I survived this one."

"So you're walkin' back to the base."

"At least I was until you picked me up. Much obliged."

"Don't mention it."

They rumbled down the road. In the distance Johnny could see the familiar arched shapes of the hangars.

"Are you gonna get one of them new aeroplanes?" the driver asked.

"New aeroplanes?"

"Them Spad 11s or 12s or 13s that was just delivered."

"The Spad 13s have been delivered?" Johnny cried.

"That's what I heard. That's the reason for this extra load," he thumbed the tank behind them. "Give you boys time to get acquainted with them things before you go after them Huns."

Leaning out the window, Johnny scanned the airfield looking for the new planes. There were several rows of aircraft. From this distance, it was difficult to tell if any of them were the newly arrived Spads.

"So what are you?" the driver asked.

"A lieutenant."

With his cigar wedged between his fingers he waved a hand. "No, no . . . what are you? You're not an ace, are you? My guess would be you're either a vulture or a buzzard."

Johnny understood the question now. A vulture was a pilot who was waiting for an aeroplane. A buzzard was a pilot who had an aeroplane, but no kills. An ace was a pilot with five or more kills.

"I'm a vulture."

The driver slapped the steering wheel. "Thought so!" he cried. "You know what gave you away?"

"What?"

"The way you drooled when I mentioned those Spads."

"You weren't kidding me about the Spads having arrived, were you?"

The cigar, clamped firmly between upper and lower gums, swung back and forth. "I wouldn't kid about something like that."

When they pulled up in front of a hanger, Johnny's door was open and he was out of the cab before the truck came to a stop. He was in such a hurry, he forgot to thank the driver for the ride.

"Hope you get one of them new Spads!" the driver called after him.

Johnny Morgan rapped on his commanding officer's door. "Enter!"

The door flew open. Johnny saluted Captain Eastman, then said, "I heard the Spad 13s have arrived. I would like to request one of them, sir."

Eastman sat behind a small desk. With pen in hand, he worked on an array of papers the edges of which bent over the sides of the desk. His head was lowered, his back ramrod straight as he wrote.

"Morgan, I didn't hear you come in."

"I knocked, sir."

Eastman looked up. "That's not what I meant. I didn't hear your aeroplane land."

"It's in a field fifteen miles from here."

"Condition?"

"Strut damage. Propeller broken. That's all the damage I was able to assess. The engine cut out and died at 7,000 feet. I would like to request one of the new Spads, sir."

Eastman slapped down his pen. "One thing at a time, Morgan!" he shouted. "What caused the engine to cut out?"

"Would you like me to make a guess, sir?"

"Give me your opinion as a pilot!"

"Fouled spark plugs. Possibly cracked spark plug wires."

Eastman nodded. "Fill out a report and inform the hangar foreman of the location of your aeroplane."

"Sir, I request that I be given . . ."

"You have an aeroplane, Morgan."

"Sir! I may have an aeroplane, but it has no weapons!"

Eastman was unmoved.

"Sir!" Johnny said. "I respectfully request . . . "

"They've already been assigned. You'll have to wait until the next shipment arrives."

"Assigned! To who?"

Eastman shot out of his chair. "To qualified pilots!" he shouted. "It's my decision to make and I made it!"

"But I'm more qualified than . . . "

"That will be all, Morgan!"

"Sir, I . . . "

"That will be all!" Eastman shouted.

Saluting, Johnny turned and opened the door to leave.

"Morgan!"

"Yes, sir?"

"I want you to ride back with the hangar foreman to retrieve your aeroplane. I want you to take good care of it, because it's the only one you'll have for a long, long time."

It took Johnny a great deal of self-control to keep from slamming the captain's door.

"Johnny! Johnny!"

Percy came running across the field toward him.

"Aren't they great?"

Johnny walked purposefully toward the hangar. "You're referring to the new Spads."

"Of course I am!" Percy cried. "Have you seen yours yet?"

"You got one?" Johnny cried.

Sensing something was wrong, Percy nodded, but hesitantly.

"Who else? Who else got one?"

"Mott, Wisehart, Oldfield, Bickers . . . "

Johnny threw his jacket to the ground in disgust. "I'm better than the lot of them!" he shouted.

Percy stared at him, aware now of the source of Johnny's anger. "You didn't get one of the new Spads!" he said.

"No, I didn't! Eastman gave them to clowns instead! What did he do? Start at the bottom of the competency list and work his way up? I can't believe this!"

Percy's face clouded with anger. It was a rare occasion, but unmistakable when it did. "I may not be the best," he seethed, "but I'm a good pilot."

"Of course you are," Johnny said.

"You called me incompetent."

"What are you talking about?"

"You inferred I was at the bottom of the list of qualified fliers."

It was beginning to dawn on Johnny what Percy was talking about. "Wait, Percy, I didn't mean you. I was referring to the others."

"The other incompetent pilots?"

Johnny sighed in exasperation. "I meant to call *them* incompetent, not *you!*"

Percy was not appeased. "Bickers is a fine pilot and a good man. Wisehart is without doubt superior in skill to me. The truth is, you think I'm a bad pilot, don't you?"

"Of course I don't!" Johnny protested. "I was just . . . "

"Well, let me tell you a thing or two, Mr. Ace Pilot. There is more to being a pilot than flying skills. There is teamwork. Camaraderie. The sense that we're all in this together."

"Of course we're in this together!"

"Oh? Listening to you, one would get the impression that this is your war and all the rest of us are here for no other reason than to cheer you on."

Turning on his heel, Percy stalked away.

"One would get that impression, would one?" Johnny shouted after him. He threw his goggles and helmet into the dirt next to his jacket.

Later that afternoon, while Johnny ate dust in the back of a truck that returned him to the field where he had crashed, he looked up and saw a near perfect V formation of Spad 13s flying overhead with Captain Vernon Eastman in the lead aeroplane.

The superiority of the Spad 13s was well-documented by the time Johnny Morgan got to fly one. It had a more powerful engine, a faster climb rate, could fly faster and higher than the Spad 7, and was designed for two Vickers machine guns instead of just one. A week after the first Spad 13s were delivered, Johnny was summoned to Captain Eastman's office.

"You wanted to see me, sir?" Johnny said, standing at attention in front of the captain's cluttered desk.

Without looking up, Eastman said, "Report to Hangar 3."

"Sir, may I inquire . . . "

"I said, 'Report to Hangar 3!'" Eastman shouted. "Would you like me to draw you a map?"

"No, sir!"

Wiping greasy hands on a rag, the repair foreman—a stocky fellow who had a nervous habit of flinching his cheeks like a chipmunk when he talked—met Johnny at Hangar 3.

"Morgan!" Flinch. Flinch. Dirty fingernails pointed across the hangar. "Over there!"

A mechanic was giving the propeller bolts one last tug on a Spad 13.

"Yeah? So?" Johnny said.

"Didn't Eastman tell you?" Flinch.

"Tell me what?"

Flinch. Flinch. "The Spad. She's yours."

"Mine?"

"Unless you want to keep that flying junk pile you have

right now."

"Is she ready?" Johnny asked excitedly.

Flinch. Flinch. "Just needs someone to put her through her paces. Any volunteers?"

Within minutes Johnny was bouncing across the airfield picking up speed until he slipped the bonds of earth and soared into his atmospheric refuge. He did everything he could think of: climbed, dove, rolled, slipped, stalled. He even tried the twin Vickers guns and found them loaded. The Spad responded to his every touch.

Let's have some fun.

Pretending he was flying over an enemy aerodrome, he pitched down into a dive and pretended to strafe the aeroplanes which were lined up like soldiers on the field, executing a barrel roll as he pulled out of the dive.

Mechanics came running from the hangars. Pilots from the barracks. A crowd gathered on the field to watch him. Remembering some of the tricks he and Wachorn used to perform, Johnny put on a one-man show—looping, all kinds of turns, swooping, flying upside down, a whole array of acrobatic maneuvers. With each pass, the crowd below cheered. It was just like old times in Colorado, only with a much superior aircraft.

Having exhausted his repertoire, he landed and taxied toward the hangars. A crowd of cheering, clapping soldiers and workers came out to greet him. Including Captain Eastman. Only he wasn't clapping. Nor did his face look cheerful.

He started with a few curses, then said, "What did you think you were doing up there? This is a military base and a military machine! Contrary to what you might think, we're not a circus and you're not a clown!"

"Sir, I was just doing my duty."

"And just what duty were you performing?"

"I was instructed to put this aircraft through its paces. That's what I did."

Eastman glared at him with a look that could melt lead. Through clenched teeth, he said, "Your actions were totally irresponsible, Morgan! You can't fool me. All of this was to impress everyone with your flying abilities. Well, let me tell you this. If you want to impress someone, I suggest you impress them over a German airfield. Do you understand me?"

"Yes, sir."

The once enthusiastic crowd had withered away under Captain Eastman's tirade. When the captain turned to go back to his office, Johnny was left standing beside his aeroplane alone. He stood there until Eastman had disappeared around the side of the hangar.

Climbing back into his aeroplane, Johnny strapped on his helmet and took off once more. He flew across enemy lines to the nearest German airfield. On his first pass, he strafed the aircraft lined up on the ground. Pilots and repairmen emerged from the hangars and barracks to see who it was that was attacking them. On his second pass, Johnny flew over the assembled crowd upside down.

Then, he returned to his own airfield. Once again, Captain Eastman came storming onto the field demanding to know where Johnny had gone.

"Just doing what you told me to do, sir."

Johnny was given eight days of house arrest for obeying Captain Eastman's orders.

Chapter 26

JOHNNY Morgan despised flying in formation. The way he described it to Percy, "There's an added responsibility in a formation that doesn't work for me. It's so much easier when you have only yourself to worry about."

Captain Eastman knew Johnny despised flying in formation. And Captain Eastman despised Johnny. So naturally, Johnny was surprised when the captain did not assign him to a formation group. Instead, he was given scout responsibilities.

He hung high in the clouds, circling like the buzzard that he was—a pilot with an aeroplane, but no kills. Waiting. Waiting for a victim.

Far below him, a different kind of war was being waged. He watched as swarms of infantry in French trenches poured into no-man's land. From this high above the action, the mass of soldiers looked like a liquid spilling over a rim and flooding the plains. Puffs of smoke of various sizes appeared on the German side. Light at first, then heavier. The French tide was stemmed. Halted midway. Then, the liquid motion began to reverse itself and flow the other way until the last little drop was back over the ridge. A heavy residue was left on the field. Johnny knew these were the dead and dying.

Then, a new development. More puffs of smoke appeared.

These sailed through the air with wiggly tails and landed close to the French side. This smoke was different from the artillery puffs. It was thinner, wispy, and—Johnny knew— deadly. Canisters of poison gas. Johnny could only imagine the frantic actions of those below in the French trenches as they donned gas masks. Their eyes stinging. Lungs and throats burning.

Without warning, the gas changed direction and blew toward the German side. The wind had changed. Now it was the Germans' turn to don the masks, to choke, to burn, to die. That was the problem with an indiscriminate weapon, it didn't matter who it killed, the one at whom the canister was thrown, or the one who threw the canister.

Watching the drama of infantry warfare, Johnny concluded he preferred the air to the ground. He had his own set of dangers—laboring for breath in the rarefied air of high altitudes, suffering agonizing cold, inhaling the sickening fumes of rotary engines' castor oil, smeared goggles at crucial moments, guns jamming, burning to death, falling out of the aeroplane to your death, or falling with it to your death. But here in the sky, he could fly like an eagle (or a buzzard); while on the ground, they lived in the dirt like gophers.

A small movement below caught his eye. It was crossing quickly over the battlefield, from the French side to the German side, casting a shadow on the ground beneath it.

His target!

Shoving the stick forward and hitting a hard right pedal, he spiraled downward to lose altitude quickly. When he was low enough, he took a position that put him between the aeroplane he was chasing and the sun. Approaching from the sun would give him the element of surprise.

He identified his prey. A German Albatross scout. More maneuverable than his Spad, but not as fast. Couldn't sustain deep dives. The lower wings had a tendency to fall off.

Just as Johnny was about to close in, a second Albatross joined it; then a third.

Three to one odds, Johnny thought. I pity those other pilots. They're outnumbered!

Diving down on top of them, Johnny targeted the middle scout. With his first burst of fire, all three of the German pilots reacted.

The two side scouts split off. The middle scout tried to outrun him.

"No you don't!" Johnny said, once again on his tail. He was keeping an eye on the location of the other two scouts. Both were circling around to get in behind him.

Johnny let them get into position, then just as they were about to close in, he pulled up hard. One of the trailing planes followed him, the other stayed with the original scout. Pulling around, Johnny came after the two that were together, using his superior speed to keep ahead of his pursuer. He strafed the two planes.

Tack . . . tack . . . tack . . . tack . . . tack.

The one scout started smoking and peeled off, heading for a lower altitude. The original scout continued on his way.

Tack . . . tack . . . tack . . . tack . . . tack.

Bullets whizzed by him. The third scout! Johnny spun into a dive, knowing the Albatross couldn't follow him. When he leveled out, both aeroplanes were above him. His attacker circling around for another pass.

Johnny aimed straight for the original scout, the one the other two were protecting for some reason. The attacking Albatross lined up to come at him from the side.

While he closed on the tail of the original scout, the attacking scout closed on him. Johnny took aim.

Tack . . . tack . . . tack . . . tack . . . tack.

Out of the corner of his eye, he saw his attacker reach for

his guns. Johnny turned into him. It was a dangerous move in that he crossed directly into the path of the attacker, but only for a second. Had he turned away, the attacker would have fallen in behind him with an opportunity for repeated and extended blasts.

Johnny climbed at a nearly vertical ascent. Just as he was about to stall, he hit the rudder bar and fell over, coming down on top of his attacker.

Tack . . . tack . . . tack . . . tack . . . tack.

The Albatross suffered critical, but not fatal damage. He fell to a lower altitude to escape. Again, Johnny let him go. There was something about the original scout plane that intrigued him. Now, it was just the two of them.

He fell in behind the scout. The German pilot zigged and zagged and climbed and dove, but nothing he did was able to shake Johnny from his tail.

Johnny checked his guns. He flew in closer and took aim.

Tack . . . tack . . . tack . . . tack . . . tack.

Fabric and splinters erupted from the tail.

Tack . . . tack . . . tack . . . tack . . . tack.

The plane dove. Johnny stayed with it.

Tack . . . tack . . . tack . . . tack . . . tack.

Smoke started pouring out of the Albatross' engine. Johnny could feel the exhilaration. He was going to get his first kill!

The Albatross was crippled, but could still fly.

They were down to a couple hundred feet. Johnny took aim again.

Tack . . . tack . . . tack . . . tack . . . tack.

More smoke. Then, Johnny saw what the German pilot was doing! He was attempting to land! Johnny couldn't have that!

Tack . . . tack . . . tack . . . tack . . . tack.

The Albatross shuddered, then fell nose down. It crashed

onto a field, the softest crash Johnny had ever seen, but a crash! He had downed a German aeroplane! His first kill!

Johnny swooped upward and spun around several times in joy. He circled the field to get a look at his handiwork. The pilot was climbing out of the wreckage.

Johnny had an idea.

Circling around, he landed in the field and taxied toward the crashed Albatross and the pilot. His hand rested on his guns. The pilot saw him coming and reached for a sidearm. Johnny squeezed the trigger of his gun.

Tack . . . tack . . . tack . . . tack . . . tack.

Pieces of the downed Albatross flew into the air. It was enough to convince the pilot to drop his pistol. Johnny motioned for the pilot to come to him.

With his hands raised, the German pilot approached the Spad.

Captain Eastman's voice could be heard from the other side of the door.

"Come in!" he barked.

Johnny opened the door and stepped inside.

"Sir," Johnny said, "I wish to report my first kill."

Eastman looked at him skeptically. "Tell me about it."

Johnny described the encounter. Him against three German Albatross pilots, how he chased two away and downed the third.

"That's some story, Morgan," Eastman said.

"It's factual, sir."

"That may be, but without corroboration, I can't give you credit for a kill."

"Corroboration?"

"Someone else has to witness it."

"But, sir, I'm a scout. It's not like flying in a formation. There are not always other pilots around to corroborate."

"Those are the breaks, Morgan. But without verification, I can't give you credit for the kill."

"Sir, would you accept another form of corroboration?"

"What did you have in mind?"

Johnny reached inside his jacket and pulled out a piece of paper. He handed it to Eastman who read it.

Captain Eastman,

Let it be known that on this day, Mr. Johnny Morgan disabled my two escort aeroplanes and shot down my plane.

Hermann Goering

KATY would always remember this day as a day of contrasts: natural beauty and the ugliness of humanity; fear and hope; life and death. It began with a luxurious, rosy-pink sunrise and ended in a dank, black cave.

The morning orb had yet to make its appearance. The eastern sky blushed with early light. Bands of color stretched across the horizon beginning with a pale white strip that outlined the contour of the land. It blended with a luminous ribbon of coral which gave way to azure, which formed the final link between the coming day and the passing night with its spatter of stars overhead.

Laura and Katy sat behind a small white ornamented cast-iron lawn table facing dawn's early glow. It was a rare moment of personal relaxation for them, borrowed from their meager ration of sleeping time. Mrs. Jones had requested an early meeting with them before they started a new shift, then was called away unexpectedly. The two younger women decided to redeem the time with a second cup of tea on the hospital lawn.

Cupping the warm drink in both hands, Katy smelled the freshly brewed tea before sipping the milky brown liquid. She smiled at the pleasing warm sensation as it went down. It was one of those perfect little moments. The splash of colors in the sky. The chill of morning against her skin. The aroma and flavor of a good cup of English tea. A feast of senses.

Beside her, Laura sipped her tea while reading a letter from Percy. The letter had been waiting for them at the hospital upon their return. The postal markings indicated he had mailed it the day before they parted in Paris. Laura had already read aloud the opening line to her. Percy had skipped the salutation. None was needed.

> *I already miss you. And I couldn't bear the thought that you would go back to your duties without so much as a reminder of how much I care for you. So I wrote this before you left Paris in the hope that the postal service would be kind and a part of me would be waiting for you at the hospital upon your return.*

"Isn't that so sweet?" Laura smiled. She was looking at Katy, but her eyes were filled with Percy.

"Very thoughtful," Katy agreed. She observed her younger partner as Laura returned to the letter.

Laura's eyes bounced happily from line to line. She devoured every word. As she worked her way down the page, her joy increased until she was literally glowing. There was a sense of young love radiating around her that rivaled the warmth and richness of the hues of the rising sun.

For some reason, Katy's next sip of tea was not as soothing. And the colors in the sky had washed out into a nondescript hazy yellow. With black specks.

Had Katy been wearing glasses, she would have removed and cleaned them. Squinting into the distance she counted more than two dozen specks dotting the horizon. They were uniformly spaced. Shaped in a series of inverted Vs.

A chill of terror swept aside the morning's good feelings.

"Laura!"

"Mmmmmm?" Smiling eyes were reluctant to detach from Percy's words.

"Aeroplanes!" Katy cried, pointing to the sky. "In formation. From the east!"

The last phrase snapped the bond that held Laura's attention to the letter. She looked to the horizon. "God help us!" she cried.

The black specks were larger now. The percussive popping of antiaircraft artillery could be heard.

Katy's cast-iron chair tumbled backward against the grass as she jumped up. "Let's alert the staff," she said.

Laura folded her letter, stuffing it in her apron pocket. She grabbed her teacup and both women ran inside, but not before taking one last look at the black specks that marred the morning sky.

The hospital window exploded. Pieces of glass showered patients in their beds, many who were not yet awake.

"Cover those over there with blankets! Get these to the basement!" Katy shouted orders to the nurses on duty. Throwing back the covers of a young man with a bandaged head, she proceeded to help him out of the bed. He was a willing participant. Too willing and not wise.

"Slippers!" Katy shouted. "There's glass all over the floor. Unless you want bloody feet, put on your slippers!"

A thunderous boom was followed instantly by more flying glass.

Katy and her patient ducked. Bits of window pelted them in the back. Tiny pieces stuck in Katy's hair.

Through the jagged glass wave after wave of German bombers flew over the hospital. The hospital itself did not seem to be the target. They were bombing the surrounding neighborhood. But errant bombs were finding their way onto hospital grounds.

Mrs. Graham Jones came running into the ward.

"Get Laura!" she ordered. "The cellar is full."

"What are we going to do?"

"There are some caves about a mile away. We'll transport the remaining patients to that location."

Mrs. Jones relieved Katy of her patient.

Katy found Laura one floor beneath her, on one end of a stretcher that bore a rather large patient. Laura's arms and neck were straining from the load. Katy assisted her as the patient was loaded onto a wheeled cart.

"Thanks," Laura said. "Carrying him was one thing. Halfway there I was beginning to wonder how I was going to lift my end onto the cart."

"We have transport duties," Katy said. "I'll fill you in on the way."

Katy drove the third of three ambulances. There was a full load in back. With every rut, or jolt, or bomb blast came cries of pain and fear. One additional patient, his arm in a sling, sat in the front between Katy and Laura.

"This is worse than no-man's land," he said, staring at the destruction on both sides of the road.

Some of the houses were leveled completely. A foundation and jagged remnants that once were walls was the only indication that there had once been a building there. Other houses had gaping holes in them through which flames of fire danced.

Everywhere, displaced families sifted through the rubble for missing loved ones or treasures. Hundreds of them, having bundled in sheets or blankets what few personal items remained, clogged the roads as they attempted to escape the destruction on foot.

BOOM!

A geyser of dirt and debris erupted a hundred yards to

the right of the ambulance, literally shoving it a foot or two sideways. Rock projectiles pelted the side of the ambulance. Katy's ears rang from the percussion.

One of the patients began weeping openly, pleading with the German bombers to stop. Laura turned in her seat and tried unsuccessfully to soothe him.

Bombs rained all around them as Katy steered around shell holes and debris and pedestrians and bodies. The clear sky overhead swarmed with enemy bombers like gnats on a summer day.

BOOM!

The blast was right in front of them. A direct hit on ambulance number two. Like a toy, the vehicle flew into the air—tumbling as it rose, its driver tossed free from the vehicle, a ragged black hole in the top, wheels turned upward, fire in the undercarriage, crashing down, skidding into a ditch beside the road, landing on its roof, the sides crunching together like an accordion, coming to a halt in a cloud of dust, just before it burst into flames.

The impact of the bomb slammed Katy, Laura, and their front-seat passenger back against the seat, then forward as though they ran into an invisible brick wall. The ambulance skidded sideways.

Katy turned into the direction of the skid.

The ambulance began to tip. Momentum was working against her. The driver's side wheels lifted off the road.

The horizon was turning sideways. The ambulance was tipping over and there was nothing she could do to stop it. A cacophony of male screams and cries arose from the back. There was a moment of hesitation when it seemed like their momentum had died just short of a rollover; then, WHAM! The vehicle whomped over on its side like an elephant brought down by a big game hunter.

Katy figured she must have passed out, but only for a

moment. The first thing she remembered was the thump, thump, thump of distant bombs exploding. Her head throbbed. Her ears rang. There was a warm sensation against her cheek, a rounded shaft of some sort dug into her side. Muted moans and whimpers came from beneath her.

When her eyes fluttered open and she raised herself up, Katy saw that she'd landed on top of the soldier patient who'd been riding next to her. Her cheek was pressed against his forehead. It was his elbow that was poking her side. But if she was on top of him, then he must be . . .

Laura!

Seeing the steering wheel above her, set against the blue sky which was still busy with bombers, she reached for it to pull herself up. A face appeared sideways above the windscreen. It was one of the nurses from ambulance one.

She was young, with black short-cropped hair. She was on her hands and knees. Her eyes were wide in anticipation of what she might find inside the cab of the ambulance.

"Katy!" she cried. "Are you alive?"

"Laura is under me! Help me up!"

With the help of the young nurse, Katy climbed out of the cab, doing her best not to step on those who were underneath her. Just as she was working herself free, the soldier let out a low moan. He was coming around.

"Is anything broken?" the young nurse asked him.

His response was another moan.

"I'll take care of them," Katy said to the nurse. "You check on the patients in back."

The young nurse backed away and Katy took her place.

"Laura?" she shouted. She winced. It hurt to shout.

There was no sound coming from beneath the soldier patient. Katy could see a tiny portion of Laura's apron. There were bright red stains on it. A little of Laura's hair was visible under the soldier's neck. But that was all. The rest of her was covered by the patient who was hovering midway between consciousness and unconsciousness.

"Soldier!" Katy cried, not remembering his name. When he didn't respond, she reached in and slapped his face lightly, trying to bring him around. "Soldier! Can you hear me?"

He moaned.

She slapped him again. "You've got to get up!"

His head fell side-to-side. As it did, Katy could see a little more of Laura. The side of her face. Eyes closed. A trickle of blood from the corner of her mouth.

British soldiers appeared behind Katy, about a dozen of them.

"You and you," Katy barked, pointing to two of them. "Get him out of there!" She ordered two others to stand by to get Laura. The rest were to help remove the patients from the back of the ambulance.

The soldier was hauled out of the cab in short order. Then, Laura was extracted. She was laid beside the soldier in a bed of wild daisies that covered everything on that side of the road for several hundred feet.

Overhead, the skies had cleared of bomber activity. They had turned their attention to an unknown target several miles up the road.

Katy bent over the soldier. He was coming around. Coughing. Opening his eyes.

She turned to Laura. She was breathing, but still unconscious. The blood from her mouth was a split lip. The apron blood had come from a cut on the soldier's arm.

"Will she be all right?" a raspy voice asked. It was the soldier. His head was turned toward Laura. He stared at her through a forest of daisy stems.

The shadow of the young nurse fell over Laura. Katy looked up.

"Two are dead," the nurse reported. "The others will

make it."

A British sergeant appeared beside the nurse. To Katy, he said, "Is that your ambulance?"

Katy acknowledged that it was indeed her ambulance.

"Would you like me and the boys to right it?"

"Can you do that?" Katy asked.

"Consider it done."

Laura moaned. She turned her head side-to-side, the brightness of the sun bothered her. Katy moved so that her shadow blocked the sun.

"Where does it hurt?" Katy asked.

Laura's eyes worked back and forth as she performed a quick inventory of herself. "All over," she replied. She touched her lip with the back of her hand, wiped away the blood, and stared at it. "Other than my lip, no place in particular. It just feels like a rhinoceros sat on me."

"I've been called a lot of things in my life, but never a rhinoceros." The soldier, obviously feeling better himself, had propped himself up on one arm.

"You're only half of one," Katy said. "I'm the other half." To Laura: "Are you sure you're fine?"

She needed assistance, but she sat up. For a moment, her eyes appeared to be woozy, but they quickly cleared.

Behind them, the sergeant was counting out time as his soldiers rocked the ambulance back and forth. After establishing momentum, with one final heave, the ambulance was once again set upright.

The sergeant jumped behind the wheel. It took three attempts, but he was able to bring the engine to life. He tried first gear and reverse, and turned the wheels side-to-side. Jumping out, he declared the vehicle in suitable shape to drive, at least until a mechanic was able to take a good look at it.

"Would you like us to load the wounded in the back

again?" he asked.

Katy nodded. "I want to check each of them as you do, Sergeant." To Laura, "Stay here. I'll be right back."

Laura started to get up. "I can help," she said.

"You just lie there for a few minutes," Katy said. "I'll have Nurse . . . " she looked up at the young nurse.

"Watkins," said the young lady.

"I'll have Nurse Watkins assist me."

"You'll call me if you need me," Laura said.

"I'll call."

It wasn't long before the patients were loaded again. Katy relayed a message to ambulance number one that ambulance three was ready to resume their journey. The young nurse went running off.

"Anything else, ma'am?" asked the sergeant.

"Ambulance two . . . " Katy asked.

The sergeant shook his head, indicating that there were no survivors. "I'm sorry," he said.

Katy thanked him for his assistance, then turned his attention to helping the soldier and Laura back into the cab. Laura insisted she didn't need any help. It was only a headache and minor bruises and scratches, that was all. With the two of them in the cab, Katy turned her attention to the ambulance while she waited for word from ambulance one that they were ready to move out.

She lifted the bonnet of the truck and checked hoses and belts and the radiator. Everything seemed to be in working order. *We'll find out soon enough.* Closing the bonnet, she looked for a signal from ambulance one. Its bonnet was open. A pair of legs dangled out the side while the young nurse looked on.

Katy took a deep breath to steady her nerves.

Not far from her lay the charred and still burning remains of ambulance two. She walked slowly toward the now blackened monument to death. She hadn't known the drivers. They were new. Arrived while she and Laura were in Paris.

The sun beat down warmly upon her. A perfect spring day. It was the kind of day that songwriters attempted to capture with their music, that poets loved to describe with words. How utterly insane it was that a day of such beauty was the backdrop for war and death.

Black smoke from the ambulance circled merrily as it rose into a picture-perfect blue sky. Birds that just a few minutes earlier had been drowned out by the sound of explosions or the monotonous droning of aeroplanes, chirped happily nearby. The fragrance of spring daisies commingled with the odor of burning rubber. Huge sections of the wild flowers had been trampled under heavy boots. Some of their yellow and white and purple petals were splattered with blood. A monarch butterfly, its orange wings flitting happily, oblivious to the political differences between the human belligerents, bounced from flower to flower and landed on the back of a dead man who was lying facedown in the field.

Untold beauty and hideous human misery. On this spring day they shared the same tiny corner of the world.

The two surviving ambulances limped along the road, barely a mile from the caves when the German bombers struck again. Katy didn't know if she could survive another close hit. She found herself wishing that if a bomb were to land anywhere near her, that it would land on her head so that it would all be over quickly.

Instead, the bombs fell at distances of 50, 100, 200 yards. Safe enough not to cause physical damage, but close enough to wear her nerves down to next to nothing. By the time they reached the caves, she was shaking uncontrollably. She jumped at the slightest sound. She felt more like one who required care than who gave it.

They found the caves already occupied when they arrived. A field hospital had moved in eight days previous. However, with an adjustment here and there, enough room was found for everyone.

Against her wishes, Laura was made to lie down for a time as a patient. Katy wanted to keep her under observation for a couple of hours. Once all her patients were settled, Katy slumped down against the wall of the cave next to Laura. The chill of the wall penetrated her clothing. A single kerosene lamp placed on a small rock outcropping provided the only light.

She could still hear the bombs pounding away outside the cave. They were not as loud, but still they continued to wear on her like the steady drip of a faucet. For the first time since leaving the hospital, she didn't have anything to do. It gave her emotions sufficient excuse to rise to the surface and threaten to spill over.

A middle-aged nurse approached Katy. She extended her hand. "Don't get up," she said. "My name is Ella."

"I'm Katy." The two women squeezed each other's hand.

Ella was a stocky British woman with a proper accent. She had large forearms and legs which attached to a barrel of a body. She didn't smile readily, but neither did Katy get the impression that the woman was an unfriendly sort.

Motioning to Laura, who was sleeping, Ella said, "Your partner?"

"And friend."

"Hear you had a difficult time coming in."

Katy nodded. "That we did." She did her best to still her shaking hands so that Ella would not notice. Failing that, she folded her arms to hide them.

"How long do you plan on staying?"

"Just until the bombing stops."

"Ah! 'Til the war ends," Ella joked.

Katy smiled. It was a weak smile for a weak joke.

Looking around the cave, Ella said, "Would you believe I haven't been in the light for eight days? You probably noticed that the stench in this cave is quite awful."

Katy noticed.

"It permeates everything after a while. Clothes. Food. Even a person's skin. Then there are the kerosene lamps for light. Hardly sufficient to do most nursing duties. The conditions get more crowded with each offensive. Most of the time the cots are so close together you can just barely squeeze a foot between them."

"From what I noticed earlier, you have a wide variety of patients."

Ella nodded. "Side-by-side I have Americans, English, Scotch, Irish, and French. I even have a few Boche in the corner. There's no fighting soldiers here. They lay there and watch each other die."

"I noticed sections of the cave are curtained off with blankets," Katy said.

"We have an operating area and a dressing-room area. One part of the cave is curtained off for officers."

"How long do your patients stay here before being transported to a hospital?"

"Most stay for about twenty-four hours. We want to send them off as quickly as possible, because even this cave is a dangerous place. If it's not a bombing raid, it's cannon fire, with the shells breaking over and around us."

"Aren't you afraid?"

"Don't have time to be," Ella replied. "Fact is, I feel guilty having stolen this little time from the wounded to chat with you." She paused for a moment as a thought struck her. "Maybe we can redeem this time. Do you have a minute? I'd be most grateful if you would examine a patient for me. He's not responding to our treatments and, quite frankly, we're all a bit stymied over this case. Perhaps an objective viewpoint is what is needed in this situation. Do you mind?"

Katy glanced over at Laura. She was still sleeping.

"What's the nature of your patient's injury?" Katy asked, boosting herself up from the floor of the cave.

When Katy returned, she found Laura sitting up on her cot. The younger woman's cheeks were wet with tears.

"What's wrong, dear?" Katy asked.

Laura wiped off her cheeks. "It's nothing," she said.

"Are you in pain?"

"No. I'm feeling strong enough to do my share of the duties."

Katy studied her friend quizzically. "Laura, what's wrong?"

"It's nothing . . . it's silly."

"Nonsense! Whatever is troubling you, it's serious enough to cause you to cry."

Laura's hands fumbled in her pockets. Standing next to the cot, Katy hid her own hands in her pockets, not wanting Laura to see them trembling. She thought she knew what was troubling Laura—the poor girl was frightened to death by the bombs just like her—but Katy wanted Laura to put her fear into words.

"It's gone," Laura said.

Puzzled, Katy said, "What's gone?"

Tears came despite Laura's best efforts to stop them. Her hands continued to fumble in her pockets.

"Percy's letter," she said. "It's gone. And I hadn't finished reading it."

Katy wrapped her arms around Laura, who was sobbing openly now. Her anguish was understandable.

Together, they wept over Laura's loss.

For three days the caves served as home to the refugee patients from the hospital. On the third day, the road back was a tour through human suffering.

Homes gutted. Farmlands razed by fire. Dead animals lying everywhere. Graves freshly filled. Orphans crying. Entire families living in temporary shelters built out of whatever material could be salvaged from the rubble.

In comparison, the hospital was relatively unscathed. It suffered no direct hits. Most of the windows were blown out, but that was the extent of the damage. With the exception of some minor cuts from flying glass, the patients too fared well.

When the hospital building came into view, Katy prayed a prayer of thanksgiving for the comfort of her quarters. Cramped and dark, she had often referred to her room as the cave. No more. From now on, it was her palace.

A third ambulance had been sent to transport some of the cave patients to better facilities. So when Katy and Laura returned, once again, they were the third in a line of three vehicles.

"Isn't that Fred Radcliff?" Laura asked.

She pointed to a British lieutenant who ran to the first ambulance arriving back at the hospital. He jumped on the running board and poked his head in the driver's side of the cab.

"It looks like him," Katy said, "though at this distance I can't be sure. What is he doing?"

The lieutenant pulled his head out of the first cab and looked to the second. No sooner had it pulled to the unloading area when he jumped onto the running board and once again poked his head into the cab.

"That *is* Radcliff!" Katy cried. She pulled in behind the second ambulance and braked to a stop just as Radcliff pulled away from the second cab and ran toward her.

His face appeared in the driver's side window. His was a comical expression, the kind Katy had always pictured appearing on the faces of the people in the Bible who saw angels—wanting to believe that what they saw was true, yet hesitant to believe lest they make fools of themselves.

Radcliff's first expression dissolved into one of pure relief and joy. He closed his eyes and lifted his face heavenward. "Thank God! Thank God!" he cried.

Then, taking Katy completely by surprise, he grabbed her face with both hands and planted a kiss directly on her mouth.

Katy pulled away. "Mr. Radcliff!" she cried. "How dare you!"

Laura thought it was funny. She was laughing.

"I fail to see the humor in this!" Katy fumed.

Fred Radcliff was instantly apologetic. "Please forgive me," he cried, holding up his hands in a defenseless posture. "It's just that I got carried away, that's all . . . "

"I should say so!" Katy cried.

"Three days ago we received a report that one of three ambulances had been shelled. That there were no survivors. So for the last three days I have been trying to learn the identity of the driver of that ambulance. I tried everywhere! Nobody knew. So for three days I've been forced to live with the fear that you had been snatched away from me forever, and this without you ever knowing what I feel for you."

"How sweet!" Laura cooed. "Tell her now, Lieutenant Radcliff."

"Laura!" Katy objected. Opening her door, she pushed Radcliff away. She walked past him as if he was not there to the back of the ambulance where the hospital staff was already unloading the patients.

Radcliff followed her. "Is there a time when I can speak

with you?"

Pointing to one of the patients, Katy instructed the two stretcher-bearers. "Take him to the second ward. Tell the nurses he needs his bandages changed immediately."

"Katy!" Laura said, appearing from the other side of the ambulance. "Lieutenant Radcliff is talking to you."

With a sigh, Katy turned toward Radcliff. Still using her nursing tone, she said, "Thank you for your concern, Lieutenant. Truly, it is appreciated. But I have work to do at the moment."

"Katy!" Laura cried in disbelief.

"I understand duty," Radcliff replied, "just tell me when you end your shift and I'll come back then."

"I'll be sleeping then."

"How about tomorrow?"

Katy swung around, fully intending to put an end to this nonsense once for all. However, there was something about the level of earnestness in his eyes that stopped her. Never before had a man been so intent on wanting to be with her.

"Tomorrow," she said. "Ten o'clock. At the garden lawn."

The joy in his eyes compounded tenfold. It was enough to take her breath away.

"Ten o'clock," he said.

By nine o'clock the next morning, Katy was regretting she'd agreed to meet Lieutenant Radcliff. By 9:15, she was auditioning excuses why she would have to miss the meeting, to see which one sounded most believable. By 9:30, she wished she had never agreed to take Maggie Thomas' tea cakes to the London hospital in the first place. By 9:45, she had resigned herself to the meeting and promised herself that it would be one of the briefest encounters between a man and a woman in all human history.

Lieutenant Fred Radcliff was waiting for her when she

arrived fifteen minutes late. He was holding a single yellow rose which he gave to her before a single word was said. Making no mention of her tardiness, he offered her a seat at the white cast-iron table.

She stood.

"Fred, let me say I'm very flattered by your attention, but . . . "

Radcliff held up a hand and stopped her. "I think I know how you feel," he said. "You have been straightforward with me from the first day we met."

"Then you understand . . . "

Again he stopped her. "I'll be brief," he said. "I have loved you from the first moment I saw you walk into the hospital ward carrying Maggie Thomas' tea cakes. From that day until now, I have never stopped loving you. I'm fully aware that your life's goals leave no room for romance. I've told myself that a thousand times. A million times! But for some reason, I can't stop feeling about you the way I do.

"I'm not here to attempt to change your mind. It's just that these last three days when I feared you might have been killed in that transport . . . " his eyes became glassy with tears, " . . . I just couldn't bear the thought that you had died not knowing how much I love you. I don't ask your love in return. I just want you to know how I feel."

Katy held the rose close to her. "I'm sorry, Fred. I knew you had feelings for me, but I never knew they were to this extent. And I wish I could return them, but . . . "

Radcliff shrugged, "There's no need to state the obvious."

"What I wanted to say," Katy persisted, "was that I can't promise my feelings for you will ever change."

"I'm not asking for any promises."

"Maybe promise isn't the right word then," Katy said. "Fred, you're a wonderful man who deserves a wife who will love you with the same intensity with which you love her. I would hate to see you miss the opportunity to find such a woman by spending your life hoping for something that can never be."

Radcliff's voice was firm when he spoke next. "Maybe I'm not making myself clear," he said. "Katy Morgan, you may never love me. But I can't help loving you. God knows, I've tried. But if there is one thing of which I am sure in this life, it is this: I will love you forever. God help me, but this is a truth I will live with until the day I die."

Chapter 28

JOHNNY lay in the dark, his hands behind his head, and stared at the ceiling. Percy lay in the bed on the other side of the room. A sliver of French moonlight split the window curtains and streaked across the wooden floor between them.

All was quiet in the room. Percy was awake. Had he been asleep, Johnny would have heard some form of rhythmic breathing, from a soft sonorous slumbering to a window-rattling, nose-clearing, full-blast snore.

"You thinking about Mott?"

The question hung in the dark. For a good long time it hung there without a response to claim it. Johnny began to wonder if he'd been mistaken and Percy was asleep after all.

"Yeah."

So Percy was awake.

"Me too," Johnny said.

"Every time I close my eyes I see him standing on the wing. Then . . . "

Richard Mott was the first battle-related death among the pilots of the 59th Squadron. A tracer bullet had pierced his gas tank, setting the aeroplane on fire. In an attempt to save himself and his craft, Mott had climbed onto the wing of his burning machine. Reaching into the cockpit, he then tried to sideslip the aeroplane to the ground. The theory was that a pilot could thus fan the flames away from the cockpit and keep from burning to death. His feat was not unique. A valiant effort, but ill-fated.

Mott's aeroplane exploded. Both pilot and machine fell to the ground in flames.

"Some pilots jump rather than burn," Johnny said.

"Which would you do?" Percy asked.

"Sideslip."

"That was a quick answer. You must have thought about this before."

"No. Arrogance, plain and simple."

Percy laughed. "Explain. Not the fact that you're arrogant, I already know that. Explain how arrogance determined your answer."

"It's simple. By jumping out of the aeroplane, you concede your death. You admit to having failed and choose to die by slamming against the ground rather than burning up in the aeroplane. Me? I hate to lose. I'll fight death to the very end. And as long as my hand is on that control stick, I like to think I still have a chance to win. How about you? What would you do?"

"I'd jump."

"Really?"

"No. But if you're up there jousting with death, I don't want to be anywhere near either one of you."

It was Johnny's turn to laugh.

After his laughter died out, it was silent and dark again for a time. Then, out of the darkness came Percy's voice. It was somber and heavy.

"Mott's death has forced me—all of us pilots—to think about all the things that can go wrong up there. It's a wonder we haven't all died by now."

"I prefer to think about strategy and victories," Johnny said. "That's what will keep me alive. Let the Huns think about death."

Percy mused, "The way I see it, sooner or later all of us are going to get into a battle where the odds are too long against us. Or perhaps we'll meet up with a stray bullet from ground artillery fire. Or maybe, our engine will cut out while we're flying low strafing trenches."

"You make it sound like flying aeroplanes is dangerous," Johnny quipped.

"Like I said, Mott's death got me to thinking."

Silence again for a while.

"Percy?"

"Yeah?"

"The other day. I didn't mean to suggest you were an incompetent pilot. It's just that I was furious with Eastman because he didn't give me . . ."

"Forget it."

"You're a good pilot."

"The best."

"Now who's being arrogant?"

Percy chuckled again.

It felt good to be talking to Percy again. He was the only person in the squadron who talked with Johnny on a regular basis. The other pilots looked at him askance and talked more behind his back than to his face. That didn't bother him. He hadn't come to France to be social. He came to shoot down Huns and become an ace. Still, it was good that Percy was talking to him again.

"Do you know what I'm reminded of?" Johnny asked.

"What?"

"That first night in Columbus at your father's hotel. It was just like this. We lay in the dark and talked."

"Do you remember what we talked about?"

"What else? Aeroplanes."

"Figures."

After a moment or so, Percy sighed. "I miss them," he said.

"Your parents?"

"Yeah. I wish they were still alive so I could introduce Laura to them. They'd fall in love with her. I know it. And she'd love them too."

"I'm sure they would," Johnny said. "But if they were still alive, do you think you'd be a pilot today?"

A moment of thought. "Naw. I probably would have joined up with the infantry though once we got into the war."

"You were saved from life in the trenches!"

"But at what cost?" Percy asked.

"Look at it this way. If things had worked out like you say, and you joined the infantry, you probably wouldn't have met Laura."

"Probably. But . . . well, I don't know . . . it just seems we were destined for each other. Even if I were in the infantry, I could have been on furlough in Paris at that same time and still met Laura."

"But she wouldn't have been attracted to you."

"Why not?"

"You would have been one of a thousand doughboys! It's the wings that attract the females."

"Yeah, I've noticed how you have to keep brushing beautiful women aside everywhere you go."

"I'm different."

"That's for sure."

Johnny laughed. "I mean, I'm different in that I let them know right away they're wasting their time. I'm not interested."

It was quiet for a good long time. Johnny wondered if Percy had drifted off. Then, out of the darkness came a voice.

"Johnny?"

"Yeah?"

"What do you think of her?"

"Of who?"

"Of Laura!"

Until this moment, Johnny hadn't given the girl much thought. "She's all right, I guess."

"That's high praise coming from Johnny Morgan!"

Johnny laughed. "What I meant was, I'm not sure I'd ever be attracted to her. But I think she's perfect for *you.*"

"Thanks," Percy said. "I think so too."

He tracked the German Albatross single-seater through the clouds. The German pilot gave no indication he knew he was being tracked.

Step right up to the window, ladies and gentlemen! Witness Johnny Morgan's second kill on his way to becoming America's greatest ace!

Several layers of cloud formation made the skies ideal for a game of cat-and-mouse. Ducking behind clouds. Tracking the Albatross at times by his shadow. Maneuvering closer. Positioning for a shot. And still not spotted. On a clear day, it could never be this easy.

Johnny had picked him up as the German scout climbed after having strafed the American trenches. Had the Albatross circled around for another pass, Johnny would have gone after him then. But the attacker flew toward the German lines.

Antiaircraft fire was heavy. So, rather than risk getting hit by his own antiaircraft—he wouldn't be the first pilot to do so—he followed the Albatross until it was clear. Secretly, he was hoping the American gunners were off their mark today. Had they downed the Albatross, he would have been deprived of kill number two.

So, the game began. The German pilot was probably thinking about the ale he would have with his squadron buddies when he landed. He'd tell them about his victory. How he strafed the Americans.

Not today, Boche. You won't be doing any celebrating at the expense of American lives today. Or ever again.

Below him, his prey continued on, unaware that death was close at hand. Johnny flew in and out of a series of clouds. So did the Albatross.

Now you see him, now you don't.

He checked his guns.

Ready or not.

A shadow caught his eye. It flashed against a cloud. Then it was gone. There! No . . . Yes, there!

His shadow? *No!*

Hard right. Forward. The Spad responded. Nose down and away.

Tack . . . tack . . . tack . . . tack . . . tack.

Bullets, tracers, split the air so close to his head he thought he could feel their heat. He glanced over his shoulder. A Fokker triplane!

Hard left. Johnny was slammed hard against his seat, his head thrown back. The wind pressing hard against his goggles.

Tack . . . tack . . . tack . . . tack . . . tack.

Not as close this time. He'd gained a little distance. Johnny pulled out the throttle. Speed. He needed more speed.

Stubby and slow, the Fokker triplane would not win any races. But it had so much wing surface that it could out-turn or out-climb any Allied aircraft. In a dive, its integrity was questionable. So Johnny had done exactly the right thing: steep dive and speed.

But he was lucky. Very lucky. All this time, the tracker was being tracked.

Turning toward the battlefront, Johnny withdrew, racing away from the triplane. Low and fast. He increased the distance between him and the Fokker without giving the other pilot another opportunity to shoot.

The Fokker pilot, seeing he had no chance of catching the faster aeroplane, broke off and headed back to the German side.

Johnny circled around to go after him, berating himself all the while for his near-fatal mistake.

Complacency will get you killed! Stay sharp! Stay sharp!

Once again, the cat-and-mouse game began. This time, however, the cat watched his back lest any more mice sneak up from behind.

He flew to 17,000 feet. Shivering. His joints aching from the cold, he scanned the clouds beneath him for the Fokker.

Patches of cloud and shadow. Dark and light. Visibility unlimited one moment, blind the next.

Watch your shadow. Don't let it give you away.

Condensation formed on his instrument panel. He checked his watch. Given the Fokker's speed and his own, he should have caught up with the Fokker by now. Johnny strained for any sign of the aeroplane's presence.

Where are you? Where are you?

Clouds. Patches of ground. Shadow. But no Fokker.

Suddenly, his heart seized. A chill shot through him and it had nothing to do with the frigid temperature. He looked behind him, craned his neck hard to the right, fully expecting to be looking through the wrong side of two German Spandau gun sights.

He saw nothing but sky and cloud.

Relieved but far from relaxed, he continued his search below him for the Fokker.

Where are you, Monsieur Boche? Why won't you come out and play with me? You didn't by chance change course on me, did you?

Far below, he saw the shape of an aeroplane skirting the ground. Black. A shadow. His own.

Then, he saw another aeroplane shape directly in front of the shadow. This was the real thing. His Fokker!

Johnny began his descent.

He was so close to the Fokker by the time he fired, he could have placed the bullets in the enemy aeroplane by hand.

Tack . . . tack . . . tack . . . tack . . . tack.

The Fokker's rudder erupted into splinters and bits of fabric. The German pilot glanced back to see who was attacking him. The shock and surprise on his face was reward enough. But Johnny wanted more.

You deprived me of my Albatross. Just as well. A Fokker triplane is even better.

Tack . . . tack . . . tack . . . tack . . . tack.

Bullet holes ripped up the side of the Fokker's fuselage.

The Fokker pulled up. Johnny stayed on his tail. He banked right, then left. Johnny matched his every move.

Tack . . . tack . . . tack . . . tack . . . tack.

More holes in the fuselage. The pilot grabbed his shoulder.

Tack . . . tack . . . tack . . . tack . . . tack.

The Fokker nosed down. It was no escape maneuver. Johnny followed after it nevertheless. When black smoke and fire spewed from the craft, Johnny broke off the pursuit. Kill number two was imminent.

Spiraling out of control, the Fokker plummeted toward the earth. Whether the pilot jumped or was thrown free, Johnny never knew. To him it was odd to see the two separated from each other. Both falling at identical speeds. The Fokker falling like a giant torch; the pilot twirling slowly beside, his arms and legs fully extended.

A fireball signaled their demise and Johnny's second victory.

He didn't think of the pilot as a human being. All he could feel was one thing: Victory! Triumph! Victory! Blood coursed through his chest in mighty bursts. He circled the downed aeroplane several times, admiring the kill.

Corroboration! I need corroboration. But, from where? A note won't do in this instance . . .

Just then, he spotted three Spads flying in formation in the distance.

How to get their attention? Something unusual. Something . . .

Flying parallel to their course, Johnny pulled up like he was going to perform a loop; halfway up the climb, he fell off. He pulled up again, and fell off; pulled up, fell off, like a porpoise jumping out of the water.

It worked. The formation changed course to intercept him. When they reached his location, he circled the downed Fokker. The lead pilot acknowledged what had happened. Just to be sure, Johnny took note of the squadron's designation on the side of the three aeroplanes. He smiled. The 103rd squadron, formerly the Lafayette Escadrille.

Saluting each other, the pilots returned to their separate squadrons with Johnny two fifths of the way to becoming an ace American pilot.

Johnny Morgan's third kill came less than a week later.

Before the mission, he was tied for the lead in his squadron with Captain Eastman, who also had two kills to his credit. Four other pilots in the squadron, including Percy, had one kill apiece. As for casualties, two more pilots of the 59th Squadron, Allsop and Follmer, had recently taken up residence next to Mott in the airfield's graveyard.

With their loss, Captain Eastman pulled Johnny back into the squadron formation to fill one of the gaps. Johnny saw it differently.

"He wants to ensure that I won't get more kills than him," he said to Percy as the two of them approached the briefing room. "You'll see I'm right. He'll keep me busy as a decoy while he swoops down for the attack."

Swinging open the door, Percy preceded Johnny into the briefing room. Pilots of the 59th filled the small room. They lounged in chairs, perched on the edge of tables, or sat in the sills of open windows. A chorus of greetings met Percy as he crossed the threshold. Johnny was greeted by a nod or two, and only from those he looked at directly or from younger pilots who knew him only for his number of kills.

Eastman burst through the door immediately behind them. The squadron captain marched to the front of the room, squared his shoulders, and spoke in clipped sentences. Their objective was to draw out the German pursuit planes located at the Cambrai aerodrome. To do that, Percy Hill and Johnny Morgan would get their attention by strafing the German trenches. Eastman himself would then lead the remainder of the squadron in formation at a higher elevation ready to attack.

Eastman stared directly at Johnny when he said, "Hill and Morgan, you will be the decoys."

Johnny and Percy exchanged glances.

In the air, Johnny and Percy flew wing tip to wing tip. With a nod, Percy banked left to begin the strafing run. Johnny followed, but not without first glancing up at the tiny V formation of aeroplanes high overhead.

He readied his guns. Percy was pulling up, completing his run. Johnny nosed his Spad into a dive. Beneath him, a zigzagging line of earthen trenches stretched for miles to the horizon. German soldiers, having already felt the sting of Percy's run, were scurrying out of the trench or diving into side caves or taking a stand by aiming at the approaching aeroplane with their rifles.

Tack . . . tack . . . tack . . . tack . . . tack.

Soldiers clutched their chests and arms and faces and fell backward. Small splashes of dirt exploded from the sides of the trench where stray bullets hit. To Johnny, it was all a blur of activity.

Tack . . . tack . . . tack . . . tack . . . tack.

Having completed his run, he pulled up and circled around for another approach. Off to his side, Percy was entering his second run. To the east, there was no sign that they'd attracted the attention of the aerodrome.

Yet.

As he began his second approach, Johnny spotted the fuel truck.

If it's attention you want . . .

Altering his course slightly, Johnny strayed from the trenches. The fuel truck loomed ahead.

Tack . . . tack . . . tack . . . tack . . . tack.

KA-BOOM!

Billowing fire and black smoke formed a mushroom shape that ascended skyward in a pyrotechnic display.

Yeeeehawwwww! Johnny shouted.

Antiaircraft guns spit shells in earnest. Heavy rifle fire rained bullets heavenward. Black specks appeared on the eastern horizon. Pursuit fighters. The decoys had certainly gotten everyone's attention.

Johnny and Percy climbed to a higher altitude to escape the ground fire. Within minutes, the German pursuit squadron barreled down on top of them. As they approached, Johnny counted twenty-four fighters. Twelve to one.

Like shooting fish in a barrel. How can you miss?

With the battle at hand, Johnny looked to the higher altitudes for their reinforcements. The sky was clear! He scanned the heavens from horizon to horizon. It was possible the squadron was hidden behind a couple of heavy cloud banks. But they were a good distance away. Right now Eastman and the others should be jumping all over the Germans.

He looked all around him for Percy. The only other Spad in the vicinity wasn't hard to find. He was being chased by two Fokker biplanes with two more maneuvering to cut off his escape route.

Tack . . . tack . . . tack . . . tack . . . tack.

Johnny had problems of his own. The Fokker behind him was firing from too great a distance. A beginner's mistake. The other pilot would expect him to dive and run, so instead . . .

Johnny pulled back on the stick, climbed to the German squadron's attack elevation, and flew straight into the path of the bulk of the aeroplanes. Fokkers scattered everywhere to avoid a head-on collision.

That bought him some time, but not much. Again he glanced high overhead looking for Eastman and the 59th. They were still nowhere in sight.

He urged his Spad into a steep climb. Just before stalling, he rolled the aeroplane over and re-entered the fray, his guns blazing.

Tack . . . tack . . . tack . . . tack . . . tack.

Again, he split the group. So far, he'd managed to keep them guessing. No one had been able to slip in behind him. Not so with Percy. A Fokker was on his tail, peppering the other Spad with gunfire.

Johnny banked that direction and targeted Percy's pursuer.

Tack . . . tack . . . tack . . . tack . . . tack.

Tack . . . tack . . . tack . . . tack . . . tack.

Riddled with bullets through its wings and fuselage, the attacker broke away. But there was no fire, and he didn't go down. No kill.

Tack . . . tack . . . tack . . . tack . . . tack . . . tack . . . tack . . . tack . . . tack.

While Johnny was maneuvering to rescue Percy, a Fokker had slipped behind him. The barrage was heavy. His attacker was right on top of him.

Burning metal sliced through Johnny's left shoulder. His head flew back in pain as he screamed. Beneath his jacket, his shirt was sticky with blood.

Tack . . . tack . . . tack . . . tack . . . tack.

Expecting another hit, Johnny banked hard left. His eye caught sight of another Spad and another and another.

The squadron had finally arrived.

He pulled out of his dive.

Tack . . . tack . . . tack . . . tack . . . tack.

His attacker was right behind him.

All right, let's see if you can follow this . . .

He pulled into another steep climb. As before, the Spad slowed and was about to stall. The Fokker, expecting him to repeat the earlier renversement which concludes by turning the aeroplane in the opposite direction, continued forward. He would then circle back and re-engage, once again on Johnny's tail. However, this time, Johnny rolled the aircraft and looped over the top. Instead of reversing direction, he looped around and continued in the same direction—now on the Fokker's tail!

Surprised, the German pilot glanced repeatedly over one shoulder, then the other. He couldn't believe he'd lost the advantage and was now in the Spad's line of fire. He tried several frantic evasive maneuvers which Johnny matched.

Patiently, Johnny drew in closer. With his injured arm burning with pain, he readied the guns. When he was close enough that he couldn't possibly miss, he muttered, *Kill number three,* and pulled the trigger.

Nothing happened.

The gun was jammed! He reset it. Still jammed.

Craning his neck, the German pilot recognized what was happening. He grinned, knowing that fortune had smiled upon him. He waved a friendly gesture as if to say, "Better luck next time."

For a pilot whose guns are jammed, the prudent thing to do is to head home. But Johnny couldn't ever remember doing a prudent thing in his life and he wasn't about to experience prudence today.

He increased his speed and climbed to a slightly higher altitude, flying directly over the German Fokker. Then, he descended.

He descended until his wheels were on top of the Fokker's top wing. The German couldn't bank one way or the other without entangling the aeroplanes with one another, which would certainly result in both of them crashing. Likewise, if he tried to climb, Johnny's wheels would cut through the fabric and they would both crash. His only course of action was to descend, which he did.

Johnny matched his descent. The German pilot was in the same predicament, only lower. He tried again. Johnny matched him again.

After flying like this for a while with the German helpless to perform any maneuver without endangering himself, Johnny forced him down. Foot by foot. Lower and lower and lower.

Johnny Morgan earned his third kill when he forced a German Fokker to crash into a row of trees. He didn't have to worry about corroboration. Half the squadron saw him do it. They couldn't stop talking about it for months.

Chapter 29

PERCY leaned close to Johnny's ear. In a low voice, he said, "We could teach these Brits a thing or two about airfields. I think my kidneys are lodged in my throat."

"Shut up, Hill!" Eastman barked. "All of you, come over here!"

With their leather helmets and goggles dangling from their hands, Percy and Johnny and two other pilots from the 59th Squadron gathered around their commander, their aeroplanes lined up smartly behind them.

"Listen, gentlemen . . . "

Johnny hated when Eastman called them gentlemen. He used it in such a demeaning manner, like a mother talking to a four-year-old child.

". . . are you listening to me, Morgan?"

"Yessir."

"As I was saying, gentlemen . . . we're guests here at St. Marie Cappel and I want everyone to be on his best behavior. Everything you do and say reflects on our entire squadron. Do you understand?"

A smattering of *yessirs* made the rounds.

"Morgan?"

"I said, *yessir,* sir." He appealed to Percy beside him. "Didn't I say, *yessir?*"

"Yes, sir," Percy said to Eastman. "He said, *yessir,* sir."

The approach of a British general saved Percy and Johnny from their commander's expected verbal retribution. Cordial introductions were made, after which the general led them to a nearby hangar where more introductions were made. Then, while Captain Eastman was led off to confer with other commanders, the four pilots were introduced to their hosts by a tall, lanky captain who must have been at least six foot tall with his nose being half that size.

"Morgan and Hill?"

Percy and Johnny identified themselves.

"I don't know what you two chaps have done to warrant special treatment," said Captain Long Nose, "but you are to be hosted by one of our finest. My information says he requested you specifically. Care to enlighten me?"

The two American pilots stared at each other. Percy pointed to Johnny. "He's our best pilot. I'm a nobody."

The tall Brit looked Johnny up and down with an appraising, and not too complimentary, eye. "Yes, well, be that as it may . . . ah, here comes your host now."

A confident-looking British lieutenant with a prominent jaw approached them. He was of average height and sported a neatly trimmed mustache.

"Gentlemen. Your host: Lieutenant Radcliff."

Without waiting for the introductions to continue, Radcliff extended a hand to Percy. "Lieutenant Hill," he said, "welcome to St. Marie Cappel. I hope your stay is pleasant."

Percy returned thanks with a confused expression.

"And Lieutenant Morgan . . . Johnny . . . it's a pleasure meeting you. I've heard a good deal about you."

Now it was Johnny's turn to look puzzled.

"Shall we?" Radcliff motioned for them to follow him.

Without waiting for a response, Radcliff stepped away smartly. Percy and Johnny trailed in his wake. They had to hurry to keep up with him.

"Who is this fellow?" Percy whispered to Johnny.

"I was hoping *you* knew."

"Me? He called you by your first name."

"So? All that means is that he knows my first name, that doesn't mean I know his!"

"Strange. Very strange."

"All I know is that if he requested us personally, he can't be all bad."

A troubled expression formed on Percy's face. Johnny recognized it as one of Percy's what-has-Johnny-gotten-us-into expressions. Johnny didn't hold the feeling against him. If past history were any indication of what lay ahead, it wouldn't be the first time Percy received a bum deal because of his association with Johnny.

Radcliff led them to the Red Cross canteen. He opened the door for them.

"Lieutenant Hill," he said, "I believe there is someone in here you know."

Inside, seated at a small table, was Laura Kelton. No sooner had Percy stepped through the doorway when she raced across the floor and flew into his arms.

Radcliff beamed. The puzzled expression on Johnny's face grew deeper.

"Who are you?" he cried.

Before Radcliff could answer, Laura broke away from Percy. She gave Johnny a hug and a kiss on the cheek. "It's so good to see you again, Johnny!"

The hug and kiss stunned him. Johnny honestly couldn't remember the last time a woman had kissed him. The softness of her cheek and lips pressed against his cheek, the whiff of her perfume . . . it surprised him, that was all. She meant nothing romantic by it, and he read nothing romantic into it. But for a fellow whose existence consisted of metal and fabric and fuel and grease and guns and men who were either competing with him or trying to kill him, an unexpected kiss from a beautiful young lady was nothing less than stunning. Powerfully stunning.

Holding onto Percy's arm like a lifeline, Laura patted Radcliff on the shoulder. "This dear man," she said, "arranged all this! When he heard that the American 59th Squadron had been chosen to take part in this pilot exchange program, it was he who contacted your Captain Eastman, specifically requesting the two of you."

"No small feat, I might add," Radcliff said with a half-grin. "By the way, we need to talk about that sometime. What have the two of you done to your poor commander?"

"Don't get us started!" Percy said with a laugh.

Laura directed her next comment to Johnny. "Lieutenant Radcliff is a good friend of Katy's . . . "

Johnny took a fresh look at Radcliff. *A British aviator and his sister. His sister with any aviator. It just didn't fit.*

". . . who, unfortunately, couldn't break away to be here right now . . . after all, there is a war on, you know. But we'll all get together soon."

"There you have it!" Radcliff said, rubbing his hands. "Now that everything is out in the open, you two gentlemen can stop wondering who I am and what designs I have on you."

"Big mouth!" Johnny said, poking Percy.

"Lieutenant Morgan," Radcliff said, "how about if you and I sit over there." He motioned to a table beside a large window that overlooked the airfield. "I'm sure Percy and Laura would prefer being alone for a time. And this will give me a chance to get to know you."

Once more, Laura thanked Radcliff. Then she and Percy retreated to a small table in the corner where they huddled and whispered and smiled a lot.

Other than the Red Cross worker, a middle-aged woman

who occupied herself by stacking the shelves with cigarettes and candy, the four of them had the canteen to themselves.

The conversation between Radcliff and Johnny was far from fluid. At least the view of the airfield gave them something to look at during the dead times in their conversation, which came frequently.

"Saw you fly in," Radcliff said. "Those are Spad 13s, aren't they?"

"Yeah."

"Handle well?"

"Faster than the 7s. And more reliable than the Nieuports, which had a nasty habit of shedding their lower wings on a steep dive."

"Could ruin your day."

"I'll say."

Johnny watched a repairman roll a wheel past the window toward a hangar.

"Katy said you flew back in the States. Curtiss Jenny?"

"Yeah."

"That's what I thought. Slow. Clumsy."

"Yeah. But if there's nothing else . . ."

"My sentiments as well."

Three Sopwith triplanes took off from the airfield in a three-across formation.

"Is that what you fly?" Johnny asked.

Radcliff looked out the window. "Naw. I prefer the Camel."

"Really? What about the torque?"

Radcliff laughed. "It's brutal! With the weight concentrated in the nose, it pushes the center of gravity well forward. Add to that a powerful engine and a light body. . .

". . . and you get a lot of new furrows plowed in your airfield," Johnny concluded.

Radcliff laughed again.

"I don't know if I'd like an aeroplane with such a strong torque."

"That's what's so great about her! To the right, she can out-turn anything in the sky."

"Even a Fokker Dr. I?"

"On a good day," Radcliff said.

An amplified scratch caught both men's attention. Its origin was the far side of the canteen where Percy and Laura had discovered a Victrola. Laura was shuffling through a handful of the thick vinyl discs while Percy positioned the player's arm on a disc spinning atop the turntable.

"Do you mind?" Percy asked.

"Not at all," Radcliff replied.

Johnny shook his head. He didn't mind either. In fact, the music provided one more convenient distraction for him. Radcliff and Johnny sat back in their seats, listening to the music and avoiding eye contact with each other.

There's a long, long trail a-winding
Into the land of my dreams,
Where the nightingales are singing
And a white moon beams;
There's a long, long night of waiting
Until my dreams all come true;
Till the day when I'll be going down
That long, long trail with you.

"I got my third kill a few days ago," Johnny said.

"Is that so?"

"Two more to go."

"Then what?"

"I'll be an ace."

"That's right," Radcliff said as though it was nothing unusual.

The scratching of the Victrola introduced another song.

> *It's a long way to Tipperary; it's a long way to go;*
>> *It's a long way to Tipperary, to the sweetest girl I*
>> *know!*
> *Good-bye, Piccadilly, farewell, Leicester Square,*
>> *It's a long, long way to Tipperary,*
> *But my heart's right there.*

"How many kills do you have?" Johnny asked.

Radcliff gave him a look that Johnny might have expected if he'd asked the man's underwear size, or something else of a highly personal nature. Maybe the Brit pilots didn't like to compare records. There was nothing he could do about it now. The question had been asked. Besides, he wanted to know.

"You and your sister have a lot in common, do you know that?"

It wasn't the answer Johnny expected. And though he didn't know what Radcliff meant by the remark, he knew he didn't like the implication. He and his sister were nothing alike. This was probably Radcliff's way of avoiding his question. The bloke's record was probably an embarrassment to him. Radcliff struck Johnny as the kind of a man you'd expect to find behind a desk rather than a control stick.

"Twenty-two."

"Twenty-two?" Johnny cried. "Twenty-two kills?"

Radcliff shrugged. "We've been at it a lot longer than you chaps."

> *Oh, Mademoiselle from Armentieres, parlez-vous?*
>> *Oh, Mademoiselle from Armentieres, parlez-vous?*
> *Oh, Mademoiselle from Armentieres*
>> *She hasn't been kissed in forty years.*

Hinky Dinky, parlez-vous?

Radcliff gestured happily to Percy and Laura. "Have you heard this version of the song?" He sang lustily, if not on key:

> *Oh, the General got the Croix de Guerre; parlez-vous?*
> > *Oh, the General got the Croix de Guerre; parlez-vous?*
> *Oh, the General got the Croix de Guerre,*
> > *But the son-of-a-gun was never there!*
> *Hinky Dinky, parlez-vous?*

Laura clapped her hands and laughed. Percy joined her. Johnny stared incredulously at the man who sat across the table from him. He had never met anyone with twenty-two kills. How could the bloke be so casual about it?

It felt good to be in the air after so many receptions. For a day and a half there had been nothing but introduction after introduction, exchanges of pleasantries, enough toasts to drown them all, and smiles. Miles and miles and miles of smiles. If for no other reason than he no longer had to smile, Johnny felt good to be alone in his mount again. If he had to choose between the droning of his engine and the droning of one official after another, he'd choose the engine any day of the week.

As hosts, the British aeroplanes took the lead. The briefing for the morning flight had reminded Johnny more of a parade than a military mission. Untold hours had been spent arranging the formation. This had become painfully clear to him when it took the commanders over an hour to explain its arrangement.

For Johnny, the formation was simple. He was in the last slot on the longest side of the final V formation. Clearly, this was Eastman's contribution. For added emphasis, Eastman had pulled him aside following the briefing and warned him that he was not to break formation under any circumstances. Before Johnny could voice it, Eastman addressed the single exception. If by chance they were attacked by German aeroplanes and there was no longer any formation to maintain, then Johnny was given permission to break off. But as long as there were two aeroplanes flying in formation, Johnny was to be one of them.

The sector they were to fly over was quiet; this too according to plan. The initial joint foray was intended to be nothing more than an in-the-air handshake between the two forces. Not until the afternoon mission would they actually fly in the direction of the enemy.

Johnny checked his distance to Percy's wing. Perfect. A novice could do this. He sat back comfortably with an armada of allied aeroplanes arrayed before him. It was such a nice day, he was in no particular hurry. He was content in the knowledge that he'd get his chance for kill number four this afternoon.

Eastman and the other commanders would be pleased. The mission was proceeding as planned. The British were proudly displaying their territory and the Americans were getting a tour of the Northern European terrain. Johnny chuckled as he remembered a part of the briefing. The Americans had been instructed to observe their hosts and acquaint themselves with the characteristics of the British pilot. But if there was a difference between a British climb and an American climb, Johnny had failed to notice it.

With a casual glance over the side, he spotted something that caused him to lean over and look harder. A Fokker triplane. Tracing the course of a river. Flying a couple hundred feet above it at best. Johnny figured the pilot was lost and was using the river to find his way back home. The Fokker didn't seem to be in any hurry. Probably wasn't even aware of the armada sailing over him.

Johnny looked around to see if any of the other fliers had spotted the Fokker. Percy was the only pilot with whom it was possible to make eye contact. His head was tilted downward. He was preoccupied with something on his instrument panel.

The joint mission proceeded flawlessly on course.

Below, the Fokker strafed a three-arched stone bridge. The German pilot's intent was unclear. There was no one on or below the bridge that Johnny could see. Flying over the bridge, the Fokker continued following the river. Bored? Or was he testing his guns?

Johnny looked to Percy again. All he could see was the back side of his friend's leather helmet. Wiggling his stick side-to-side, he waggled his wings. That did it. Percy looked back.

Johnny pointed at the Fokker. Leaning over, Percy saw it too. His reaction was to shake his head in warning.

What kind of fool does he think I am? I'm not going to break formation for a single Fokker.

Impressive with its power of two nations combined as one, the joint mission droned onward through clear skies. Johnny couldn't help but wonder how many other pilots saw the Fokker below.

With nothing else to do, he kept an eye on the German aeroplane. At one point, the Fokker departed from the river to strafe a flock of sheep. Johnny felt his ire rise as he counted seven sheep dead.

What kind of pilot strafes sheep?

Johnny waggled his wings. Again, he pointed at the Fokker. Again, Percy shook his head side-to-side, this time emphatically.

Does he really think I'm going to break formation because a few sheep are killed?

The Fokker returned to the river, but only for a short time. Veering off again, he attacked a farmer who was plowing a field. On the first pass, one of the farmer's oxen was hit. It crumpled to the ground. When the farmer saw the Fokker circle back, he ran for the house. Splashes of dirt indicated the Fokker was firing. The splashes approached the farmer from behind. The farmer collapsed.

"No!" Johnny shouted.

As the Fokker passed over, the farmer jumped to his feet and continued running. The German pilot circled for a third pass.

Johnny broke formation.

Forward and right went the control stick. His Spad nosed into a dive.

He couldn't help taking one look at the formation as he left it. Eastman saw him. The commander's lips formed recognizable unkind words.

In a full dive, Johnny aimed to intercept the Fokker. Having completed his circle, the German aeroplane was once again spitting bullets at the fleeing farmer.

Surely, that Boche is blind! He still doesn't see me!

As the Fokker's sting drew closer to the farmer, Johnny decided he needed to make his presence known. He reached for his guns. His left arm complained. It was still hurting from his wound. But not enough to prevent him from firing.

Tack . . . tack . . . tack . . . tack . . . tack.

The streams of bullets crossed paths. Two patterns of dirt erupted. It caught the German pilot's attention. He broke off his attack before reaching the farmer.

Johnny was right behind him. He reached for his guns. Then stopped. He needed to get closer. There were pilots from two nations directly overhead who were undoubtedly watching by now. It wasn't that he wanted to impress them, but at the same time he didn't want to appear that he lacked skill either.

The Fokker had turned eastward and was running. Johnny took up behind him. The closer he got, the more frantic were the Fokker pilot's actions. The Boche had to be a novice. And an immature one at that. Dead sheep and a frightened farmer were testimony to his character. Johnny drew closer to his target.

Seeing that he couldn't outrun the Spad, the Fokker executed a sudden climb and roll. Johnny would have loved to see the pilot's face when he turned into an entire armada of enemy ships. Never had Johnny seen a triplane turn so sharply.

Right into Johnny's path. The Fokker fired wildly.

The two aeroplanes passed each other. Johnny climbed, turned, and came down upon the Fokker's tail.

It's time to say good-night.

With a twinge of pain in his shoulder, Johnny reached for his guns. He waited until he was right on top of the Fokker. At this distance, he could have recorded the kill with a handgun.

Tack . . . tack . . . tack . . . tack . . . tack.

The Fokker pilot slumped over. His craft spiraled downward and crashed. A pillar of fire consumed the aircraft.

Johnny had kill number four. A combined squadron of British and American pilots had witnessed it. Now, all he had to do was survive Captain Eastman's wrath to get credit for it.

Chapter 30

A CROWD of pilots greeted Johnny when he landed. He'd never had so many hands slapping his back all at once in his life. Congratulations and commentary surrounded him.

"Glad one of us had the nerve to break formation and get that Boche!"

"Did you see the way he strafed those sheep? What kind of men are they recruiting for pilots over there anyway?"

"That was one happy farmer. I thought his arm was going to fall off, he was waving it so hard!"

"Well done, chap! Well done!"

"I have a question," a grinning Radcliff said. "What was this maneuver once the Fokker was down?" A flat hand represented the aeroplane. He swooped it up and down like a porpoise.

"That's his victory celebration!" Percy said. "He's done it ever since his second kill!"

"Really?" Radcliff said. "After doing such a fine job on that Boche, I thought, 'What a shame! The poor chap's having engine trouble!'"

The sea of pilots parted as Eastman and the British commander approached. Eastman's face was tense. Johnny had seen the look before. Rage lurked immediately beneath its surface.

"Are you the pilot who shot down the Fokker?" the British commander asked.

"Yessir," Johnny replied.

The British commander extended his hand. "Well done, son!" he cried. Cheers from his men rose all around them. "I wanted to go after him myself," said the commander. "But I thought if I did, the entire joint squadron would follow me down!"

Johnny was engulfed in laughter.

Captain Eastman did his best to join the festivities. But it was asking too much. The best he could manage was a weak smile.

The afternoon mission had a more military bent to it. The large group was broken into smaller formations of four aeroplanes. Each was given a sector to patrol. Johnny's group consisted of Radcliff, Eastman, Percy, and himself.

Captain Eastman's presence made Johnny uneasy. He didn't know why the commander had chosen his group. Maybe it was just as well. If he knew the reason, he'd probably feel even worse.

They flew four across. Eastman and Radcliff had the center. Percy and Johnny had the sides. Naturally, Johnny was on Eastman's side.

Most of the afternoon went without incident. Stalemate characterized the ground forces below as each side was deeply entrenched and seemed content to be that way, at least for the day. The air above them was equally uneventful.

The three Spads and Sopwith Camel journeyed the length of their sector and back again twice without seeing any enemy aircraft. Nor did they encounter significant anti-aircraft fire from the German side.

Johnny consoled himself with the fact that he'd already earned a kill that day. In all the excitement that followed it, he'd allowed his hopes to rise. This could well be the day he would become an ace pilot. All he needed was one more kill.

He checked his gauges. Fuel was getting low. So were his spirits. It didn't look like this would be the day after all.

As Radcliff brought them around to a heading that would lead them back to the airfield, Johnny checked his wing distance to Eastman. Glancing up, he saw on his commander's face an expression of abject horror. Eastman's eyes were fixed on something at a higher elevation.

Johnny looked that direction. He saw it too.

The German equivalent of their morning armada! There must have been fifty aeroplanes coming toward them. Radcliff saw them. So did Percy.

A moment later they were swimming in Fokkers. Eastman was the first to react. With full throttle, he did his best to outrun them.

Radcliff had a Fokker on his tail. So did Percy.

With Eastman off to a good start, Johnny turned toward the Fokker on Radcliff's tail.

Tack . . . tack . . . tack . . . tack . . . tack.

The Fokker pilot didn't discourage easily. He was firing at Radcliff. Johnny took aim again.

Tack . . . tack . . . tack . . . tack . . . tack.

This time, the Fokker pilot got the message. With his right wing tattered, he pulled up and away.

Radcliff signaled Johnny his thanks. He too gave his craft full throttle and headed for home. Johnny turned toward Percy.

Tack . . . tack . . . tack . . . tack . . . tack.

The Albatross that was chasing Percy took a hit in the side. His plane was leaking fuel. He broke off his attack.

Tack . . . tack . . . tack . . . tack . . . tack.

Johnny flinched as bullets ripped across his wings. He banked hard left.

Tack . . . tack . . . tack . . . tack . . . tack.

Hit again! He climbed. Looped. The German stayed with him.

Tack . . . tack . . . tack . . . tack . . . tack.

Tack . . . tack . . . tack . . . tack . . . tack.

His engine started smoking. Shoving his stick forward, Johnny went into a spiral dive. The Fokker fell away, thinking he had a kill. Johnny went into a straight dive and pulled up.

All right, where is that Boche?

Percy was having a time of it. There was another Albatross on his tail with a Fokker closing in.

Be right with you, friend. I've got to get the Boche who thought he had me first!

Johnny spotted the Fokker that had left him for dead. His engine no longer smoking, he went after the Fokker full throttle.

Kill number five coming up!

The Fokker attacking Percy started firing, joining the Albatross.

Come on, Percy! Stay with it! I'll be there in a minute!

Falling in behind the Fokker that had shot at him, Johnny pulled in close. He readied his guns. Placed his hand on the trigger.

The Fokker climbed up and away!

Johnny wasn't quick enough. He flew right under his prey. The Fokker looped over to get on Johnny's tail. Johnny countered by climbing and looping himself. It was too steep an angle for the Fokker. Johnny came down on his tail.

Tack . . . tack . . . tack . . . tack . . . tack.

The Fokker's rudder assembly exploded.

Tack . . . tack . . . tack . . . tack . . . tack.

His fuselage was hit. White smoke began to pour out.

Tack . . . tack . . . tack . . . tack . . . tack.

The Fokker burst into flames. The pilot climbed out of the cockpit and onto the wing. Johnny took aim again.

KA-BOOM!

It was unnecessary. The Fokker exploded in the sky.

"NUMBER FIVE!" Johnny shouted. "Number five! Ace Johnny Morgan!"

He turned toward Percy and his two attackers.

Here I come, old friend . . . America's newest ace to your rescue!

Percy and the two German planes came into sight.

Almost there . . . hold on . . .

The Albatross fired.

Tack . . . tack . . . tack . . . tack . . . tack.

Percy slumped to the side. His Spad nosed over.

NO!

The Fokker fired. Percy's Spad burst into flames. It plummeted earthward trailing a thick column of black smoke. Suddenly, Percy was thrown from his mount. He fell beside the plane. This time Johnny saw a human being fall to his death.

Not an enemy.

Not some pilot with no name.

It was Percy.

His only friend.

Johnny Morgan recorded three kills that day. Two Fokkers and an Albatross. Enough to make him an ace. But there was no celebrating. Percy Hill was dead.

J.S.T. Fullard	*Chapel St.*	*Southampton*
Jas. Whistler	*Hardman St.*	*Bath*
Henry Minifie	*Quay St.*	*Ipswich*
Wm. Clayson	*Worsley St.*	*Manchester*

LAYING his pen down with a groan, Jesse slumped back in his chair and rubbed his eyes. Tedious. That was the word that best described the spy business. Tedious. He reached for his pocket watch then stopped short of pulling it out.

He didn't need a watch to tell him it was well past midnight. Every part of his body was telling him the hour was late—his eyes told him it was time to pull the shades and close up shop; his back and neck told him it was time to lie down if he expected them to function in the morning; and his legs told him they went to sleep without him thirty minutes ago.

"Just a couple more names . . ." he muttered.

Arching his back, he picked up a pen and forced tired eyes to focus on the next set of numbers. The first number in the series was *4529324.*

He referred to the code strip which had arrived separately. It was the fourth handwritten strip he'd received from Bruno. Each new strip rendered the previous one obsolete. Scanning down the list of numbers, he located a partial match: 4529. The sixth number from the top. That meant 324 was the page number. Snatching the dictionary, which had become well-worn in a short period of time, he flipped to page 324, matched the code strip to the entries. The sixth word from the top, opposite 4529 was: **mag** *n.* (1796): magazine.

Three letters! A bonus. He recorded them on his list.

Because this particular message consisted of personal names, Bruno's code system was slow and clumsy. Most of the names had to be spelled out letter-by-letter.

Next number: 5555152. Page 152. The code number 5555 was at the top of the list. It translated into the letter G.

Jesse yawned as he appended this letter to the previous three letters.

By attempting to communicate with Bruno, Jesse nearly burned the bridge between them.

He could think of only one place to start—discover the identity of the intermediary who delivered the messages to his door at night. Renting the apartment across the hallway, Jesse bored a small hole through the wall and a hallway painting. The painting's busy floral theme obscured the hall-way side of the hole. From this vantage point he watched his apartment door.

For two weeks he spied and waited. No message came. Until now, rarely had a week gone by when he hadn't received a message. *Had his source dried up?* He waited one more week. Still no message.

Pulling the plug on his self-surveillance, he returned to his regular activities, taking up residence in his apartment again.

A message was slipped under his door that night. ALLIANCE UNRAVELING MORE SOON. *Alliance? What alliance? The international alliance of nations against Germany? What would Bruno expect him to do about that? What other alliance was there? What about a personal alliance? The alliance between him and Bruno. A warning?*

It disturbed him that this message was different from all the prior messages which gave him concrete information—names, places, dates. This message sounded more like a prophecy.

Still, Jesse saw in it seeds of hope that he might yet discover Bruno's intermediary. It said MORE SOON. MORE meant another message would be sent. SOON meant he wouldn't have to wait long. Hopefully.

He didn't.

Two days later, having manned the peephole once again, Jesse received another message, this one delivered under the door of the apartment opposite his. The door next to the peephole! To make matters worse, Jesse was watching at the time it was delivered and still he didn't see who delivered it.

His vision restricted to his own doorway, someone sneaked directly under his peephole and delivered the message. Jesse felt like an amateur. And a foolish one at that. Whoever had slipped him the message knew where he was and what he was doing. Jesse's ineptness probably cost him contact with Bruno.

He stormed across the hallway into his apartment. Using the dictionary, he decoded the message: TRUST ERODING. MISS LIBERTY WEDNESDAY TWO P.M.

Arriving at the statue thirty minutes early, Jesse stood at the monument's massive base and waited. Two o'clock came and went.

By 4 P.M. Jesse had meandered across every square inch of the island, had climbed the steps, had watched ships go by, had climbed the steps again, and had looked expectantly into every face that he passed. No contact. He waited until five o'clock before concluding that his contact wasn't going to show.

Jesse was leaning dejectedly against the railing of the ferry when someone bumped into him from behind. His first thought was landlubber legs. That's why he always stood by the railing. He knew if he walked about, he'd inevitably wind up in someone's lap. With a forgiving smile plastered on his face, he began to turn around.

Someone shoved him against the railing. Forcefully.

"Don't turn around. Keep your eyes on the bridge."

A gravelly whisper disguised a deep male voice.

"Anything you say," Jesse said. "It's a lovely view."

The body that pressed against him was bulky and unyielding.

"Bruno is disappointed," the voice said.

"Understandable. My efforts to contact him were clumsy. But it is imperative that I communicate with him. Can you help me?"

"Bruno doesn't have ears. Only a mouth."

"Does Bruno have eyes? Because if he does, he should be able to see that we have worked well together and that he can trust me."

The ferry bobbed as it approached the Manhattan landing. The silent presence behind Jesse kept him pinned against the railing.

"Mutual friends in England need our help."

"What do you want from Bruno?"

"Information."

Deckhands tossed ropes to waiting workers ashore. There was a bump and the soft screech of wood against wood as the ferry nestled against the pier.

Close to Jesse's ear, the gravelly voice whispered, "Put your request into code. Slip it under your apartment door at 2

A.M. But I warn you, if anyone is watching, it will not be picked up and you will never hear from Bruno again."

One more generous shove against the railing took Jesse's breath away. The voice wanted to make sure he had Jesse's attention. He did.

"Don't turn around. Don't get off. People who are truly friends of freedom would have no objection to seeing Miss Liberty twice in one day."

"No objection at all," Jesse wheezed.

That night, after his second trip to Bedloe Island, Jesse wrote out his request for information regarding German agents in England. Seven days later a coded message of suspected agents was slipped under his apartment door.

Jesse's eyes refused to focus. Best to get some sleep and a fresh start in the morning. In the afternoon he would place a call to Colonel House and arrange to relay the information to the Federal Secret Service.

As he gathered up his dictionary, decoding slip, and writing instruments, he picked up the list, taking one last glance. All those hours and what did he have to show for his effort? One, two, three, four, five names. Five names! There must be at least that many more names on Bruno's list yet to be de . . .

Wait a minute!

His eyes fell on the last name. Something about it struck a familiar chord.

How could I have missed that?

Blaming the near-miss on fatigue wasn't good enough. If his suspicions were correct, that familiar chord he heard could very well be a death knell—for Emily.

Ripping open a side drawer on the desk, he rifled through its contents. What was it Emily had said in her letter? *She has a secret side to her that she tries to keep hidden from me.*

Where is it . . . where is it . . . ? He pulled an envelope from
the drawer. His interest lay in the return address:

> Mrs. Emily Morgan
> c/o Mrs. Maggie Thomas
> 23 Lumley Lane
> London, England

An icy claw gripped Jesse's heart. He compared the return
address with the last decoded name on Bruno's list of suspected German agents. The claw in his chest squeezed
harder. His fear was confirmed.

Maggie Eisenbein Lumley Lane   London

"Emily dear, are you sure you won't stay longer?" Maggie
said. "I've grown so accustomed to having you around the
house, I don't know what I'll do with myself once you're
gone!"

Emily folded a skirt and laid it in her travel bag. "You're
such a dear to have put up with me all this time!"

"Nonsense! Your presence has been an elixir for this old
lady."

Clutching a folded sweater against her chest, Emily
laughed. "Old lady, indeed! I only hope I'm as active and
spry when I'm a decade younger than you." She placed the
sweater in her bag. "Besides, Jesse's been by himself too long.
There's no telling what kind of trouble he's gotten himself
into by now. It's time I went home and started acting like a
wife. That is, if I still remember how!"

Maggie leaned against the bedroom doorjamb as she
watched Emily pack. "Has Jesse been dropping hints in his
letters?"

"Oh, no . . . Jesse isn't one to hint. He'd come right out and tell me if he wanted me to come home. That's not to say he doesn't miss me . . . he does." She looked up at her host with a warm smile. "Which is one more reason I'm in your debt. The last time I went away for more than a week, he treated me like royalty when I returned! At least for a while."

Maggie grinned. "What about his work? Is he still keeping odd hours?"

"There are no such things as regular hours in Washington."

"But won't it be dangerous for you? I mean, with his international espionage work and all. It just stands to reason that his enemies would do anything to stop him. Aren't you afraid that they might come after you to get to him?"

Emily placed her hands on her hips and thought. "I suppose that comes with the job. There was that danger even when he was a security agent in Denver. To protect me, Jesse would never tell me about his jobs. He became even more tight-lipped when he went to Washington." She laughed as she remembered something. "I must confess that it is hilarious at times to watch him start to say something, then swallow his words. At times he aches to tell me what he did that day. But he won't. It's like watching a man try to keep from scratching when you know he has a powerful itch."

Maggie laughed with Emily. "Have you told him about me?"

"Told Jesse about you? I've told him plenty! I've told him you're a dear, dear friend and that I'm trying to drag you back to the States with me."

"I mean about my clandestine activities."

Out of instinct, Emily checked the window, then whispered, "Your other identity?"

Maggie nodded and winked.

"No, that's not my place."

With a chuckle, Maggie said, "Not that it would have made any difference had you told him. With your husband's resources, I'm sure he knows all about me."

Emily closed her travel bag. "Are you sure I can't talk you into coming home with me?"

"Only as far as Queenstown this time, my dear. A trip to the colonies will have to wait until after this wretched conflict comes to an end."

Jesse didn't sleep that night. The first thing he did was to send a cable to Emily.

> DEAREST EMILY.
> BAD NEWS. BROTHER SLATE CLOSE TO DEATH. COME HOME SOONEST.
> JESSE.

It was a message Emily alone would understand. She had no brother. Slate was the name she used for herself when, as a young runaway, she joined a wagon train heading west, disguised as a boy. Since Emily and Slate were one and the same, Jesse hoped she would understand from the message that her life was in danger.

The second thing he did was to cable British Intelligence, relay his suspicions, and ask them to put the Lumley house under surveillance.

The third thing Jesse did, as soon as the Cunard offices were open, was to buy a ticket to London. He considered requesting permission to travel by navy vessel. But this was a personal matter, and considering the bureaucracy involved in such a request, this was by far the faster method.

"Did you inform Jesse you were coming home or do you intend to surprise him?"

"I posted a letter two days before we left London."

The women stood shoulder-to-shoulder in the ticket line at the Queenstown Cunard terminal. Considering her previous eventful crossing, Emily thought she might feel nervous about boarding a ship again once she reached the wharf. She didn't. The business-as-usual atmosphere of both workers and passengers in the terminal helped. There were still the reminders that it was wartime—posters, notices—but now that America had entered the conflict the U-boats were concentrating on military targets and leaving the passenger lines alone.

The young lady who assisted Emily at the ticket window couldn't have looked more Irish if she'd tried. A full head of fiery red hair was set off by her green blazer and pale, freckled complexion. Pale green eyes glanced up frequently at Emily.

"So!" Maggie said as Emily departed the ticket window, "you're really going to leave me, aren't you?"

"Don't make this any harder than it already is for me," Emily pleaded.

"At least I have you for one more night."

"Do you think we'll get to see the Morehouses?"

Maggie stopped. She placed a hand on Emily's arm. "Didn't I tell you, dear?" she said, her face drawn. "Their house burned to the ground with them in it not more than a month after you saw them at Bryn's house."

"I'm so sorry to hear that!"

Flashes of memory came to mind. Ian Morehouse's bulbous nose and squinty eyes spying on her in the dark. Ethel Morehouse with her thick glasses.

"Oh, dear," Maggie exclaimed. "I never thought to ask you until now."

"Ask me what?"

"You don't have reservations about staying the night at

Bryn's house, do you?"

Emily had already given the matter some thought. All her memories of Bryn's house were warm ones. She had no qualms about staying there at all.

"If you're concerned about the dust," Maggie said, "you can rest assured. I've seen to it that the house would be kept up."

Emily linked her arm inside Maggie's arm and squeezed. "I can't think of a place I'd rather stay on my last night before returning home. Besides, I'll be with you, won't I?"

A gray-haired man who looked too old to be riding bicycles braked to a stop in front of 23 Lumley Lane. Carrying a cable message in his upraised palm as though it was a royal summons, he approached the door and knocked. When there was no answer, he knocked louder. When there was still no answer, he circled the house. Encountering no one in front or back, he peered into a side window. He even knocked on it.

Returning to his bicycle, he did not leave the cable unattended on the doorstep. It required a signature from the recipient. When he climbed onto his bicycle he was confronted by two hefty men dressed in black who appeared from nowhere. They stood on either side of him and questioned him for fifteen minutes before letting him continue making deliveries.

It was late afternoon by the time they reached Bryn's old house. Bouncing down the rutted dirt road in a taxicab, Emily peered at the approaching stone cottage through the taxi's glass window. Feelings of nostalgia swept over her that brought her close to tears. It seemed odd to her that the house could have this kind of effect on her. She hadn't spent all that much time in it. She supposed it was the trauma associated with her stay at the house that extracted such strong emotions from her.

As they climbed out of the taxi, Maggie called happily to her travel partner, "Emily, dear, the door should be unlocked. Go on in, while I pay the cabbie."

With her travel bag in hand, Emily swung open the front door and stepped inside. The heavy odor of pipe smoke greeted her. Not stale, as before when she had stayed here. Fresh. So fresh in fact, that it still swirled in the air. Particularly over the rocking chair.

She gasped and clutched her throat.

This can't be!

She saw a man seated in the rocking chair! Wisps of thin gray hair stretched across a tanned scalp. Even before he turned and looked at her, even though she had never seen the man before, she knew who he was!

But that's impossible! He's . . .

Responding to the opening of the door, the man in the rocking chair turned to see who it was. If Emily had any doubts about his identity, they were swept away. He looked exactly like she'd imagined he would look.

Like the pipe smoke over the chair, confusion and fear and disbelief swirled inside Emily's head.

This can't be! It can't be! It can't be!

The man stood and faced her.

Emily stepped backward. A bony hand planted itself in the small of her back and shoved her into the room. The door slammed shut.

"Emily," Maggie said in a strangely cold tone of voice, "I'd like you to meet my brother, Bryn."

Chapter 32

FACING a squadron of German Fokkers single-hand-edly was preferable to what Johnny had to do. With the Fokkers the worst that could happen would be that they shot you down and you died. Telling Laura that he was responsible for Percy's death was worse than dying. It was wanting to die and not being allowed to.

She was waiting for him when he arrived. So was Katy. He hadn't expected her to be there. Her presence would only make this more difficult than it already was.

They were both dressed in their nurse's uniforms and were seated next to each other on a stone bench at the edge of a large grassy expanse between two wings of the hospital. An empty white cast-iron lawn chair was positioned facing them.

A witness stand?

That would make them the jury.

My life in my sister's hands. Now there's a horrifying thought. I'd have better odds against the Fokker squadron.

"Laura . . . Katy." Greeting them, he sat in the witness chair.

Dabbing red, swollen eyes, Laura attempted a smile. It was disrupted by sobs.

Johnny lowered his head and gave her time to compose herself. Katy sat with her hands folded in her lap. She stared at Johnny with unfeeling eyes.

Suddenly, Laura was off the bench. Wrapping her arms around Johnny's neck, she pressed her wet cheek against his face and cried. Not knowing what to do with his hands, Johnny left one on the arm of the chair and patted Laura gently on the back with the other.

Katy's stare was relentlessly locked on him.

After a time, Laura apologized and took her seat on the bench.

"Don't apologize," Johnny said. "There's no need to."

Laura sniffed and dabbed her eyes again. Johnny cleared his throat. Katy stared.

"Thank you for coming," Laura sniffed.

"I wish . . . I wish . . . " Johnny stammered.

What did he wish? That Percy hadn't been shot out of the sky? Of course he wished that. Everybody wished it. More than anybody he wished Percy was alive. He wished he'd had the good sense to help his friend out when he needed it. But wishing for things changed nothing. Who cared what he wished?

"What I mean to say is, I'm sorry."

A struggling smile appeared as Laura said, "Thank you, Johnny. But there is no reason for you to apologize."

No reason! Didn't Radcliff tell you? It's because of me that Percy is dead!

Fighting back his emotions, Johnny said, "I am responsible for Percy's death."

Laura's brow knotted up. "How are you responsible?"

Johnny's insides twisted horribly, like a piece of laundry being wrung out. "Didn't Radcliff tell you?" he asked.

"Tell me what?"

"That Percy is dead because of me?"

Laura shook her head. "He told me no such thing. Lieutenant Radcliff told me that if it had not been for you, he would have been shot down . . . "

"That may be . . . I was able to . . . "

". . . he told me that the sky was swarming with German aeroplanes and that it was fortunate any of you survived . . . "

"Yes, there were over fifty . . . "

". . . he told me how you risked your life by landing next to the wreckage, and how, while German aeroplanes strafed you, you picked up Percy's body and carried him back to your aeroplane and flew him home."

Johnny exploded out of his chair. "Will you listen to me for one moment!" he shouted.

It was a completely spontaneous outburst. And now that he stood over Laura and Katy and they stared up at him with shocked looks on their faces, he wished he hadn't done it. But then, he was doing a lot of things lately he wished he hadn't done.

He could hold back his emotions no longer. Kneeling before Laura he said, "There were two aeroplanes on Percy's tail. Instead of helping him, I chased after another aeroplane that had shot at me. I wanted that pilot to be my fifth kill."

Laura looked at him innocently.

"Don't you understand what I'm saying? I could have helped Percy sooner! But I didn't! I was more concerned about becoming an ace than I was about my friend!"

Laura sat quietly for a while. She looked down at Johnny and bit her lower lip as she thought.

"If you had gone to help Percy first," she said, "he would still be alive?"

"That's what I'm saying."

"Isn't that rather arrogant of you, Lieutenant Morgan?"

Her question blind sided him. "Arrogant? I don't know what . . . "

"Tell me if I'm incorrect. Captain Eastman was in the air, was he not?"

"Yes, but he was . . . "

"And Lieutenant Radcliff. He was up there with you?"

"Yes . . . he had just broken away . . . "

"And yet you say that only *you* could have saved Percy?"

Johnny nodded. "I had position. All I had to do was swing around and . . . "

"And what? Could you have stopped both of those pilots from firing? And what about the other forty-eight aeroplanes? Could you have saved Percy from them as well?"

"Laura, I understand what you're trying to do. But the fact remains. At that moment in the sky I valued a title more than I valued the life of my friend. I can't help but believe that if I had chosen otherwise, Percy would be here today. And I don't know how I'm going to live with that knowledge."

Putting one hand on his shoulder and cupping his face with the other, she said, "Johnny Morgan, Percy admired you like you were a brother. He loved you. I cannot bring myself to believe that he blames you for his death. And neither do I."

With his head down, he said, "I wish I could share that sentiment. But I don't think I'll ever be able to forgive myself."

"There is one thing you can do."

He looked up hopefully. "I'll do whatever is in my power."

"For the rest of this war, you can fight in memory of Percy."

All expression drained from Johnny's face. "You're asking me to do the one thing I can't do. It is because of Percy's memory that I will never fly again."

Laura looked at him with sad eyes. "Then the Germans downed two of America's pilots that day."

After Johnny had gone, Laura said to Katy, "You were awfully quiet."

"There was no place for me in that conversation."

"What do you think? He's taking this pretty hard."

"Percy was Johnny's best, and possibly only, friend," Katy said. "I expected him to feel sad."

"Katy! The way you talk, you make your brother out to be some kind of unfeeling animal."

"It's not that he doesn't have feelings," Katy said. "It's just that my brother has never let his feelings get in the way of doing what he wants to do."

"So then, what did you expect Johnny to do today?"

"I thought he'd come looking for comfort. Looking for someone to tell him everything was all right. And you did that for him."

"It didn't seem to do him much good."

"No, it didn't. And that's what surprises me."

"And turning in his wings?"

Katy shook her head in wonder. "For Johnny to give up flying? Now that's astonishing. I never thought I'd see the day. And that's what convinces me that something inside him has changed. Laura, I think my brother is turning into a human being."

Johnny was sitting in the corner of the Red Cross canteen when she entered. Had he known Laura was coming, he never would have chosen that particular seat. It was "their" corner. The corner where Percy and Laura had huddled and whispered and listened to music. Johnny had chosen the corner for a different reason. It had the farthest table from the large window overlooking the airfield.

Laura looked spectacular in a simple yellow cotton dress. It never ceased to amaze him how different she looked when she was wearing something other than her nurse's uniform.

"May I sit down?"

She pulled out a chair opposite him and sat down. "Soda water?" she asked, pointing to his empty glass.

"Would you like one?"

"Please."

His chair scraped loudly on the floor. A minute later he returned with two soda waters.

"You really did it, didn't you?" she said.

"Did what?"

"Turned in your wings?"

A slight nod laid claim to the action. He tried not to look directly at her. It was painful for him. Every time he did, he expected to see Percy appear by her side.

"Have you spoken to Lieutenant Radcliff today?"

"If you mean, 'Has Lieutenant Radcliff tried to talk me out of it,' then the answer is yes."

Laura took a dainty sip. Setting down her glass, she said, "I simply asked you a question; you don't have to be rude about it."

Johnny mumbled a halfhearted apology.

"Did your commander try to talk you out of it too?"

That was funny. He laughed. "Right now, Captain Eastman is the happiest man in this aerodrome. He's probably the happiest man on this side of the front!"

Laura took another dainty sip. She looked at him disapprovingly over the rim of her glass.

"Rude. Sorry," Johnny said. "No, he didn't try to talk me out of it."

"And the rest of the pilots in your squadron?"

Johnny leaned forward. "What do you want from me?"

"That's better," Laura said. "I'm glad you asked. I want you to rejoin your squadron."

"I can't do that."

"Why not?"

"You know why not."

She took another sip of soda water. "So then, what are you going to do?"

"I don't know yet."

"Go back to Colorado?"

"I don't know."

"Join your father in Washington?"

"I don't know."

"Last I heard, your mother is still in . . . "

Johnny stood up so fast, his chair crashed backward.

"Is our conversation over?" Laura asked.

"What are you doing here?" he asked.

"I thought I'd have a pleasant conversation with a friend."

Friend. He'd never thought of Laura as a friend. She was Percy's girl. That's how he was introduced to her and that's all she had ever been. Percy's girl.

"Do friends drive other friends crazy?" he asked.

With an impish grin, Laura said, "Sometimes."

Setting his chair upright, Johnny sat at the table again.

"You met Percy when you were flying over his hometown, didn't you?" she asked.

"Columbus, New Mexico."

"And the two of you did something for the expeditionary force . . . "

"We were mechanics."

"For aeroplanes."

He nodded. Those days seemed so long ago.

"And then you joined flight school together."

"College Park, Maryland."

Laura smiled. "I remember Percy telling me how you used to coach him at night. The way he told it, every day after classes, you would say something like, 'Remember what the instructor told you today about . . . well, don't believe him!' Then you would tell him what it was really like to fly."

Johnny laughed in spite of himself.

"He said he never would have graduated from flight school if it hadn't been for you."

"An exaggeration. He would have caught on. He was as

good as any of those other fellows."

"And then you came here together. Percy told me that it was you who saw to it that you would be shipped out to the same squadron."

Johnny smiled. "We'd come too far by then to go separate ways."

"So why are you so determined to go separate ways now?"

Just when he was starting to have a good time, she had to go and say something like that. *What did she want him to do? Die, so that he and Percy could be together?*

"Let's not get into this again," he said.

"We have to get into this," Laura insisted. "Because I'm not about to let you cast a black shadow over the life of the man I love."

Johnny looked away. He didn't want to fight with her.

She reached across the table and took his hands. "You're an aviator," she said. "And if Percy's assessment of you is right, one of the best in the world. That's what he loved about you! He was proud to fly with you. It would hurt him deeply to know that he was the reason you stopped flying."

Johnny stared at the tabletop.

"Look at me," Laura said softly.

He tried. But couldn't.

"Look at me!"

Slowly, he raised his chin. Their eyes met. And once they did, he no longer found it difficult to look at her. There was forgiveness there. And love.

"My course is already set," he said. "I couldn't change it now if I wanted to."

Releasing his hands, Laura reached down into her handbag. She tossed a pair of wings onto the table. "I've already spoken to Captain Eastman," she said. "The wings are yours if you want them."

Chapter 33

JOHNNY lay in his bed in the dark. A splash of French moonlight spilled through the curtains and wet the wooden planks with a silvery-blue light. There was just enough illumination to outline the empty bed on the other side of the room.

"Percy."

The darkness magnified his name, bouncing it against black featureless walls until it came back to him.

"Percy."

He didn't expect an answer. He just felt the need to say it, to hear it. Saying Percy's name out loud meant that a part of his friend was still alive.

"Percy. Percy. Percy. Percy. Percy. Percy."

They flew in tight formation. Captain Eastman, with nine kills to his name (two more than Johnny), flew the point. At his own request, Johnny flew the tail position.

This position served two purposes for him. First, Percy's memory was honored in that he was still flying. Second, it gave him the edge he needed to stay alive, without giving in to his competitive nature.

Since Percy's death, he'd lost that competitive edge. In a dogfight, timidity was suicide. He compensated by creating the role of squadron shepherd. In essence, he meant to do for the rest of the squadron what he failed to do for Percy.

He let Captain Eastman and the others be the aggressors while he held back and kept a lookout for trouble. If an enemy aeroplane gained an advantage over one of his pilots and was closing in for the kill, Johnny attacked the enemy aeroplane with the fury of a shepherd protecting his sheep from a predator.

To remind him of his duty, Johnny taped a couple of Bible verses on his instrument panel.

> *Whosoever will be great among you, shall be your minister: And whosoever of you will be the chiefest, shall be servant of all. For even the Son of man came not to be ministered unto, but to minister, and to give his life a ransom for many.*—Mark 10:43-45

It was the second verse that gave him an image for the role he'd adopted for himself.

> *I am the good shepherd: the good shepherd giveth his life for the sheep.*—John 10:11

Eastman spotted the Fokkers below them. Five of them flying in a V formation. He didn't attack immediately, choosing instead to position the squadron so that its approach came out of the sun.

Like hawks they swooped down upon the German aeroplanes. The Fokker pilots didn't see them until Eastman opened fire. Within seconds after the attack, he had his first kill of the day. Bickers got the second kill a few minutes later.

As was his new practice, Johnny held back and watched his flock. It soon became evident that all but the lead German pilot had little experience. That meant that flying skill, not bullets, would win the day. Pilots had their hands full just to keep from colliding with one another.

The lead German Fokker, however, demonstrated superior flying skill. Executing an impressive split-S maneuver, the German pilot rolled his aircraft until it was inverted, then pulled back to complete half a loop. He was right on Bickers' tail, firing furiously.

Johnny dove to intercept the attacking Fokker.

At this point novices are easy targets. In the heat of pursuit, they ignore all else around them, concentrating solely on getting their sights on the fleeing enemy aeroplane. A surprise burst of bullets from behind usually breaks them of this bad habit—if they live.

Such was not the case with this Fokker pilot.

Before Johnny had a chance to reach for his guns, the Fokker took an evasive turn. Johnny stayed with him. At least the Boche was off Bickers' tail.

The Fokker climbed. Johnny climbed. He dove. Johnny dove.

Patience. Stay with him. Don't fire until you're right on top of him.

These were the flying virtues that had paid off well for Johnny. The Fokker was in his sights, but not close enough for a shot. *Patience.* He tried to move in closer. The German pilot was unpredictable. He managed to stay out of Johnny's range.

Give the man credit. He's good. He's very good.

A flash of wing caught the corner of Johnny's eye. Some fool novice pilot. Johnny had to bank hard left and dive to keep from colliding with him. Uttering a quick sigh, Johnny pulled out of the dive.

Tack . . . tack . . . tack . . . tack . . . tack.

Bullets whizzed past Johnny's head. He turned to see who was firing at him. It was the same German pilot he'd been chasing! When Johnny dove the other pilot saw his chance and dove after him. He was in position. Firing!

Tack . . . tack . . . tack . . . tack . . . tack.

Johnny plummeted several thousand feet. The Fokker was right behind him.

Tack . . . tack . . . tack . . . tack . . . tack.

The Spad's right wing took several hits. Johnny pulled up hard, did a barrel roll, and fell off into another dive. He looked behind him. The German pilot was still there.

This Boche is good!

Tack . . . tack . . . tack . . . tack . . . tack.

Nothing Johnny did could shake the Fokker pilot from his tail. So far, the only reason he hadn't suffered fatal hits was because he'd at least managed to keep the German a good distance away.

But for how much longer? Those bullets would soon find their mark unless he did something to get this Boche off his tail.

Tack . . . tack . . . tack . . . tack . . . tack.

More perforations in Johnny's right wing!

Since conventional methods weren't working, Johnny decided to try the unconventional. Playing the role of dare-devil, he zoomed precariously close to the remaining Fokkers, cutting between them, streaking in front of them, surprising them with a pass over their head. Hopefully, the tactic would keep the experienced pilot too busy flying to fire his guns. And, with any luck, one of the inexperienced pilots would overreact and crash into his own commander.

Tack . . . tack . . . tack . . . tack . . . tack.

His tactic wasn't working. The German Fokker ducked and dove and squeezed through every situation Johnny put him in. Worse yet, Johnny had just broken into the clear. The Fokker was on his tail. At point-blank range.

Johnny braced himself.

The bullets never came.

Looking behind him, Johnny saw the German pilot setting and resetting his guns. He tried to fire. Nothing. His guns were jammed!

Taking advantage of this moment of distraction, Johnny pulled up suddenly into a near stall, then looped around behind the pursuing Fokker. A moment of inattention was the only mistake the Boche pilot had made. Johnny was determined to make it his last.

The tables were turned. Johnny closed in on his prey.

Now it was the Boche pilot's turn to climb and dive and loop and roll to get Johnny off his tail. But Johnny stayed with him.

Reaching for his gun, Johnny curled his finger around the trigger. Number eight coming up! Pride surged in his chest. The thrill of victory pumped his heart. He'd met a worthy opponent and bested him. A skilled aviator, but today the German pilot's luck ran out.

The German stared behind him. The two pilots' eyes met, peering through opposite ends of the Spad 13s gun sights.

I am the good shepherd . . .

Johnny lowered his gun hand.

He had already accomplished what he'd set out to do. With the Fokker's guns jammed, the predator was no longer a threat to any of his sheep.

Swinging wide, Johnny pulled up alongside the German Fokker. At 10,000 feet, the two warriors faced each other. Johnny offered a salute which the German pilot returned. Banking right, Johnny turned toward home.

The summer storm arrived sooner than expected. Johnny was alone in his Spad scouting his designated sector when the rain began to fall. The rain hit his goggles and face with force. The goggles clouded, blinding him. He ripped them off. Raindrops stung his eyes and cheeks.

The rain was only part of his problem. Winds swirled unpredictably. If the Spad wasn't caught in an updraft, it was slammed by a downdraft. He was either flying into the wind making no progress or being pushed along at incredible speeds. Johnny felt he was riding atop a dandelion seed.

CRACK!

Lightning streaked the sky. It was close. Close enough that Johnny could smell it. The hair on the back of his neck tingled with the charge.

He was blind. Half the time he wasn't in control of the aeroplane. And now he was dodging thunderbolts. He had no choice. He had to set down.

On second thought . . . he was behind enemy lines. Maybe he should try to make it . . .

CRACK!

Another thunderbolt. This one closer.

Battle the Boche or battle thunderbolts?

Johnny began his descent. He had to get below the clouds which, at the moment, had a dangerously low ceiling. He passed through clouds. In and out, in and out. Between patches he could see the ground. Inside the clouds, well, that was a unique and unnerving experience.

To be surrounded by milky moisture. To hear the engine throbbing and feel the wind against your face, yet for lack of visual reference to appear as if you are not moving at all. To have your sight limited to a few feet in front of the propeller, knowing that you are traveling at a speed of over eighty miles per hour, that should you happen to see something solid, it will be the last thing you ever see.

The cloud around him thinned and cleared. He was no more than fifty feet above the ground. There was a small town. A church steeple. Outlying farms.

THE ALLIES § 402

A sudden downward wind pushed him toward the town. Johnny banked to miss the church steeple. An updraft sent him sailing several hundred feet high.

These winds will make for one interesting landing.

He descended again, looking for a suitable field, hoping he hadn't waited so long that the fields were muddy. If they were too soft, he'd tumble tail over engine.

Maybe a road would be safer. He spotted a farm road. It was rutted, like all farm roads, but the ruts seemed a safer bet than a soggy field. Lining up his approach, he descended.

Fifty feet. Forty. Thirty. Ten.

The road looked to be in better shape than he'd originally thought.

He flew into a down draft. The Spad slammed against the ground. A light flashed in Johnny's head as bright as any of the lightning bolts he'd seen. It nearly knocked him senseless.

He tried to keep the wheels on the ground. The Spad lifted up, then slammed into the ground again.

This time, his wheels stayed down. As his senses cleared, he took stock of his situation. He was on the ground. That was good. Taxiing down a country road behind enemy lines. That was bad. Surely, someone had heard or seen him.

He taxied for what seemed an eternity, looking for someplace to pull off. After a mile, he saw a small patch of trees. It gave him an idea.

It was the flight training contest all over again. Only, instead of having a teammate, he was alone. And if he failed to act quickly enough, he did more than lose a few dollars to Calahan; he could very well lose his life.

He cut the engine just a few yards from the trees. Jumping out of the cockpit, he checked the terrain. The rain fell from slate-gray skies mercilessly.

No one in his right mind should be out in this weather!

As far as he could see, no one was. Grabbing his toolbox

from the floor of the cockpit, he began to disassemble his aeroplane.

With the wings off, he pulled the fuselage into the trees. He carried the wings in next, propping them against the side of the fuselage. He then pulled branches and limbs from trees and covered up his aircraft to keep it from being seen from the road. The rain did an adequate job erasing the tracks his wheels had made.

Satisfied that everything was concealed, he climbed into the cockpit, hunkered down into the seat, and prepared to wait out the storm.

Covering themselves as best they could from the rain, Katy and Laura had loaded the last of their supplies into the ambulance when a motorcycle roared up beside them. The rider lifted his goggles. It was Fred Radcliff.

Peering from beneath her hood, Laura cried happily, "Look who's here!"

"It's a little dangerous to be riding that thing in the rain, isn't it?" Katy said.

A disconsolate expression was the first indication that he had not stopped by for a friendly visit.

"I'm afraid I have some bad news," he said.

Katy straightened her shoulders. Laura covered her mouth with her hand.

"Johnny didn't return from patrol."

"How long has he been missing?" Katy asked.

Radcliff looked at his watch. "He's six hours overdue."

"And in this storm," Laura added.

"Exactly."

"Did anyone see him go down?" Katy asked.

"An artillery outpost in that sector reported hearing an aeroplane fly over them. It was flying low. They couldn't see it because the cloud cover was less than a hundred feet.

They said it sounded like a Spad, but that it was headed in the wrong direction. Toward Agneau. Either they were mistaken as to the aeroplane's identity, or the pilot was turned around—which isn't hard to do given these weather conditions."

Laura's eyes misted over. Katy wore her professional nurse's expression.

Fiddling with the strap of his motorcycle goggles, Radcliff said, "All we can do now is wait for the weather to clear. I've already gotten permission to fly a search mission once it does."

"You're a good friend, Fred. Thank you," Laura said.

Observing Radcliff's wrinkled brow and busy hands, Katy said, "Is there something you're not telling us? There is, isn't there?"

Radcliff looked surprised, like a little boy caught in a lie who couldn't believe he'd been caught.

"We're adults, we can take it," Katy said testily.

Radcliff protested her inference. "I wasn't trying to conceal information from you," he said. "It's not confirmed. More along the level of a rumor. Something one of the artillery soldiers said he thought he heard. His buddies said it was just thunder."

"What did this soldier say he heard?" Katy asked.

With lowered eyes, Radcliff said, "He said he thought he heard an aeroplane crashing. But, like I said, other men heard the same thing and said it was thunder."

Katy's eyes softened. "Thank you, Fred. It was decent of you to come out here in this weather to tell us personally. Only next time, drive a car. Motorcycles are dangerous even in good weather. Only a pilot would drive one in weather like this."

Donning his goggles, Radcliff said to Katy, "I'm beginning to grow on you, aren't I? You're starting to care for me."

"What are you talking about?"

"My safety. You're concerned for my welfare. You care!"

He revved the motorcycle engine and roared away.

"I'm a nurse!" Katy yelled after him. "I'm trained to care! It's my job!"

Doing its imitation of a bucking bronco, the ambulance bounced and jumped and jolted all over the road.

"Slow down, Katy!" Laura cried.

"I'm anxious to get there and get back," Katy said. "Aren't you?"

"Of course I am! But I'd prefer riding in front of the ambulance as a nurse, not in back as a patient!"

Katy didn't respond. Neither did she slow down.

Rain pelted the top of the covered truck. The day was gray and cold. Visibility was poor. The road was muddy and slick. Fortunately, there wasn't much traffic. Only a few local vendors pushing carts and a mule-drawn supply wagon.

"Maybe I should drive," Laura said.

"I'm doing fine!"

"No, you're not! You're driving angry."

"Angry! I'm not angry."

Katy looked over at Laura. The younger woman wasn't convinced.

"Pull over," Laura said. "I'm driving."

Pursing her lips, Katy let out a frustrated sigh. "If I slow down, will that make you happy?"

"Maybe. It depends on how much you slow down."

Katy eased up on the throttle. "Better?" she asked.

Laura nodded. "Do you want to know what would truly make me happy?"

"No. You're too happy already. I'm of the opinion that too much happiness is not a good thing."

Laura ignored the remark as more of Katy's sass. She said,

"It would make me happy if we could talk about Lieutenant Radcliff. You're developing feelings for him, aren't you?"

"No!" Katy said emphatically.

"I don't understand why you're so reluctant to give in to your feelings. It's obvious he cares for you and that you care for him."

Katy sniffed. "I don't care for him."

"But you have to admit he cares for you, don't you?"

Katy said nothing.

An exquisitely pleased look sparkled in Laura's eyes. "He's told you, hasn't he?"

Still Katy said nothing.

"He has! He has! Has he told you he loves you?"

Gripping the wheel tightly, Katy concentrated on the road ahead.

Laura bounced in her seat and it had nothing to do with the road's condition. "What did you say to him?"

Katy pursed her lips. She didn't want to have this discussion, but Laura seemed to be having it without her. And she was coming to the wrong conclusions. "I told him I couldn't return his affections."

The bounce went out of Laura. "Poor Lieutenant Radcliff. That must have been painful for him to hear."

"If it was, it didn't last very long," Katy said. "It hasn't changed a single thing. He still does the same things he's always done."

"That proves he loves you!" Laura cried.

"Let's change the subject, shall we?"

"Do you love him?"

"Can we please change the subject?"

"I know you do," Laura said. "That's why you've been so angry lately. You don't want to love Lieutenant Radcliff, but you can't help yourself. So you get angry."

"I'm not angry!" Katy insisted.

"It's the same with Johnny."

"I don't have to listen to this."

"He's your brother and you love him."

"I don't love Johnny."

"Yes, you do, very deeply. That's why you get so angry with him and treat him so mean. If you didn't have feelings for him, you wouldn't care what he did."

"We're almost to the cathedral."

"What are you going to do, now that Johnny is changing? It's going to get harder and harder for you to stay angry with him."

"If he's still alive," Katy said.

Laura sobered instantly. She turned forward and placed nervous hands in her lap. "You're right," she said. "If he's still alive."

Passing through the bombed-out remains of the town which had once boasted a magnificent cathedral, Laura grew silent. Meditative. Suddenly, she turned to Katy and said, "Pull over to the side of the street."

"Why? We're almost there."

"Katy, stop!"

The ambulance slowed to a standstill. "What is it?"

"Lieutenant Radcliff mentioned a small town," Laura replied. "He said Johnny's aeroplane went down close to it."

"Agneau."

"Yes! That's it!" Laura reached under the ambulance seat and pulled out their road map. Unfolding it, she spread it across the interior of the cab.

"What are you looking for?"

"Agneau."

"I think it's east, maybe northeast of here . . . wait a minute!"

"Here it is!" Laura cried. "Here we are . . . and here's Agneau . . . "

"And here's the line that separates the Germans and British running right between the two places!" Katy shouted.

"Remember that field where we rescued Lieutenant Radcliff's commander? It's right here." Laura pointed to the spot on the map.

"Where a sniper shot at us!" Katy reminded her.

"Agneau is only ten, maybe twelve kilometers beyond that field."

"On the German side of the lines!"

Laura folded the map. "Katy . . . let's go try to find him."

Katy sat back against the seat, her head tilted toward the clouds. "I can't believe what you're suggesting."

"It's only ten kilometers away!" Laura pleaded.

"It's only on the German side of the war!" Katy cried.

"What's the worst that could happen to us?"

"I don't even want to think about that!"

"If we get caught, we can just say we got lost! We're in a hospital vehicle, wearing nurses' uniforms, with no weapons, no secret plans. How hard would it be to convince them that two women took a wrong turn? And if they do detain us. . . ."

"Detain us?"

". . . surely the Red Cross will come to our aid!"

"Out of the question!" Katy said. "It's simply out of the question!"

Laura stopped arguing. For a time, neither woman spoke. The only sound was that of the rain against the top of the ambulance.

"I see him in my mind," Laura said. "Pinned beneath his aeroplane engine like Captain Quigley. Bleeding. Losing consciousness. With no one there to help him."

"We don't know for sure that he even crashed."

"We'll take a look around; if we don't see him, we'll come right back."

"You're talking crazy."

"Katy, he's your brother! How can you sit there and do nothing knowing that he may be so close?"

"Do you realize what could happen to us?"

With a quiet voice, barely audible over the drumming of rain on the roof, Laura said, "Yes, Katy, I do. And do you realize how you've changed? How different you sound? Remember, you were the one who was bored in London. You were the one who wanted to do something exciting and worthwhile. Now you have your chance."

Memories of the London hospital flooded into her mind:

"For me, the most inspirational missionary is Mary Moffat."

Suddenly Laura sat up straight. "You are exactly how I've always pictured Mary Moffat would look!"

"I consider myself to be one of Edith Cavell's girls, and pledge to God that I will live a life worthy of that calling."

"Occasions of adversity best discover how great virtue and strength each one has. For occasions do not make a man frail, but they shew what he is."

Katy's own words convicted her:

"Do you realize what could happen to us?"

These were not the words of a disciple of Mary Moffat or Edith Cavell.

Pushing the clutch to the floor, Katy slipped the ambulance into first gear. She said, "Let's go get Johnny."

Chapter 34

STANDING next to his rocking chair, Bryn Thomas was a larger man than Emily had imagined him being, and she had imagined a large man. His hair was gray and thin to the point of extinction. Small eyes hid behind wrinkled lids. His jowls were thick, his hands massive, a feature accentuated by his pipe. Huge sausage fingers held it. The pipe looked like a child's toy in his hands.

"Though I am understandably shocked to meet you, Mr. Thomas," Emily said, "it does give me the chance to do something I never thought I'd get a chance to do this side of heaven."

Bryn's bushy eyebrows pulled together in puzzlement.

"I would like to thank you for saving my life, and that of the child as well."

"You're welcome," he said. His speech was thick, his voice deep. The hint of a smile indicated her gratitude was appreciated. Slowly, he then turned and took his place in the rocker.

Turning around, Emily looked at the woman who had been her English host ever since the sinking of the *Lusitania*. "Maggie Thomas," she said, "I do believe you're a spy. A German spy."

An arched eyebrow indicated Maggie was impressed. "Very good!" she said.

Her reaction was far different from the previous time

Emily accused her of being a spy. Probably due to their location. Maggie felt safer here. They were miles from the nearest person, so there was no need for pretense. A fact which did not bode well for Emily.

"I assume I am your hostage," Emily said.

"Right again!"

Emily looked at the door behind Maggie. "And if I should force my way past you and attempt to escape?"

Maggie patted her bag. "All good spies carry a weapon," she said with a smile. "But surely our friendship will not deteriorate to the point that we are forced to use such crude measures, will it? Besides, even if you got out the door, Bryn would saddle a horse and retrieve you before you got far. Shall we have some tea?"

While Bryn rocked and smoked and stared at the sea, Maggie heated water and Emily arranged cakes on a platter. It occurred to Emily that she had been a hostage all this time. The only reason Maggie had invited her and Katy to her house in England was so that she could keep an eye on Emily. Her friendship, kindness, and generosity were nothing more than bars to a cage.

"It's Jesse, isn't it?" Emily said. "All this time I thought you were interested in my family. But your interest was in my husband."

"A personal aide to the President of the United States!" Maggie said, pouring the tea. "A man that close to the President must know a lot of important information. Which, sadly for me, he never saw fit to relay to his lovely wife."

"I must be a real disappointment to you."

"On the contrary! You have been great fun. A wonderful companion. And Katy! A lovely young lady! I am truly sad to see ..."

"Katy ... she's all right, isn't she?"

Maggie waved an inconsequential hand. "She holds no interest for us, unless, of course, something unforeseen should happen. But as long as we have you, we have all we need. And the fact that we haven't reaped any fruit from this endeavor doesn't mean there is no fruit to be reaped. We simply have to try another method of harvesting."

Ignoring Bryn, Maggie set the cups on a small tea table that had not been there during Emily's previous visit. There were only two chairs at the table. Emily wondered if Maggie had purchased the table specifically for her. Teatime had been the highlight of their days together.

Maggie sat in one chair and began preparing her tea. She assumed Emily would sit in the other.

Thou preparest a table before me in the presence of mine enemies.

Emily took the seat opposite Maggie, hoping the rest of the psalm would hold true. If there ever was a time she needed goodness and mercy, it was now.

"Blackmail," Emily said, adding sugar to her tea.

"Why, of course, dear!" Maggie said cheerfully. "Do be a dear and pass the cream."

"Jesse won't give you what you want."

"You underestimate his love for you, Emily. He'll gladly trade information for his lovely wife. But let's talk about something else, shall we? Oh, by the way, I'll need your ticket for the ship."

"My ticket?"

"Naturally, we'll have to have you board the ship. Otherwise, if someone were to attempt to track you, they would stop here in Queenstown, and we can't have that, can we?"

"Someone will impersonate me on the ship?'

"Yes, dear." She made a sour face. "These cakes aren't as good as mine, are they?"

As the reality of her predicament and the danger to Jesse began to settle in her mind, Emily grew quiet. Turning inward was her way of concentrating on a problem.

"My dear," Maggie cooed, "don't look so glum! After the war, when I come to visit you and your lovely family in the colonies, you'll look back on this time and realize you had nothing to fear at all!"

"Is this some kind of sport for you?" Emily asked.

"Adventure, dear, adventure! I couldn't bear to think that Georg . . . oh, I haven't told you about Georg, have I? Georg is my husband . . . "

"And he's not a farmer in Belgium."

"Heaven's no, dear. You'd laugh if you saw him. He's not the farmer-type at all. No, actually, Georg is Lieutenant Colonel Georg Eisenbein of the 32nd German Artillery unit. And as I was saying, I couldn't bear to think of him going off to war and having all the fun while I was left behind to all the rationing and dreariness of the home front. Being the doting husband that he is, he asked me what I wanted to do during the war, and I said, 'Darling, I want to be a spy, of course!'"

"Of course," Emily echoed.

"With my English heritage, it was nothing for the army to set up my cover with all the proper documents. And it's such a wonderful life! A person must be constantly thinking and scheming. You'd love it, dear. You really should give it a go sometime."

Emily peered over the rim of her cup. "I'll give it some thought."

"You'd be so good at it! That's why I think you and I hit it off so famously; we're so much alike!"

"I used to think that," Emily said. "But I'm not so sure anymore. I don't think I could murder a harmless elderly couple like the Morehouses."

In his rocking chair, Bryn stirred and grunted. The pace of his rocker increased from leisurely to determined.

"Admittedly, that was unfortunate," Maggie said with a disappointed tone in her voice. "It was entirely Bryn's fault."

Another grunt came from the rocking chair. This one was louder.

Talking to the back of the chair, Maggie said, "It was your fault, dear brother. You simply must accept that."

Smoke rose from behind the rocker in furious puffs.

In a voice loud enough for Bryn to hear, and in a tone that sounded like a mother, Maggie said, "Bryn never should have gone after those shipwrecked people in the first place." To Emily: "Do you know why he didn't come back after bringing you and the baby here? When he went back for more survivors, a British agent with whom we'd had a previous encounter recognized him. Fortunately for us, we were able to silence the agent before he passed along his sighting."

"Another killing?"

Maggie looked annoyed. "My dear, don't be so tiresome about killings. They're part of being a spy, that's all. Anyway, to continue, we had made provisional cover by crashing Bryn's boat and faking his death. As it turned out, it wasn't needed. But then, there were the Morehouses. You can imagine how they reacted when Bryn came back from the dead."

"So you killed them and covered your tracks by setting their house on fire."

"Loose ends," Maggie said, wagging a finger playfully at Emily. "A spy has to watch the loose ends, otherwise the whole fabric will begin to unravel."

Emily sipped her tea.

A British government car pulled up in front of the house at 23 Lumley Lane. Two secret service agents climbed out of the car. Jesse Morgan was right behind them.

A pair of darkly clad men appeared from the house across the street.

"There was no one in the house when we arrived. And there has been no activity since then."

"None at all?" Jesse asked.

"Only a cable messenger. He arrived shortly after we did the first day."

Emily never received his cable. "Can I look inside?" Jesse asked.

The interior was small and neat. The pantry meager. Jesse could find no evidence that Emily had been in the house at all.

"She may have gone home, sir," one of the agents said to Jesse.

"Can you arrange for transportation for me to Queenstown?" Jesse asked.

"The Cunard Line?"

"Yes."

"Consider it done, sir."

For nearly a fortnight Emily had been held hostage at Bryn Thomas' cottage while Maggie made attempts to contact Jesse Morgan. So far, she'd been unsuccessful. Her cables had gone unanswered.

Several times a day Maggie left Emily alone with Bryn while she conducted business in Queenstown. Emily saw in this her opportunity to escape. Not in spite of Bryn, but with his help.

"I feel like I've known you a long time," Emily said to him.

Bryn said nothing. He rarely did. Not that he was mentally or physically deficient, he was just slow and accustomed to living alone.

"When you left me and the baby here and then didn't

come back. After a couple of days, I began to wonder what kind of person would risk his life to save others and then not even show up for so much as a thank-you."

Pipe smoke drifted in circles toward the ceiling.

"Thinking you might never come back, I decided to poke around through your things to see what kind of a person you were. I hope you don't mind. It's not the kind of thing I would normally do. But, you have to understand, naturally I was interested."

Not knowing if he was even listening, she continued anyway.

"So I asked myself, 'What can I learn about the man who saved me, just from his everyday surroundings?' Do you know what I learned about you?"

Emily waited for a response. And waited. Should she continue, or should she . . .

"What did you learn?" the deep voice from the rocker asked.

Emily smiled. "I learned you probably were sitting right where you are now when you saw the *Lusitania* start to go down. And that you probably got up and took a closer look from this telescope."

Silence. Then, "How did you know that?"

Patting the telescope, Emily said, "This was still pointing in the general direction of where the ship sank."

"What else did you learn?"

"Well, let's see. That a man lived here. From the size of the clothing in the drawer, a big man. That you lived here alone . . ."

"How did you know that?"

"The single bed, for one thing," Emily answered. "There were no women's clothes anywhere. And, there was a single plate and cup and fork set out to dry."

A huge head appeared from behind the rocker.

"You're smart," he said. "Are you smarter than Maggie?"

"Everyone is smart in different ways," Emily said.

"Not me. I've never been smart."

"You're smarter than you think," Emily said.

"Nah. Maggie's smart. Not me."

"You're smart enough to love good music," Emily said. "I want to thank you for sharing it with me. It really helped me when the nights got lonely."

"Me too."

"My favorite is 'The Roses of Picardy.'"

"Mine too."

Bryn stood and faced Emily with the expression of a man who was discovering he had a lot of things in common with a new friend.

"You're smart enough to read your Bible," Emily said.

"I try. But it's hard."

"But do you know what it is that I liked most about you?"

"What?"

"The way you loved Clare."

Hearing his wife's name shocked him. "How did you know Clare's name?"

"Your Bible," Emily replied. "Please understand, I wasn't snooping. I picked up the Bible to read it one night and I saw what you wrote in the front about Clare. I think it's very sweet."

Bryn looked at the Bible on the stand.

"It's evident you loved your wife very much."

"I never told her," Bryn said.

"I think she knows."

"Think so?"

Emily nodded her head.

"But there's one thing that troubles me, Bryn."

"What's that?"

"That a man as good and sensitive as you can kill people."

"It's not me. Maggie does that."

"But you're part of it."

He was getting heated. "No! Maggie does that, not me!"

"Do you know what else I can't understand? Why you would save me from drowning in the ocean only to kill me when you're done with me."

"We won't kill you. Maggie promised."

"You have no choice, Bryn! You have to kill me! I know all about the spy operation. I know more about it than the Morehouses, and you killed them!"

"Maggie killed them!" Bryn thundered. "Not me! Maggie!"

"Whether you kill me or Maggie kills me, I'll be dead."

"Maggie won't kill you!" Bryn insisted.

"She has no choice now! And neither do you. You have to kill me."

"I won't let her."

"Bryn, there's only one way you can stop her."

"How?"

"You have to let me go."

Bryn shook his head. "Maggie would be mad."

"If you don't let me go, she'll kill me. Just like the Morehouses."

Bryn shook his head emphatically. "I won't let her! I won't let her!"

Jesse stood at the counter of the Cunard terminal at Queenstown.

"Are you sure it was my wife?" Jesse asked.

The red-haired counter girl nodded. "Your wife is not an easy person to forget!" she said. "All anyone has to do around here to put tears in everyone's eyes is to tell the story about how she came in here carrying that baby from the *Lusitania.*"

"And you're sure she boarded the ship?"

"No, sir. I didn't see her get on board, but as you can see, her ticket was canceled."

The ticket lay between them on the counter.

"I'd like to cable the ship," Jesse said.

"We can arrange that, sir."

After sending two cables, one to ship security and one to Emily, Jesse stepped out into the sunshine. His British escort stood beside him.

"That just about wraps it up, doesn't it, sir? We've done everything we could do."

"Looks like it, anyway," Jesse said. "At least she's safely on her way home."

"You don't look very happy about it, sir."

"I just have a feeling I can't get rid of."

"I know the feeling, sir. Nine times out of ten it's indigestion."

Jesse laughed. "That's been my average too." Then he said, "Wait here just a minute."

He went back inside and spoke to the ticket counter girl.

"If you don't mind," he said when he returned, "I'd like to make one last stop. It might give us a lead on our elusive Maggie Eisenbein."

"Bryn! What are you doing? Where's Emily?"

Maggie stood in the open barn door. Behind her, a taxi-cab pulled away from the house leaving behind it plumes of dust. Bryn held a bridle in his hand, frozen at the sight of his sister. He looked down, unable to match her gaze.

"I'm taking Emily to Queenstown," Bryn mumbled.

"What?" Maggie thundered. "I'd say you were out of your mind if you had one!"

Emily appeared from the interior of the barn. She held a pitchfork with the pronged end pointed at Maggie.

In return, Maggie reached into her bag and produced a pistol. "Friends don't do things like this to each other,

Emily, dear."

"Friends don't hold friends hostage and blackmail their husbands, Maggie, dear."

Bryn stepped between them. "You can't kill Emily. I promised!"

Maggie, laughed mockingly. "Get out of the way, you big oaf! I'm not going to kill her."

Bryn turned toward Emily triumphantly. "See?" he cried. "I told you she wouldn't kill you!"

"She's lying to you, Bryn," Emily said. "She may not kill me today, but once she has what she wants, she'll have no choice but to kill me."

"Emily! How can you say that? I'm your friend!"

Maggie's face was sincerely puzzled.

"You're a German agent," Emily said. "My husband is an American official. Our two countries are at war, that's how I can say it."

A look of exasperation covered Maggie's face. "Is that what's bothering you? I thought you understood by now. Emily, I don't care a thing about German politics, or English, or American for that matter. Now Georg. . . well, he's a different story. He's a Kaiser stooge. But I don't do the things I do for Germany. Nor am I doing what I do because I hate America. I do it for the adventure, the fun . . . can't you understand that? For me, it's the thrill of getting and passing information without getting caught . . . like gossiping about others without them finding out about it. This is nothing more than a parlor game to me!"

"And was it a parlor game for the Morehouses? And the British agent?"

"Can't you get past that?" Maggie cried, exasperated. "They were trying to ruin my game."

"Like I'm trying to ruin the game now?"

"And it's all so unnecessary!" Maggie cried. "What's an

American memo or a German coded message between friends? They're slips of paper, that's all! Put down that silly fork, you look absolutely ridiculous, and come inside." Her eyes brightened as she lifted her bag. "I was able to obtain some of that Chelsea tea you like so well."

Emily was stumped. She was caught in the middle of Maggie's game and didn't know how to get out. Truth was, she could envision herself and Maggie after the war sitting on her Denver porch with Jesse and reminiscing about all the fun times they'd had together. After all, this was the same Maggie she'd grown to love. However, there was another side to this whole affair that had to be considered. Emily doubted seriously that Maggie's superiors were as playful as Maggie.

Emily felt the rough wooden handle of the pitchfork in her hand. She didn't want to hurt Maggie. But then, she couldn't let this game continue any longer. It had already gotten out of control with the Morehouses. Who could predict what would happen if it got out of control again?

"I'm sorry, Maggie," she said. "I want to go home."

Maggie raised the pistol that had fallen limp in her hand. "I can't let you do that, dear. That would spoil the game."

"Bryn," Emily said, "would you hitch up the carriage for me? I would like to leave now."

Glancing cautiously at his sister, Bryn turned toward the carriage.

BLAM!

The big man flinched at the sound. So did Emily.

Maggie stood determinedly with the pistol aimed at the ground. Wispy gray-white smoke swirled menacingly in front of her.

Looking down the hollow end of a firearm was daunting enough; hearing its thunderous bark increased Emily's fear tenfold. She re-gripped the pitchfork, knowing it was no match against Maggie's weapon.

Out of control. The situation had escalated to the point of being out of control. Better to give in now and wait for a better opportunity.

Just as she was about to toss the pitchfork aside and agree to a quiet afternoon tea, Bryn once again stepped between her and Maggie.

"How can you kill your friend?" he asked.

"That was a warning shot! If I'd wanted to kill Emily, she'd be dead now."

"I'm not dumb, Maggie," Bryn said. "Just slow."

"You're as dumb as a fence post!" Maggie yelled. "Now get out of the way."

"Bryn is a good man," Emily said. "And wise in his own way. I'm surprised you don't know your brother better, Maggie."

"For the last time," Maggie said to Emily. "Get inside the house."

All I have to do is toss the pitchfork aside and this will end.

Emily couldn't do it. This had to end. Today. Now.

"Those days that I was here alone," she said, "I got to know your brother. He's a kind and sensitive man, Maggie. He won't be able to go along with your game much longer."

"He'll do whatever I tell him to do!"

"Bryn," Emily said, "I also feel like I got to know Clare."

"Shut up, Emily!" Maggie screamed. The gun in her hand began to shake.

"She was a fine Christian woman, Bryn. If she were still alive today, do you think she would be holding a gun on a houseguest?"

"I'm warning you, Emily!" The gun shook so hard in Maggie's hand, Emily feared it might go off unintentionally.

"No more killing, Maggie!" Bryn said. "No more killing." With one step he'd covered the distance between him and his sister. He reached for the gun. His hand enveloped the barrel and half of Maggie's hand.

"I didn't rescue Emily for you to shoot her," he said.

"Let go, you fool! You're ruining everything!"

With his hand securely around the gun, he just held it while Maggie tried to take it away from him. She struggled. Set her feet. Pulled backward with all her might.

BLAM!

The blast reverberated throughout the barn.

Bryn's eyes opened wide. His mouth dropped in shock. Gun smoke separated brother and sister. Maggie screamed. She jumped back, letting go of the gun.

A red spot appeared in the middle of Bryn's chest. It grew steadily. He stumbled back a step and fell to one knee, looking in amazement at the gun in his hand, then at his sister.

"Look what you did!" he said. Then, something beyond Maggie seemed to catch his eye. He smiled. "Clare . . . " he cried.

Bryn slumped to the ground, the gun still in his hand.

Staring at the lifeless giant who had pulled her from certain death, Emily fought off a team of emotions—anger, remorse, sorrow, grief—knowing that if she gave in to them now, Bryn would have saved her in vain. This was her chance. Maggie was empty-handed while she held a pitchfork.

Maggie too saw that the advantage had swung to Emily's side. Spying the gun in her dead brother's hand, she made a move for it.

Emily jumped to intercept her, stopping her short of the gun. The pitchfork's pointed prongs were leveled at Maggie's throat.

At first, Maggie recoiled slightly. Then, with a knowing smile, she said, "Emily, dear, friends don't run their friends through with a pitchfork." Slowly, she began to reach for the pistol.

All Emily had to do was thrust and it would be over. The

nightmare would come to an end. But she couldn't do it! She could not bring herself to run Maggie through with a pitchfork. She knew it. And worse yet, Maggie knew it.

Tossing the pitchfork aside, Emily lunged for the gun.

Maggie was on it an instant before Emily got there, but not in time to snatch it away cleanly. While Maggie's hand gripped the gun, Emily's hands gripped Maggie's hands. Struggling, leaning, pushing, they fought for possession. Maggie managed to work her hands to the butt of the pistol. Emily was left with the barrel. The two women were on their knees playing tug-of-war with the weapon.

Just like Bryn and Maggie. And just like the dead Bryn, Emily was holding the wrong end. The losing end. If she pulled harder, it could go off. If she let loose, she'd be a hostage again.

Don't pull! Don't pull. That's what Bryn did. He pulled back and look where it got him. But don't let go either. Don't give in. Lose and you die. It's as simple as that. But if I can't pull, how can I win? If I can't pull... Push? Push! That's it! Push! She's countering the pull. Push instead. Push the gun to one side. Knock her to the ground.

With all her might, Emily dove forward. She caught Maggie by surprise. The older woman flew backward. Emily landed on top of her. A startled expression formed on Maggie's face.

Emily thought she'd knocked the breath out of the woman. She saw quickly it was more than that. Maggie's mouth fell open in shock. Her hand went limp.

The gun was free!

Emily jumped to her feet and pointed the gun at Maggie, puzzled at her opponent's lack of reaction. She didn't seem to care. The woman's head leaned awkwardly to one side, resting against the handle of the pitchfork.

The prongs of the pitchfork were beneath her.

"Emily, dear," Maggie said weakly. "Friends don't kill friends." With a blank stare, Maggie breathed her last.

The shakes came. Emily began trembling uncontrollably.

Just then, she saw a black automobile coming up the dirt road toward the barn and the stone cottage. Trailing dust swirled relentlessly on both sides.

I doubt that Maggie's superiors are as playful as Maggie.

"O Lord, when will it end?" she cried. Her first instinct was to run. Hide. But if she hid, they would find her; if she ran, they would catch her.

Out of control. Everything was out of control. Now, it was a matter of survival.

Her rage over the death of the kindly Bryn pushed her to the edge of reason and understanding. Hurt and feelings of betrayal over Maggie's death pushed her over the edge. She would fight them. She might not win, but she would fight them. There was no doubt in her mind. She could pull the trigger. She could kill.

Standing in the open barn door, she aimed the pistol at the oncoming automobile as it loomed larger and larger.

From which side would they first appear? Right side? Left side? It didn't matter. Emily was prepared to shoot at the first threatening person she saw.

The automobile came to a stop. Its trailing dust caught up with and engulfed it.

Emily could see two men in the front seat. Big. Burly. Both were dressed in black with black hats. She'd never seen either of them before.

They stared at her. Their mouths moved though she couldn't hear what they were saying. The man on the passenger side aimed a few words toward the back seat, but never once did he take his eyes off Emily. For what seemed an eternity, the automobile sat there while the men talked and argued.

Emily shook with fear. *What are they waiting for? How many are in there?*

Finally, a back door opened on the passenger side.

Emily swung her aim that direction.

Hands appeared first.

Emily... be on your guard...

Her heart began to sink. She wanted them to attack outright. It would be easier for her to defend herself. If they stepped out one-by-one and came at her with their arms raised, spread apart, she knew she just couldn't gun them down. But then if there were four or five of them, and they all drew their guns simultaneously, could she shoot all of them before one of them shot her?

Out of control. Don't let the situation get out of control!

Beneath the door, a pair of feet stepped out of the automobile. Then the head appeared over the top of the back door.

No, it can't be! I'm seeing things! I'm tired, distraught...it can't be... it can't be!

The passenger casually draped both arms over the rear door of the automobile. "What's the matter, Emily?" he said. "Lose your police whistle?"

"Jesse? JESSE!" Emily cried.

But how? He couldn't have known...

Abandoning her questions, forsaking reason, giving in to her emotion and desire, Emily let the pistol fall to the ground. She ran toward the automobile and Jesse. He met her halfway.

Chapter 35

SHIVERING in his cockpit, Johnny had plenty of time to plan his escape once the weather cleared. He was soaked and chilled. His fingers and joints were stiff despite his continuous efforts to keep them flexible. Speed would be of the essence when the time came to reassemble the aeroplane.

Determining that time was the riskiest part of the proposition, he had to anticipate the storm's passing. If he guessed too early, he'd be unable to take off and would be forced to sit conspicuously in the field. If he waited too long and the locals were out and about, he could be captured while re-attaching the wings. Darkness was another factor. If the storm didn't let up soon, he'd be forced to spend the night and wait until morning.

From under his covering, Johnny peered out at the cold, dark, gray, wet world. The rain seemed to be letting up. He'd give it a few more minutes. If it slowed any further, he'd risk assembling the aircraft.

Within minutes the storm got its second breath. The rain came down harder than ever. The gray day was turning dark. He had no choice but to hunker down in his cockpit and wait until morning. Lightning splashed stark white light against the trees like a photographer's flash. Thunder rattled the fuselage frame.

Johnny sniffed, flexed his hands, and pulled his jacket more tightly around him. It was going to be a long night.

About an hour before dawn, Johnny began stripping away the forest covering from around the fuselage. The rain had stopped. Moisture still fell, but it came from the limbs and leaves of the trees. Lifting the tail, he pushed the Spad out of the woods. Placing the wings in position beside the fuselage, he rushed to re-attach them. With only a single pair of hands, he had to use rocks and branches to support the wings while he attached them.

Out in the open he was vulnerable. And he felt it. Every few seconds he checked the field and the road expecting to see someone as night's darkness began to fade.

His fear drove him to move faster than he'd anticipated. It was still too dark to take off by the time he'd re-assembled the aeroplane. He had no choice but to wait for the light.

Without his exertion to warm him, the cold invaded his clothing. To fight the encroaching chill, he paced around the aeroplane, checking the eastern sky with each completed lap. It seemed it was never going to show a hint of friendly light.

A motorized vehicle of some sort was coming! Though he didn't see it yet, he could hear it chugging along the dirt road. As fortune would have it, at that same time the cloud cover broke overhead. Shafts of early morning moonlight highlighted the field, the trees, and his aircraft.

Just then, the vehicle came into view. A truck emerged from the portion of road concealed by the forest's edge. It rattled and splashed its way along the rain-ravaged road, its headlights illuminating the puddles and ruts that lay in its path. Johnny hid himself behind the fuselage and watched, hoping the truck would continue on its way toward town.

With a squeaking of brakes, the truck pulled to a stop. A silhouetted form appeared from the driver's side of the cab.

The figure walked around the front of the truck. Headlights gave the black shape form and color. It was a man in brown pants, a blue shirt, and braces. He carried a rifle.

He shouted something in the direction of the aeroplane. Something in French.

Not understanding what was said, Johnny chose to remain silent and concealed. A moment later, the man climbed back into the truck. With the grinding of gears, it started forward down the road again, then swung into the field, its headlights illuminating the aeroplane *and* Johnny!

Jumping onto the wing, Johnny reached into the cockpit and set it for engine start. He ran to the propeller, grabbed it, and pulled to prime the engine. The truck's headlights illuminated his every movement.

With a kick of his leg, he tried to start the aeroplane.

The engine coughed, but it didn't start.

Please, baby, don't be temperamental today.

The truck's engine raced. But instead of accelerating, its back tires slipped and slid.

Another kick. This time the Spad's engine caught on. Its roar shattered the early morning stillness.

Removing the logs he used as wheel blocks, Johnny clambered into the cockpit.

Suddenly, the truck changed course. Instead of coming straight toward him, it raced to get in front of him, to prevent him from taking off.

Johnny pulled back on the throttle. The Spad responded by moving forward, sluggishly, mired in the muddy field.

The truck moved into his path. The driver was climbing out, dragging his rifle behind him. He used the top of the truck's cab to steady his rifle.

Johnny gave the Spad full throttle. He was picking up speed.

The driver of the truck pressed his cheek against the rifle

barrel and aimed.

Johnny pulled back on the control stick. The craft started to lift up its nose. He was coming up on the truck fast. It was going to be close.

A bounce. Another. Johnny pulled back a little more on the stick.

The aeroplane leaped off the ground just before it reached the truck.

Johnny never knew whether the closeness of the encounter knocked the driver down into the muddy field, or whether the man just slipped, but as the Spad rose from the field, the driver lay sprawled beside the open door of his truck.

Looking around to get his bearings, Johnny was at first confused. Everything was turned around from the way he thought it should be. Flying blind in the storm had seen to that. Making the necessary corrections, he headed for the front line. Minutes later, German artillery fire confirmed his position. He climbed higher to get above the cloud cover.

Though his first objective was to get home safely, he didn't forget his original scouting mission. Making the most of his last few moments of ground visibility, he scanned the terrain for troop and artillery placements. He took note of their position for his report.

Then, just before a cloud swallowed him up, he saw something unusual. Beside a major road, laying in the ditch on its side was a hospital ambulance, the kind the British used. He saw no sign of life anywhere around it.

Visibility turned to zero as he climbed above the clouds.

"How is your arm?" Laura whispered.

In their cramped quarters Katy flexed her wrist and rotated her shoulder. A full-faced wince indicated there was some pain. "I can use it," she said, flexing them again.

The two nurses were crouched beneath a ledge in the corner of a chicken coop. A steady level of clucking circulated around them as did floating feathers.

"We could have chosen a better smelling hiding place," Laura said, laughing.

"I'm glad you can find humor in this. Will you still be laughing when they shoot us for spying?"

"We haven't been caught yet!"

"Well, it's only a matter of time before we will be caught!" Katy said. "The ambulance will tip them off that we're in the vicinity, and we're probably the only two people in the entire town parading around in British nurses' uniforms."

"I'll admit our outlook is bleak, but it's not hopeless. We'll just stick to our story. In the storm, we got lost . . . "

"And drove the ambulance into the ditch," Katy completed the sentence with a disgruntled tone.

"Don't be so hard on yourself. Neither one of us could see where we were going. You just happened to be behind the wheel at the time."

"That's my point. I was behind the wheel. I'm responsible for our predicament. We would be back on our side of the line had I not driven us into that ditch."

"Well, I prefer to look on the bright side," Laura said. "At least this time when the ambulance fell on its side, I got to land on you."

Katy stared incredulously at her partner. Laura smiled sweetly and winked.

Both women got to laughing.

The door of the chicken coop opened and slammed shut again.

Instantly falling silent, Katy and Laura pressed back into the corner as far as they could manage.

"Bonjour!"

A sweet-looking little girl stood in front of them. She must have been seven or eight years old. Her blond hair was cut short. A basket for gathering eggs was draped over one arm. Katy was perplexed by her greeting and lack of fear. You would have thought she encountered nurses crouching in the corner of the chicken coop on a daily basis.

Katy nudged Laura to respond. She had the superior language ability.

Speaking in French, Laura said, "Hello! You are a pretty little girl. We were caught in the rain and came in here to get dry."

The girl's face scrunched up. "Your French is horrible, Miss!" she said in English. "Speaking like that, you will get caught for sure. You are from the ambulance that crashed near here, aren't you?"

"You could tell by our uniforms," Katy said.

"No, Miss, I could tell by the lady's British accent."

Laura leaned forward and took a closer look at the girl. Whispering to Katy, she said, "Look at her eyes."

"Yes, Miss," said the little girl quite happily. "I am blind."

"Forgive me," Laura said. "I did not mean to be rude . . . "

"No offense, Miss!" said the little girl.

Katy stood, but not without a few grunts and groans. Her legs and back were stiff. Laura was right beside her.

"Thank you for sharing your chicken coop with us," Katy said. "We'll be on our way now."

"Oh, no, Miss! You cannot! They are looking for you!"

Katy and Laura exchanged glances, not knowing what course to take next.

"Come with me," said the girl. "Grandmama can help you." The little girl turned to go.

"Wait!" Laura cried. "We don't know your name."

With a happy smile, the girl turned back to them. "My name is Allegra."

"Allegra!" Laura said. "It means 'cheerful.' A suitable name for such a pretty young lady, don't you think, Katy?"

"And what are your names?" the girl asked.

Again, Katy and Laura exchanged glances. Katy nodded.

"My name is Laura Kelton."

The girl smiled brightly in acknowledgment.

"And my name is Katy Morgan."

A surprised look formed on the girl's face. She cocked her head slightly to one side. Her eyes moved back and forth in thought for just a moment.

"Come!" she cried, more excited than ever. "Come! Grandmama will want to meet you!"

"What do you mean, you think they went after me?" Johnny shouted.

After landing and reporting to Captain Eastman, Johnny had gone to the Red Cross canteen for a cup of coffee to warm himself up. He hadn't been there more than five minutes when Fred Radcliff came storming in and sat at the table opposite him.

"Katy and Laura are missing. The last person to see them is a Sergeant Gillette at a field hospital near the front. They were supposed to pick up patients for transport from him. He said he saw the ambulance with Katy driving. It was headed toward the front. They never stopped at the field hospital. The only thing we can figure is that they were hoping to find you."

"Me?"

Radcliff nodded. "The reports we got regarding you were mixed. One of them said that you had crashed."

Johnny stared at his coffee. "It was their ambulance," he said.

"You saw their ambulance?"

Johnny nodded. "When I flew out. There was an ambulance laying on its side in a ditch."

A worried look crossed Radcliff's face. "Did you see

any . . . " he couldn't bring himself to say bodies, ". . . anyone?"

Johnny shook his head. He stared hard at his coffee.

Radcliff stood. "I'll report what you just told me."

"I've already done that."

"But they may not have pieced it together like we have."

Johnny didn't respond. Nor did he raise his eyes from his coffee.

"Where are you going to be?" Radcliff asked.

"You don't want to know."

Entering the house by way of a summer porch, Allegra nimbly pulled the two nurses in her wake. "Hurry!" she whispered. "Before anyone sees you!"

From the porch they entered a kitchen. Katy detected the pot of stew on the stove before she saw it. Its meaty odor prompted a rumble from her stomach.

An elderly woman appeared through a doorway at the other end of the kitchen. The instant she spotted Katy and Laura, she stopped dead in her tracks and said, "Oh, my!"

"Look who I found in our chicken coop, Grandmama!" Allegra cried happily. "This is Laura Kelton," she said.

Laura greeted the woman with a sheepish nod, unsure as to the reception she would get.

"And this is Katy Morgan," Allegra said, completing the introductions. Only, she didn't stop there. "The daughter of Jesse and Emily Morgan of Denver, Colorado; the same Jesse Morgan who is currently serving as an aide to President Wilson while Emily is in England visiting . . . "

"Sh . . . sh . . . sh . . . sh!" The older woman scolded.

"But Grandmama! Isn't this such a wonderful surprise!"

"Sh . . . sh . . . sh . . . sh!"

Katy and Laura stared dumbly at Allegra, who had now sensed her grandmother's rebuke and displeasure.

"How did she know all that?" Katy asked.

"Don't mind her," the older woman cried. "She was just prattling on . . ."

Katy stepped forward. Intently serious. Genuinely perplexed. "That was not idle prattle," she insisted. "How does this little girl whom I met minutes ago know all that about me?"

The older woman stared hard at Katy. "You are indeed Katy Morgan?" she asked.

Katy nodded.

"And the two of you . . . the ambulance that crashed."

"That's ours," Laura said.

"They're searching for you," the old woman said. "Only for some reason they are looking for men, don't ask me why, I don't know. However, should they see you in those uniforms . . . come with me."

"You didn't answer my question," Katy said.

"And I may never get to answer your question if you are found!" The old woman said most insistently, "First, we get you a change of clothes. Then, we talk."

Katy looked to Laura who nodded.

From a surprisingly well-stocked trunk of clothing, the old woman found a pink dress for Laura and a blue skirt and a cream blouse for Katy. She waited for the women to remove their uniforms which she spirited away. After they had finished changing, they returned to the kitchen.

The old woman was stirring the pot of stew. She held two glass vials in her left hand. Allegra sat at the kitchen table happily munching a cookie.

Before Katy had a chance to utter a word, someone pounded on the porch door. Not waiting for a response, a German colonel stormed into the kitchen.

"Iva!" he spoke in French. Katy caught only a few words: "I could smell your . . . soup . . ." Now she wished she'd studied harder in Paris.

The colonel stopped when he saw Katy and Laura. He was broad-shouldered and had a small waist. His forehead was prominently square, his eyes a sharp blue. A rifle was strapped over his shoulder. While his attention was diverted on the ladies, the old woman slipped the glass vials into the stew and pushed them to the bottom with the ladle.

"Well! Iva," he leered, "... who are these ... ?"

The woman at the stove turned around happily. "Colonel ... my niece ... and my niece ... Brussels ... Antwerp ... "

"*Bonjour!*" said the Colonel, slinging his rifle from his shoulder and setting it in a corner.

Katy and Laura returned the greeting, smiling sweetly. Pretending to be shy, Katy's greeting was very soft. She prayed with all her might that he didn't attempt to engage them in conversation.

Iva, for that was what the colonel called her, took charge. Grabbing a bowl she ladled out the soup and ordered the colonel to sit down and eat it.

Looking down his nose into the bowl, the colonel took it from her hand. Grabbing the ladle himself, he spoke, "... soup, I like ... meat ... meat."

The ladle scraped the bottom of the pot. He eagerly plopped the chunks of meat into his bowl and went back for more. Iva grabbed the ladle from his hand and shoved him playfully aside. "... some ... Allegra and me ... our guests" were all the words Katy could translate from the woman's response.

The colonel shrugged and winked at Laura.

While he carried his overflowing bowl to the table, Iva shooed Katy and Laura away with her hands. They returned to the bedroom where they'd changed.

It was nearly ten minutes before Iva returned for them. It was the longest ten minutes of Katy's life. The entire time she and Laura sat side-by-side on the bed and prayed.

"He's gone," Iva said, none too pleased.

Back in the kitchen, she served each of them, and Allegra, a bowl of soup.

"Now tell me what you're doing here," she demanded. "You're going to ruin everything!"

She sat down in the remaining chair. She did not eat. Folding her arms, she scowled at Katy and Laura.

Katy guessed her to be in her late sixties at least. Her hair was gray and pulled up into a bun on the back of her head. Her cheeks were wrinkled and full. She looked like a woman accustomed to smiling, though she wasn't smiling now.

"You haven't told me how Allegra knows so much about me," Katy said.

"First things first. What are you doing here?"

This was a woman who was used to being in charge, and who, if Katy's intuition was correct, usually got her way in things.

Allegra sat quietly sipping her soup. Though her head didn't turn from person to person during the conversation, it was still clear by her reactive facial expressions that she was listening.

"All right," Katy said. "We received a report that my brother's aeroplane had gone down in this area . . ."

"Johnny Morgan," Allegra said, "59th Squadron, nine kills to his rec . . ."

"Sh . . . sh . . . sh . . . sh!"

The little girl stopped, but she was clearly displeased.

Increasingly frustrated, Katy said, "How does she . . ."

Iva cut her off. "That explains the aeroplane this morning."

"They found the wreckage?" Laura cried.

Iva shook her head. "An aeroplane took off from a local field this morning. One of our townspeople spotted it and tried to stop it."

"The aeroplane got away?" Laura asked.

Iva nodded.

"Thank God!" Laura cried happily.

"Amen," said Allegra, fearing a rebuke but not getting one.

"You Morgans are certainly busy people," Iva sighed.

Laura shook her head, "It's amazing, isn't it? I could tell you so many stories!"

Katy interrupted. "Now it's your turn," she said to Iva.

"I'm not done," Iva said. "What did you expect to do? Drive here, pick up your brother, and drive back . . . simple as that?"

"We thought he might be injured," Laura said.

"He's my brother," Katy said firmly. "That's reason enough to try."

Her comment brought an awed stare from Laura, but a pleased one.

"Now, no more stalling. Why is it that Allegra knows so much about us?" Katy demanded.

Iva sat back in her chair. For a long time she stared at Katy as though she were weighing out in her mind the measure of information she would hand over and the measure she would withhold. "On occasion, we have done business with your father. We are part of the French underground movement."

"And you would involve a small child like Allegra in this dangerous work?" Laura cried. "Are her parents aware . . . "

"My mother and father are dead," Allegra said.

"As are her grandparents," Iva added. "She has no family."

"Except you, Grandmama," the little girl said.

Iva grinned. "Allegra's grandmother and I were best of friends. Had been since we were girls."

"But to use Allegra in espionage . . . with her disability!" Katy said.

Iva looked lovingly at Allegra. "It wasn't an easy choice.

But without her, there would be no resistance in Agneau. We would be just one of many occupied towns in France. As for her disability... I assume you're talking about her blindness."

"Of course, her blindness!" Katy said.

"You've seen how she gets around," Iva said. "Have you noticed any difference between her and a sighted person? Have you seen her walk with her hands in front of her? Have you seen her hesitate at steps?"

Now that it had been pointed out to them, Katy and Laura had to admit Allegra was as mobile as they were.

"How do you do it?" Laura asked.

Allegra was pleased she was asked. "I count steps," she said.

Astonished, Katy and Laura looked to Iva, who nodded. "Allegra has a wonderful mind. She never forgets anything. She has instant recall."

To prove her ability, Allegra named all the states of Europe, their capitals, their rulers, and the date they assumed power. She named all the Presidents of the United States and their terms of office. She named the Senators and Congressmen and could have named their secretaries had Katy and Laura not heard enough.

"Whenever we come across valuable information, we tell it to Allegra. When we need it, we ask her."

"But why would she know about me?" Katy asked.

"As I mentioned, we have done business with your father. Naturally, we would not be doing so if we didn't trust him. That entails getting to know a little about his background, family, and that sort of thing. Allegra was particularly impressed with you."

The girl smiled broadly.

"That's why she hasn't been able to keep her mouth closed. She is excited to meet you."

"Me?" Katy asked Allegra. "Why me?"

"Because you and your mother were helping people in Belgium. And because you wanted to be a missionary and when you couldn't you worked as a nurse in London even before America was in the war. I want to be like you. I want to help other people."

Katy didn't know what to say.

Chapter 36

"I N Belgium, you will meet a contact who will get you across the border to Holland." Iva sat on the edge of an overstuffed chair as she spoke.

"But we're so close to the front!" Katy said. "Is it really necessary for us to go to Holland?"

"I couldn't slip a flea over to the free French side right now," Iva insisted.

"I suppose you're right."

"Of course I'm right. I've been doing this for years. There is no room for mistakes."

Katy sat back in her chair. It was night. The windows were dark. Allegra was sitting next to her. Laura had a chair of her own next to the front door of the house.

With a sly grin Katy turned to the little girl beside her. "My mother's maiden name!" she cried.

"Austin," Allegra said with a grin. "Franklin and Eleanor Austin. They live on Fifth Avenue in New York on the corner of Thirty-eighth Street. Mr. Austin is president of Austin Enterprises and Mrs. Austin . . . "

"I surrender!" Katy cried. "You are truly amazing!"

Allegra smiled appreciably.

"Time for bed," Iva said to the girl. Then, when Allegra began to object: "Do it quickly and without fuss and you may come back down to say good-night."

"Yes, Grandmama," Allegra said, scooting out of the chair. A moment later she disappeared up a flight of stairs.

Katy smiled warmly. "I must apologize for the inconvenience," she said to Iva, "but I wouldn't have missed this for the world. Do you realize how much this means to me? All my life I've dreamed of being a role model for girls like Allegra. I've wanted to be for them what Mary Moffat and Edith Cavell have been to me."

Resting plump hands across an ample midsection, Iva stared at Katy. "Is that why you do the things you do?" she asked.

Katy nodded, still feeling the warmth of being an inspiration to a girl like Allegra. "I remember hearing stories about strong, faithful women in Sunday School . . ."

"And you hope someday Sunday School teachers will tell stories about you?" A discordant tone was attached to the sentence, one that made Katy realize Iva was not sharing in the warmth of the moment.

"Well, I just want to help other young ladies raise their sights and try to make something of their lives. I think it's important for them to have positive female . . ."

"Let me ask you a question," Iva said.

"All right."

"If nobody ever heard of you or anything you did, if you lived and died in complete obscurity, would you still do things that helped others at your own expense?"

Katy stammered, "I suppose I . . ."

"Let me put it another way," Iva said. "If you had to choose between two assignments where one would place you in a field of service for a period of time and afterward you could go back to America and tell others about the hardships you suffered, and where the other assignment meant only hardship, and suffering, and giving, with no acknowledgment about the life you lived, which one would you choose?"

Laura listened with interest.

"But surely it is no sin to want others to be encouraged by what you do," Katy said, catching Iva's implications.

"I guess it depends on how important it is to you that other people find out," Iva said. "It sounds to me that you are more interested in what people hear about you than you are in the people you've been sent to help. That's why I asked the question. Could you labor year after year without recognition, content in the fact that you are faithful with the gifts given you?"

Katy sat quietly in her chair. She had no immediate response.

BAM! BAM! BAM!

The door to the house flew open. A bewhiskered man stepped inside without waiting for an invitation. He was supporting a younger man with a severely injured leg.

"Johnny!" Laura screamed.

"Johnny Morgan! Born September 24, 1896, 59th Squadron . . . "

"Not now, Allegra!" Iva called to the girl on the stairs. To the man assisting Johnny, she said, "Etienne, get him into the kitchen."

"He crashed in my field," the older man said. "I didn't know what else to do with him."

"You did the right thing, Etienne," Iva said. "This is his sister."

"His sister?"

"An active family, aren't they?" Iva said with half of a grin.

While they bandaged Johnny's leg, he told them how he and Radcliff took two unauthorized aeroplanes in an effort to rescue Katy and Laura.

"Radcliff? Fred Radcliff broke the rules?" Katy cried.

"I told you he liked you," Laura said.

"We ran into three Fokkers on our way here. I managed to down one and break away. Radcliff was keeping the other two busy. He motioned for me to leave."

"You left him?" Katy said. "Just like you left . . . "

"Katy!" Laura cut her off. "This was different. He left Lieutenant Radcliff to come rescue us. If you ask me, it was very brave of both of them."

"Thank you, Laura," Johnny said.

"You'll have to leave tonight," Iva said. "By morning, the Germans will be going house-to-house looking for a downed pilot."

Laura said to Johnny, "Do you think you can make it?"

"What other choice is there?" he replied.

Iva outlined the escape plan to Johnny. Etienne would take them in the back of his truck tonight. They would be handed over to a friendly contact at the train station in the morning.

"I only got to know Katy for one day!" Allegra complained.

Kneeling down beside the little girl, Katy gave her a hug. "We'll see each other again," she said.

"Soon?"

"God willing."

As Laura and Johnny followed Etienne to the truck, Iva held out her hand and dropped two small glass vials in Katy's hand. "Give these to your father," she said. "At least something good can come from this."

"From Allegra's mind to these vials. So that's how you pass along the information."

Iva nodded.

"Something good has already come from this," Katy added. "Until tonight I never realized that I was doing the right things for the wrong reasons. Thank you for making me aware of it."

Iva smiled warmly. "God bless you, my dear," she said.

"And the two of you," Katy replied.

A canvas tarp was thrown over the three of them as they lay down in the back of Etienne's truck. They bounced against one another for kilometer after kilometer.

Etienne's barn served as their resting place until just before dawn, then they were loaded up again. "It's going to be a long way home," Laura said over the noise of the truck.

"Too long, if you ask me," Johnny said.

"Iva knows what she's doing," Katy added. "Our best chance is to follow the plan she has outlined."

Johnny rose up and lifted the tarp just enough to catch a glimpse of their surroundings. "Maybe there's a better way . . ." he said. Throwing back the canvas, he banged against the glass separating the cab from the bed. His appearance was so sudden and unexpected, it gave Etienne quite a start. He nearly drove off the road.

"Pull over!" Johnny yelled.

Katy sat up. "Johnny, what are you . . . "

She stopped mid-sentence. Laura saw what she was looking at too. It was clear what Johnny had in mind.

"I don't like this idea, Johnny!" Katy said.

"Trust me! It'll work!"

The truck stopped. Johnny motioned them to run toward covering, some densely packed large bushes near the roadside.

"Thank you, Etienne!" Johnny cried. "We'll take it from here!"

Etienne turned around in his seat. He saw what the girls saw. "That's not a good idea, son!" he cried.

But Johnny was already out of the back of the truck.

Glancing around nervously, Etienne pulled back onto the road without looking back.

Several hundred yards distant loomed a German aerodrome with nearly a hundred Fokker aeroplanes lined up side-by-side.

"I'll get the aeroplane," Johnny said. "Once I get it started, I'll swing by here. The two of you get in as fast as you can."

"Will we all fit?" Laura asked.

"I'll get an aeroplane with two cockpits. You can both fit in the back. The tricky part will be strapping in. You'll have to figure out a way to do that so both of you are secure. I'd hate to lose one of you halfway home."

He was looking at Laura when he said it.

"Do you think you can just walk up to an aeroplane and take it?"

"Sure," Johnny said. "Why not? If you act like you know what you're doing, most people will leave you alone."

Without further word, Johnny limped into the open toward the line of Fokkers.

There was some kind of meeting going on near the hangar. Pilots were standing about idly while an officer addressed them. An occasional mechanic wandered in and out of the hangar, but other than that there wasn't much traffic.

The Fokkers were lined up in three rows facing away from the hangar. Johnny selected an aeroplane from the row farthest from the hangar. He didn't want to appear to be loitering, that would certainly get attention. So he jumped onto the wing and into the cockpit. Here, he was hidden while he studied the configuration of instruments on the panel. He worked the throttle and set the starter switch.

Hopping out of the aeroplane, rather gingerly because of his leg, he approached the propeller. One of the pilots was casually surveying the line of Fokkers when he was supposed to be listening to the instructing officer. He saw Johnny.

Johnny waved at the pilot. The pilot returned the wave and resumed listening.

Grabbing the propeller, Johnny pulled. The engine didn't so much as cough. He'd checked the fuel gauge. Until this

447 § THIRTY-SIX

moment he hadn't considered it might be broken. He pulled again. Still nothing.

The bored German pilot was looking at him again, this time with more interest.

Johnny pulled. Nothing.

He wasn't putting enough kick into it, because of his injured leg.

A commotion caught his attention. Now the entire group of pilots was looking at him. Several were pointing.

Johnny kicked his leg and pulled.

The engine coughed, sputtered, and died.

Just like me if I don't get this thing in the air.

To a man, the German pilots were running toward him. Several were reaching for a sidearm.

Johnny kicked and pulled.

The engine coughed, belched smoke, and started!

He limped toward the cockpit.

BLAM! BLAM! BLAM!

Small-arm fire whistled past him.

He clambered into the cockpit.

A bullet whizzed by his ear, striking the engine cowling and ricocheting off.

They were too close, he had to slow them down long enough to pick up the girls. He pulled the throttle out and hit the rudder bar as hard as he could. The Fokker swung around. Johnny reached for the Fokker's guns.

Tack . . . tack . . . tack . . . tack . . . tack . . . tack.

Because of the angle of the aeroplane on the ground, all the bullets went high. But the sound of bullets flying overhead was enough to drop the pilots to the ground.

Swinging around again, Johnny taxied toward the girls.

They were waiting for him. As soon as he passed, they climbed aboard from the back of the wing.

BLAM! BLAM! BLAM! BLAM!

Some of the pilots were on their feet again, chasing him. Others were donning helmets and goggles, getting ready to pursue him.

"Hurry!" he yelled as the girls climbed aboard.

Laura was in the cockpit first, then Katy.

"Straps! Straps!" he reminded them. "And quickly!"

BLAM! BLAM! BLAM!

He yanked the throttle. With the majority of the field behind him, he didn't have the luxury of a normal takeoff. A hundred feet away was the road. On the other side of it was an empty field. The bushes blocked his view of traffic to the right.

With German pilots in foot pursuit, and Laura and Katy busily trying to strap themselves in the back cockpit, Johnny raced across the road, right in front of an automobile.

The driver of the automobile hit the brakes. His vehicle spun three times around before coming to a stop. He was a foot or so from the tip of the wing as the aeroplane passed in front of him.

They hit a ditch on the far side of the road with such a jolt, Johnny thought for sure he'd damaged the landing gear. But it didn't collapse on him. Giving the Fokker more throttle, Johnny pulled back on the stick.

It was an impressive climb.

He could hear Katy and Laura screaming behind him.

Looping, he circled around and approached the aerodrome.

Tack . . . tack . . . tack . . . tack . . . tack . . . tack.

He strafed the pilots who were still firing at him with pistols.

Tack . . . tack . . . tack . . . tack . . . tack . . . tack.

He went down the row of aeroplanes on the ground, pumping bullets into them, bits of wood and fabric and metal flying everywhere.

Tack . . . tack . . . tack . . . tack . . . tack . . . tack.

He fired at the aeroplanes attempting to take off. Two were still taxiing. He hit them both. The engine of one caught fire, the other started spinning around and around in circles. A third aeroplane had just left the ground.

Tack . . . tack . . . tack . . . tack . . . tack . . . tack.

Johnny hit it as it was climbing. It turned over and crashed into the ground.

He circled around, making one last pass.

Tack . . . tack . . . tack . . . tack . . . tack . . . tack.

Not a single German aeroplane had gotten into the air to pursue him.

Still, they weren't home yet. There were other aerodromes and other aeroplanes.

He turned around to check his cargo. Laura and Katy were huddled together, their arms encircling each other, their eyes open with a combination of terror and fascination.

The remainder of the trip was without incident. They managed to pass over the front lines without artillery fire of any kind. No other Fokkers attempted to intercept them. And when Johnny saw a squadron of British aeroplanes, he knew they were home safe.

Tack . . . tack . . . tack . . . tack . . . tack . . . tack.

"What do they think they're doing?" he cried.

Tack . . . tack . . . tack . . . tack . . . tack . . . tack.

Two Sopwith Pup aeroplanes buzzed around him like flies.

We're on your side!

Tack . . . tack . . . tack . . . tack . . . tack . . . tack.

Johnny swung hard right. The Fokker pulled into a tight turn.

The Fokker!

"They don't know I'm on their side!"

Tack . . . tack . . . tack . . . tack . . . tack . . . tack.

Johnny banked left. On the horizon six more British aeroplanes, Sopwith Camels, were coming toward him.

Think, Johnny, think! How do I convince them?

He couldn't fire at them no matter what happened. He tried waggling his wings.

Tack . . . tack . . . tack . . . tack . . . tack . . . tack.

Bullets ripped through the fabric of his left wings.

"Johnny! Make them stop shooting!" Katy cried from behind.

The ladies were a hindrance. How could he perform escape maneuvers with them back there? He couldn't spiral out of control or attempt to land without risking perforation holes through all of them.

Tack . . . tack . . . tack . . . tack . . . tack . . . tack.

The Camels were closing in on firing range.

He had an idea! He only hoped someone would remember it.

He began to porpoise. Pull up, fall off. Pull up, fall off.

"Johnny, what are you doing?"

Pull up, fall off. Pull up, fall off.

One of you remember! Please remember!

Pull up, fall off. Pull up, fall off.

One of the Sopwith Camels waggled his wings. Johnny waggled his wings.

Pull up, fall off. Pull up, fall off.

The waggling Camel fell off and away, with a roar of increased speed. The others continued their attack intercept.

It's not working.

Pull up, fall off. Pull up, fall off.

Just as the other Camels were about to attack, the aeroplane that had broken off flew right in front of their path, firing and doing a barrel roll. The other Camels broke off.

Tack . . . tack . . . tack . . . tack . . . tack . . . tack.

The Sopwith Pups!

The Fokker took a hit in the side. Johnny could smell

gasoline.

Tack . . . tack . . . tack . . . tack . . . tack . . . tack.

This time it was the Sopwith Camel, not firing at him, but at the Pups! When they backed away, the Camel drew up alongside of the Fokker.

Johnny turned around to get the ladies' attention. He pointed at the pilot next to them.

Lieutenant Radcliff.

The Fokker began to smoke.

Fire!

Flames licked the edge of the fuselage in front of the front cockpit. Like orange snake tongues, the flames flicked at him. Burning his hand and arm and one side of his face.

What would you do if your aeroplane was on fire?

Sideslip.

It was his only option.

Johnny unstrapped himself.

"What are you doing?" Katy cried.

Lifting himself up, he climbed over the edge of the cockpit and out onto the wing.

"Johnny!" Laura cried.

With his hand still on the control stick, he slipped the plane through the wind in a descent that kept the flames from burning him.

The landing field came into view. Johnny Morgan slipped the plane toward the field.

Hold on, hold on.

As they reached the field, Radcliff was right beside him. Sending him hand signals.

One hundred feet.

Fifty feet.

Twenty feet.

Ten feet.

Johnny prepared himself for a jolt. Standing on the wing,

leaning into the cockpit. Not your usual landing. He shoved the throttle in some and pulled up on the aeroplane, a little less throttle, a little more stick.

The aeroplane hit. Bounced. Hit again.

Johnny had only one thought. Stop the aeroplane and get the women away.

"Unstrap!" he yelled.

Laura and Katy worked feverishly on the leather straps.

Johnny signaled for them to get ready to jump out. They understood. He shoved in the throttle completely and killed the engine.

"Now! Everyone out!"

With the aeroplane still moving, Laura climbed on the wing. She jumped and rolled in the field. Katy was next. She jumped, and she too rolled in the field.

Johnny was right behind her. Pain shot up his leg like never before.

The explosion that consumed the stolen Fokker did not do justice to his leg which, had there been a visual picture of it, would have put the aeroplane explosion to shame.

He rolled and rolled, finally stopping face up, staring at the blue sky.

The next thing he knew, Katy and Laura were on top of him.

"We did it! We did it!" Laura shouted.

"That was wonderful!" Katy screamed. "When are you going to teach me to fly?"

EPILOGUE

Drew Morgan, 1630, Zechariah 4:6
Christopher Morgan, 1654, Matthew 28:19
Philip Morgan, 1729, Philippians 2:3-4
Jared Morgan, 1741, John 15:13
Jacob Morgan, Esau's brother, 1786, 1 John 2:10
Seth Morgan, 1804, 2 Timothy 2:15
Jeremiah Morgan, 1833, Hebrews 4:1
Benjamin McKenna Morgan, 1865, Romans 8:28
Jesse Morgan, 1892, Genesis 50:20

J ESSE Morgan stood on the grassy hillock and looked at the small gathering. They assembled in the midst of several rows of white crosses, each one representing the death of a soldier in the Great War.

Emily stood at her husband's side. Katy stood with Lieutenant Fred Radcliff, and Laura Kelton stood next to Johnny. On Johnny's other side, in attendance at his request, was Captain Vernon Eastman.

"We gather at this spot at my son's request," Jesse said. "For when I asked him who he wanted to invite to this ceremony, he said, 'Father, I can't think of anyone I would want to be there more than Percy Hill.' And so it is fitting that we gather here in France at the final resting place of Lieutenant Percy Hill, my son's best friend."

Jesse continued, "It is the tradition of our family to pass along this Bible which has been a family heirloom for almost three centuries. In the front of the Bible is recorded a list of names which I have just read to you. These are Morgans who have gone before us. Each one of them at some point in his life was responsible for the care of this Bible and with it, the care of the Morgan family faith in God.

"To be completely honest, I must confess that I have not been the best example of keeping this tradition alive. And so when my son gave evidence of not caring for our family heritage, I determined to return the Bible to another line of Morgans that they might bear the responsibility of this tradition.

"However, events of late have changed my mind. So it is without hesitation and with unbridled joy that I have added my son's name to this distinguished list.

"Reading from the front cover again, I have written:

Johnny Morgan, 1918, Mark 10:43-45

"The Scripture reads: 'Whosoever will be great among you, shall be your minister: And whosoever of you will be the chiefest, shall be servant of all. For even the Son of man came not to be ministered unto, but to minister, and to give his life a ransom for many.'"

Slowly Jesse closed the Bible. "Captain Eastman has asked if he could say a word."

Eastman stepped forward. "Mr. and Mrs. Morgan, it is with pleasure that I tell you about your son. At the end of the Great War, he is without doubt the greatest pilot in my squadron. Although he would be the first to downplay the significance of these achievements, when the war came to an end, he had a record of eighteen kills, more than any other pilot in the squadron, myself included. He has been awarded the Distinguished Flying Cross by the Royal Flying Corps and Croix de Guerre by the nation of France. In our squadron, he is affectionately known as the Shepherd of the Skies for the unselfish way in which he watches over the other pilots and, like a shepherd, risks his life to ensure that they all return home safely."

Eastman paused and cleared his throat. "I must admit also, that when I first met Johnny Morgan, I did not like him. But since that time, I have learned many lessons from him. Some in the air. Some on the ground. But the best thing I can say about him is this: It is a privilege for me to count him as a friend."

Standing in front of Johnny, Captain Eastman saluted him. Johnny returned the salute. Then, both men shook hands.

All eyes returned to Jesse. "The final part of this ceremony gets longer and longer each time, for it is an account of our family which has been handed down from generation to generation. So, Johnny, listen closely because I'm only going to say this once . . . Our story begins at Windsor Castle, the day Drew Morgan met Bishop Laud. For it was on that day his life began its downward direction . . . "

When the story was complete, Jesse prayed for the family and then declared the official portion of the gathering closed.

"Not so fast!" Johnny said. "This being a family gathering, there is some other family news that needs to be announced. Katy . . . "

Katy tried to shoo him away like she would a fly. "Not now! This is your day."

"Correction. This is a day for the whole family. Your news is a significant milestone for the family and I think you should announce it now."

"Announce what?" Emily cried.

"Have you been holding back on me, Katy?" Laura said.

"Johnny!" Katy complained.

"You have to tell them now."

"All right . . . " She took Radcliff by the arm and said, "Fred and I have been appointed missionaries to South Africa by the London Missionary Society."

Cheers went up all around.

"Katy! That's so wonderful!" Laura cried.

"We're so proud of you, dear!" Emily hugged her daughter while the men congratulated Radcliff with handshakes.

"When do you leave?" Jesse asked.

"First, of course, there's the wedding in September. Then, we have about a year of training. We will probably be in South Africa by the summer or fall of 1920."

The rest of the afternoon was spent enjoying the French scenery and one another. An occasional aeroplane wandered overhead from the nearby aerodrome.

Jesse and Emily strolled arm-in-arm as the sun cast long shadows across the natural emerald carpet. Fishing in his pocket, Jesse pulled something out.

"That's where that is!" he said. "I thought I'd lost it."

"What?"

He showed it to her. It was a small glass vial with a tiny scrap of paper inside. "The coded message that Katy brought back with her from Iva and Allegra." He unrolled the tissue paper. A series of handwritten numbers were printed on it.

"What did it say again?" Emily asked.

"If I thought you were going to ask me to decode something, I would have brought my dictionary with me."

Emily punched him playfully in the arm.

"If I remember correctly, it said something like: Lost Sheep Found, Returned. Compliments Bruno."

"Their story is amazing," Emily said. "So, which one was Bruno? The old woman or the young girl?"

"Both, and more. Bruno consisted of nearly the entire village. That's why he was such an extensive source. Nearly everybody was in on it. Iva was the mastermind when it came to communicating the information and Allegra was the repository of the information."

Emily shook her head in wonder. "And nobody knows where Iva and Allegra are now?"

Jesse shook his head. They disappeared shortly after Katy and Johnny and Laura left them. Nobody knows where they went."

"She must have been an amazing little girl! I wish I could have met her."

Jesse nodded. "That makes two of us."

Emily squeezed his arm tightly. "Look over there," she said.

Jesse followed her gaze.

Johnny and Laura were strolling arm-in-arm. She rested her head against his shoulder. Bathed in the French sunlight, he reached down, lifted her chin, and kissed her.

"Do you think they'll get together?" Emily asked.

"He had to go behind German lines to get her. He'd better not lose her now."

AFTERWORD

CONSIDERING the number of momentous events that occurred in the first part of this century which were often separated by large gaps of time, for the purpose of this novel I chose a patchwork approach to record these events rather than a strict chronological approach. There remains a general forward movement of events from the beginning of the conflict to its end; however, there are times when alternating chapters skip back and forth in time.

For example, while Johnny's story is started early in the book, the events of Pershing's Punitive Expedition didn't occur until 1916 while the sinking of the Cunard luxury liner *Lusitania* and William Jennings Bryan's resignation took place in 1915. Had I followed a strict chronology, the story line of the novel would have suffered. I blended these major events together for effect, so that the reader could experience the mounting emotions of our nation which Americans living at that time experienced over several years. For those who are ardent history buffs, my apologies if I have offended your sensibilities; for those who are reading primarily for the story, you're welcome.

Pancho Villa's raid on Columbus, New Mexico is factual. Oscar and Pearl's hotel, as well as the Hills themselves, are fictitious. Villa's men raided the small town as indicated in the story, though the revolutionary leader's exact whereabouts that night are subject to debate. Buildings that have survived the raid to the present day include the adobe Hoover Hotel, the railroad depot (restored), and the U.S. Customs Service building. The customs house is now the Pancho Villa State Park visitor center.

The punitive expedition was the last significant military use of the cavalry and the first significant appearance of mechanized tools—specifically, trucks and airplanes. First Aero Squadron's early successes and failures are narrated historically. Major Benjamin D. Foulois is a historical character while Captain Vernon Eastman is fictitious. The First Aero Squadron was comprised of eight Curtiss Jenny planes and eleven pilots.

One other historical character that I included in a cameo appearance was Captain Harry T. Cavenaugh. Records list him as belonging to the Truck Train Company of the 10th Cavalry. Though he is no relation to me, I couldn't resist sticking him in the novel.

Edith Cavell's story is fact. After her martyrdom and the other German atrocities in Belgium, it was impossible for America to remain neutral. Miss Cavell's love of the devotional book *Of the Imitation of Christ* is also historical fact. The passages quoted in the story are passages she had marked in her copy of the book. All told, there are eighty-four underlinings in her copy. Her letters to the nurses and the account of her death is a matter of historical record. She was a courageous woman whose name is, sadly, generally unknown today. Her inclusion in this narrative is deliberate. I wanted to do my small part in resurrecting the memory of this selfless woman.

The devotional treatise, *Of the Imitation of Christ,* was

written by Thomas à Kempis, a German monk and writer (c. 1379–1471), and is still influencing people's spiritual lives today. It can be purchased at most bookstores under the title, *The Imitation of Christ* or sometimes simply *Imitation of Christ.* I used the longer title which is on my copy, printed in 1871.

Throughout the book I use the spelling of aeroplane as a personal preference. This particular spelling helps create the mood of early flight. Our more familiar spelling—airplane—was used as early as 1907.

The 59th Pursuit Squadron is fictional. I merely transposed the numbers of the first American air unit to reach France, which was the 95th Pursuit Squadron. Other famous American squadrons included the 49th, commanded by Raoul Lufbery, and the 103rd Pursuit Squadron formed from the legendary Lafayette Escadrille.

The Zeppelins' bombing of London was a composite taken from several eyewitness accounts.

The description of ambulances and their women drivers is based on historical fact. Mrs. Graham Jones, a historical person, is credited with training and leading these brave volunteers.

Miss Lena Ashwell is a historical character also. Her concerts and plays as described in the narrative were a blessing to servicemen who would leave the misery of the trenches to be refreshed by this woman's vision and organizational skill.

The personalities and espionage surrounding the explosion at the Black Tom factory are a matter of record, as well as the extent of the blast reaching to and marring the Statue of Liberty.

Historical characters with whom Jesse Morgan interacts include Secretary of State Williams Jennings Bryan and his expressed viewpoints, Colonel Edward House, and of course, President Woodrow Wilson. I used actual excerpts from President Wilson's speech calling for a declaration of war as it was recorded and printed in the *New York Times,* April 3, 1917.

Jack Cavanaugh
San Diego, March 1997

The Morgan Family

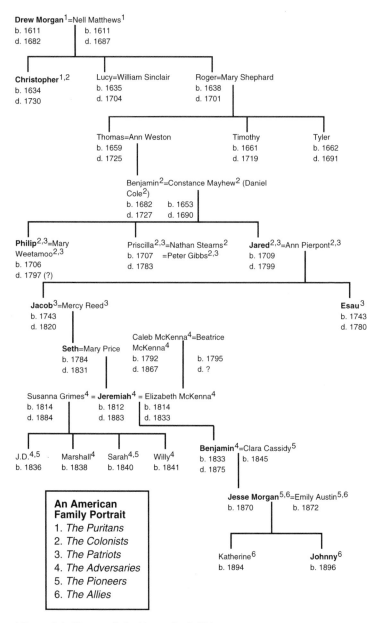

Drew Morgan[1]=Nell Matthews[1]
b. 1611   b. 1611
d. 1682   d. 1687

Christopher[1,2]   Lucy=William Sinclair   Roger=Mary Shephard
b. 1634   b. 1635   b. 1638
d. 1730   d. 1704   d. 1701

Thomas=Ann Weston   Timothy   Tyler
b. 1659   b. 1661   b. 1662
d. 1725   d. 1719   d. 1691

Benjamin[2]=Constance Mayhew[2] (Daniel Cole[2])
b. 1682   b. 1653
d. 1727   d. 1690

Philip[2,3]=Mary Weetamoo[2,3]   Priscilla[2,3]=Nathan Stearns[2]   **Jared**[2,3]=Ann Pierpont[2,3]
b. 1706   b. 1707   =Peter Gibbs[2,3]   b. 1709
d. 1797 (?)   d. 1783   d. 1799

Jacob[3]=Mercy Reed[3]   **Esau**[3]
b. 1743   b. 1743
d. 1820   d. 1780

Caleb McKenna[4]=Beatrice McKenna[4]
Seth=Mary Price   b. 1792   b. 1795
b. 1784   d. 1867   d. ?
d. 1831

Susanna Grimes[4] = **Jeremiah**[4] = Elizabeth McKenna[4]
b. 1814   b. 1812   b. 1814
d. 1884   d. 1883   d. 1833

J.D.[4,5]   Marshall[4]   Sarah[4,5]   Willy[4]   **Benjamin**[4]=Clara Cassidy[5]
b. 1836   b. 1838   b. 1840   b. 1841   b. 1833   b. 1845
d. 1875

Jesse Morgan[5,6]=Emily Austin[5,6]
b. 1870   b. 1872

Katherine[6]   **Johnny**[6]
b. 1894   b. 1896

**An American
Family Portrait**
1. *The Puritans*
2. *The Colonists*
3. *The Patriots*
4. *The Adversaries*
5. *The Pioneers*
6. *The Allies*

* Names in **bold** appear in the Morgan family Bible.

* Superscript numbers indicate which characters appear in which books.